SPARGO'S CONFESSION

A novel
of Cornwall 1810-22
by

Donald R. Rawe

also by DONALD R. RAWE

LOOKING FOR LOVE IN A GREAT CITY
novel Jonathan Cape (as Daniel Trevose)
CORNISH VILLAGES
(history and topography) Robert Hale
CORNISH HAUNTINGS AND HAPPENINGS
(occult) Robert Hale
A PROSPECT OF CORNWALL
(history, topography,) Robert Hale
THE MERMAID OF PADSTOW
Stories and poems Lodenek Press
THE CREATION OF THE WORLD
(tr. from the Cornish) medieval drama Lodenek Press
EGLOSOW KERNOW- CORNISH CHURCH POEMS
Lodenek Press.

Plays performed in Cornwall and Devon including:

HAWKER OF MORWENSTOW
(commissioned by the Orchard Theatre);
MURDER AT BOHELLAND
(Kernow Productions) and
THE LAST VOYAGE OF ALFRED WALLIS.

SPARGO'S CONFESSION

A novel
of Cornwall 1810-22
by

Donald R. Rawe

Lodenek Press

First published 2010

ISBN 978-0-946143-30-6

Published by Lodenek Press, Woodlands, Bodieve
Wadebridge PL27 6EY

Tel: 01208-895290

Typeset by Chris J. Berry
Printed and bound by TJ International

SPARGO'S CONFESSION

Contents

To HELEN
With Love and Gratitude

CHAPTER 1

AN APOLOGIA

In this year of our Lord 1861, the twenty-fourth of the reign of her Majesty Queen Victoria, I, James Spargo, Bachelor of Arts, Clerk in Holy Orders and Rector of Forrabury-with-Minster in Cornwall, take up my pen to confess my past misdeeds and unlawful exploits.

Whether these be sins, cardinal or venial, or not, I leave it to merciful Heaven and my fellow men to judge; but since, during these past forty years, they have weighed increasingly heavily on my conscience, I have concluded after much prayer that I shall find true peace of mind only by writing them down, so that the world may hear of them if it will.

Here in my study looking out upon the cliffs and sea, and the north Cornish coast which I know so well from my seafaring days, I recall those times of my youth, when were sown the seeds of my involvement with free-trading: that is, the persistent avoidance of those onerous duties imposed by the Treasury of the day; in a word, and not to ignore its direst implications, smuggling.

CHAPTER 2

A CHIP OFF AN OLD SPAR

It began, I recall, when I was ten years old, and became an unwitting accomplice in my father's business with contraband goods. Today smuggling is a dying, if not dead, enterprise, due to the numerous excisemen and coastguards now employed, and also the lowering of duties in this era of legal free trade. But then, back in the year 1810, it was rife, and hardly looked upon as a reprehensible activity, certainly not by our own sort of people in the little North Cornish port of Lodenek.

Our family, the Spargos, had for generations been seafarers of one kind or another: fishermen, coastal traders, ferrymen, naval seamen and warrant officers. They sailed across the globe with Anson, Hawke, Boscawen and Nelson; they explored the West Indies, Africa and the Americas. Yet they never left Lodenek to settle elsewhere, always returning home, if only to die a slow death of palsy or recurring fever. When the French Wars broke out after that bloody Revolution, and duties on wines, spirits, tea, sugar, salt and tobacco remained high, it seemed natural enough to those of our menfolk who escaped the Press Gang to engage in smuggling. They sailed their barques and fishing ketches around Lands End (provided they had fair weather— for going around land, as we say, is still today an undertaking to be seriously considered) to Roscoff or Brest: there to trade fish, corn, copper and lead for those items which could be profitably sold to our gentry, farmers and merchants, at prices well below those of fully taxed goods.

In that period salt was taxed at threepence the pound, tea at five shillings the pound, sugar at eightpence the pound, spirits sixteen shillings a keg, and wine eight shillings the hogshead. And it was a fortunate fisherman, or sailmaker or shipwright, who could earn more than five silver shillings in a week at that time. I never thought to question the right of our people to such free-trading, until I heard our Vicar, the Reverend William Rowlands, preach against it, on the grounds that our Lord Jesus Christ had counselled us to render to Caesar the things that were Caesar's. And, thundered the Vicar, Caesar or King George III, or the Prince Regent, it made no difference: 'He that will cheat the King will be led to cheat his own brother, his father, his wife and children. He will sink into the mire of dishonesty and immorality that will surely damn him.' A passionate Evangelical was Mr Rowlands; perhaps he had heard the Reverend John Wesley fulminate against free trade, for down the road at the Methodist Chapel ministers also often exhorted their flock to eschew smuggling, though rather more on the grounds that access to cheaper alcoholic beverages and tobacco would corrupt those who brought in such goods.

My father had no time for these sentiments; moral considerations, he said, were all very fine for those who could afford them. 'Life is hard here in Cornwall, boy,' he said to me when I questioned him about the sermon we had all heard, 'and we must earn our few pence by whatever means the Lord sees fit to provide for us.' There was then a strong resentment of the edicts of

Governments in far off London, which deny independent Cornish people the right to live as they see fit: a resentment which still surfaces in hard times.

My mother was even less sympathetic to the Vicar's views. She was Irish, born near Cork, and came of a race even more exploited, deprived and trodden down by his Majesty's laws and ordinances. 'Bad cess to his Reverence,' she said, listening to our conversation round our cottage hearth that night, 'if he do want to take the bread out of the mouths of half-starvin' children.'

Lodenek is but a good day's sail or so from Cork or Waterford, and our port has always had its share of Irish people who have left their green isle for a better life elsewhere. Even in those days, long before the terrible potato famines of the 1840s, the Irish farm labourers lived little better than animals, being sorely oppressed by the landlords and the Militia. Small wonder then, that Wolfe Tone and the Fenians tried by force of arms to win their freedom for their nation. I say all this because it explains (though it does not condone), the background against which I grew up, and the activities into which I was drawn, even before I had reached my teens.

CHAPTER 3

GALLEY MONKEY

My father, Edward Spargo, was a skilled mariner who had been employed for some years as master of the brigantine Galatea, which traded out of Lodenek across the Irish sea to Dublin and Cork, to Bristol and the growing port of Liverpool, and north to Glasgow and Leith. In days of peace (for we must remember that too often the activities of the Emperor Napoleon prevented our ships using the English Channel) she would voyage as far as Christiana and the Baltic ports, bringing back cargoes of new timber for her owner, Mr Thomas Rowlands. Even in wartime she was, on occasions, when good pitch pine for ship building was scarce, sent to Sweden, voyaging around John o' Groats and back the same way. Thomas, brother to the Reverend William, was of a breed of businessman new to our part of the world. Here was no mundane unimaginative merchant content to remain in the limitations of the trade to which he had been apprenticed. His father had come down to St. Columb in Cornwall from Gloucestershire, bought a mill and farm, and set up as an agricultural merchant. Prospering, he sent his eldest son to Oxford and made him a parson; the second son, Thomas, showing great aptitude in business matters, he set up as a general merchant in Lodenek, in the year 1790. By the turn of the century Thomas had become the dominant businessman in the port, owning six ships and a shipyard which built and repaired brigs, barques and ketches; later he acquired three farms, two inns, some rows of cottages, and a gracious Queen Anne house where he and his growing family lived. One of his lucrative activities was to buy from the Duchy of Cornwall agent the cargoes of ships that too often foundered on our cruel cliffs, and to sell them off by auction. My father always spoke of Thomas with wonder and deep respect. ‘You never know what he’ll be up to next,’ he would say, ‘except that ’twill always be something to the profit of Thomas Rowlands.’ At the age of thirty-two Thomas was appointed a magistrate, and sat on the bench with the gouty and choleric old squire Devereaux— Sir Robert Rochester Devereaux, Colonel of his Majesty’s Cornish Light Dragoons, and High Sheriff of Cornwall.

What the old Squire thought of Thomas I cannot be sure, but evidently he avoided as much as he could the society of this upstart; it was said that he predicted Thomas’s downfall, but small town people will always exaggerate after the event and make too much of little. At all events it was a matter of amazement and disbelief when, on the old Squire’s death, Thomas not only succeeded him as chairman of the bench but became for two years High Sheriff. That was when I was twelve years old, I well remember; and further, his business ventures still prospering despite (or indeed, as I found later, because of) the French Wars, he began to build himself a grand new Mansion at a place above the town, known as Sandry’s Hill. Thus he would look across the town to Devereaux Place on the opposite valleyside, where the Squires had been ensconced since Norman times. It was a great impudence; it was flying in the face of the established order; it was almost blasphemy. Even my father was aghast at such a piece of colossal audacity.

'The Devereauxs will never allow it,' he said. 'They'll find a way to stopping it. They won't put up with two manor houses in Lodenek.'

But I run ahead of myself; I must deal with the feud between the Rowlands and the Devereaux families later in this narrative. I return to myself at the ripe age of ten, a boy with generations of the salt sea in his veins, eager, as all Lodenek boys who lived around the quayside were, to be a sailor. For months I had kept badgering my father before each of his voyages, to take me with him. My mother was all against this, fearing to lose me, her eldest son (only my sister Joan was older among us children), as so many Lodenek youths and men had been lost at sea. But in the end my father said, 'Well, Harriet, there'll be no stopping him soon— he'll run away to sail with somebody else. I should rather have him with me to keep my eye on. We'll be sailing for St Ives and Falmouth in a week, just a short trip. Anyway, my dear, with any luck at all he'll be sick as a pup and want no more of it.'

Needless to say I took to the water only too well; I was in my natural element, once we had left the estuary on which Lodenek lies and were out among the rolling billows of the Atlantic. I was not pleased, however, with the job I was given, of helping Tom Permewan in the galley of the Galatea, peeling potatoes and 'scrowling' pilchards— that is, splitting them open and grilling them over the stove— and making tea laced with rum for the crew.

The family had been greatly excited at the prospect of my first voyage. Mother and Joan between them had made me an oilskin jacket, cutting and sewing the linen cloth to my size and hanging it up on the line in our back yard to give it six coats of linseed oil, each one drying out in the wind and sun before the next was applied. Father presented me with a pair of canvas boots, which he taught me to grease with lard and tallow. His own mother, dear old Grandma Spargo, knitted me a Guernsey frock, with her own special pattern across the chest, in navy blue Welsh wool; and each of my brothers and sisters gave me something and kissed me solemnly, and wished me a good voyage and safe return. My nine-year old brother Reuben presented me with a single-bladed pocket knife with a bone handle, his dearest possession; Emma, aged eight, with a large tin box to keep my dry shirts and breeches in; Susannah, nearly five years old, a large red handkerchief with white spots on it; and little Daniel, who would not be two until Christmas, came toddling up with a paper twist of strong humbugs that Mr George Hicks the grocer sold. Yes, I was the hero of the family, and was determined not to disgrace myself in their eyes. Sea sickness?— I did not know what the word meant. It was not until three years later, tossed about in a storm for two days and nights off Ushant that I found out.

Meanwhile we were sailing slowly down the Cornish coast, veering and tacking against a cold nor' westerly in the month of March. Now and then a sharp shower of rain mixed with hail would sweep over us and be gone, having hardly had time to wet my new oilskin—which I wore only when I was able to go on deck, and that was not so often as I had wished or expected. For after Tom and I had prepared and served each meal to the crew of twelve, there was only an hour at the most before we had to begin on the next: I scrubbing carrots, peeling potatoes, and chopping up onions for a stew, or measuring out meal or kneading dough for a great hobbin or dough-cake to be baked hard like a vast biscuit, so that men on watch in the foc'sle or the rigging could carry it with them and nibble when they wished.

Sometime in the early hours of the next morning, when Tom woke me and told me to stoke up the slab stove and get water boiling, we entered St Ives Bay; and looking out of the galley door as we slackened sail, I saw the sun glowing in a mist as it rose above Carn Brea, seven miles inland. A glorious sight it was to see it struggling through the grey and purple vapours of the dawn, which I realised pretty soon was actually a huge pall of smoke hanging over the district of Camborne and Redruth, put up by scores of massive steam engines pumping out water from mines. Then Tom roared at me and gave me a kick on the shins— not very hard, to tell the truth; after all, I was the skipper's son, though he had been told not to show me any favours. 'We'll be in port in less than twenty minutes and all hands'll be called on deck— they'll want their sup of tea afore that, you idle monkey!'

And there we all were, the crew in line with their pewter mugs ready and I sloshing out steaming tea from the bucket to each as they came, when my father emerged from his cabin abaft, dressed for the shore in his high-buttoned sailcloth jacket and a blue bandana wound around his neck. 'Working the rascal hard, eh, Tom?' he said, looking at me sternly.

'Pretty hard, Cap'n,' said Tom, who had only one

ear and a jagged scar across his left cheek. 'Can't get 'un movin' in the mornin' very fast, it do seem.'

'He'll settle down, I dare say. He'd better, or there'll be no more voyaging for Master James.' A shadow of a wink flickered in his eye, as he stared down at me , and I was about to smile back, but thought better of it.

'Hoy there, Galatea! Excise to come aboard!'

A revenue cutter with a Tide Waiter was alongside.

CHAPTER 4

A QUESTION OF GEOGRAPHY

I saw my father's face tighten, and he glanced at Enoch Penberthy, the mate. They went to the bulwark and looked down.

'Only coastal bound to Falmouth, Officer,' Father said. 'But come up if you will.'

'Send the rope down, Captain.'

Father nodded to one of the men, who let down the rope ladder to the pinnace riding beside us. The Tide Waiter came aboard with his sword-stick and book, puffing heartily, for he was a man of about fifty. 'Won't take long, then, Captain…?'

'Spargo. Galatea of Lodenek, trading round land and back.'

'You'll have a bill of lading aboard?'

'Certainly.' Father went to his cabin and brought out a long document which the Revenue man perused closely, sighing still through his teeth. 'Welsh steam coal and pit props. Yes. Nothing else to declare? I could do with a tot of brandy.' The Officer wrote an entry in his book and closed it with a snap. He grinned pleasantly.

'We could all do with some o' that,' Enoch muttered.

The Tide Waiter looked disappointed. 'Well, I'll be ashore for my breakfast. Morning to you, Captain.' And he was over the side, lowering himself slowly and reaching out with a foot stretched out behind him as the pinnace bobbed and swayed.

We landed the coal and props on the quayside, helped by four men the local merchant had employed. Then, taking on board several tons of silvery grey lead ore and fifty hogsheads of salted pilchards, we re-embarked on the afternoon tide; for Falmouth, as I thought.

But after we had passed Gurnard's Head, Cape Cornwall and Land's End, leaving the dreaded Wolf Rock on our starboard, we soon lost sight of land. We were going a long way out to sea, it seemed, to reach Falmouth. I thought little of it at first, being as busy as usual in the galley. My knowledge of geography was scanty— at the Dame School which I attended only the basic three Rs were taught, apart from the composition of a well set out letter— but as night came down across the heaving purple Atlantic and no lights showed, I said to Tom, 'I should think we must be near to Falmouth now, surely.'

'Well, Cap'n do know what he's up to. Not for us to question it. Sometimes we got to lay offshore for a couple or more tides before 'tis safe to go in. Now make out the fire, boy, we'll have a last sup o' tea and biscuit and turn in.'

So I stretched out on the locker top, where a straw filled mattress was my bed, and lulled by the rocking of the ship, the creak of her timbers and the waves slapping her stern, soon slept deeply. In the morning when Tom woke me I saw land nearby, a harbour wall made of great boulders, and various craft, tall ships and fishing vessels, riding inside; a bustle on the quayside and a grey huddled town of stone houses and cottages with tiled roofs behind. 'Falmouth?' I said.

'No, boy, ted'nt Falmouth. Now look— there've been a change of plan. This here's Roscoff, do 'ee knaw where thass too? Tis Brittany— France.'

'Where the crabbers and onion sellers come from?'

'Ess, that's of it. And remember, England's at war with France. Now all you got to do is say nothing to nobody when you get home. Don't mention a word, specially to yer Da.'

'But he brought us here, didn't he?'

'Course he did. And 'e do knaw what 'e's doing. Best skipper in Lodenek, your Da. But 'e've got his reasons, you'll knaw all about it in time. If you do want to go to sea with we again, then just keep silent 'bout where we've bin. And next time we sail you'll be doin' something better than just galley monkey, I can promise 'ee that.'

CHAPTER 5

A DAY AT ROSCOFF

My boyish sense of adventure rose in me as I gazed at the forbidden port— Roscoff, which I had heard talked of since I was a tot, as the source of most of the contraband goods brought into Cornwall, both during war and peace. The present conflict had begun ten years before, the year I was born, when Napoleon Bonaparte had made himself Emperor of France and begun a conquest of Europe. Spain, Portugal, Austria, Italy and Germany had succumbed to his all-conquering armies. Now he was about to attack Russia, although of course we did not know it at the time.

But we were welcome enough in Roscoff, as I found when we went ashore. Brittany was a long way by horse and coach from Paris and the French Government, and Roscoff is on the north-west tip of Brittany; the ordinances of the Emperor, forbidding trade with the so-called enemy across the English Channel (which they preferred to call the British sea, meaning that the Bretons owned it as much as the islanders opposite) had very little effect here. And the age-old links with Cornwall still held; those of us Cornish who could still speak a measure of our old Celtic tongue found they were understood by their Breton-speaking cousins, who for centuries had come and gone as freely in our towns and parishes as in their own. Later, after a number of trading visits, I was struck by the Saints names in the district— St Pol or Paul, as at Mousehole; St Carantec, as at Crantock; St Petreuc, as at Lodenek and Little Petherick.

And so on. Those venerable holy men had preached to men and women of the same race on both sides of the British Sea.

My father, having berthed the brig, called to me. 'Now, my son, we're going ashore, you and me. Look lively, now. There's a certain merchant here we must see… Damme if he isn't there waiting for us on the quay.'

I looked across at the quayside and saw, standing by the granite bollard to which our painter was tied, a round full-faced man in black knee-breeches, white stockings, long black coat, white shirt with a frilled neck and a black tricorn hat edged with gold lace.

'Captain Spargo— *bienvenu,*' he said, clasping both my father's hands in his own as we came ashore. 'And zis is your own son?'

'Yes, he's big enough to be a galley monkey. I'm hoping to make something of him one day. His first voyage, you understand.' My father smiled down at me, and I stood as sturdily erect as I could, thinking of what Tom had said. I could see a fine career as a deckhand, midshipman, lookout, navigator, and finally master, stretching ahead of me.

'My oldest boy, James. This is Monsieur Renan, James.'

M. Renan took my hand in his large warm one stained with snuff and tobacco. '*Enchantè, James.*' He pronounced the name '*Zhamm,*' which immensely intrigued me. Then to my father he said, 'You will come *chez-nous* and take something, *comme d'habitude?*'

We walked through the narrow streets with the shuttered houses looming over us, past butchers' and bakers' shops and vegetable stalls, to an open square in which trees grew, and approached a large house with blue painted shutters. Two girls with white frilled aprons over their long black dresses were arguing in Breton, a strange tongue to me, as they played with their dolls on the steps.

'Charlotte, Iseut, *pas de bruit, s'il vous plait.*'

They fell silent and stared at us. Charlotte, I saw, was about my age; her eyes widened as she noticed me, and followed our progress into the house with open interest. The other, small and darker, stared sullenly at the ground and would not look up.

We were ushered into a shady room with a long oak table and a huge dresser stacked with plates, jugs, and a large bowl of fruit, some of which I had seen seldom— such as oranges and grapes— and others, like melons, never. M. Renan was pouring out wine for my father. '*Un verre pour monsieur Jammes?*'

I looked questioningly at my father, who said, '*Un peu, m'sieur.*'

So I had my first taste of Muscadet, which, to tell the truth, was somewhat sharp, and rather put me off such beverage for several years. Afterwards I concluded that my father had deliberately intended that.

'*Du fruit, peut-être?*' M. Renan indicated the bowl. I selected a ripe pear, and retreated to the window seat to sink my teeth into it.

'Now, James, boy, we've got some important business to do,' Father said with a glance at M. Renan. The Breton merchant put his glass down and said, smiling. 'But of course. Perhaps you would like to see our small town?' Then without waiting for an answer he opened the door and called, 'Charlotte! Iseut! *Venez ici.*' The two girls, who must have been just outside in the stone-flagged passage, perhaps listening at the door, appeared. '*Un promenade avec Monsieur Jammes Spargo par la ville, hein?*'

They curtsied dutifully. 'My two daughters will conduct you. *Retournez entre une demi-heure,*' he bade them. I went off still clutching my half-eaten pear, and was taken by the hand of Charlotte, who looked amused at my bewilderment; whilst the quiet dark Iseut walked beside her on the other side, occasionally peeping around her sister at me but dropping her eyes bashfully when they caught mine.

We crossed the square to a large church with three bells in its open lantern belfry. *L'Egalize Notre Dame de Kroaz Baz.*' Charlotte announced firmly. '*La plus grande èglise de Roscoff.*' She strode away, pulling me after her, and we went down a side street towards the harbour. On the way we stopped at a small well in a stone housing by a carved wooden Calvary— Christ on a cross, the two thieves, and praying disciples. '*Le Calvaire et Fontaine de Sainte Eglantine,*' said Charlotte. I stared at the agonized but elongated and formal sculptures, noble in their passion like El Greco figures; I had never seen such representations before. Evidently however, the girls thought little enough of them, except that they both stooped and, dipping a hand in the well water, sprinkled a few drops over the Calvary group and their own foreheads. They indicated that I should do the same, which, after a little hesitation, I did. Both then smiled and gabbled various comments at me in Breton. Charlotte began to run, followed by the giggling Iseut, and I followed in pursuit; so developed a game of hide-

and-seek, with the two girls hiding behind corners or in doorways and jumping out at me, squealing with laughter and running off again down narrow alleyways like our Lodenek 'drangs', or along paths behind houses and over small bridges crossing the streams which carried refuse and night soil and smelled high like our town leat at home.

We ran across the quayside, jumping over the lobster pots and piles of nets, running in amongst the sails spread out to dry or being repaired, over baulks of timber and past chandlers and fishwives loading their baskets with mackerel ready for selling. No-one took any notice of us, whereas when I indulged in such escapades along Lodenek quay I was soon sworn at, cuffed and sent off. And of course, at home I would be ashamed to be seen chasing two girls, but here it did not seem to matter. I was mightily enjoying myself after being cooped up in the galley of the Galatea.

Finally we ended up chasing each other round the trees in the square before the house of Renan, and I caught little Iseut, who ran (intentionally I think) into my arms.

'*Un baiser, un baiser*!' demanded Charlotte, and her sister held up her face, lips puckered, so I kissed her, as I was evidently expected to do. Iseut immediately cast her eyes down, blushing under her brown complexion, then unexpectedly smiled up at me. She was pretty in an elfin manner; at that age it hardly registered with me. Yet that quick smiling glance stayed in my mind, to be remembered over the years.

'James! James!' My father was coming out of the house with M. Renan. Giggling, with a rush of petticoats and aprons, the two girls rushed past them into the house. 'Back to the ship, boy. Work to do. *Au revoir, m'sieur.*'

'*A bientôt,*' the Breton bade us as we set off across the square. I noticed there was no sign of Madame Renan, and said so to my father; who told me that M Renan was a widower.

The Galatea was being unloaded, her hold half-empty now as the labourers carried lead ore in wheelbarrows up the gang plank, to be reloaded into horse-drawn carts. The barrels of pilchards had already been discharged. I was puzzled, having understood that this had all been intended for Falmouth; but remembering Tom's words about being silent, said nothing to my father. Presumably, I thought, one could not tell a Customs Official one's real destination, considering the embargo on trade with France. Later I was to discover a further reason for not revealing our intentions. By mid afternoon, after a considerable cargo of early potatoes, cauliflowers and asparagus had been loaded into our hold, men were rolling pipes of port and casks of brandy across the quayside, to be stowed in upon the roots; these were followed by chests of tea, a couple of bales of tobacco and a dozen sacks of salt.

I stood watching wide-eyed, knowing well that this was the main object of our voyage. What if we were intercepted on the way back? What if, on arrival in Cornwall, the Excise were waiting to take us all prisoner and confiscate this contraband? A shiver of fear and delight went down my back. But father and his crew went about seeing to the stowing of this cargo as unconcernedly as if it had been coal or timber: the men chewing tobacco and spitting over the side, the Mate giving directions as to the stowing, Father marking off the various items against one of the bills of lading. There were actually two bills, as I learned later, one to be shown on arrival at Lodenek for the roots and declared to be from Falmouth; the other, to be kept in the inner pocket of father's jacket, for the free trade goods.

Finally M. Renan appeared on the quayside, and was invited aboard to the Captain's quarters, where a toast to the prosperity of the trade was drunk. Then as the evening closed in we went ashore to eat and drink at a harbourside *auberge* before re-embarking for Cornwall. I can remember now the taste of that steaming hot lobster soup with *croutons* and pieces of onion floating in it, and the delicious fish pie and *crèpes* with honey which followed. Our fare at home was better than most Lodenek quayside families had, but these delicacies were quite outside my experience.

Later that evening we weighed anchor and slid out of Roscoff on a strong favourable wind that by four in the morning bore us to Land's End, under a fitful moon sailing among broken clouds. Two ships passed us well out on the starboard. but there was no challenge to identify ourselves.

'Most likely free-traders shipping over to Roscoff their selves,' commented Tom.

It took us all the following day, the wind having slackened and gone round to the east, to sail up the north Cornish coast to reach our landing place. Near midnight, before the moon rose over the moorland peaks of Bron Welly and Roughtor, we were lying off Porthcothan Bay, and a small fleet of boats appeared along side. Quietly, without fuss, the illicit cargo was let down, bag by bag, cask by cask, over the side into those skiffs and bumboats. Then slowly, on a pearl grey swell, the contraband was taken ashore to be stored in caves, crevices and barns until teams of horses and wagons could be assembled at night to load and drive it to destinations across Cornwall and into Devon.

At ten the next morning the Galatea rode off Stepper Point awaiting the turn of the tide to enter the estuary; a Customs cutter from Lodenek met us. Again we were inspected, this time the Officers (three elderly men and a raw youth with a limp) examining the fo'csle and the crew's bunks, the galley, and the Captain's cabin. The cargo of roots was examined and some of it prodded as a gesture toward looking for contraband goods It all seemed somewhat perfunctory, however, as if they expected to find nothing.

So we were allowed to proceed; and soon, the wind dropping as we approached Lodenek quay we were pulled into harbour on the rising half tide by two of Thomas Rowland's shipyard gigs. On the quayside, waiting to welcome Father and myself home were my mother, holding little Daniel tightly by the hand in case he should fall into the dock, and my elder brothers and sisters. They were all so glad to see me, and for days afterwards I was pressed to recount to them everything I had seen and done; but my father's warnings, and the meaning of Tom Permewan's words, stopped me short of giving Reuben and Emma (who, being next oldest to me, wanted to know most) any account of our activities, and prevented me from even mentioning the name of our actual destination.

CHAPTER 6

MR THOMAS ROWLANDS

I found life in Lodenek tame enough then for a few months. But I went fishing with Tom Permewan, when the Galatea was in port, and with other fishermen who owned their own boats. One day Tom and I and Reuben (who was as excited about this venture as I had been going to sea) went in Tom's dinghy down to the Doom Bar, a great sand bar stretching across the estuary, on which so many ships had foundered, so that pieces of their masts and gunwhales could often be seen among the shifting sands; and by stretching a net across the channel at low water we caught three score of floundering quivering grey mullet which fed among the shallows. We sold them for three shillings, sharing between us at one and sixpence for Tom and ninepence each for us boys, plus four of the fattest mullet to take home to mother.

In July I went out to join the seiners at Harlyn Bay, and helped to bring ashore a handsome shoal of ten thousand pilchards. These were carried up in scoops, buckets and wheelbarrows by the local populace of St. Merryn parish to the fish 'Palace' or cellars on the cliffs. Then I witnessed the pressing and packing of these tiny silver fish, bulked against the stone walls and pressed down into barrels with granite weights, until the train oil ran out of them and into the stone gutter from which it was collected. Most of our cottages were lit at night by rudimentary lamps filled with that reeking fuel— a smell I recall now fifty years later, and which seems to resurrect before me our cramped cottage and the quayside smelling of fish and tarred ropes.

In the autumn I was taken on another run to Roscoff, during which there was some real excitement. First, I was taken up the rigging by the foretopman, a slim youth of about sixteen called Davey Bligh, and helped him to do his watch in that eyrie, swaying above the sails and buffeted by the winds. Fortunately, though at first terrified, I found I had a good head for heights and was thrilled to the core by the experience. Looking down at the deck though the billowing cracking canvases, I was amazed how small the Galatea seemed; she was a minute chip of wood floating on the great Western sea, as insignificant as an insect, and the men below on deck were like little marionettes. Of course my own small size made the world look larger, and I felt I was on the highest pinnacle one could ever attain (though our little ship's mast could not be compared, for instance, with those of the great East Indiamen and China Clippers now sailing). But the vastness of the Atlantic, stretching and heaving beyond us as far as we could see, gave me my first idea of infinity: of how we are all stray souls upon the ocean of God's boundless mercy, allowed to make our own impudent voyages only at his benign sufferance.

We got to Roscoff and M.Renan, where I was again presented with fruits to choose from; so I had my first luscious peach, a great luxury. And I played as before with the two girls, only this time Charlotte made sure she was the one who got caught and whom I had to kiss. They taught me a few words of French and Breton; I could say '*Je t'aime*' and '*Voulez vous me baiser,*' '*Dez da,*' and '*Noz da.*'

On the return voyage, whilst I was in the galley peeling potatoes and minding the soup simmering on the stove, we were challenged by a British naval sloop. Father gave orders to clap on more sail and we ignored her command to heave to. She fired several shots at us; one ball carried away half our mainsail yard arm. But we were lucky: after an hour's pursuit off the coast near the Lizard a thick mist descended on us, and the sloop let us go. The Galatea lay off Mullion until the next morning when the fog cleared, and returned to the North coast the next day. Meanwhile, our ship's boat had landed Enoch Penberthy at the tiny cove below Mullion, where he had obtained a horse and ridden up to Porthcothan to tell the waiting boats we were delayed.

My days now passed in hanging about the quayside, being employed at odd jobs around the discharging luggers and schooners, running errands for my father when he was in port, and for Mr George Courtney, who had a sail loft where I earned a few pence helping with cutting and folding the Irish linen cloth from newly imported bales. As I had learned to read and write at Miss Maria Tonkyn's school I was useful to a variety of tradesmen and captains around the harbour, and by the time I was eleven had a reputation for being a ready clerk and amanuensis. I often took down letters and documents at the dictation of some old salt who had come into Lodenek port on a trader, and who wanted to write to his family, or make a will. I remember my first encounter with Mr Thomas Rowlands himself, on that very account.

I was sitting on the deck of the Galatea, pen and paper in hand, my ink bottle with cork stopper placed on the windlass, carefully writing out a letter for Davey (who had received little schooling, partly through his own lack of application to study, and partly because his family were so poor as to need him to earn from a very early age). The letter was to his grandfather at Boscastle who, he said, was now too old and feeble to journey to see him and his mother. A shadow fell across the paper, and I looked up to see, staring down at me with a slight frown, Mr Rowlands. Coming to meet him along the deck was my father.

'What's your name, young man?' Mr Rowlands enquired. He was a thickset man with a grey impassive face, and deep set eyes that seemed to miss nothing. He wore spotless tight-fitting white trousers, a long blue coat and a small powdered wig: as gentlemen, and those aspiring to be gentlemen, did in those days.

'James Spargo, sir,' I said, standing up hastily and accidentally knocking against the windlass, upsetting my inkwell; I stooped hastily to retrieve it as it fell to the deck. but half the tiny bottle was spilled on the scrubbed beech wood planks. Davey Bligh sniggered and hid his mouth with his hands.

'Your lad, Mr Spargo?' enquired Mr Rowlands of my father as he reached us.

'Mine indeed, Mr Rowlands. I'm bringing him along in the way of being a mariner. He's done a couple of trips with us already.'

'A handy sort of fellow to have about, I should say.' The merchant nodded affably at me. 'Writes a good clear hand from what I can see. Well now, Captain, there's a point or two I want to discuss with you.' And they retired to the cabin together.

'Dam' lucky you didn't spill ink over his breeches,' said Davey. 'You wouldn't get no compliments for that, young Jim.' I studied the splash of ink on the whitened deck, so often scrubbed and holy-stoned, and went to get a bucket of water and some salt from the galley to try to remove it.

The upshot of the encounter was that Mr Rowlands recommended Father to get me more education, and some sort of agreement was struck that the great merchant would contribute something extra to the Captain's salary to cover it. Thus from that time I was marked out as a youngster of rising talent, to be encouraged and brought along to take part in the manifold business and seafaring interests of the Rowland's empire.

CHAPTER 7

NATIONAL SCHOOL

Since the age of eight years I had been a choirboy at the church of St.Petroc's on the hill above the port. I was encouraged to go partly because choirboys were paid a penny for attending choir practice and two services each Sunday (with another penny whenever there was a wedding or a funeral important enough to engage the choir), and partly because my father believed it was essential to gain the esteem of those who ordered the world we lived in. The Vicar, Reverend William Rowlands, was after all his employer's brother; and the Vicar had been appointed to the living by Squire Devereaux, who was patron of the parish.

I had a good true voice, though it was never loud. The choir master, Mr Josiah Tremain, was a kind if somewhat dreamy tutor; we small boys would often pass objects among us, including pet mice, frogs and newts, whilst he was expounding how we should sing the hymn or psalm. Occasionally some object, perhaps a clay marble or conker, would be dropped onto the floor of the choir stalls, arousing him to momentary anger; if he was satisfied he had the culprit he would dart forward, grab the boy by the scruff of his neck and march him out the church, telling him he was not fit to grace God's house and would forfeit his penny for that week. Such punishment was once my lot for allowing my pet white rat Horatio (named after Lord Nelson) to escape, running along the altar and sitting up cleaning his whiskers between the tall candles, to our loud merriment.

But generally I progressed well and, at the time when I was thirteen and my voice beginning to break, so that I could not sing except in a strange harsh croak (like the ravens I had seen flying off the cliffs near Guddra Gorge), Mr Tremain was very understanding. 'You mustn't force it, my son,' he would say. 'Sing with the tenors, but keep it soft and gentle, or you'll damage your vocal chords. In six months time 'twill come all right.' And so it did.

One evening in September, in the year Napoleon retreated from Moscow and Wellington drove the French out of Spain, we were practising the 100th psalm, accompanied by two serpents, a bassoon and a clarionette (church organs had not made their appearance in our part of the world, and would not for another thirty or forty years) when, as the evening sun faded from the upper traceries of the west window, the Vicar himself came into church. It was an event not entirely unknown, but certainly unlooked for, and we fell silent and stopped our shuffling and surreptitious squabbling as he walked up the aisle.

Reverend Rowlands was taller than Mr Tremain, and rather more florid (he was fond of his port); he carried his tall hat in his hand and his white clerical stock was wound high about his throat. 'Just a word with our songsters, Mr Tremain, if you please.' He stood on the chancel steps surveying us all with his steady grey eyes beneath thick whitening eyebrows. We held our breath. There were no underhand amusements in the choir stalls when the Vicar took the service.

'Boys,' he said. 'You are fortunate to live in this enlightened age. How many of you have attended school— any sort of school?'

About half of us raised our hands.

'I rejoice to see that some of you have had an introduction to education. But now you will all have the opportunity to avail yourselves of it— and at a very modest fee. The National Society for the Education of the Poor is to establish a school here in Lodenek. We have secured suitable premises in Venton Lane, where the boys' class will be opening under the master we have engaged, Mr Henry Nanskivell, next Monday. I recommend you all to take advantage of this, and not to linger in ignorance any longer than is necessary. I advise you all to tell your parents, and if they can possibly spare you from your home or whatever duties you undertake by day, come to school as soon as possible. The fee is only sixpence per term; the first term will end a week before Christmas.'

He paused to let all this register well in our minds. It sounded rather grand to us— a National Society: quite a cut above Miss Tonkyn's school, held in her kitchen among the steaming pans and kettles, and her old dog scratching himself for fleas before the hearth. But there was more.

'I am looking for two, possibly three, older boys who will be able to act as monitors. It is a very important position. Monitors will go to the school at eight in the morning and will be taught the lessons for the day by the Master. Then, from nine to twelve, they will teach what they have learned to the younger boys. Monitors will, in fact, when they have satisfied the Master of their proficiency, be paid a shilling per week. How many boys have we here, Mr Tremain, who are twelve years of age or more?'

There were three of us; myself, my brother Reuben, and Matthew Pook, who was a little older than I. None of us were blockheads; so on Mr Tremain's recommendation we were all asked to report to Mr Nanskivell on the Monday morning following, to be instructed in the art and science of monitoring.

The Monitorial system is now falling into disuse, but at that time it was the one effective method of teaching literally thousands of pupils to acquire the elements of education. And there were then some thousands of such schools set up by the National Society, in towns and cities all over the United Kingdom, daily instructing boys and girls who would otherwise have been unable to study the most basic requirements such as reading, good handwriting and elementary arithmetic. But our National School for the Education of the Poor according to the Principles of the Church of England, to give it its proper title, went beyond these first requirements. It would teach us to improve ourselves and be able to earn our bread; but it would teach us also moral precepts, Bible study, prayer and daily worship.

At five minutes to eight o' clock on a wet Monday morning Reuben and I trudged up the hill from the harbour, meeting Matthew as we went, and made our way to the wooden steps ascending to a long room over three tiny cottages, dwellings for elderly people on parish relief, who could no longer work to support themselves. For an hour we were instructed by Mr Nanskivell, learning the simple lessons to teach the pupils in our classes. Then, at nine, the pupils came clattering up the wooden steps— some thirty boys, soon to grow to sixty or so as the school found favour with the community of Lodenek. There was a quarter of an hour of prayers, followed by a hymn, and lessons proper began. An hour of arithmetic; half an hour of religious instruction, during which one of us monitors read from the Bible and Mr Nanskivell expounded upon the text; ten minutes break or playtime, during which we were allowed out to visit the earth closets in the tiny garden outside; half an hour of spelling and writing practice, then, reading lessons for the six and seven year-olds, and set reading exercises from improving works for the older boys who could read. Among these, I remember well, were extracts from The Pilgrim's Progress, Paradise Lost, and Johnson's Rasselas; with Gray's Elegy and Scott's Lay of the Last Minstrel our chief diet in verse.

Mr Nanskivell was an enthusiastic young man, a born teacher who could hold us entranced for hours, it seemed, when he talked on subjects that interested him personally. When the dry bread, as he called it, of the morning subjects, was digested, he would gather the whole class— somewhat truncated, for sometimes half the boys would be given work to do by their parents in the afternoon— and teach them whatever came into his head. I now think he was very much advanced for his time; the idea that young working-class children could be interested in, and would benefit from, such subjects as singing, poetry, drawing, nature studies, even debating, was in those days almost unknown, though happily we did not know this. The general view among statesmen, churchmen and those in authority was that such activities were strictly for the rich and well-to-do; we were to be taught the bare skills of learning in order to fit ourselves for a trade, and ought to have nothing to do with such refinements.

Fortunately the Reverend Rowlands, when he called to inspect the school, always came in the mornings; once satisfied the three R's were being taught correctly and insisting that daily devotions were carried out he left us severely alone. Then Mr Nanskivell, with two golden hours left to please himself and us, came into his own.

It was he who gave me my first insight into romantic poetry, something I have loved ever since, and also, in my modest way, attempted to write. He got us monitors to read to the others, so they might learn William Wordsworth's 'Daffodils' and his Lucy poems; and he enthralled us by reading us the whole of Coleridge's 'The Ancient Mariner.' I recall the scene well: a dark louring afternoon lit by sudden blinks of distant lightning, and the muttering of thunder coming down the estuary from St. Breock Downs; and thirty boys, all who knew a good deal about the sea, having from infancy gone fishing and even, like myself, voyaged across the Western Approaches out of sight of land, all drinking in every word– drunk, indeed, upon those fantastic adventures into the hell of the Southern Seas.

With sloping masts and dipping prow
   As who pursued with yell and blow,
Still treads the shadow of his foe,
   And forward bends his head,
The ship drove fast; loud roared the blast
   And southward aye we fled.

I was myself terrified, dreaming every night for perhaps a week, of that unforgettable scene in the doldrums:

The moving moon went up the sky,
  And nowhere did abide;
Softly she was going up
  And a star or two besides –

Her beams bemocked the sultry main,
  Like April hoar frost spread;
But where the ship's huge shadow lay
  The charméd water burned away
A still and awful red.

Beyond the shadow of the ship
  I watched the water snakes;
They moved in tracks of shining white,
  And when they reared, the elfish light
Fell off in hoary flakes.

It still comes back vividly to me now, and even now I occasionally dream of that lurid scene; I am there myself, amid the desolate wastes of the Southern Sea. But though I retain that strange feeling of dread, the experience is somewhat at a remove now, and less of a nightmare than it was then in my youth.

On Wednesday afternoons we had singing practice, and as I was in the church choir, I was put in charge of a group of smaller boys to teach them the treble parts of songs such as 'Rule Britannia!', 'Hearts of Oak', and 'Where the Bee Sucks' by Dr Arne. Mr Nanskivell, himself possessing a pleasant tenor voice, would then train the older boys to sing ‘Where e’er you Walk’, ‘Drink to me Only’ and ‘There is a Lady Sweet and Kind.’

Near Christmas we would practice carols, and in the evenings would all go out with Mr Nanskivell, singing before the Squire at Devereaux House, the Vicar, and gentry such as old Rear Admiral Polkinghorne, aged ninety, who lived in a quiet Georgian house along Skidney Lane, and Mr Thomas Rowlands and his family at St. Petroc’s house— an activity pleasurably anticipated because we expected to be rewarded with hot mince pies and mulled ale.

But sometimes vociferous and over enthusiastic singing in schooltime upset the old people who lived below. Then there would be an irate banging of a walking stick upon the ceiling below us, and Mr Nanskivell would break off, saying ‘Sorry boys; we’re getting carried away,’ and direct us with an apologetic smile to the quieter realms of nature study or drawing.

CHAPTER 8

WHITSUNTIDE SPORTS

One of the great events of the Lodenek year was at Whitsuntide, when the National Schools and others (that is the British and Foreign School run by Nonconformists, and Miss Tonkyn's school), and Mr Rounceval's Academy for the improving of Merchant's Sons all had a holiday. There was a grand children's tea-treat laid out on the trestle tables under the oaks on the green outside Devereaux House. All families of any substance contributed something towards it, whether only plates of Cornish splitters, pots of home made blackberry or raspberry jam, or perhaps a screw of tea or sugar (both which of course were very dear then, at least if they were duty paid). The gentry were expected to shoulder most, and trays of yeast buns and almond- flavoured tartlets, pounds of butter and several gallons of milk were always forthcoming from the great House. And Mr Thomas Rowlands, not to be outdone, would send up dozens of stoneware bottles of fizzy ginger beer, and scores of brandy snaps and biscuits baked especially for the occasion by the cook at St. Petroc's.

After the tea-treat, under the blazing sun which never seemed to fail us on those occasions, there were races. It was at one of those sporting events that I became first acquainted with Miss Emily Rowlands, Thomas's eldest daughter.

She was tall for her age, which was fourteen; I knew her by sight, of course, for she sat each Sunday with her father and mother in their family pew just across the aisle from the choir stalls. Often I had gazed at her in mute admiration, though she studiously and (it seemed to me) rather contemptuously avoided my gaze. Her gleaming light auburn hair, done into little ringlets hanging around her face; her soft fair complexion, her violet eyes, her pert little turned-up nose, all presented a picture of growing girlhood being trained and taught towards lady-likeness, yet still capable of being leavened by outbreaks of coquetry and contrariness; her flowing cambric or silk dresses (the material no doubt imported clandestinely from across the water— I had seen bales being taken on board the Galatea at Roscoff) — all combined to present an image of unattainable feminine beauty before which I could only wonder, contemplate and despair.

Yet she was not, as I found, so unattainable. Like me, Emily had been persuaded to help at the National School, in her case by becoming one of the first monitors at the girl's section in Ruther's Lane. So when we marched behind the Sea-Fencible's fife and drum band through the town and up to Devereaux Place, I, with Reuben and Matthew Pook, was at the head of the boys behind Mr Nanskivell; and following us, behind Miss Julyan, the school mistress, was Emily and two other girl monitors. I suppose, looking back now, that Mr Rowlands might well have sent Emily away to a young ladies' academy or boarding school— indeed, later, when she was eighteen, she went to Bath for a year or two to learn French and other accomplishments; but perhaps he saw it as his duty, and Emily's, that she should in the meantime help the town of Lodenek in this way.

When the races were announced, and we all trooped up the lane to the closely mowed field opened by the Squire Devereaux for the occasion, walking with Matthew and Reuben I became suddenly aware of the three girls ahead of us, two of them from time to time turning to stare at me and then being overcome with a fit of the giggles, as they confided some comment to the one in the middle; who did not deign to turn her head. I realised that the lofty one was Emily; and wondered what on earth they were saying to her. After a while, just before we all reached the sports field, which bore considerable evidence of sheep being pastured there recently, Emily stopped, and said loudly in a mock-exasperated tone, 'Very well then. I shall dare to. See if I don't!'

At which the others, glancing behind me, also stood still, plainly expectant.

'Master Spargo, I believe,' said Emily, as I came level with her. I noticed Reuben stopping, amazed, as I myself halted.

'I have a favour to ask.' The two other girls simpered and sniggered: she gave them a stern glance that silenced them.

'A favour?' I said.

'Yes. Will you enter the wheelbarrow race with me?'

I understood at once the significance of this. Of all events at the sports the wheelbarrow race, being the only event which girls were allowed to enter with boys, had a special interest. In it, 'the barrow' was the boy, who, his legs gripped by the girl partner and raised off the ground, 'walked' or 'ran' using his arms and hands as fast as he could go over the mere thirty yards stretch to the finishing line. The situation of being handled by a girl, with every ones' eyes upon one, meant that a sort of declaration was being made. All very innocent, and looked upon by adults with amusement; but boys who still wanted nothing to do with girls would refuse to enter, even quitting the field until the race itself was on: whereas those who entered were quite clearly thought to be courting, particularly by the young females they submitted to in the race. Often afterwards I thought that marriage itself is much like a wheelbarrow race, with wives supporting and directing their husbands, who puff and perspire under the onerous course to which they have committed themselves.

Should I allow myself to be thought 'sweet on' Miss Rowlands, whom I admired greatly but of whom I had never thought myself remotely worthy; or should I refuse, not only throwing away a glorious opportunity to gain her acquaintance, but earning her scorn and despite? There was no question in my mind as to the answer.

'Very well, Miss Emily. I'll be your barrow.'

She smiled upon me. Behind her the other girls held their breath. She turned to glance at them, as much as to say, 'See— I told you so;' then said to me, 'Good luck in the other races. I'll be watching and cheering you on.' Then they were gone, she and the others, lost in the melée of white frocks and bonnets and best suits, cocked hats and the uniforms of the Fencibles.

Reuben was staring at me as if I were a strange being from another world. 'Well, come on, Reub,' I said. 'I couldn't very well say 'no', could I?'

'No,' said Reuben, blinking in wonder. 'But... after all... Emily Rowlands!'

'She's only a girl, like the others.' I tried to sound careless, but inwardly I was glowing with pride that she had chosen me.

'A bit saucy, that one, I reckon,' said Matthew. 'I like young Jane better.' Jane Pellow was one of Emily's giggling companions.

'Why not ask her to go in for the wheelbarrow with you?' I suggested.

'Well, damme, p'raps I will. Why shouldn't I?' He looked at Reuben. I looked at Reuben.

'What about Mildred, then Reub?'

Reuben, aged nearly twelve, blushed scarlet and mumbled something indistinct.

'Come on, boy, she can't eat you. Only a girl,' I coaxed.

'Don't hold much with 'em,' Reuben muttered unhappily.

'Tis only a bit of fun,' said Matthew. 'Can't hurt 'ee— 'less you paddle into a cow pat like Dick Derry last year.'

'Rather not, Jim,' Reuben said. 'Don't push me, eh?'

'All right, Reub. But I'll wager in a year or two you'll be looking for a nice little maid to enter with. You just wait and see if I'm right.'

We entered the field and went up to the blackboard on which were chalked the various events. Mr Nanskivell, in his best white trousers and serge cut-away coat with tails, was arranging some six year old boys for a fifty yard race: he was the starter, and had a large white handkerchief which he held high, shouting, ‘Ready— Steady— Go!’ And as the handkerchief came down, off they went; the winner breasting a string held across the finishing line by Mr Tremayne, the organist, and William Williams, the leading bass in the choir.

For the older boys there were the hundred yards sprint for twelve years and under; the hundred yards for the over twelves; two hundred yards and the quarter of a mile hurdles; the three legged race; the sack race; the blindfold race, which, like the two latter ones was a joke event since the entrants were spun around three times blind folded, before they started, and had to get their bearings by touch and hearing before they could run in the right direction. There were archery and bowling at ninepins. And there was the pillow fight on the greasy pole, projecting over a trough of water from the farm wagon to which it was fixed.

For the girls, who were expected to indulge in less rowdy pursuits, there was throwing quoits to encircle stone figures (three hits gave a prize, usually sweets or an apple); there was the egg-and-spoon race (bring your own hard-boiled egg, usually a bantam’s or a pullet’s); there was a pail full of water on which floated apples, which had to be got up by using your mouth and teeth only— an activity that ruined many a pretty ringlet; and, of course, the wheelbarrow race, which was always the last event of the afternoon.

It was, without doubt, my day of triumph. Perhaps inspired by Emily’s encouragement, I excelled at nearly everything I entered. I won the senior hundred yard sprint, drawing ahead of Matthew Pook at the last few seconds to breast the tape. Matthew gave me a close challenge in the two hundred yards, but again I reached the string a split second before him. The next event was the hurdles where I was up against a taller choirboy named Job Peters; his stride was much longer and he seemed to walk, rather than jump over the wicker sheep hurdles spread at intervals along the course. But although he soon drew ahead I could see he was careless, and sure enough, he knocked the third from last hurdle down and lost his rhythm; I jumped clear over mine and sped past him to claim another victory. As I reached the finishing line I saw Emily and her two cohorts clapping me and crying, 'Bravo! Bravo!'

The greasy pole was something I had not intended to enter; larded until slippery as glass, it meant spoiling one's best suit unless one went into the corner behind the sacking screens, where men and boys went to relieve themselves against the hedge, and changing into old clothes. I had no old clothes with me, and was content to watch the fun as successive pairs of boys swung wild blows with feather pillows at each other— sometimes missing and falling off into the trough with a splash, producing great merriment among the spectators; sometimes connecting and bursting their pillows, sending a shower of feathers flying like snow.

It was as I stood there watching with Matthew and Reuben that Job Peters, still evidently smarting at being defeated by a smaller and younger opponent, taunted me to enter.

' 'Fraid of spoiling your nice Sunday clo'se eh? Bet you couldn't last twenty seconds on that there pole, young Spargo.' I saw Emily and her friends approaching. Again I was faced with the challenge, either to cry off and be held a coward, or to rise to the bait and go through with it, come what may. Flushed with my previous successes, conscious of the gazes of my brother (who considered me a great hero), and Matthew and various other listening bystanders who now included Emily, I said, 'Right. Come on, then, Peters, we'll go in for it.'

'And may the best man win,' said Emily, loudly. I looked at her: she was smiling at me wickedly, apparently urging me on, as if to my doom. 'I'll show her as well,' I thought; then noticed Reuben glancing nervously across the gathered spectators. There were mother and father, just arriving at the gate and paying their silver threepences as entry fees. Reuben looked at me, worried; he knew I was about to ruin my best Sunday trousers. I shrugged; it couldn't be helped. Peters and I went up to Mr Nanskivell, who was now in charge of this event, put our names down and divested ourselves of our jackets and shoes in readiness.

First round winners got a small reward, an apple or pear or a small bag of sweetmeats, and a chance to go on to the second round and to beat other winners; and so on until the two final contestants remained to take the big prizes: for the overall winner, a navy blue cocked hat with real gold braid around it; and for the runner-up, a silver shilling. Peters went on the pole first and easily knocked his opponent, a scrawny boy, off his perch and into the long trough, some four feet deep, dug into the ground and filled with water. Now I took my turn; and was conscious of my mother's horrified face as I inched my way along the pole gripping it with my knees. I faced my opponent, who was slightly bigger than I was, and took one swing with my pillow, which burst as it hit him; he stayed there undismayed, and in a whirl of feathers aimed a huge swipe at me, which if it had connected would no doubt have finished me then and there. But I managed to arch myself back an inch or two and was gratified to feel his pillow brush past my nose: he lost his balance with the force of the swing and went down into the muddy water, to a great yell of laughter from all watching, including my father; who was evidently trying to get my mother to forget about my once spotless linen trousers, now so splashed and greasy.

After being victorious in two further contests, in the final I was faced with Job Peters, stripped to the waist. He was brawny and bronzed, appearing like a young Hercules as he sat easily on the pole, gripping it lightly with his knees as if he was quite at home and could stay there comfortably all night. Armed with a fresh pillow and having made sure that the ticking was good and strong, I aimed the first blow, vertically down on his head, which I thought might surprise him. He warded it off easily with his free arm and caught me a fast sure blow on the side of the head that knocked me over. But I had locked my ankles and knees together, and though suspended from the pole I hung on; and even to his surprise, managed to aim a blow at his legs while he pounded down on to my crossed feet, the only part of me still above the pole.

How does one regain an upright position in such a situation? I tried swinging myself from side to side, whilst holding on to the pole with my hand (a fiendishly difficult business in itself), and gripping my pillow with the other, while Peters sat back laughing at me; indeed soon the whole crowd was guffawing at my antics, sure that at any second I would loosen my grip and fall. But them Master Job made his great mistake: he leaned rather too far forward and tried to beat me on the body as I swung about, vainly attempting to get myself up. I saw the pillow coming and thrashed at it, blindly enough, with my own; the two entwined together momentarily, enough to pull him to one side; and suddenly, with an almighty splash, it was he who entered the trough and came up spluttering. So, still hanging there upside down, I was declared the winner. I came off, and still dishevelled and sweating, received the cocked hat, which I put on, and bowed to the crowd; who cheered loud and long.

My mother came up to me and said, 'I was going to give you a good hiding for spoiling your clothes, my son, but your father forbids it. He's too soft-hearted by half.' She was smiling, though, and said, ' 'Tis all such nonsense, James. Haven't you had enough of it yet?'

'I doubt it very much; eh, James?' said my father, who had now arrived, exuding evident pride.

'There's still the wheelbarrow race, mother.'

Reuben at my side, said, 'He's going in it with Miss Emily Rowlands.' I saw my mother and father exchange glances; they were impressed. And indeed, at that moment Emily herself came up, straight from the refreshment table under the trees, and said, 'Well done, James Spargo. D'you like lemonade?' She held out a mug of the beverage to me, and, mumbling my thanks, I drank long and deep. 'Don't forget the wheelbarrow race,' she said, and went off with her giggling escorts.

I decided not to enter any other events in the meantime, but encouraged Reuben to try the archery, in which he did tolerably well, scoring two inners and a near bull's-eye; and cheered Matthew on in the sack race, which he won by sprawling over the finishing line a foot or two ahead of his nearest pursuers. I was surprised then to find Mildred Morcom, the third of Emily's friends, beside me, also cheering. She looked at me, blushing prettily with admiration, and said, 'You're certainly having a field day, James. I'm glad you brought that great bufflehead Job Peters down. Can I try your hat on?' The hat was a trifle too big for me, and I doubted if it would fit Mildred— she had a fine head of hair, and a mass of ringlets; I was trying to explain this to her when Emily appeared with a large bun covered in dark treacle, and thrust it into my mouth, effectively silencing me and making me look foolish. Then she took Mildred off, both of them laughing at me, whilst I struggled with the bun, nearly choking. I could not decide then, or afterwards, whether she had taken it into her head to do this to spite Mildred, or whether they were both party to the prank.

It was now about four o'clock, and the shadows of the beech and oak trees around the field began to stretch out across the grass. A few more events followed, notably the egg-and-spoon race for girls, which was won by Jane Pellow, with Emily and Mildred standing along the route crying her on. Then it was the wheelbarrow race, the last contest of all.

Because Lodenek was much interested in who would pair with who, few people had left the ground. I saw my mother and father turn from the refreshments, mugs in hand, to see me doff my cocked hat and tight jacket, and my shoes, and prepare to be a wheelbarrow with Emily at the helm. Matthew got his wish, for having found the courage to speak up he had Jane to steer him. Poor Reuben, dreadfully teased and subjected to a barrage of pleas and cajolings, had submitted to be a barrow for Mildred. But further along the line of the other contestants I could see Job Peters, who had a strapping girl called Rebecca O'Rourke as his handler. I reflected that Job, with his wide shoulders and brawny arms (for he worked as a sawyer at the lower shipyard, half a mile below Lodenek harbour) would be a likely winner; and Rebecca, who helped her mother do the washing and mangling for all the Devereaux family, would keep his legs firmly tucked up under her arms and not fail him for the duration of the course.

And so it proved. Those two went ahead immediately the handkerchief came down, and we were soon all struggling to pursue them. Pounding the turf with my hands, pushing myself fiercely and almost dragging Emily after me, I got nearest to them; only ten yards from the finish, to collapse when my left wrist gave way and Emily sprawled on top of me, shrieking with laughter.

I found my head buried in her voluminous underwear— white calico unmentionables, satin petticoat, white cotton stockings, and at least two frilled underskirts; nothing, of course, to what our grand ladies are subject to now in Queen Victoria's third decade, but, even so, quite considerable. I had become familiar with what my mother and sisters wore by seeing their under garments dancing on the line in the yard behind our cottage, but this was another matter altogether; a quite fortuitous glimpse of intimate things I had not looked for and was immediately ashamed to be presented with. I hasten now to add, as a man long married (though my dear wife, God rest her soul, is not here to read this), who has always honoured and respected the opposite sex, I am not proud of recording this occurrence; but it did have various results which affected my life afterwards, and so as a matter of truth I set it down.

Emily, as the winners were being presented with their prizes, rolled over and freed me, still convulsed with merriment, which increased on seeing my violently flaming and embarrassed face; and kneeling up before all those bystanders including my parents (most of them also laughing), kissed me fully on the lips. Helping me to my feet, she dusted me off in as possessive a manner as any young wife declaring to the world her new husband; then arm in arm, she led me back to help me on with my jacket and cocked hat. Finally she became unexpectedly solicitous about my wrist, which was by now swelling painfully, and gravely relinquished me to the care of my mother, father and brother, expressing the hope that they would get me home to administer a cold water compress as soon as possible.

CHAPTER 9

THE PORTHCOTHAN AFFAIR

My sprained wrist soon healed, and during the summer, when school was not held (we had all August to ourselves), I went on the Galatea for several runs to Roscoff. I was now promoted to foretopman, Davy having got himself taken on as an able seaman on a larger vessel sailing from Falmouth. My eyesight was excellent, and, my voice developing more power after breaking, I was able to bellow sufficiently loudly from the crow's-nest to make myself heard in all but the worst gales; during which, in any case, I was not sent aloft.

Often, as I did my watch up there above the ship as she moved west or south-west, I would think of Emily and her remarkable behaviour at Whitsun. I could not but conclude that in a strange sort of way she was making a favourite of me; but what the future could bring for us both I could only guess. I realised that her father (who was now High Sheriff of Cornwall) would expect her in time to make a good match with some well-to-do landowner's son, or at least a rising young man in the world of mining or commerce; and I doubted if Thomas would ever entertain any consideration of me as a son-in-law. If I could become a reliable captain and business man like my father I should, of course, command a good deal of respect in his eyes. That, my eventual aim, was therefore reinforced by frequent thoughts of the challenging, baffling Emily.

Meanwhile, at Roscoff, I had little time for

amorous adventures, though I did accompany Father to M. Renan's house. This time I was offered wine, to drink with the two men, and had an introduction to the business side of the voyages.

My father, in addition to captaining Mr Rowland's ship, acted also as agent, handling the buying of goods to be taken back. Few sea captains had the commercial ability to discharge both duties; so I knew that Father was an important and valued servant in Thomas' enterprise.

With M. Renan we went to the great warehouse he owned on one of the Roscoff wharves. I was amazed to see the long lines of casks of spirits, brandy, rum and Geneva; of wine— mainly port, sherry and claret; bales of tobacco in the leaf, chest after chest of tea, barrels of salt and sugar; baulks of silks, satins, calico, bales of cotton; hundreds of boxes of currants, raisins and sultanas, spices, and pepper; and sacks of cocoa and coffee beans. All goods which bore duties, mostly onerous, in King George's domain.

My father had a list of goods to purchase, and the wherewithal to pay for it: golden guineas. Later I realised that Mr Rowlands, proprietor and managing director of the Lodenek fleet, had provided the cash. Since gold coins were especially needed by the Emperor Napoleon to finance his wars, this huge and continued trade in contraband goods with his enemies across the channel was encouraged for his benefit, despite edicts to the contrary

'So that's another reason why we're always received as friends here,' I thought, as Father gave his orders.

'A hundred and twenty ankers of rum, Monsieur; and fifty of cognac. Five chests of tea, Assam or Darjeeling, packed into your usual watertight bags. Ten sacks of sugar...five of salt. Quelle prix?'

'*Trois guineas le sac, de vingt kilo*.'

Father nodded, and continued, 'Twenty-four boxes of currants, twelve of dates. Sixty kilos of pepper...'

The order was written down by M. Renan, who retired to a little office hardly bigger than a cupboard, where, to my surprise, I saw a now familiar figure seated writing at a tiny desk: Iseut. Evidently her father was employing her as a clerk. She looked up and gave me a half longing, half rueful smile, as if thinking she would rather be out in the sunshine and playing hide-and-seek along the quays.

'*Bonjour, Iseut*,' I said, trying out my French.

'*Bonjour, comment vas-tu, Jammes*?'

'*Très bien, merci. Où est Charlotte*?'

'*Charlotte est allée à Paris avec notre tante, à voir la grande cité*.' Again the sad little smile; but perhaps her turn would soon come, I thought, to see the world and Paris.

She was growing up, quite a little woman now, with a firm bosom and head held high, her black hair (neither too long and straight) now tightly coiled; she had already bid childhood adieu with evident regret, and could see, so far, only a new tyranny, or at least drudgery, in doing her father's accounts. There was no sense of adventure, of a world opening up for her, as there was for me. I wished I could help her, console her, and perhaps love her. But business called us, and I had to leave with Father to see to the watering and provisioning of the Galatea for the return voyage.

The ship was loaded that afternoon; I noticed that the ankers of spirits— containing eight gallons each— aboard already roped in such fashion that they could be easily handled and borne, one on a man's back and one on his chest, or one each side of a mule or donkey. The tea was in oilskin bags weighing each about five pounds; they could if necessary be dropped overboard and could lie for days in a channel, to be later dragged or 'crept' up with grapples.

Not that we actually expected to do such a thing at that time; the Revenue officers along the north coast of Cornwall were much extended, and some (as I found later) actually received extra inducements from Mr Thomas Rowlands not to interfere with his free-trading; but one was never sure that a new and zealous Riding Officer with several armed dragoons would not chance upon us as we discharged our clandestine cargo, or even be informed of the intended operation in response to generous rewards offered for information; although in the main none of our people would dream of such treachery to their own kind. After all, their access to such goods depended on our enterprises; they could never have afforded enough duty-paid goods to enjoy even a semblance of civilised living.

We had an uneventful voyage home, apart from running into a fierce squall off Cape Cornwall, riding it out with sails hastily struck; and by one o'clock in the morning approached Porthcothan Bay, where, the clouds having obscured even the most brilliant stars, I was ordered to give the signal of our arrival from the crow's-nest.

The lantern had green glass in it. As I was instructed to do, once I had climbed the rigging and got into the lookout barrel, I lit it with my flint and tinder-box, keeping it facing away from the land; then turned it towards the shore, exposing the light for three seconds; turned it away, counting three slowly; then completed the signal by a further exposure towards land for three further seconds. Almost immediately this was done a small light, a mere pinprick it seemed, showed twice from the hillside above the Bay.

'All clear,' I shouted to my father and Enoch Penberthy, who were waiting directly below.

'Shorten the mizzen— we'll go farther in,' I heard Father order. I peered towards the white sands of the beach, which showed dimly ahead beyond the line of breakers massing and moving in relentlessly to spend themselves on the sands. Soon dark shapes could be discerned, dinghies and bumboats being rowed out towards us; voices hailed us and ropes and ladders were let down from the Galatea's bulwarks. Soon the discharging was taking place, in a quiet businesslike manner, as well organized as ever, it seemed.

But as the first boats laden with ankers of rum and brandy reached the shore, the clouds moved apart enough to allow a weak moon to illuminate the beach itself and the dark steep cliffs around it. A horse appeared on the sands, a grey ridden by a uniformed figure, down near the tideline. A voice cried, 'Halt— stay where you are; or I fire.'

The horseman, in a red coat which appeared purple in the moonlight, was holding a long pistol. I saw the men in the foremost bumboat turn and stare; they were rowing hard to get through the breakers and beach their craft as high on the sands as possible, so it was a futile order to give, I reflected. Just then the moon was blanketed out by another swathe of cloud, and a shot rang out, echoing round the cliffs.

I heard curses, arguments and recriminations, but could make nothing of it; my father was giving orders for the Galatea to clap on sail and move off, which we very smartly did. As we made way to the open sea, with some of our free-trade goods still aboard, we heard several other shots from the shore. I wanted to watch the fracas, but knew that my first duty was to search the sea ahead of us for oncoming vessels, so I turned from the shore and stared nor'-east, as we passed Treyarnon and Constantine Bay and rounded Trevose Head. It became very cold in the crow's-nest, the wind rising off the sea and screeching through the gaps between the staves of the barrel; I drew my oilskin tightly around me and was glad to sip from the little flask of rum and water I was allowed. Soon the white shadowy tower of the Daymark above Stepper Point, guarding the entrance to our estuary, showed up. 'Daymark on starboard ahead,' I sang out. The wind was getting up now, a strong north-westerly; the waves were running before us, showing white crests in the intense gloom.

We entered between the Points and, before we reached Hawker's Cove, a small fishing settlement on our larboard, I heard orders being given and, in the sudden hush under the lee of Stepper, witnessed the remaining ankers and bags of tea being deposited over board, to sink into the channel. A boat was lowered, loaded with the last few sacks of sugar and salt, and some boxes of dried fruit, and rowed into the cove, to be concealed in some pilot's cottage, well or cellar until (as we used to say) the coast was clear. The Galatea then dropped anchor to await morning and the flowing tide, when our gigs would come out to help tow us in.

The Porthcothan affair was great news in Lodenek the following day. The Riding Officer, it appeared, had been alerted by the Comptroller, second-in-Command of the Custom House at the port, and sent out to do his duty; his chief, the Collector of Customs, being on annual leave. It was commonly thought in Lodenek that there was a measure of collusion between Mr Thomas Rowlands and Mr Mackenzie, the Collector; they were certainly firm friends on the same close social standing, often entertaining each other and their families. Whether this amounted to bribery and corruption can never be proved; certainly no evidence was ever adduced to that effect, and if the Collector benefited from Thomas' enterprises it was, as far as Lodenek knew for certain, only by open purchase of legitimate duty-paid goods, albeit at the sort of discount which any merchant might accord to a good customer. Nevertheless, until that morning when the Galatea berthed alongside the north quay, it had been remarkable that she was never searched except when she had no contraband on board, and that such searches appeared, though apparently diligent, to be mere formalities.

Now, with the Collector away for a month, the young Comptroller had decided to earn himself likely promotion by attempting to have various smugglers apprehended. So on coming ashore with the Galatea's cargo the oarsmen at Porthcothan had been challenged; the shots we heard had been interchanges of fire between our landing party and the Riding Officer, backed by six armed Revenue men who were waiting on the cliff top. The Riding Officer had been shot through the shoulders, and two oarsmen had been arrested and were now charged with attempted murder, in addition to importing goods without paying duty.

On berthing we ourselves were subject to close inspection by the Comptroller, Mr Piers Baldrick, his Landing Waiter, and two Revenue men; who insisted on going over the ship from crow's-nest to keel, and stem to stern. This, certainly was no formality; I could see my father and Enoch standing there watching solemn-faced as the men went about their duties, opening every container, chest and locker, poking and prying with their swordsticks, even cutting open the lifebelts we carried; for, it transpired, a ship had recently been apprehended at Falmouth, carrying tobacco rolled tightly inside the covers of such utilities.

'No cargo— and no ballast, Captain?' I heard Mr Baldrick say, for all to hear. He stood there in the full morning sunlight, the braid glittering on his epaulettes and three-cornered hat. 'Where d'you say you sailed from?'

'Wexford,' my father said. 'We took across a consignment of pilchards from St.Ives, but there was no return cargo for us; and with the weather beating up I decided to run for home rather than make for Kings Town or Bristol.' It sounded a likely enough story, for the nor 'wester had increased to gale force outside the estuary.

Baldrick stared down into the hold. 'Can't smell any fish,' he said. 'Must have been well packed.'

'In hogsheads,' Father said. 'They have some excellent coopers in St.Ives.'

'Well, I shall send down to get a report on it, you may be assured of that,' Baldrick said. 'Found anything, Harris?'

'A jar of brandy in the Captain's cabin, another in the Mate's.' Harris, the Searcher, carried two narrow-necked stoneware bottles.

'Duty paid, Captain?'

'Got 'em at the Britannia, the day we set sail,' said Father. 'One for me, one for Enoch; ask John Button. Baldrick nodded, as if thinking, 'As I expected you to say.' It would he useless to question John Button, the landlord, who would merely confirm what Father had said. The double irony of it was that the brandy had almost certainly been delivered by free-traders to the back door of the inn.

'Well, Captain Spargo, I bid you good day. But I warn you now and anyone else here who might be tempted to bring in uncustomed goods that while I'm in charge here my duty will be discharged to its utmost.'

The two men accused of murder, both fishermen, one from St. Merryn parish and the other from St.Eval, were tried later that week before Mr Thomas Rowlands, chairman of the bench, and two other magistrates, Rear Admiral Polkinhorne and young Mr Alwyn Bassett of Harlyn House. Without doubt, all of them benefited from the free trading that went on. The two accused swore they carried no arms and therefore could not have shot the riding officer. They were found not guilty. They were also discharged by the Magistrates (after a brief retirement to discuss the case) from the charge of bringing in contraband, despite evidence sworn by the Revenue men that they had been seen rowing bum boats full of ankers.

And as for the cargo itself, after the skirmish, when the Revenue men had hastily retired from the scene to minister to the Riding Officer, it was rapidly landed, taken up from the beach by a score of waiting men (who were each paid ten shillings for their endeavours) and carried a mile or more up the valley where it was stowed in the long tunnel or recess known as the Vugha; the entrance of which was cleverly sealed up with stones, turves and furze so that the Revenue men returning with a detachment of King's Light Dragoons from Bodmin Barracks the next day failed to find it.

Three weeks later, after the return of Mr Mackenzie, mule trains and wagons drawn by horses with muffled hooves removed most of the goods, driving them far across Cornwall and into Devon; but a good number of ankers, and much of the tea and dried fruit, were distributed to inns, shops, farms and the houses of the gentry and clergy, over several parishes of our own district.

Mr Piers Baldrick had, however, one consolation to set against these frustrations. He was acute enough to send the two Revenue pinnaces down river on the next tide after the Galatea had berthed, with grapples and drags; and they 'creeped up' most of the ankers and bags of tea we had jettisoned on our arrival inside the Points.

No accusations were made, since there were no witnesses forthcoming and no evidence attached to the goods as to who had deposited them there. We knew, and he and his men knew, why they were there. And so the matter rested.

CHAPTER 10

AN INVITATION TO A BALL

So the years passed, and I was growing up to know the sea and ships, how to handle them, and how to navigate. My father was an excellent teacher, strict but never unreasonable. The trade we engaged in was at times legitimate— taking tin ingots to Cardiff and bringing back coal, exporting malt or wheat to Norway and returning with pitchpine for ship building or pit props for Cornish mines— and at times illegitimate, as our voyages to Roscoff undoubtedly were. The difference meant little to me then, and I never thought to question seriously what we were doing. Sometimes I eyed the Galatea's ten brass guns (each capable of sending a five pound ball smashing into the riggings or bulwarks of an American or French privateer) with considerable speculation, wondering whether they would ever be used against another enemy- the Revenue Cutters which were now increasingly operating around our coasts.

Napoleon had abdicated in 1814, when the Allies finally entered Paris, after some eleven years of almost continual war; confined then to Elba, the Emperor escaped to France the next year, raised another enthusiastic army and, with 74,000 men, most of them seasoned veterans, met 25,000 veterans of the British Army under Wellington at Waterloo, with Blucher's Prussians arriving at the last moment. The world now knows the outcome of that great battle; to us then it was above all a great relief to lay the bogey of Bonaparte, to see him exiled to St.Helena, and to have finally done with a conflict for which few people, even in the most loyal parts of England, had much stomach any more.

Ours were mixed feelings in Cornwall. The end of the war meant that the London government was now able to devote more money and resources to combating free-trading. Prices of bread and meat and most food were still ruinously high, and would remain high, despite an often starving rural population, for years. Duties on imported goods increased rather than shrank— in 1815 more than 2,000 articles were listed on the Statute Book as dutiable.

Men disbanded from the Navy were now being offered posts in the Revenue, where they would almost certainly come into conflict with their own friends, even their own kin, who were intent on perpetuating the golden age of smuggling. The incident I had witnessed at Porthcothan was a straw in the wind, a significant pointer to what would follow.

Meanwhile I was growing tall for my age and broadening in the shoulders and chest, after several months as deck hand on the Galatea. I was not often at school now, having handed on the duties of monitor to others; and Reuben was now following in my footsteps, doing spells as galley-monkey and foretopman. Soon after my sixteenth birthday, when I was third mate on the Galatea (entrusted with her command during two watches of four hours in the twenty-four), I received an invitation to the birthday ball to be given for Miss Emily Rowlands, at the grand mansion her father was building on Sandry's Hill.

The fortunes of Thomas Rowlands had never ridden higher than in that year, 1816. The shipbuilding and trading activities, the success of his Lodenek Bank (backed by Coutts and Company of London, who held deeds on much of his property), the rents of houses, inns and farms he owned, all led him to decide that St.Petroc's, that homely Queen Anne house on the hill just above the harbour, was too small for his family of eleven children, his wife and servants; so he had, the year before, began to build a large new porticoed house in the Regency style, with four bays and two wings, farther up the slope with a view of the whole town, and looking, eye to eye as it seemed, at Devereaux Place on the hill opposite, with the church tower rising between them as if to keep the two peacefully apart.

As Sandry's Hill House rose stone by quarried stone to its crenellated top, and the Ionic pillars of the gracious portico were added, Lodenek was agog at the achievement: the Devereaux family might look down their noses and avert their gaze, but here was a real challenge, a *nouveau riche* merchant intent on becoming Lord and Squire, indeed, having already been appointed High Sheriff and Chairman of the Bench. Lodenek was, in fact, split down the middle, as much as it had been by religious factions: divided into those who supported Arthur Devereaux, Major of the King's Cornish Light Dragoons— either through holding employment under him or by renting houses from him— and those who admired the panache and brilliant business methods of Thomas Rowlands, or who held jobs or tenancies from him. Of course we Spargos were all for Thomas, despite my father's native caution and doubts; it would have been ungrateful for us to be otherwise. So when, that September, the Invitation arrived, written in a flowing hand upon rag paper stiff as a board and sealed with wax and a signet ring, addressed to myself, I could not but feel honoured, and read it out to them all at home.

'Miss Emily Lavinia Rowlands requests the pleasure of the company of Mr James Spargo on the occasion of her 16th birthday Ball.

At Sandry's Hill House at half past six o'clock on the evening of Friday 10th September, 1816. R.S.V.P.'

'What does R.S.V.P. mean?' asked my sister Emma.

'*Respondez s'il vous plait*,' I answered, more or less accurately. 'Reply please' .1 must write a note to say I'm coming.'

'What will you wear, James?' Reuben wanted to know.

That, indeed, was a question. I had already outgrown the best clothes I had almost ruined that glorious day at Whitsun the year before. The pay I had from the Galatea would never be enough to cover a new jacket and trousers and shoes, but I could see that it was either that or make an excuse not to go, and forgo Emily's favour for ever. My mother saw me frowning and said, 'We'll manage somehow. Emma's a good needle woman; she and I will make you new trousers, and I'll have a word with your Da.' The upshot was that father lent me a guinea for a new jacket, which I had made to measure by Mr Benjamin Oatey, generally recognised as the best tailor in town, of navy-blue west country broadcloth: the best he stocked. It was my first tail-coat, cut away at the waist with broad lapels and a high collar; I felt a genuine Regency buck when I tried it on. That left only the shoes, which I could afford myself, and were ordered from Mr Thomas Henry Curgenven, who made shoes for all our family at his little cobbler's shop just off the quay, not twenty yards from our cottage: they were square-toed with two straps over the insteps and shining tin buckles. I laboured long at my reply to the invitation, not to be outdone by Emily's flourishes: my pride in my own hand writing taught me by Miss Tonkyn (God rest her soul) came to the fore as I wrote:

'Mr James Spargo begs to accept your most kind invitation and will be delighted to attend the Ball on the 10th September next.'

Reuben, wide-eyed at this latest honour, had volunteered to deliver the reply; but first I had to seal it, and had nothing to impress the wax. Reuben himself came to the rescue, producing a brass button with a raised anchor on it, which he had from Matthew Pook, in exchange for his prize conker pickled in vinegar and baked in hot ashes, which (Reuben reckoned) had demolished a hundred and fifty opponents.

CHAPTER 11

SANDRY'S HILL HOUSE

It was a quiet balmy evening as I went up the hill to the great new house. Sounds of an orchestra filtered out through the portico as I entered the drive among newly planted laurels and almond trees. Several carriages drove past me, bringing guests from another parish. Ahead of me, until I caught him up, was Matthew Pook, looking uncomfortable in a new suit rather too large for him; his parents had evidently had it made with an eye to the future.

Emily was at the door, with her mother, receiving the guests and their presents. Mrs Rowlands, a stately buxom lady, I knew only by sight; she did not appear much in the town itself. Perhaps because Emily had told her about me she smiled graciously, inspecting me closely. Long afterwards I learned that she was a Trenance from St.Wenn, and was heiress to a considerable estate there; her money, or credit, had helped her husband Thomas to build up his business.

Emily wore a dress of brilliant blue taffeta with little tucks and flounces across the bosom, and at the half sleeves: high waisted, and flowing long, as they wore them then. Her auburn hair, although still done in ringlets at the sides, was gathered up at the back exposing a long swanlike neck. She appeared very grown up to me now, quit unlike the daring boisterous girl I knew at Whitsun the year before. When she saw me she coloured slightly, and gave me her hand to kiss, coyly fluttering her eyelids, as if she had been practicing this art especially for the occasion.

'So glad you could come, James Spargo,' she said, in a manner intended to suggest a Duchess at a garden party.

I mumbled, 'Very many happy returns of the day, Miss Em'ly,' and handed her a little package containing three cambric handkerchiefs embroidered with the letter E in pink by my sister Emma. She hardly glanced at it, but gave it to her mother to dispose of, and greeted Matthew.

Inside the hall I could see the musicians, a group of local talents including three members of our church orchestra: two fiddlers, a flautist, a clarinettist, and a cellist. They were led by a middle-aged man with a shock of wild grey hair, always getting into his eyes; he was of Italian extraction, of the name of Boldini (being known irreverently as Professor Baloney), and he was playing a fortepiano. This last was something of a novelty to us in Lodenek; the only keyboard instruments I had ever had the excruciating bad fortune to hear until then were various harpsichord and spinets, usually poorly tuned, and played by young pupils of very little or no talent. Professor Boloney's new forte-piano was well in tune and he could certainly play it; though from time to time he would break off, rising to conduct the others for a space, then sit down to resume his brilliant trills and chords again. I stood there quite fascinated, until Mildred Morcom said shyly at my elbow, 'Hello, James. I wondered if you'd come.'

Mildred, too, was suddenly grown to an adult, it seemed, as I looked at her pale complexion, her fair hair also done up into a bun, and her fashionable dress in sea green. Her china blue eyes stared at me; I knew she admired me, but this only irritated me.

'Hello, Mildred. Didn't you think I'd be here?'

'I wasn't sure. You sailor boys don't always like this sort of occasion.'

True, I thought; very near the mark, in fact, for I was regarding the other guests with some apprehension as they entered the hall with such lordly assurance that it was obvious they were well used to moving in these circles or even in greater ones. The young men— not so much older than myself, as I realised afterwards— were sons of neighbouring gentry and merchants, used to conducting themselves before others with the ease that public school education brings. And I was only a clumsy sailor lad, a National schoolboy; how could I compete with them on such an occasion? Only the thought that Emily herself had been a monitor like me gave me any confidence.

The orchestra now burst into the Military Two-step, marking the arrival of several dashing young blades in the dress uniform of the Dragoons: tight short black jackets with gold—braided epaulettes, and red trousers with gold seam stripes. Emily was greeting them, and I saw she had a card in her hand on which she was marking down various dances she would engage to have with them. She was evidently extremely impressed by these young officer cadets. Not to seem an utter coward, I went up to her and said 'I obliged you in the wheelbarrow race last year, Miss Em'ly. Will you oblige me now by dancing with me?'

Her eyes, I saw now under the glare of the chandeliers, each carrying fifty blazing candles, were a strange mixture of emerald and violet; indeed they did not quite match, the right one being greener than the left. 'Ah yes,' she said, touching my arm. 'How is your wrist now?'

'Quite recovered. No ill effects, thank you.'

She nodded and examined her card. 'You may have the Six Hand Reel and the Lancers, James,' she said, marking the card with a little pencil; and turned to welcome the next arrival.

Two footmen passed by, each bearing a tray of glasses, one of brandy punch with fruit floating in it, the other of claret cup. I took a glass of the punch and went over to Mildred. 'Have you got a card?' I asked.

'Yes, James.' I could see that she had only a few dances marked on it. 'The first dance, the Valeta, is vacant,' she informed me. I undertook to have it with her, and also a waltz, though I had only a vague notion as to what a waltz really was.

I did quite well in the Valeta, which after all is simple enough, and easily picked up by watching others; Mildred glowed with inordinate pride at being squired by me. Then came the Reel with Emily, at which I acquitted myself tolerably well, only putting a foot wrong here and there, and managing to avoid knocking into her or stepping on her foot: which I sensed, with mortal dread, would be the end of my endeavours in this society. I held my hand up high and twirled her about, swinging her recklessly as she closed with me to promenade, causing an amused shock to appear on her face. The dance was over too soon, I felt: suddenly the music finished and she was curtsying, giving me a roguish smile as I bowed to her.

Syllabubs, mince pies with clotted cream, jelly with cherries in it, blancmange and meringues were then served, and after three or more dances had run their course, an interval was announced. Emily was laughing vivaciously to two of the cadets who seemed to monopolize her. I took some blancmange, a mince pie and another glass of brandy punch, and found Matthew eating jelly by the grand staircase which spiralled up to the bedrooms; he looked as if he were being slowly boiled alive in his serge coat and choker, and was trying to spit out cherry stones unobtrusively on the side of his plate.

'Well, Matthew; what do you make of it all?'

'Don't know, James, don't know at all. Never seen anything like this before. Some great house 'tis, you, id'n it. Be years before 'tis finished.'

I said, 'Well, they certainly do things well. It'll give the Devereauxs something to think about.

I was still watching Emily, passing from one admirer to the next, smiling and making little comments or jokes. One tall cadet, with a tiny fair moustache, kissed her hand, and passed her a note, which she secreted inside the tucks of her sleeve, with the beginnings of a blush upon her, as she turned from him quickly; looking up, she caught my eye, and stared boldly at me, smiling faintly and raising her eyebrows. So much competition, I thought; what could I do to outshine them all? I could see her slipping away out of my world, where I could never follow her.

The dancing began again with a Cornish Furry, followed by a Three Handed Reel, both of which I danced reasonably well with a plump farmer's daughter from St.Issey; then the Waltz was announced. I found Mildred, and holding her by her waist as I saw other men do with their partners, launched upon the floor. But I could not get the rhythm right; my feet slithered about hopelessly and the poor girl could not follow my shuffling. 'One two three, one two three,' I heard her count, and I tried desperately to keep the beat of the music. I turned, swinging her out, and she seemed to anticipate this; but we barged into another couple, then, oh horror! I stepped on her little satin covered toe and she cried out agonisedly. 'Damnation,' I muttered. 'Sorry, Mildred, I'm a clumsy oaf.'

'No, 'tis all right,' she breathed, forgiving me readily. But the dance was ruined for me, and we almost came to a standstill there in the centre of the hall where the other gaily dancing couples could move about us without our harming them. When it ended I walked her back, in sheer misery, to her seat and bowed, saying, 'Can I get you anything?'

She shook her head, looking at me with a mixture of pity and adoration. 'Don't worry, James. You couldn't expect to...'

But I turned and rushed away from her, grabbed a glass of claret from the nearest flunkey, and went to sit on the stairs. I stared across the floor as they went into an old Court Dance, in which there was a great deal of twirling, bowing and curtseying between the partners. I could have done that one, I thought, seeing Matthew squire Jane Pellew through it, smiling upon her with an idiotic fixed expression. Looking up, I saw several of the younger Rowlands children watching the proceedings from between the railings of the balustrade on the first floor; it seemed to me they were grinning at my discomfort.

Dancing lessons, that would be the answer, I thought. Who taught dancing? At the same time I wished I were well out of this brilliant strange world, out on the high seas with the Galatea ploughing through the rollers on a trip to Roscoff or Russia. That, I knew, was a real life, a man's life, the life I was best fitted for. Sailors got married, didn't they? And surely they couldn't all dance well. Women were said to admire sailors, to think them heroes. But Emily... would she ever think well of me now? She must have seen what had happened. And now, soon, there would be the Lancers. I had no idea whether it would be an easy dance to learn like the Valeta, or something quite beyond me. I could only wait in my agony, drinking another glass of claret to keep up my courage, and hope it would be the former.

But, of course, it was indeed beyond me. The first figure amazed me with its intricacy as I tried in my hopeless manner to step it with them, threading in and out of the others with their help as I was pushed here and there; but it seemed to me I had suddenly acquired three feet, and couldn't put any of them where they were wanted. Emily started to laugh, and I could see the others, two of whom were cadets, smiling; I grinned foolishly, striving to do what was wanted, but it was useless. As soon as the figure was ended I said to Emily, 'Sorry - I think I'm going to be sick,' and left the floor, staggering dizzily, as much from embarrassment as from the effect of the drinks I had had. I saw Emily beckon to another cadet, who had been watching the confusion; he readily joined the set, and soon they were going through the second figure with nonchalant ease as the orchestra played faster and livelier, and Professor Baloney gesticulated more vigorously from his forte-piano, his hair at times appearing to stand on end.

I went outside on the portico, needing air. My face was sweating great drops that splashed on to the steps, and I actually did feel nausea rising in my stomach. I leaned against one of the great pillars carved out of blocks of Portland limestone, some of which we had brought back to Lodenek in the Galatea. Gradually I recovered, vowing never to go dancing again whatever the attractions were, and wandered slowly along the drive and down a path leading off it.

A cool night wind came from the west, calming me; little white moths flickered about the roses and late flowering Michaelmas daisies, and a big furry creature with beautiful orange and brown wings settled momentarily on my coat sleeve. A consideration arose in my mind, causing an upsurge of anger against Emily. She must have realised beforehand that, unskilled at dancing as I was, I could never have executed the Lancers: why had she deliberately engaged me for it, unless she wanted me to make an utter clown of myself before everyone? Was this another strange quirk of her humour? Perhaps indeed, back at that Whitsun, she had secretly hoped that I would bungle the wheelbarrow race— which in a certain sense I had done.

A plantation of young beech and plane trees lay before me, through which the path wound along to the parish church: it was planned as the Rowlands' private way to Sunday Service. I decided now to quietly slip away, not wishing to re-enter and face the further banter and amusement of all within. But on reaching the gate leading into the churchyard I found it locked. I was considering climbing up over it when I heard footsteps behind me, crunching on the gravel of the path, and turned to find Mr Rowlands himself approaching.

'Well young man, and where do you think you are going?'

'I... want to go home. I'm not feeling too well, Sir.'

'I see. Well now; Mr Spargo, isn't it?'

'James Spargo, Sir.'

'I remember you. The amenuensis. And how are you faring now at sea?'

'I'm third mate on the Galatea, Sir.'

'Are you, indeed. A good ship, the Galatea— my best vessel, I think. And your father is a very respected Captain. You wouldn't want to let him down, now, will you?'

'Let him down, Mr Rowlands?'

'I mean in public. I saw what happened in the Lancers. It's nothing to disturb yourself over, James, my boy; I've made a fool of myself at dancing in the past. What does it matter? You'll be forgiven, perhaps even admired if you come back with me now, and stroll in as if nothing has happened. Simply laugh it off as a piece of bad luck, eh?'

I stood there in the half-light, staring at him. He was smiling gently, one hand in the pocket of his tight grey trousers, but looking at me keenly, with some of that challenging stare I had seen on Emily.

'There'll be another interval about now, I should guess,' he said. 'They'll be cutting the birthday cake and handing it around. Come and have a piece, eh?' And indeed, I realised that the music, which until now could be heard from the house, drifting down over the hillside, had ceased. 'But I shouldn't take any more brandy punch or wine if I was you,' he advised.

We turned back, walking still in a leisurely fashion among the growing young trees interspersed with shrubs. He mused, half to himself it seemed, 'Dancing, balls, girls— what do they really count for? They're only a means for the women to get to know young men, and make matches. You don't want to think of marriage yet, do you? How old are you James?'

'Sixteen, sir.'

'Hmmm. When I was your age I was interested in horses, farming, and business, in that order. Didn't look for a wife until I was nearly thirty. Now I've got eleven children. It will all come to you in due course, lad. No need to hurry. Emily looks well tonight, don't she?'

'Oh yes. Quite lovely,' I opined.

'The Belle of the Ball. But she don't know what she wants, yet, you see. Don't you let her lead you a dance any more— you've had your lesson, eh?'

I admitted that I had.

'Stick to ships and the sea,' he told me, as he mounted the steps under the grand portico. 'I expect great things of you, James. Dancing? Pff!...' He gave a derisory snort, clapped me on the back, and left me.

Emily, seeing me at the door, beckoned me over to where she was dispensing pieces from a great two-tiered iced cake dressed with ribbons and bearing sixteen candles, recently blown out. 'James,' she said, in that considerate, slightly worried tone she had used when I had sprained my wrist, 'are you feeling better? Can you eat some of this? Or would you rather take it home with you?'

'I'm sorry I spoiled your Lancers,' I said, accepting the plate, and eyeing the cake doubtfully.

'Oh, nonsense, that was of no account whatever. Stupid of me to put you down for it - I didn't realise you had never danced it before. I say, would you like to put it right by partnering me in the Boscastle Square? It's very easy, I promise you.'

I was conscious of Mildred just behind her, staring at me with some anxiety. But Emily's violet and green gaze was upon me and I submitted. 'Very well, Emily. I'll do my best,' I said.

I went over to the refreshment table and asked for a glass of lemonade, and crumbling some of the icing of the cake, ate and drank a little.

'Good old Jim,' Matthew said, coming to my side. 'Feel better? What a sheenanigans you made at the Lancers. Like a bull in a china shop.'

I nodded and shrugged. 'Try anything once,' I said. 'But some things only once.' Professor Boloney raised his hands, struck a chord, and the dancing began once more.

An hour later, after stepping through the Boscastle Square Dance without further mishap, and taking part in the hilarious Serpent Dance which ended the evening, I was ready to leave. Emily and her mother and father were all at the door, seeing everyone off. As I took my leave, thanking them for a wonderful evening with a somewhat rueful smile, I saw Thomas Rowlands give me a faint but discernible nod, accompanied by the ghost of a wink.

CHAPTER 12

SMUGGLERS AND SEARCHERS

I stuck to the sea, as Mr Rowlands advised, and had very little to do with girls for nearly two years. I did see Iseut from time to time when we berthed at Roscoff, but only during the course of business, and once her sister Charlotte— who was actually, at the age of seventeen, now betrothed to the son of a Roscoff wine merchant. At this time the increase in the number of Revenue cutters, and fast sloops of the Royal Navy itself (now no longer occupied with war against the French), caused us to alter our free-trading arrangements: sometimes the Galatea sailed to St.Peter Port in Guernsey, where clandestine warehouses were offering uncustomed goods, or to Cherbourg; occasionally we visited Brest. This was to give pursuing vessels the slip and keep them guessing as to our true intention.

On several voyages, sailing as far as Bordeaux, we loaded with casks of burgundy and cognac and boxes of lace, sewn up in waterproof bags; then called at St.Nazaire, where we took on cauliflowers, artichokes and melons. We sailed into Lodenek, and under the watching eyes of the Landing Waiters, discharged the fruit and vegetables, paying the relatively low duties on them. Our first cargo was hidden deep in the hull under a false bottom, and on our next voyage out we landed this contraband at Harlyn Bay, Porthcothan, or, if the sea were calm enough, at Porthmeor Cove, where we anchored just outside the dark savage rocks that guard the entrance thereto.

Mr McKenzie, for ten years Collector of Customs at Lodenek, had now retired; he was over sixty and in poor health, and his masters in the Revenue Service had offered him a favourable pension to step down. In his place they put the over-zealous Piers Baldrick, who was quite incorruptible, being paid a salary of nearly twice that which McKenzie had received. Mr Thomas Rowlands did attempt to cultivate Baldrick's society, inviting him to one or two gatherings at Sandry's Hill House; but it led to nothing, and the acquaintance did not prosper.

On several occasions, having landed our goods and stowed them in the Vugha, it was found that Revenue men were encamped on the valley side opposite, watching day and night for over a week, and the free trade cargo could not be removed without revealing the hiding place. Various ruses were then resorted to. Incoming smuggled goods were, for a while, dispersed around the various farm houses and cottages of the district, hidden in cupboards, cellars, lofts, wells, and furze-ricks— for every farmer and cottager then cut furze in the summer and autumn to burn on his hearth in winter, wood being sparse and too valuable on our bare north coast to use as fuel. Underground, over a period of four months, work was done in the Vugha itself, extending its chamber through the hillside until it came out in the floor of a barn at Trevemedar farm, half a mile away; so that both exits could be used to distribute goods stowed there. The Excise never found either of them.

We had many a laugh at the expense of the 'Searchers,' as we generally called all Revenue men. Part of one cargo of tobacco, hotly pursued by the Collector's men, was driven by two brothers in a dray to the Ring o' Bells inn at St.Issey where, before the arrival of the Searchers, it was transferred into a large coffin and taken into the church; candles were lit and placed about it, the brothers then kneeling in vigil about it. Having searched the inn and the dray and found nothing, the Excisemen, seeing lights in the church, entered, but were asked by the verger not to disturb the men, who he declared had just lost their father after a long illness. They left the brothers unchallenged, to run the goods far across country later that night.

The Reverend William Rowlands, called late at night to the death-bed of a parishioner at St. Cadoc above Harlyn Bay, was mounting his horse after administering the last rites when he witnessed a train of eight carts loaded up with ankers of spirits and bales of tobacco, and forty horses each carrying three bags of tea weighing fifty-six pounds. The smugglers were well-armed, and the Vicar could only watch and later report what he had seen to the Collector, as he considered it his duty to do, as soon as he reached Lodenek, naming various riders he had seen go past; but no charges could be preferred as no other evidence or witnesses were available, and magistrates and juries were still finding for the defendants in most cases of this kind.

Various battles were fought up and down the coast between the free-traders and the Searchers, several woundings being the result; though there were only two fatalities, these being the steeds of Riding Officers. A quantity of thirty tubs of brandy, seized from a visiting French vessel off the entrance of the estuary, was brought into Lodenek itself and locked in the Custom House store. Two nights later the store was broken into and the whole cargo removed by boat at high tide, the Tide Waiters who had been on duty being found dead drunk afterwards.

CHAPTER 13

AN ENCOUNTER ON THE CLIFFS

It was at this time, when I was nearly eighteen, that a chance meeting occurred which, more than any other, was to change my life. It was in early May; the Galatea, on which I was now second mate, was on the stocks at the Higher shipyard, having her hull stripped of barnacles and weed and being re-caulked. I had little to do until she was ready for her next voyage, and, the day being very fine, one of those wonderful early summer days when the world appears to be completely renewed, and the skies washed clean of every impurity, I decided to indulge in one of my boyhood passions and go looking for gulls' eggs along the cliffs at Stepper Point.

Gulls' eggs are not exactly a delicacy, being very strong and peculiarly fishy in flavour, the herring gull in particular being hardly a finicky feeder; but for many generations, indeed no doubt centuries, the eggs had been regarded as a welcome supplement to the family diet of the poor, especially in times, as now obtained, when the price of a wheaten loaf rose to sixpence, a tenth of a man's weekly wages, and some families were reduced to seeking their main sustenance in the form of mussels and limpets gathered from the rocks of the sea-shore. So I strode away down the path beside the estuary, along the sands of the beach near Hawker's Cove, and out above the main channel to the mighty cliff towering at the western end of our river, where it met the Atlantic Ocean.

The upper part of the cliff from here on was clad in flying bent grass, among which nodded and trembled hundreds of sea-pinks, or thrift: one of the glorious annual sights of our western land. Among the tussocks around which the narrow paths and sheep tracks wound, were the tiny ice-blue flowers of vernal squill and the first yellow buddings of kidney vetch; and masses of butter-yellow furze flowers glowed and burned along the banks, giving off their unique warm and haunting perfume.

Looking back, I realise now that at such places I was always uplifted into communion with another and vaster, more impersonal world than the one I moved in at home, around the quayside and on the Galatea, much as I loved that bustling seafaring life. Here was a world that thrust me suddenly into splendour, into the magnificence of an existence that mere man himself had little effect upon, and indeed, was privileged to share in. It was God's world, revealed in all its pristine, fortuitous glory: sometimes, standing on a pinnacle of rock and viewing the clashing sea below, the stately eminence of volcanic cliff rising in frozen majesty from the waters, the profusions of flowers and the wonders of bird song— for the sky would often be full of larks, all singing the Creator's praise, so it seemed to me— then I would feel tears of wonder and joy welling into my eyes and running down my face in the salt-laden breeze.

I was probably the only youth in Lodenek who drew such emotions from the scenes I moved in. Others might walk the paths and climb intent on getting eggs or picking samphire, to fish for bass from the rocks, or to drive adits into the cliff-face, mining for copper, lead or silver; but if they ever stopped to stare and appreciate the natural splendours before them, they never talked about it. My father, on the one or two occasions upon which I had hinted at my joy in all this, had looked at me in a questioning, faintly anxious manner, and immediately passed on to some matter of practical concern, as if to imply that my thoughts should be directed away from such romantic dreaming. So, believing myself to be something of an oddity in a world of keen commerce, dangers and hardships, I ceased to refer to these secret indulgences, in case I should be thought idle and untrustworthy. Sometimes on a voyage I wished I were still foretopman, aloft and alone in the lookout barrel, able to commune unhindered with the stupendous infinities I saw about me.

That day I had managed to climb a hundred feet or so down the rocks beyond the terrifying black chasm in the cliffs known as Pepper Hole, to where, on a ledge above the crawling sea, several gulls had made their untidy nests of sticks and seaweed; and had robbed them of three eggs, fighting off the vicious attack of a hen bird in order to do so. Panting from my exertions, the eggs stowed carefully in the deep pockets of my sailcloth smock (which I had taken off, to carry carefully, I was so hot with my efforts) I mounted the steep purple and green cliff face on the other side of that Round Hole, at the bottom of which the surging waves slapped and spouted with the incoming tide; and, gaining the turf above, came over a ridge to the landward and saw, below me in a natural amphitheatre in the cliffside, a young woman sitting, gazing out over the sea towards Gunver and

Trevose Heads. In her hand was a paint brush, and on her knee a small board with sketching paper pinned upon it. I must have startled her, a wild apparition suddenly appearing a few yards from her in a shirt opened down to my waist (it was one of my father's cast-offs, a decent garment in its time but now fraying at the cuffs, and much patched):

I heard her breath drawn in with a sharp sound, but she sat there, staring at me with liquid dark eyes. I recognized her as Miss Lucretia Devereaux, who came every Sunday to sit in the Squire's pew with her father and mother and various brothers and sisters. She, I knew, was the lame one who walked with a hobbling gait up the aisle, due to a hip deformity she had had from birth. We seldom, if ever, saw her in the town itself. I noticed, cropping the short grass of the turf some way off, a pony with a side-saddle, tethered to a gate post in the slate hedge.

'I'm sorry, Miss Devereaux, if I frightened you,' I said, still panting. 'I was climbing up the cliffs— been looking for gull's eggs.'

She frowned, regarding me closely. 'You're one of the choristers, aren't you?'

Indeed I was, I assured her; she seemed to relax somewhat, as if considering I was no threat to her, a solitary maiden lady on those cliffs. For a year now I had been the leading tenor in the choir each Sunday, except when the Galatea had undertaken lengthy voyages. I stared down at the picture she had been doing: a water-colour sketch of the coast before her, with Trevose Head and its attendant islands in the distance, and Gulland Rock in a brilliant blue-green sea in the right foreground.

I had never seen a landscape painting before. It had never occurred to me that anyone might want to paint a picture purely of such scenes as I moved among, without any person or ship as its main subject; my face must have shown surprise and admiration for, unfinished as it was, it was already recognizably a work of some art.

'Do you like pictures?' she asked, smiling at my innocent reaction.

'Yes, but I don't see many,' I said. I thought of the oil painting of a man o' war, the frigate H.M.S. Arethusa, which Mr Nanskivell had brought to the school one day for a history lesson, and which we had been set to copy for one of our drawing lessons.

'No,' she said, '1 don't suppose you do. Can you draw?'

'Only ships, and vases, and marble statuettes, as we used to at the National School,' I told her. My gaze now fell on an open book beside her on the grass, showing a page of poetry. My keen eyes recognized the lines:

She dwelt among the untrodden ways
Beside the springs of Dove —
A maid whom there were none to praise
And very few to love.

'I know that poem,' I volunteered. 'Tis by William Wordsworth.'

It was her turn to be surprised. 'You do? What other poems do you know?'

'Daffodils, and Gray's Elegy, and The Ancient Mariner. That's a terrible poem, though I like it.'

'Why do you say it's terrible?' She laid her painting down and sat back at ease on the turf. Below us a flock of oystercatchers flew piping shrilly out to sea with their black and white chevron-marked wings flashing.

I half-squatted down, not daring to sit in her presence, but to be closer so that she might hear me tell her of the nightmares I had had, and which still occurred, though less intensely, on occasions.

'It is certainly a strange and wonderful piece of writing,' she agreed. 'It disturbs me too, whenever I read it. Mr Coleridge has a vivid imagination— perhaps, at times, too feverish.' She took up another book and read aloud:

'In Xanadu did Kublai Khan
A stately pleasure-dome decree;
Where Alph, the Sacred river, ran
Through caverns measureless to man
Down to a sunless sea.'

'Another dream,' she commented, 'perhaps less terrible, but just as vivid. What is your name?' She looked up with a sudden darting glance.

'James Spargo. Miss.'

'Well James, you seem to have had some sort of education. What do you intend to do for a career?'

'I'm second mate on the brigantine Galatea. I want to be a master mariner, like my father.'

'The Galatea— isn't that one of Thomas Rowlands' ships?'

I admitted that she was. A thoughtful look came over her and she stared out to sea. A red-brown kestrel hung over the cliff beyond the deep echoing inlet we called Butter Hole, hovering as it studied the cliffside for the movements of rabbits or small birds.

'I have heard,' she said, 'that the Galatea, like other vessels owned by Mr Rowlands, does a considerable amount of free-trading.' She turned on me such an earnest penetrating gaze that I could only stare at her: with black shining hair drawn severely back on each side of her head and plaited into a dense bun at the back, her large Roman, almost aquiline nose, and her dark eyes burning into me, she seemed then more of a stern school-mistress than a young woman of only twenty-two. 'You don't deny it,' she went on. 'Of course it is rife, though it is a dangerous commerce, from what one learns in the newspapers. The Government is sending more Revenue craft, and recruiting many more men to the Excise. They will soon be watching every stretch of the cliffs and shore.'

'We can outwit them,' I said, finding my tongue at last. 'We've got a few tricks up our sleeve.'

She smiled. 'Don't misunderstand me, James. I am not preaching, like our Vicar, against smuggling. I realise what natural temptation it is to avoid these unjust duties. My own father does not condemn it, and I am sure that much of the wine and brandy in our cellar at the House is brought in by free-traders. I do not take sides. I only caution you: it will become much more difficult and dangerous as time goes on.'

She began to gather her things together, putting her paint box, brushes and water bottle into a soft straw bag or 'frail', and with an effort got up. 'It is time I went now.' I handed her the sketching board, with half-finished picture pinned on it, and the two books. 'Perhaps,' she said, 'you would like to have this little volume? It is an old one, and I have the same poems in other books at home.'

I murmured my thanks, and we went slowly across to the pony, which now ceased his cropping and looked up to regard her with large amber eyes. I had some idea of helping her mount, but she untethered the animal skilfully and, by stepping on a large granite stone beside the gate, was up in the saddle before I could make a move to assist her. She paused for a moment, looking around at the sea swirling on the off-shore rocks, at the waves sweeping in slowly, the seabirds circling and crying. 'It is natural, of course, for an adventurous young man to want to go to sea,' she said, smiling down at me. 'But do not forget the natural beauties of the land, James. They are great treasures, beyond price, as Wordsworth knew. Perhaps we shall meet again along this coast; I often come here.'

And she moved off, with the slightest of kicks on the pony's ribs, along the pathway through the fields of young corn as I held the gate open for her.

I walked home in an entranced state, so oblivious of what I had set out for in the morning that I carelessly tried to squeeze through between a wagon and a wall in Ruther's Lane and broke my gull's eggs. Fortunately the book was in the other pocket of my smock. I felt I had suddenly found a great friend, who shared my love of cliffs and seashore. That it should be someone so much beyond our local society and our modest station in life, seemed to me nothing short of a miracle. I did not know if I *admired* Miss Devereaux; she was far from being the beauty of the family, but a lady she undeniably was, and so gracious and understanding to me (when she might have imperiously scorned me or waved me away with a word or gesture) that I could only feel gratitude, wonder and a great warming glow in response to her actions.

Looking back now through all the intervening years, I believe I can discern in that encounter the beginnings of my love for her. It was not the usual love of a man for a young woman he has just met, full of romantic aspirations mingled with natural desires and the attraction of one sex for the other. Nothing of that, I am sure, crossed my mind or stirred in my heart. As for the possibility of a friendship leading to marriage, it did not remotely occur to me: persons of my standing simply did not marry into circles as exalted as the Devereaux family; the idea would have been impossible had it then arisen.

I took off my smock, stained and caked with egg yolk, and rinsed and rubbed it under the pump on the quayside. My mother, examining it when I reached home, said, 'You can't leave it like that - it needs warm water and soap. I shall have to scrub it out; anyhow, 'tis dirty, it may have to go into the boil next Monday.' I escaped to the attic bedroom, which I shared with Reuben and young Daniel, and finding neither at home, lay on the feather bed we all three slept in together, and opened the book: *Lyrical Ballads*, by William Wordsworth and Samuel Taylor Coleridge. Among those paeans to nature and its beneficence, I found these lines, underlined in pencil, surely by Miss Lucretia herself:

For I have learned
  To look on nature, not as in the hour
Of thoughtless youth; but hearing oftentimes
  The still, sad music of humanity,
Nor harsh nor grating, though of ample power
  To chasten and subdue. And I have felt
A presence that disturbs me with the joy
  Of elevated thoughts; a sense sublime
Of something far more deeply interfused
  Whose dwelling is the light of setting suns,
And the round ocean and the living air,
  And the blue sky, and in the mind of man:
A motion and a spirit, that impels
  All thinking things, all objects of all thought,
And rolls through all things. Therefore I am still
  A lover of the meadows and the woods,
And mountains; and of all that we behold
  From this green earth; of all the mighty world
Of eye, and ear, - both what they half create,
  And what perceive; well pleased to recognize
In nature and the language of the sense
  The anchor of my purest thoughts, the nurse,
The guide, the guardian of my heart, and soul
  Of all my moral being.

I read the passage over and over, hardly understanding it, but enjoying it as pure sound and poetry, feeling rather than comprehending the sentiments behind it. I am sure it was because she had chosen to underline these words that they became, from that day onwards, to this very time when I write them down here, the dearest and most precious of all poetic utterances to me. Now that I fully understand them, I see what a deep sympathetic mind and spirit she had then, even when young; and how she applied such verse and sentiments to the world she and I were both born into, and especially that part of her family estate (for the Devereauxs owned all those cliff lands) which we could both share, in equal measure, since we both loved it in all weathers and at all times of the passing year.

CHAPTER 14

CAPTAIN DICK AND THE SPRITE

Quite soon after the foregoing encounter my father, although professing himself satisfied with my progress as second mate on the Galatea, advised me that it would be my best course if I served under another master for a few years, to gain further experience and fit myself for a command. Accordingly, after a discussion with her owner, Mr Thomas Rowlands, I was given a place as first mate on the lugger Sprite, under Captain Dick Stribley. I had now turned eighteen, and thought of myself in all respects a man, except that I was not married, nor even had a regular sweetheart. However I was mindful of Mr Rowlands' own words on the subject, and saw the wisdom of not becoming too set on any one maiden at that stage of my life.

The Sprite had a crew of ten, and carried six guns; it was rumoured that Captain Stribley was not averse to using the latter when challenged. Miss Lucretia's warning came home to me soon enough, for on my second voyage in the Sprite we ran into some trouble off Land's End, when returning from Brest with a cargo of Bourdeaux wine and brandy, among other dutiable items.

The Sprite was ninety tons in capacity, about half the size of the Galatea, but she was nearly twice as fast, drawing much less water. Even so, fully laden and with a north-westerly holding us back as we sailed up past the headland of Pedn-Mên-an-Mere, it was plain that when we were challenged by two Revenue cutters from Falmouth, who fired warning shots across our bows, that something extra in the way of seamanship or other devices would be required to pull us out of a difficult situation. I was highly interested, therefore, in the Master's response.

Captain Dick was a small portly man with a stubbly grey beard, hooked nose, and small red eyes; his only beverage was rum, which he drank on awakening in the morning and before sleeping at night, and steadily, at every opportunity, during the day, whether on duty or not. I never saw him take more than a nip or two, but never a half hour passed, it appeared, that he did not have his nip. I never saw him drunk. In his high-pitched voice he now cried to me, as I stood beside him on the bridge, 'Mister Mate, sight the larboard guns on their rigging!'

I relayed the order to the bos'un, who saw that the three brass guns along our port bulwark were trained on the sails of the two cutters, now fast approaching us with the wind in their favour. Our mizzen sail was close-hauled, and our jib sails, useless in such a wind, had been slackened and dropped. The leading cutter hoisted signal flags which read 'Heave to.' As she came within range, a small enough target in herself since she was bow-on to us, our guns spoke and three jagged holes appeared in her fore and main sails. The force of the wind behind her began to rend these holes into jagged tears, and we saw her deck hands hauling them down. As we continued close-hauling northwards her guns fired on us; I saw four brief flames and heard a ball buzz just above my head like some red hot dumbledory, or cockchafer. Another passed over our stern, a third sent water spouting up just ahead of us; a fourth smashed into our bulwarks, splintering wood and recoiling into the waves. But we were past her and rapidly getting out of range; the damaged cutter fell back, leaving the second to pursue us.

Captain Dick was chuckling to himself, a sound like a rooster chasing his favourite hen, enjoying the chase. 'Thass fixed one of the bounders,' he shouted to me and took a quick swig from his rum flask. 'Keep your eye on the other one, James.' Ahead of us the Longships lighthouse on its reef showed up as the October afternoon dimmed; it was about five o'clock or so, and the Trinity House men began to send out their beams. Stribley knew the inshore passages around Land's End as well as he knew our own estuary channels; he now shouted to the bos'un to tighten the foresails and slacken the rigging; then to the man at the wheel to swing her over to starboard. Thus we turned at an angle of thirty degrees and ran, the wind now in our favour, straight towards Cowloe Rocks and Sennen Cove. The cutter closed up on us, firing at us from time to time, but in a mounting swell (we were now pretty close to land) their shots either fell short or missed, ploughing into the waves beside us. We passed uncomfortably close by Cowloe, between the rocks and the cliffs, and I thought we were going to run aground as the wide arc of Whitesand Bay came closer and closer; I could see a knot of excited people, fishermen and their wives and children, watching only a couple of hundred yards away.

The cutter had slackened sail, and stood off, not daring to follow us between the reef and the cliffs. Then Captain Dick yelled out for us to go on the other tack; the jibs were struck, the mizzen tightened, and we swung about, coming broadside on to the cutter with perhaps thirty yards between us; I could see four uniformed Searchers staring at us from her bows, and then saw them dive flat down on the deck as Stribley shouted out, 'Fire!' and our larboard guns sent four balls into their rigging. Her main mast was hit, and slowly bent, from half-way up, to fold over, bringing down her stays. Her foresail was torn across by two other balls. Then as we got beyond her out towards Cape Cornwall, we saw her suddenly buck, her bow lifted clear into the air as an extra-powerful wave took her, and broke her back on a reef of rock hidden just under the surface.

'Shan't have no more trouble with they, boy,' piped the old man, delighted with himself; and took another nip, as our men cheered to see the Revenue men in the water. They were saved, we heard later, by those Sennen fishermen, who immediately pulled out in their bum boats and skiffs— the same which had been used time and again to bring contraband ashore. I reflected that it was well for us that prior to sailing from Brest we had masked the name of our craft.

On a grey January day in 1819 the Sprite sailed from Lodenek for Roscoff. It was judged safe enough to trade there now, most of the preventive activity by Revenue cutters at that time being directed against free-traders along the south coast of Cornwall— from the Fal creeks, Mevagissey, Looe, Polperro, Cawsand and Kingsand; the Cornish smugglers were now beginning to row and sail gigs and longboats across to the French coast, bringing back smaller quantities of contraband, but discharging them in tiny coves and inlets which the larger vessels could not enter; they also presented smaller targets for the cutter's guns.

I had been appointed by Mr Rowlands as Agent for our transactions. Immediately before our embarking he had come down to the shipyard and instructed me at the office, giving me a list of purchases, and an indication of the prices to which he would go, and not beyond. Golden guineas and sovereigns not now being in such demand by the French, a credit system had been set up, though it was still necessary to trade with bank notes at warehouses where we were not known. As we neared the Breton coast the following morning my thoughts turned to Iseut, whom I supposed I would see again,, and I recalled her sad imprisoned look when I last saw her in her father's store.

M.Renan welcomed me as we berthed at the quayside. '*M'sieur Jammes— Bienvenu à Roscoff. Nous ne t'avons pas vu pendant beaucoup de mois.*' He clasped both my hands in his. '*Et ton père*?' He looked at the ship as if expecting my father.

'*Mon père est bien, merci. Il est en Cornuailles. Je suis avec le Sprite maintenant, et moi, je suis l'agent.*'

'*Bravo*! 'He exclaimed, leading me by the arm, which he took in a fatherly grip. *'Au premier, les affaires; au second, tu dineras avec nous cette après-midi.'*

In the warehouse, as I expected, was Iseut, but not this time in her diminutive box of an office, but a new specially built bureau that occupied the width of one end of the large store. She looked less unhappy, and was certainly more grown-up and assured now; indeed, seeing her at the tall desk in her long black Breton dress with white apron, and a little lace coif on her head, I was struck by her dark demure beauty, enhanced by the slight frown as she concentrated on what she was writing. Then she looked up, and a coquettish smile lit her face.

'Bonjour, Jammes. Tu va bien, j' espère?'

'Très bien, Iseut, et toi?'

'*Bien, merci.*' She gave me her charming mock-shy smile again, her eyes dwelling on me a second longer than necessary. I produced my list and the ordering of the goods began, with Iseut writing them down in the large book on the desk. After it was written she would have to copy it all out again as a bill of lading for Mr Rowlands, and cost it out for payment.

'Twenty ankers of rum...forty of best brandy...six bales of tobacco in the leaf…Combien?'

'*Mille cent francs*...Twenty-one pounds.'

'*Bien.*' And so on. The church clock struck twelve, its repeated hollow notes drifting over the town and quayside. There was a noticeable lull in the various activities outside as carters, coopers, fishermen and merchants broke off for their midday meal. We soon concluded the order, and Iseut began to copy it out; but her father stopped her. '*Viens chez nous, Iseut. Écrive cela cette après-midi*,' he said. And we went, the three of us, through the narrow streets to the square where the house of Renan stood. Once inside, the merchant said, *'Du vin, Jammes? Et fromage?'*

Bread, wine and cheese were produced by Iseut, and we ate and drank at a rustic table in the courtyard at the back of the house. Beyond us the high walls enclosed urns of winter pansies and daffodils in bud, troughs of snowdrops, gold and purple crocuses and polyanthi; the pale Spring sunshine was magnified in this sheltered place, and the vines and creepers along the walls held tight buds that looked as if they were about to break open into flaming green leaves. After some desultory conversation, and having disposed of a large piece of local cheese resembling Brie and a pint or so of red wine, M. Renan retired inside to his favourite chair, to close his eyes in siesta. We were left alone, Iseut and I; she said in halting English, 'Permit me to show you our flowers.'

We walked slowly down the length of the courtyard, she naming this and that plant, smiling and giving me her half-shy, eager glances. 'You like dem?' she said. 'I learn English now, to speak to traders when dey come from your Cornuailles.'

'My Cornuailles?'

'Oui, your Cornuailles. We also have Cornuailles in Breizh, Brittany.

'*Je comprends*.'

We had turned the corner now into a smaller yard, laid out with flower beds and shrubs. In the crevices of the old crumbling walls delicate little maidenhair and hart's tongue ferns were growing amongst the moss, the ivy-leaved toadflax, and saxifrage. I felt at home, knowing similar nooks in the courts and back alleys of Lodenek.

A wooden seat was set against the only clear wall space. Iseut sat down on it and indicated the place beside her. I sat by her watching her merry brown face with slightly turned-up nose and full red lips that seemed naturally pursed as if ready to kiss; indeed, after the few glasses of wine I had taken, and remembering our childhood kissing games, the desire to embrace her now, as an adult, became almost irresistible. She was looking at the ground and smiling as if perhaps she too was remembering those childhood days; and as she turned to me to say something, I took her hand and, greatly daring, raised it to my lips.

'Ah, Jammes!' she exclaimed in a whisper that revealed to me, as if I needed proof, that she was finding that her plan was working. She raised her face to me, seeking my lips, and before I realised what was happening we were locked in a passionate embrace.

Until then kissing girls had been a kind of game that youth unthinkingly indulges in: the sweet taste of their soft lips (when not too coloured with cosmetic) had been very pleasant; the nearness of their fresh young faces, unless marred by spots or pimples, or artificially rouged and powdered, usually were quite adorable. That they should want to kiss me, as I found they did on various occasions, was always something of a surprise to me, though highly gratifying. But I had never allowed it to make me overweening or swelled-headed; each one was simply a lucky bonus, not to be expected or repeated. This kiss of Iseut's was something much more, incomparably more: the embrace of a woman, not a girl, a young woman whose whole body expressed her desire for the man she yearned for. It awakened in me desires that had been maturing, unrecognized, in my deepest self; desires that any young man must have if he is a true man, passions that are not easily mastered, but which must be bridled and led into submission, until the time comes when they may lawfully be indulged.

I write this now as a priest and married man, indeed, a widower: I look back on those heady days of my youth and young manhood as a father might look, fondly and ready to excuse, on the exploits of his favourite, but wayward son. Who, in that situation, at the age of eighteen, could have resisted such a simple, direct and innocent approach?

'Je t'aime,' she was breathing, though it was rather a moan, an imploring sighing, *'Jammes, je t'aime; aimes-tu moi un peu?'*

'Oui, je t'aime, Iseut,' I heard myself whisper, our lips meeting and lingering. *'Je t'aime beaucoup, ma chère.'*

We clung together; I petted her, kissed her neck and the tiny pink ears peeping from under her plaited hair, and whispered, half in English, half in stumbling French, fond silly phrases that seemed to come to me from out of the air, from the flowers and urgent buds about us. 'My little dove, *ma chou-fleur, mon oiseau—amant, je t'aime, je t'adore, petite mouse—* kiss me, *donne-moi un autre baiser, ma belle fleurette...*'

Gradually we calmed down. Tears stained her face: tears of shining joy and love. The bosom of her apron was damp and rumpled, the heavy velveteen of her dress creased. Gently I dabbed at her face with my red spotted kerchief, and made her blow her nose, which she did laughing and spluttering. 'I have love you from when you first come here,' she said, thinking out her English words with great care. 'I was first to kiss you when we run and hide. Do you *...souviens-toi?*'

'I remember,' I said, fondling her little brown hands with their long delicate fingers.

'*Mon père*,' she said, '*il est seul. Notre maman est morte depuis six années. Tu comprends?'*

I nodded.

'Charlotte will soon be *mariée*. My brothers and

sisters, all *mariés maintenant. Je suis la plus jeune de la_ famille.* So I must ... 'elp and be cook...'

'You must look after your father.' I understood. She was telling me that if we were to be married I must come and live in Roscoff, with herself and M. Renan. It did not appear to me to be so terrible a prospect, for if I were master of my ship I would inevitably come and go, as I would if I married a Lodenek girl. I supposed, however, that marrying a Roman Catholic would raise certain difficulties. No doubt it would shock my family and all Lodenek people; for Catholics were still at that time a people apart, traditionally suspected of loyalties other than to King and Country. They could not enter parliament, nor take commissions in the army or navy; the universities and civil service were closed against them. As for their mysterious rites, their incense burning and idolatry of statues, their servile obedience to the Pope of Rome, all those things told us as children had been calculated to cause us to recoil in horror. But here was Iseut as unspoiled and true a young maiden as ever I could wish to find, and her father, a pleasant and jovial man; I could not believe they were anything but good people.

The church bell intoned two o'clock. Iseut arose, smoothing out her apron and crumpled dress. '*Alors, il faut que je retourner aux affairs,*' she said, and held out her hands to me. I stood up, and took her into my arms again, and kissed her, this time gently on the forehead.

'I must go down to the ship and speak with Captain Stribley. *Je t'aime toujours, Iseut.*'

'*Je t'aime toujours aussi, Jammes.*' We walked back to the house in silence, holding hands.

Captain Dick came to dinner with us in the long dark dining room at five o'clock that afternoon. Also present, beside Iseut and her father, were Charlotte and Yann, her fiancé. The latter was a surly over-weight youth, who took little part in the conversation, but accounted well for himself at the repast, which was served by two elderly maid-servants. We began with a rich crab soup, with leeks, asparagus and carrots floating in it; and had then a huge mound of boiled mussels seasoned with garlic and butter, followed by a serving of succulent turbot in fennel sauce. The main dish was a tasty saddle of mutton, with mint, vegetables and gravy; but by now my appetite was failing, and I could manage but a small portion. Four varieties of cheese, with Muscadet and hot brown bread straight from the oven, and some moist Moroccan dates, with apples and tangerine oranges, completed the meal. M.Renan poured wine for everyone, and replenished our glasses at every course; except for that of Captain Stribley, who insisted on drinking rum with everything, talking in his high pitched gleeful voice in execrable French, mixed with 'damn' and 'blast it' at every other sentence and '*Votre Santé,* Down the Hatch,' each time wine was poured; at which the company responded with an increasingly loud shout at every toast, '*Yeghez Da!* (Good Health!) Down de 'atch!' All in all we had a merry, inconsequential time of it; and I was conscious throughout, on the one hand of Iseut's darkly glowing gaze upon me and every word I uttered, and on the other of Charlotte, who watched me with envy and what I took to be regret and longing, as her husband-to-be guzzled and belched and grinned oafishly at every attempt there was at humour. Both girls looked very fetching in their new silk dresses with puffed sleeves and much *décolleté*, bought for them by their aunt in Paris.

We parted about eight in the evening, all vowing to dine again together whenever the Sprite should visit Roscoff. On the steps of the house, with Captain Stribley waiting for me outside, singing a tuneless shanty to himself, I said, '*Au'voir— je t'aime*,' to Iseut, and gave her a light confused kiss because her father was watching— he slapped his thigh and laughed approvingly to see it - and heard her say, 'Come back soon, *chère Jammes. Noz da.'*

On the voyage home, the Sprite bounding and surging beneath a rising moon almost at the full, and Captain Dick snoring in his bunk, I sailed over a sea full of new promises, the memory of Iseut's eager embraces warming me as a chill south-easterly blustered round the bridge.

Yet by the time we were half-way across the Western Approaches and in sight of the Lizard light, another face was intruding on my romantic dream; one that looked out over the boundless seas, telling me to prize the treasures of Nature, and to read the new poets who were singing her praises.

CHAPTER 15

DIFFICULT TIMES - AND GOOD NEWS

The reformed Excise Service, set up mainly with ex-naval personnel, soon established an unceasing watch around our coasts, reinforcing the activities of Riding Officers, Tide and Landing Waiters, to such an effect that a considerable amount of free-trade goods were interrupted at sea, or taken on landing at various bays and inlets. Our free-traders were loath to give up the commerce (and profits) they had enjoyed for twenty or thirty years, but it was clearly becoming more difficult now to elude the Revenue men.

Various ruses were devised: rumours were deliberately whispered, and even false information blatantly given, that a landing would be made at such-an-such a cove on such a night, resulting in the Searchers lying in wait in force for the smugglers to appear; whereas they would instead effect a landing at another bay several miles away. Running battles became more frequent, both at sea between Revenue cutters and free-trade vessels, and on shore between the landing parties and the Searchers. Cases of woundings became common, and increasingly of death, from drowning or shooting. When seized, ships engaged in bringing in contraband were sawn into three parts on the beach outside the Custom House at low tide, and then dismembered and sold off in lots, in several instances effectively putting their owners out of business.

Mr Thomas Rowlands was canny enough not to

risk the Galatea, his largest ship, any further in such operations. My father was therefore much from home, voyaging to Scotland, the Baltic and St.Petersburg, to Christiana, Copenhagen, and the north German ports such as Hamburg and Lubeck, bringing back cargoes of hemp, tallow, timber, canvas and so on: all goods on which duties were paid, though relatively low. Piers Baldrick, the Collector, always had the Galatea searched thoroughly when she entered port, but never found anything concealed. Meanwhile Captain Dick and I voyaged in the Sprite to other Cornish and Devon ports, and occasionally to Brittany and France, mainly on legitimate business; though we usually acquired a small clandestine amount of spirits, tea, tobacco or silks. These were taken ashore by dinghy off Porthcothan, Porthmear or Hawker's Cove, if the coast was clear; or transferred to one of several Lodenek fishing smacks (with which we made rendezvous off Trevose Head or Stepper Point); or else the goods were concealed about the persons of the crew when they went ashore. Other vessels in the Rowlands fleet of six no doubt acted similarly, but since it was more than the worth of any crew member's employment to talk about such things, there was little or no mention of such doings in Lodenek, despite tempting sums of fifty or even a hundred pounds offered by the Excise for information leading to the apprehending of smugglers.

The year that I first met Miss Lucretia Devereaux on the cliffs proved to be one of good harvest: indeed there was too much wheat produced up and down the country, with the result that the price of corn fell and many farms could not pay their rent. Mr Thomas

Rowlands, who owned several of the farms about Lodenek, was not a harsh landlord, and gave his tenants time to pay, no doubt believing that the resources of his other ventures, his inns, his Lodenek Bank, the shipyard and the commerce of his trading ships would offset such a reverse. But since the profits from free-trading were dwindling as a result of the tighter watches of the Excise, and since farmers across the country would insist on growing more and more corn instead of grazing cattle and sheep or planting root crops, that harvest was followed by two similar ones. I am sure that all this played some considerable part in Thomas' growing difficulties. Despite the fall in prices, bread was dear enough for the poor; and the glut led to more exporting being done.

One September the Galatea was loading with wheat to be taken to Scandinavia, when her crew were confronted by a gang of angry miners from the valleys beyond Wadebridge, where the tin seams had run out, depriving them of both work and sustenance. Radical thinking had been preached to them by one of their number, who had heard Hunt speak at Manchester just before the infamous 'Battle of Peterloo', when the yeomanry had charged a huge crowd and killed eleven people. Those tinners saw no justice in the export of corn to other countries and parts of England whilst they and their families faced starvation. When she was still only three-quarters loaded, Mr Rowlands, who was on the quayside, gave the order for her to cast off and be under way; my father had to be rowed out to his own ship in one of the gigs from the yard as others pulled her out to catch the wind.

The Corn Law passed in 1815, the year of victory at Waterloo, was one of the worst features of life at that time, causing hardship to the artisans in the cities and to farm labourers and fishermen alike: for it laid down that unless the price of wheat stood at eighty shillings or less per quarter, no corn could be imported into Great Britain. Thus, there were often times of full barns and ricks, with farmers and millers hoarding corn to keep the price up, and a hungry populace unable to afford their daily bread; whilst often enough cargoes of good grain were sent abroad.

We Spargos were not too adversely affected at home, since father, myself and Reuben were all now earning reasonable wages; though we remembered times when we had been glad to eat barley bread and potatoes, and looked upon a new baked wheaten loaf as a treat. But many families, their menfolk out of work because farmers had laid them off, went on Parish Relief and even into the Workhouse. Violence spread; ricks were burned, and agricultural machinery smashed, since they did the work of several men and threw them into unemployment. A pauper girl of eighteen was hanged at Bodmin Gaol for setting fire to the wheat mow of her master, a farmer near St.Merryn: she had vowed that he should not eat wheaten bread when she and her friends had to be content with coarse glutinous barley loaves.

After I had served about a year as first mate on the Sprite, Captain Dick was taken ill, and one day I was sent for by Mr Rowlands, to see him at Sandry's Hill House. This was unusual; if it were a normal matter of business, Thomas would have seen me at the shipyard office. I walked up the hill to the great house with considerable curiosity, tinged with certain misgivings as to what I should hear when I got there.

It was a fine June morning, just before noon; the west wing of the new mansion was almost completed, and the stables at the rear were busy with horses being groomed and a carriage being got ready. Blackbirds and chaffinches were singing and searching for food in the well-grown bushes along the drive. I wondered if I should go to the main portico, but decided that modesty was the best approach and went around to the kitchen yard, where one of the servant girls I knew, Nan Thomas, was sweeping the cobbles.

'I'm here to see Mr Rowlands, Nan,' I said. 'He's expecting me.'

'Is he now, Jim. S'pose you'd better go in, then. Right through to that green baize door, you'll find Mr Simmonds the footman through there.'

I went in through the great kitchen, with its shining pans and tureens, and kettles hanging over the huge open hearth they used in those days, stared at by the red-faced cook, her kitchen maids and scullions, and down the passageway to the green baize door, which I opened. On the other side the passage widened into the circular hall where we had danced on the night four years previously on Emily's Birthday Ball. There was no one about; the sunlight flushed down through the tall Georgian windows over the staircase, casting its beams into my eyes so that I blinked, suddenly dazed. I discerned a movement across the hail, as a figure in white and peach colours came forward. Shielding my eyes from the glare I saw it was Emily herself.

'James Spargo.' She stood there contemplating

me, searching my face with a strangely anxious, almost imploring look.

'Miss Emily.'

'I am glad to see you. My father is not here yet; he went out on some business and must be delayed. Will you wait in here?' She indicated a small room, evidently used as a parlour and reading room. It was on the corner of the house and looked out, in one direction, over the growing plantation and the church, with the crenellations of the west wing of Devereaux Place rising above the trees beyond. Its other window overlooked the drive. On the walls were engravings: one of a ship in a storm, the other of three Greek or Roman goddesses facing a handsome half-clothed young man, who held in his hands an apple. Emily stood at the doorway hesitating; then she said, 'Will you take some lemonade, perhaps? I think I may have some.' She went to the plaited silk rope hanging down by the door and pulled. A bell sounded some way off down the passageway.

Emily sat down on a small upholstered chair, and I sat opposite her. 'I hear you have got on well at seafaring. My father thinks highly of you, James,' she said, still studying my face. I made some non-committal reply. She was colouring now— Emily always had a way of quickly blushing; she seemed no longer the all-commanding mistress of herself she had been. 'You have good business sense, he says. I hope you will continue in his service; it could bring you great benefits later, James.'

I stared at her, and said, 'I hope to serve him with my best endeavours, Miss Emily.'

'Please— not Miss Emily. We are old friends, are we not? Don't you remember the wheelbarrow race?'

She was smiling now, a little self-deprecatingly; I said with a cheerful grin, 'I don't suppose I shall ever forget that day.' And we burst out laughing together.

'What a termagant I was then,' she confessed. 'How could I have had the audacity even to ask you—but you didn't hesitate, did you?'

A vision of the flurrying of skirts over my head, and the closeness of her as we fell together, came back to me. 'I'd go through it again with you, even now,' I said, 'Emily.'

'I believe you would. But we are too old for such childishness now,' she sighed. 'Where is Simmonds?' She got up to pull the bell rope again. 'I long sometimes to go back to those carefree days of ours - we don't value our youth until we see it slipping away from us, do we?'

'I s'pose we don't.' I had been too busy with my mariner's career to think about any such thing; but I felt now she was right. Boys and girls in their teens are far too intent on growing up, and finding what they can for themselves as adults, to make the most of what youth has to offer. 'I wonder,' I said to her, hardly thinking about what I was saying, 'if you are happy now, Emily? You have many admirers, I dare say.'

Nan Thomas appeared, breathing heavily from running. 'Miss Emily, you rang?'

'Of course I rang. Where has Simmonds got to?'

A carriage drawn by two roans bowled past the window and down the drive; a footman in the Rowland's green and grey livery stood on the backboard.

'Gone driving with yer mother, Miss,' Nan said, pointing at the carriage. 'Can I get you something?' She looked at me in mock wonder, as if implying,

'Entertaining Jim Spargo— fancy that!'

'Bring me a jug of lemonade and two tumblers.' Emily's voice was sharp. Nan curtseyed and left the room. Emily came a step or two nearer to me. 'Yes, James, I have admirers— too many, I think. How they bore me! All they can do is dance, and pay compliments, and preen themselves like young turkey cocks! Sometimes I wish— I wish we were not rich. Sometimes I wish I had been born into such a family as yours, and could wander around the quays and do what I wished, and not have a *position* to keep up!'

I can see her there, after all these years, looking at me with such passion and petulance, such confusion and desperation: as if she wanted me to take her in my arms and bear her away to another world than the one she was born into; to a world which, fondly and quite mistakenly, she imagined would be much more real than her own. Her father's words about her sounded in the back of my mind: 'Emily doesn't know what she wants... don't be led a dance by her.' But I believe that in a second or two I would verily have clasped her to me and kissed her, and said to her the Lord only knows what extravagant things (for her sweet auburn-haired head, her violet and green eyes, her rosebud of a mouth, trembling in some agony, had as powerful an effect upon me as hitherto) — had not Nan then come back with a tray on which were a jug and two glass tumblers, and which she set down on the little table.

'Shall I pour it out, Miss?'

'No— I'll do it. Thank you, that will be all.'

Nan curtseyed, looked speculatively at me, then at Emily, and went out, but did not close the door.

'I am sorry to inflict my affairs upon you, like this,' Emily said then, pouring out the lemonade. 'Since I came home from the Young Ladies' College at Bath I can't seem to settle to anything. You know, James...' she held out to me the glass which I took, 'I think I should like to go to sea. Perhaps I can persuade Father to let me go on one of his ships.'

I sipped the lemonade, which was cold and quite bitter, but refreshing. 'I doubt if he would, Emily. There's little accommodation for a young lady on these trading vessels, except I suppose for the Galatea. And she goes to unromantic places like Liverpool and Glasgow.' I said this to discourage her.

'I shouldn't mind where she went, as long as I could travel...It would be grand, would it not, if you were on it too? You could explain to me everything about navigation and how the sails are managed...'

'Perhaps, one day, it might be arranged. Your father...'

She started up now, spilling some lemonade on her muslin dress. 'My father is coming now.' She looked alarmed and disappointed. Turning, I saw Mr Rowlands striding up the drive, a look of baleful concern, even suppressed anger on his face. Evidently Emily was in some terror of him. She dabbed at the moisture on her dress with a little lace handkerchief, quite ineffectively. I took out my red spotted, rather grubby kerchief and gave it to her; she rubbed her dress, gave it me back, then said, 'Thank you, James. We shall... always be friends, shan't we?'

'Of course. If you wish it.'

'Don't you wish it?' Her voice had a tremulous,

anxious quality.

'Yes, Emily.' I took her hand and held it, gazing at her flushed face, and conscious of her bosom rising and falling with her rapid breathing. 'I will always be your friend, never fear.'

The heavy main doors of the house were then thrown back and Mr Rowlands came striding across the hall. He paused, seeing us there in the little parlour; I had dropped Emily's hand, and was standing composedly in the middle of the room. Emily herself had sunk down on to the settee.

'Ah...James. I forgot I asked you to come. I was delayed by an argument. It has ruffled me somewhat. No matter. I hope you have been entertained by my daughter?'

'Oh yes, Mr Rowlands. We were talking of old times.'

'I see. Well, Emily my dear, if you will excuse us, there are business matters to discuss.'

'Of course, Father.' She rose, fully recovered now and smiling demurely. 'Goodbye, James...and good luck with your career. I shall follow it with much interest.' And left the room, closing the door behind her.

'Now then, James, my boy,' began Mr Rowlands, staring out of the window. His face was strained, I saw, and quite heavily lined: he looked drawn and tired, as if he had not been sleeping well these last weeks. 'I've been to see Captain Stribley,' he went on, still staring out of the window towards the town and the river. 'He is not in very good sort. Not at all. No... 'He rounded suddenly on me, frowning. 'It's a stroke. I'm quite sure he will not sail again.' His eye fell on the table, with the tray and tumblers. 'What's this?'

'Lemonade, Sir. Miss Emily ordered it.'

'Won't do for me. Sherry, I think. 'He pulled the bell rope. 'You'll take a glass?'

'Thank you, sir.'

'Good lad. Time you knew your liquor. How old are you?

'Twenty this September.'

He paused, thinking. 'Nineteen,' he said. 'At nineteen I was managing three farms. Yes...'

Nan Thomas appeared again. 'Sherry,' said Mr Rowlands. 'Where is Simmonds?'

'He went out driving with Mrs Rowlands, sir.'

'Damn. Send me Mr Pawley.'

Nan curtseyed and fled, evidently greatly in awe of her master.

'Silly girls. Useless to ask them to go to the cellar. Well, James, I've been watching your progress carefully, very carefully. Things are changing, and we need younger men now, men with ideas that are not fixed, you understand?'

'I think so, sir.'

'Adaptability, enterprise. I want men in charge of my ships who are not afraid to take responsibility, use their own initiative. Dick Stribley had initiative, confound him; you never knew what he'd he up to next. How he escaped the Revenue men as often as he did always amazes me. But that's all finished now - these damned Coastguards and cutters, the game won't be worth the candle soon...'

A tall imposing figure in black, with white stockings and silver buckled shoes, entered. His back hair was plaited into a short tail, and his side whiskers were greying. He bowed to Mr Rowlands.

'Ah, Pawley, be so good as to find me a bottle of Amontillado will you? And decant it, please.'

Without a word or flicker of an eyelid the butler bowed and silently withdrew.

'What was I saying? Sit down, my boy. Yes.' He sat down himself, staring again out of the window. 'We must stick now to legitimate business. My brother, the Vicar, doesn't approve of free-trading— not that that would stop me, all other things being equal; but he's right, we must face it, they're out to get us and we shall all end up behind bars if we continue. So now, it means sailing farther afield. And strictly no contraband— there are good ships being sunk, or sawn up, every week. You understand?'

'Yes, sir.'

'You think you can take charge of the Sprite? Sail her on your own decision from port to port, if necessary, getting cargoes where you can? You can read charts and take soundings, eh? Navigate by dead reckoning? I have spoken to your father. Best captain I could wish for. And Captain Stribley— they both agree you can do it. But if you think you want guidance, I'll engage an older man for the time and you can stay on as mate.'

My heart swelled when I heard that my father and Captain Dick thought I was ready to be ship's master. 'I'll do it, Mr Rowlands— I know I can handle her, as far afield as you wish.'

The butler returned, and with ponderous movements removed the lemonade and set a decanter of golden sherry in its place, with two tall-stemmed glasses.

'Will that be all, sir?' he said in a voice which sounded as if it came from the tomb.

'Yes, thank you, Pawley. Now...' pouring out the wine and holding up his glass, 'I drink a toast. To you, James. Captain James Spargo. Skipper of the Sprite.' Mr Rowlands sipped some of the glowing liquid. 'May your career prosper. Now try some of this.' He handed me a glassful, and I took a little; the astringent, slightly resinous taste made me cough, but I swallowed more immediately, and felt it descend, glowing like an elixir into my stomach. Captain James Spargo! I smiled at my employer, and he smiled back, suddenly shedding years as he did; I laughed, he laughed, and I saw him regard me with something that might have been envy or a fond remembrance of himself at my age, the threshold of true manhood when all things seem possible to an ambitious, aspiring youth.

'I hope,' he said, when our laughter had subsided a little, 'You remembered what I said about the women. I believe Emily has been leading you on again. You haven't become attached to anyone, have you, James?'

'No, sir,' I said. 'Not attached yet.'

'Not for want of offers, I'll warrant.'

I smiled assent. 'My career must be the first consideration, as you told me yourself.'

'Good lad. You'll do well, I'm sure of it.'

He poured out another glass of sherry for us each. My head was beginning to feel light and my senses reeled. I took a deep breath and refused to let liquor rule me, though my stomach had not taken food for four hours or more.

A little later, as he saw me to the door, I let out a

loud involuntary hiccup; as the great oak doors closed behind me I had to clasp one of those sculptured Ionic pillars to steady myself. Then, very carefully descending the steps, I walked slowly but firmly along the drive, watching my feet plant themselves one in front of the other, not daring to look back as I felt certain he would still be watching me. And so to the gates, and down the hill, giggling and laughing at times idiotically, repressing the desire to turn a cartwheel there in the middle of the street, to tell them all at home of my great good news.

CHAPTER 16

LUCRETIA AGAIN

I took the Sprite with Enoch Penberthy (for so long my father's second in command) as mate, on her next voyage: to Portreath to load copper ore and take it to Hayle to the smelters; thence with tin ore to Barry in South Wales; then with a cargo of steam coal to Dublin, where we took on flax and sheepskins to the Clyde, to supply the Scottish mills. I enjoyed charting our way around waters hitherto strange to me; at each port I went ashore and explored the town, fascinated by the clanging bustle of still-expanding industry, equally impressed by the gracious Georgian atmosphere of Dublin and the brash new zest of Glasgow.

We took ironmongery, tallow and dried herrings from the Clyde around to Newcastle-on-Tyne, then sailed across the North Sea to Stockholm with more coal. At Stockholm we loaded softwood and voyaged back to Lodenek around Land's End, berthing there after a three weeks trip with not a gill of liquor on board, beyond the keg of rum we kept for the crew, and a couple of bottles of brandy for Enoch and myself, to keep the worst of the wind out of our throats on the rather exposed bridge of the Sprite.

I felt satisfied with myself, though at that time of the year, the middle and end of July, one did not expect storms; and Enoch, whom Mr Rowlands had persuaded to leave the Galatea after more than twenty years' service on her, was a staunch support and adviser, knowing the various dangers to avoid, especially in the region of the Skagerak and Kattegat. Enoch, I knew, would devote to me the utmost loyalty, as the son of my father. He was one of those taciturn Cornishmen whose lack of idle talk concealed a deep wisdom born of experience. When he spoke he was always listened to; what he said was never to be ignored. Enoch would never be a shipmaster; he said he lacked the ability to reckon, and was no business man; but no better mate could be found I was sure. I had my father's word for that.

Throughout August and into September we plied our short hauls around Cornwall and Devon, and to Bristol, and I became familiar with several westcountry ports I had not before visited: Watchet, Minehead, Clovelly and Bude, Looe, Teignmouth and Dartmouth. I began to miss the excitement, the daring, the adventure of free-trading, and was often tempted to slip across to St.Helier or Cherbourg or Roscoff; but I knew that the risk was much too great to take on several counts, not least in brooking Mr Rowland's certain displeasure and so earning my dismissal.

I had not seen Miss Lucretia Devereaux since we had met, that unforgettable day, on the cliffs above Butter Hole; not, that is, to speak to her privately. I had beheld her in church, when I was home in Lodenek and could take my place in the choir. She made sure her gaze did not wander in my direction except once, when during a particularly long and involved sermon by the Reverend William Rowlands, my daydreaming gazing about the chancel and the pews was abruptly arrested by realising that she, also wearied by the discourse, was looking at me with a distinct smile; she quickly averted her eyes however, and perused her hymn book. I also saw her once in Devereaux Place itself, on Christmas Eve, when I joined a party of fifty carollers who mounted the hill and entered through the iron-studded door in the crenellated stone wall, to sing our own peculiar four-part Lodenek carols with revivalistic fervour, Anglican and Methodist and Bible Christian alike, to the Squire and his family. After singing two or three carols outside in the gusty dark, besplattered by rain, we were invited inside the house to sing in the hall. There we gave of our best, under the benign gaze of Major Charles Arthur Devereaux, of the Cornwall Light Dragoons, his lady, Mrs Maria Elizabeth (née Elsworthy,) and their assembled sons and daughters: Charles, Judith, Robert, Henry Fortescue (Lt.R.N., of H.M.S. Bellerophon); Lucretia herself; Sarah; and George Arthur, aged thirteen, home from Eton for the occasion. We sang, 'Sound, Sound your Instruments of Joy,' 'How Beautiful Upon the Mountains,' 'Zadok'— our own version of 'While Shepherds Watched'; and 'Jesse.'

When the youthful son of Jesse
Touched the harp with silver strains:
While the peaceful flock he tended
Grazed upon the fertile plain:
While he listened to the murmur
Of the brooklet soft and low:
Came the blessed infant Saviour
Nineteen hundred years ago.

Clap your hands for joy, ye people -
Clap your hands for joy, ye people

Clap your hands, clap your hands,
Shout Hosannah, for a Saviour's born!

The sopranos thrilled the old oak staircase, the altos swooned softly through the corridors, we tenors unleashed our passion to amaze the ancestral portraits on the walls, and the basses boomed thunderously from panelling to carved screen and up to shake the very chandeliers. I do not know what the Family really thought of it: my impression then was that though mightily amused by us erstwhile serfs sounding our bucolic arias in their domain of genteel tranquillity, they were too well-bred to allow more than a glimpse of their entertainment to be seen. They graciously smiled and congratulated Mr Tremayne, who led us, conducting from the foot of the stairs. Lucretia, who with her sisters afterwards bade us into the servant's hall to partake of mulled ale and saffron buns, maintained later to me that they all thoroughly enjoyed those innocent enthusiastic outpourings. But I wonder that people educated into the mysteries of Handel and Mozart and Beethoven should enjoy, in any honest manner, such unforced and artless music.

I had had little opportunity to go tramping around the cliffs that summer, although between voyages I had once or twice ventured as far as Stepper Point and Butter Hole; but they had not been particularly fine afternoons, and there had been no sign of Miss Devereaux. I had been reading and re-reading the book she gave me, however, and now knew all the shorter poems in it by heart, and some of the longer ones also, including large portions of the Ancient Mariner. These, with the book itself, had been my constant companions on my sea-rovings, whether in my cabin, reading by the light of a hurricane lamp, or on the bridge, reciting them to myself from memory. Poets, I think, little know the effect their verse have upon those who embrace it and take it to their hearts: many a desert or landless ocean space has been made to bloom and throb with human life, the comfort of another's mind, the mysterious realization of God's bounty given to us through remembrance and repetition of poetry by the solitary observer.

Not only this, but I had irresistibly been drawn into composing verses of my own: fumblingly at first, with awkward rhymes and jerky rhythm, like a schoolboy attempting to emulate masters far above him; then more easily, less ambitious, but truer to my own deepest feelings. And now I had written some brief stanzas which certainly pleased me, but which I had not dared to show anyone else. I knew there was but one person of my acquaintance to whom I could reveal them, and I awaited her judgement with both hope and trepidation.

By chance that early September, when the Sprite went into the shipyard to have her sails and mast replaced before the autumn gales set in, I was able to walk out to those vistas I held doubly dear to me now; and found Miss Lucretia ensconced in a natural hollow above the stream which scored its way deeply into the fold of land, to gush onto the beach beside Guddra Gorge.

As I came from Butter Hole along the green-swathed cliff top and crossed Guddra Common, I was aware of a huge iron gantry erected on the cliff-edge at Gunver Head, and a horse-whim working, drawing up kibbles or buckets of ore won from the sheer cliff face by men lowered by this means to perform such terrifying work. This was Wheal Galway, the venture of several local tradesmen and land owners (including Mr Thomas Rowlands, and also Squire Devereaux, on whose land it took place); I do not think it made anyone rich, for after some six months working it went ‘scat’, as we say; that is, bankrupt. The Squire, at least, benefited, for he had his royalties as owner of the mineral rights. It was but a small part of the mania then prevailing for digging out, streaming, raising and dressing various metal ores found, in small or great quantities, throughout the length and breadth of Cornwall. In the case of Wheal Galway it was copper, a large bronze-green streak having long been plainly observed from the seaward to exist in those towering cliffs. Copper was indeed mined there, from a third of the way down the cliff, opposite the northernmost dizzy stack of rock, the largest of three offshore masses forming the gorge. With the copper, there was a little antimony and lead; but apart from bringing a brief employment to some of our Lodenek men, and to Major Devereaux his royalties, there was little benefit in the venture, and no doubt, considerable loss in the end to the adventurers who financed it.

I was surprised to see Miss Lucretia here, some two hundred yards away from and below the miners and their engines; but as she explained, the north-east wind was striking cold off the sea that day, and she needed the shelter of the rise of land behind her, whilst being able to sit in the autumnal sun and sketch. Her pony, tethered to a gorse bush, cropped the short wiry grass near her. The cries of the gulls, the booming echoes of the blowhole on the island across the gorge as the tide forced its way into the cavity, to be rejected and flung out again, the intermittent clanking of the chain on the drum as the horse turned the whim out of sight above us, and the steady jet of stream water falling onto the rocks and shingle below, were the only sounds. As I approached she laid aside her sketchbook and smiled up at me.

'Home is the voyager, home from the sea,' she said. It sounded like a quotation; perhaps she was thinking of Odysseus or some Greek hero. 'How have you fared across the great waters?'

'Well enough, I believe,' I said. 'I'm Master of the lugger Sprite now.'

'Indeed? You *will* go far.' Her voice was light and she sounded impressed, but there was a certain mockery in her eyes.

'Thank you for the book you gave me,' I said. 'I have taken it with me, each time we sail. It has been my constant companion and friend.'

The mockery died out and a look of interest and new estimation replaced it in her gaze. 'Lyrical Ballads, was it not?' she said. 'I have more books I could lend or give you— if you can find time to read them.' She indicated that I should sit on the grass beside her.

'I would find time to read them. I would *make* time, Miss Devereaux.'

'Well, now. I must think. Have you ever read a novel?'

'You mean, stories?'

'Long stories. Concerning adventure, love, desperate circumstances.'

I shook my head. 'I should like to read one,' I said. 'But I don't know if I ought to take such a book to sea with me.'

'I should not like you to lose it. But perhaps I can find some well-worn copies. My mother and sisters and I read novels, and lend them to our friends— sometimes they are brought back to us in quite a sorry state. Tomorrow, if it is fine, I shall be here again...' She showed me her drawing, of the cliffs and Trevose Head beyond. 'I want to colour my picture in, so if this weather continues I will come here, about three o'clock; and shall have something else for you to read.'

'I have something for you to read, Miss.' I drew out of the vest pocket of my jacket my new verses, inscribed in my best copperplate handwriting.

'A poem! My dear James...did...?'

'Yes. I wrote it. For you.'

Her eyes dilated, as she glanced at it; then smiling but evidently surprised, even astonished, she said, 'I really can hardly believe...'

' 'Tis true. I wrote it. Don't know if 'tis any good, mind you. But I want you to have it.'

She held it gently between her long delicate fingers, as if it were some priceless Egyptian papyrus; then said, 'Will you read it to me?'

I had not expected this. But if that was what she wanted, that was what she should have. I took the sheet from her, cleared my throat, and read boldly:

'Upon the cliffs I wander
    Above the rushing waves
Beholding ocean's splendour
    As round the rocks it laves.

The wind-filled sky above me
  Embraces all the air,
The trembling thrift below my feet
  Disperses all my care.

Only here true freedom lives,
  I sing and shout this out –
That man's wild heart in Nature thrives,
  With beauty all about.

Not in the towns 'mid smoke and dirt,
  Nor where dark ores are mined,
But in the open air and rain
  His treasure is divined.'

I looked at her. She had turned her head away, and was looking down into the deep funnel of the narrow inlet; I saw two seals out beyond in the green and white waters, rolling over and enjoying the motion, as such creatures will do when replete with fish they have caught. On the lower shelves of rock on the island opposite us across the Gorge a cormorant was perched, holding his black wings out to dry. When Lucretia turned to me at last, I saw tears in her eyes.

'That is... quite beautiful,' she said in a whisper. 'To think that you... but why not you? Poets have come from the stables, from the farms, why not from the quayside of Lodenek? Robert Burns began as a plough boy, as did John Clare. Even Shakespeare was of no great standing socially.'

I had no real grasp of what she meant, but it pleased me greatly that she should imply that I was something of a poet.

'I have written other things, but this one seemed to me to be by far the best. The others were clumsy. I've torn most of 'em up.'

'Don't destroy any more, James. You must let me see them, all of them.'

I thought perhaps she was simply excited to make the discovery of a versifying sailor-boy, and that perhaps she would adopt me as a Deserving Cause— as a sort of mascot to boast of among her literary acquaintances. But her solemn earnest gaze, the deep brown and amber sincerity of it, quickly disabused me of such a notion.

'I shall treasure this poem for the rest of my life,' she said, taking the paper gently from me. 'You are wasted on a mariner's career. Some would say I should not tell you that, nor lend you books, nor encourage you into the realms of literature. My own father is as hard-headed a Tory hunting and shooting gentleman as you would find; God forgive him, he would say I am giving you ideas beyond your station in life.'

I sat there, frowning. 'I haven't any ambitions beyond being Master of my ship,' I said. 'Although now that I have achieved that...'

'It would be a waste, a crime, for you not to rise farther.' She clasped her hands around her knees, and stared down at the little blue autumn squills beside her. 'I shall certainly help you, if you will accept help. They cannot forbid me; I am twenty-four years old and have a little money left me by my great-aunt. As to my father, I can outwit him in any argument he may choose to use against us. Together, James, we might make a great man of you...you must study further. Latin and Greek, you know, that is the only real distinction between the upper classes and the lower ones. You poor National School boys are never taught Latin and Greek. Is it not so?'

I admitted she was right. A shadow fell across us and looking up we saw the sky darkening. I stood up, and pointed to an immense purple and puce cloud racing towards us. 'A squall coming up from the nor'east. We'd better shelter, Miss.'

'But where?'

'There are tunnels... old adits... just below. In the rock. Can you climb down?'

'If you help me.'

We gathered up her book and painting materials into her basket, which I took in one hand and, leading her by the other, we made a slow but steady descent to a narrow rock ledge twenty feet below. As we reached the adit opening in the cliff face the rain hissed down in a sudden torrent, rebounding off the rocks into the incoming tide, and within a second an impenetrable curtain of water cut off the view.

'Your pony will be soaked, of course,' I said, wiping raindrops from my face.

'Poor thing. Worse, my saddle will be drenched. It can't be helped. I really cannot be annoyed today. It has been a revelation.'

We were huddled together in that narrow dank passage, carved out of the stone and showing streaks of granite and greenstone amid the slate. But we were dry.

'What did you mean, about Latin and Greek?' I asked.' How should I go about learning them?'

'I am sure we can find someone to teach you. I could get you books, though I'd be little other help: they don't teach young ladies such things. What about the master of the National School?'

'Mr Nanskivell? He might set me on the road. I can go to him and ask. But what then, afterwards, I mean?'

'You could go to university, to Oxford or Cambridge. You could become a doctor, a lawyer, a scholar; perhaps a parson.'

Such thoughts had never before entered my head, but I saw at once that a new life on a grander scale, a life of learning and appreciation of good things, of art and music and poetry and literature, might one day be mine.

'It would mean a good deal of study,' she said. 'But I am aware that it has been done by a number of poor students. There is only one thing to prevent you. Money, or rather the lack of it.'

I stared at her. We looked, there in the dim light of that confined space, into one another's eyes, assessing the glorious new prospect we saw before us. 'How much do you think I should need?' I said.

'I don't know. Enough to keep you at College for two or three years before you could take your degree. I believe there are scholarships, or exhibitions. Our vicar would know. I could make some discreet enquiries on your behalf.'

'Miss Lucretia...' I saw now she meant much more than to give an indigent scholar a helping hand. She had my whole destiny carved out if only I would agree to it. Her melting face, and rapid breathing, sent a signal of affection, an invitation to love, throughout me. I clasped her to me, and she gave a half-laugh as we embraced.

'Lucretia. My dear...'

'My dear, dear James.'

'I've so much respected and... loved you since we first met on the cliffs.'

'And I, dear James, could not put you out of my mind.'

I can recollect now, in every detail, these many years afterwards, that first astounding embrace, so natural it seemed to me, and yet so miraculous, achieving in one bound the unattainable - Miss Lucretia Devereaux in my arms, so appealing, so frank, as if she had been waiting long years for me and me alone. I recall the nearness, the fragrance of her, the sensation of her trim light body against mine (uncorsetted, for Lucretia never believed in hampering her bodily movements any further than her disability restricted her); the very essence of her mind, body and soul flowing for the same time accepting the inescapable rightness, the divine inevitability of the situation. And I gave her some of the passion that had been transmitted to me by little Iseut in Roscoff; never had she been kissed with such fervour, such forcefulness, such commitment, if indeed she had ever been kissed at all. For Lucretia stood apart from the rest of her kind, a forbidding figure, rather because of her intellect and artistic aspirations than of her damaged hip; no would-be suitors had yet penetrated that armour of wit, wisdom and deep comprehension which met their advances. Yet I, James Spargo, a simple mariner lad with a feeling for natural beauty and some small pretensions to versifying, had succeeded where they had all signally failed. Yes; it seemed a miracle to me then. It still seems one to me now.

The rain suddenly cleared; we re-entered the

world of clashing waves, shrieking sea birds, rocks shining brilliantly now in the sun, and the incoming tide trumpeting through the Gorge. I assisted her up the steep rock face to where we had sat and talked, and thence to her pony, which gazed at us reproachfully, its back steaming in the sun. She took off the dripping side-saddle and stripped it of its velveteen cover, which she wrung out and laid across a gorse bush to dry in the wind. Then she turned to me, and took both my hands in hers, looking up at me earnestly. 'I wonder if I have said too much to you, after all. Perhaps you will go home, and away on your ship, and decide it is all an impossible dream.'

'Perhaps.' I smiled at her. 'But if I wanted a lady like you for my wife... how else could I win her?'

'Ah,' she said. 'You learn fast.'

'That's what you knew, all along. How it might be done.'

'Yes; but you have just given me proof that you will be able to do it.' She looked down into her basket and took out the now damp paper, the precise script on it now somewhat blotched and spoiled. 'I will copy this out this evening,' she said. 'You must go on, and write me more poems. You will, won't you, James?'

'I will, for you, Lucretia.'

We kissed and dallied another half-an-hour, talking of this and that, laughing and dreaming together. She read to me a poem entitled To Fancy by a new poet, John Keats, who was well thought of generally; though she said his first long poem, Endymion, had been greatly disparaged by the critics of the age. Then, putting the still-damp cover on her saddle, I helped her mount, and led the pony by its bridle up the valley path, and home, slowly, along the lanes, down to Devereaux Place. We passed through the hamlets of Crugmeer and Trethillick, where farmers' wives and labourers stared at us, well knowing who she was; but she was not too proud to be seen with me, gaily offering comments on the views all about, the slate hedgerows covered with hawthorn, ripe blackberries, sloes and rose hips. So we arrived at the main gateway into the grounds.

'We will meet again, and often,' she said. 'You will be constantly in my thoughts. We must arrange a signal - you can always send a note up to my maid Susan Roberts, when you are home and can come to our beloved haunts. Meanwhile, let us hope tomorrow will be fine, and we can meet again at Guddra.' She extended her hand which I kissed fervently.

Turning the pony's head, she rode in through the great mouldering stone archway, with pennywort and ivy growing out of it, and up the drive to the house.

CHAPTER 17

THE STUDENT

I went home, my head in a whirl of strange new thoughts and prospects, hardly able to believe my wonderful good fortune in gaining such an ally and friend as Lucretia; yet knowing that somehow I must act on her advice and better myself, or the very foundation of our newly discovered love would be undermined. At home that evening I was silent and preoccupied, trying to assess the new prospects opening up for me. I could not share my thoughts with my mother, who was busy preparing a large leek and potato pie, and in any case had more to do now that my eldest sister Joan was married and set up in a home of her own. My younger sisters' and brothers' chattering irritated me, and I was short with them. Daniel, now aged twelve, wanted me to take him fishing in the small dinghy my father owned, but hardly used; I told him the tide was not right (indeed it was then ebbing), and it would be dark inside half-an-hour. Seeing his evident disappointment I relented so far as to say that if he got me up at four the following morning we would row down the estuary and see what we could catch—bass, or mackerel, or perhaps a conger. (The conger eel, soused in vinegar, baked in a pie, or split, salted and dried for boiling in winter, was to us a special treat in those days.) After the evening meal I was glad to retire to the attic where, Reuben being away at sea, I could spend an hour or two alone.

I wondered what sort of career I could embrace,

supposing I could get to a University and take a degree. Lucretia had mentioned various possibilities. Medicine? a worthy career, yet not mine; I felt that one should be thoroughly committed to the calling, and did not feel I was made for bringing babies into the world, treating the poor with compresses for sores, dealing with epidemics or typhus and cholera, or curing the squire of his gout. The legal profession? But lawyers worked in dusty offices, seeing little sunshine and knowing few adventures outside their realm of the courts, their legal tomes, their conveyancing and will-making. I knew I could not study over long years to imprison myself thus. Scarcely more appealing to me was the career of a scholar— an historian, or literary critic, perhaps a professor or some sort: life was to be lived, I instinctively believed, not to be squeezed dry among books and sheaves of print. I might, perhaps, become a Member of Parliament and help make laws; but I reflected that one would need a great deal of money for that, to buy votes at election time, and to maintain oneself in the right style when one actually got to parliament. I doubted if ever I would be rich enough for that, even if Lucretia did have connections and some inheritance of her own.

What then? I might, perhaps, become a poet; even a novelist, or playwright; yes, that kind of literary career was the only thing that inspired me. If I could write from nature, like Wordsworth, Coleridge or Keats, I might indeed achieve something in the world, and make Lucretia proud of me.

Latin and Greek, she had said, in effect, were the keys to a higher education. Mr Nanskivell was acquainted in some measure with those mysterious tongues. The first step then, was to go and see him. I would call on him that very evening; for tomorrow might not be convenient, and the day after the Sprite was due to sail to Bristol with a load of slates from the quarry a couple of miles up river. So after a few more minutes of cogitation, eager to decide things for myself, I descended the stairs very quietly; though not quietly enough to escape my mother's notice as she sat near the oil lamp with her sewing, mending a pair of Daniel's breeches. 'Just going out for a stroll, Mother,' I said casually, and left the house.

Mr Nanskivell lived in a large old cottage he rented on the hill, at some distance from Sandrys' Hill House; those two buildings, and a farm house with several barns and byres, were the only dwellings in the fields and pastures above Lodenek itself on the south side. A half moon sailing among big mauve comfortable clouds lit my way along the lane, alongside which was a ropewalk (said to be longest in the country) where huge hawsers for mooring ships and towing them were made by four brothers, surnamed Tom. Many of their ropes had been specially ordered by the Admiralty for warships, and by upcountry merchants for East Indiamen. The church clock was striking eight, its steady notes drifting over the quiet town to me as I strode along in the still evening; over the hedges I could see the long silvery sand bars showing up in the estuary where the tide receded from them.

I reached the cottage, opened the wicket gate, and walked up the path among gnarled old apple and pear trees. I lifted the huge iron knocker with a lion's head on it and let it drop; the noise resounded through the house, startling me. I knocked again. After a few seconds, during which the echoes died, I heard footsteps from within, then the bolt being drawn back. The door opened and Mr Nanskivell, in shirt sleeves with his waistcoat open, stood there. 'Good heavens— it's James Spargo.'

'I hope it isn't too late to call on you, Mr Nanskivell. There is a personal matter which I should like your advice on.'

'Come in, James. Come in. Quite all right; I shan't get to bed much before midnight. We'll go in here— my wife's not well, you know, she retires early. I have to keep my children quiet, when they are at home.'

He was lighting a couple of candles in a room just off the passageway; on entering it I beheld, in the warm glow of their flames, books, newspapers, documents strewn across a large table, and other books on shelves around the walls. I noticed a couple of framed engravings, and a small statue of the Venus di Milo, which I remembered we had drawn at our art lessons, and which had provoked some sniggers from the younger boys— who had never before seen a representation of the female form unclothed. These comprised all the furnishings, apart from two simple wooden chairs, on which, at his gesture, we sat down.

'Excuse the muddle,' he said with a wan smile, 'I'm writing a work— a treatise— on the Antiquities of North Cornwall. The Reverend Dr Borlase has done a great deal in that line, of course, but being a West Cornwall man I believe he neglected, or perhaps could not get to, some of the remarkable sites in our district. I hope to publish it in a year or two, provided I can find enough subscribers.'

This interested me; from time to time I had wondered how exactly one went about getting a book published. 'So you pay the printers yourself?' I asked.

'I need fifty subscribers to pay me ten pounds each, and then the book will be printed.' He indicated some drawings and sketches, portraying rock piles on Roughtor, hill forts and cliff castles. 'I am doing the drawings myself, of course.' I knew from my days at the National School that he was a meticulous draughtsman. 'So far I have received twenty-two subscriptions, six of them from Lodenek itself, including Squire Devereaux, the Vicar, and Mr Thomas Rowlands.' He handed me a leaflet he had had printed, headed 'Prospectus of a Work to be entitled '*The Mysteries of Antiquity in Trigg Hundred and Northern Cornwall,* by Henry Nanskivell B.A. (Oxon,),' and outlining the material to be included in the book. B.A. I knew, meant Bachelor of Arts; which of course meant that he had been to University.

'I have to do most of my work on the book at evening, even through the night,' he said. 'School teaching becomes somewhat onerous as the term progresses, and I am glad when we have a holiday. Now, James, what can I do for you?'

I hesitated, wondering how to introduce my enquiries, and the reasons for them. Certainly I did not wish to mention Lucretia by name. 'I have become interested in poetry,' I said. 'And I've even been trying my hand at writing poems myself. I doubt if they are good, at least, not yet. But someone of my acquaintance saw one and was apparently quite impressed. Indeed I'm advised— it has been suggested— that I should try to get to a University and take a degree, like yourself, Mr

Nanskivell.' I wondered what advantages, if any, he had had from early life, or whether he had himself risen from a low station. Yet, looking about me, I doubted whether being a schoolmaster brought him much pecuniary rewards. I knew his children, the eldest of which was now nine or ten, and could not consider them particularly well dressed or over nourished. It was rumoured that his wife, poor sickly woman, was dying of consumption.

'Indeed now. I should like to see something of what you have written, James; I daresay it would help me form an opinion of how far you might go. You were a good monitor at school, of course, indeed one of the best; very quick to learn and able to pass it on to the others.'

'Yes, sir,' I said, 'I believe I can learn pretty fast. But to go to University I should need tuition in Latin and Greek, I am told.'

'Yes. Surely you would, though not to any high standards. You would have to sit the Matriculation examination, which would mean going up to Oxford or Cambridge.'

'Could you tutor me in languages?'

'I have forgotten much of what I learned, I'm afraid. One does not need Latin or Greek to teach the National Curriculum. I suppose I could help, though; I have my primers somewhere. Yes— why not? I should have to charge you some small fee, though.'

'I shall be glad to pay you.'

'Strange, I thought you were a confirmed seadog now.'

'I don't intend to give that up,' I said. 'At least not yet. But I should dearly like to better myself.'

'If you could get to Oxford or Cambridge and

read for a degree, what would be your eventual aim in life?'

I knew he would ask me that, and that I would not be able to answer. All I could see in my mind's eye was Lucretia's tears as she held, so delicately, my poem before her. 'Seafaring is in my blood, I suppose,' I said. 'I love nothing better than to be in charge of my ship on a voyage. But I want to be able to understand the world and the universe, to write poems and even books. Like you.'

'There is not necessarily much advancement in it, you know. Sometimes I wonder why I studied in order to end up here— in a small place like Lodenek.' He regarded me soberly. 'At Oxford I read the classics and English literature. I took a good degree; but then, having no patrimony or inheritance to speak of, I saw they wanted schoolmasters to run National Schools. Once here, and married, I found there was little else I could do.' He sounded weary now, old before his time, and full of regret. Evidently his income had not grown, though his family had. 'You will need money, you know, to see you through College,' he continued.

'How much would you say?'

He thought, staring at the ceiling. A large white moth entered the casement window, which was open slightly, made straight for the lamp on the table, and after fluttering round it once or twice, found its way into the chimney and expired with a small explosion. I noticed there were several somnolent daddy longlegs, or crane flies, hanging on the ceiling; one detached itself and came down, hovering above the table with soundless wings.

'If you lived simply and did not dine out, as so many undergraduates do, you might manage on a hundred pounds, say a hundred and twenty— a year,' he said. 'Usually one takes three years to read for a degree.'

'Aren't there scholarships - exhibitions, I think they're called?'

'A few. Some pay very little, even supposing you were awarded one. You would need to enquire at various Colleges. I don't wish to discourage you, James. You might well do it, with application. But the money...'

'I will raise the money,' I said, 'one way or another.'

'I sincerely hope you will, my boy. Well, I shall look out my Latin and Greek books, and we can make a start. It might be difficult, however, if you are away much at sea.'

'I shall persevere,' I said, 'if you would instruct me when I'm home. I will take my books to sea with me and study when not on duty.'

So we struck a bargain: I would pay him two shillings for each lesson of two hours, and he would give me exercises to do when I was away. I was heartened by his remarks that for Matriculation, at least, the standards were not high. Before I left he said, 'I usually take a small glass of cordial about now. Will you join me?'

I accepted. He took a bottle of dark red liquid out of the cupboard and fetched a couple of glasses. The cordial was strong, with a brandy base (I guessed) and tasted deliciously of raspberries.

'Your good health, Mr Nanskivell,' I said, raising my glass.

'And yours, James. May you have better success

in life than I have found.'

He saw me to the door, and as I left I heard a sudden violent coughing, a spasm of deeply congested lungs, from a room above. He bolted the door after me, and went upstairs, taking a candle with him; from the garden path I saw its wavering light appear in the upper chamber.

Walking home I was saddened to think of him, trapped into that life of genteel poverty. I remembered him at the School, delighted to read us poetry, expounding natural laws and scientific facts, hearing us read from selected works of literature and commenting on them so avidly, so full of the appreciation of life. Certainly it was a warning to me, to realize what he had come to. But I saw also the doors that would open for me soon, and the vision of Lucretia, with her earnest loving gaze, urging me on to great things.

There was, however, as Mr Nanskivell had pointed out, one all important unanswered question: how was I to raise the three hundred and more pounds to go to College?

CHAPTER 18

INNOCENCE AND EXPERIENCE

I thought hard about this, so hard that I barely slept that night; though when Daniel, eager to hold me to my promise, roused me a little before four in the morning when it was still dark, I had just passed into a deep exhausted slumber. The last thing I wanted just then was to be woken, but, as I should be away to sea again in a day or so, I struggled up and dressed, to accompany him down river.

I must own I had a special affection for young Daniel. He was so lively and cheerful, so wide-eyed and innocent, so eager to experience whatever life had to offer, that he reminded me of myself at his age. Indeed, unlike Reuben and my sisters, who were red-headed and took after my mother's family, he greatly resembled me in colouring, build, and facial characteristics: the same dark closely curled hair, the sharp Spargo chin, the lobeless ears. People often remarked upon these similarities we bore to each other. Like me, he was a monitor at the National School, having been selected as a keen pupil always anxious to please; like me he would often win nearly everything he entered for at the Whitsun sports. So much of myself I saw in him, so much that would never return to me now as I stood on the threshold of adulthood, that I could deny him nothing if it were in my power to give it him.

But as we put out from the quayside I could not forbear from puzzling about my own situation. I rowed mechanically; when we had dropped anchor just inside the great Doom Bar stretching across the river mouth (on which so many ships had foundered) I sat absently in the dinghy, paying little attention to my lines whilst the sun's glow strengthened over the hills and uplands to the east. Half a plan was forming in my head; I believed there was a possibility that Mr Rowlands would help me. Had he not favoured me more than once with his advice, and encouraged me to succeed in business and as a mariner? I was confident that he thought highly of me; he might conceivably be induced to lend me some money, or even a ship, wherewith to trade on my own account. An audacious idea, perhaps; but Thomas, I realised, admired enterprise and audacity. There was one consideration, however, that caused me some anxiety; and I saw I must consult Lucretia again before proceeding.

The tide was now beginning to ebb, and having caught a few mackerel and a couple of whiting, I told Daniel he must row back; but that he could pay out a couple of baited lines from the stern as he did so. In this way, we got a fine skate, just as we rounded the rocky bend of the river and came into view of the quayside at Lodenek. Daniel marched home proudly with the catch, which would fill our family's mouths for several days if the mackerel were marinated– that is, cooked in salt water and vinegar and allowed to cool with bay leaves to spice them. I was glad to go back to bed for a few hours rest.

At three in the afternoon, the weather being fine although again cooled by a northerly breeze, I was on my way out through Trethillick and Crugmeer to meet Lucretia. As I breasted the rise on which the latter hamlet sits, I saw her, on her ambling pony, a little distance from Guddra Common. She turned and saw me coming, and halted the animal so that I could overtake her.

'I have three books for you,' she said, with a welcoming smile. 'I think they will widen your interest.'

'I'm sure they will.' I walked beside her content for the moment simply to be with her, viewing the countryside, the hedgerows, the horse-whim at work up on Gunver Head, the steel-blue sea beyond fretted with the sparse foam of waves rolling towards the shore. Two ravens flew over, hoarsely coughing, and I could see several choughs probing into the bare soil of the Common with their long curved crimson beaks; after ants or grubs, no doubt.

'I shall be able to finish my picture,' Lucretia said happily. 'The glass has gone up a fair way; no rain today, I think.'

We reached the Common and turned down the narrow valley to the Gorge. Yellow flag irises and colonies of bog bean with asparagus-like heads, grew here, flanked by low sallow bushes. Stonechats perched on thin twigs, uttering their sharp metallic calls, and a flock of wheatears flew up from between furze bushes above us as we descended. When we reached the spot where she had been sketching, I told her I had been to see Mr Nanskivell, and of the agreement we had made. She said, 'I am so glad, James. I think it is important for you to begin studying as soon as possible. For several reasons.'

An impish look appeared on her face and then was gone.

'I think so too,' I said. 'I don't know how long it

will be before I can get the Matriculation.' She sat herself down and began to arrange her picture on its board, and lay paints and brushes beside her. 'Not so very long; next year, perhaps, if you can find the time to learn.'

'I will. I must find the time.' I sat down beside her. 'I owe it to you, Lucretia. For encouraging me. For making me see my proper way forward.'

'My dear.' She laid her hand on my arm, looking at me so intently, so searchingly, that I was spellbound for a moment in her serious sympathetic gaze. 'I shall be with you all times, in spirit, I mean. As you study. And when you are home, we shall find means to be together, at least for some of the time....'

I kissed her, as boldly as before, yet much more gently, holding her lips against mine for a long delicious moment, and then releasing her to see her smile at me. Indeed, to make her smile, to see the welcome and trust in her face, and the pleasure it gave her, was to me then— and also for so many years afterwards— the dearest and most fulfilling of my rewards.

'Now, James,' she said, 'you will let me finish my picture, won't you? I may not have another chance if the weather changes. Now be good, and let me do it. The books I have brought for you are there, in my basket.'

So for an hour or more I occupied myself by reading such works as opened my eyes to the new worlds of adventure, experience, and poetic delight. The first I opened was *Ivanhoe*, by Sir Walter Scott: after finding the first few pages somewhat discursive and reflective, I got into the story and went on for three or four chapters, utterly absorbed and lost to the clifflands and sunlit sea about me. Then, thinking I had better look at the other books, I examined the second: a forbidding work in three volumes, of close print, somewhat old and musty smelling; yet it proved equally fascinating, indeed full of rollicking humour and forthright speech such as I never suspected might be put between the covers of any books. It was Henry Fielding's *Tom Jones*, and I wanted to read it straight through then and there.

But I decided I must at least glance at the third volume, a very slim offering indeed, a little insignificant work in tooled leather and with an antique kind of printing inside, interspersed with strange woodcuts. I read:

> Tyger! Tyger! Burning bright
> In the forests of the night,
> What immortal hand or eye
> Could frame thy fearful symmetry?
> When the stars threw down their spears
> And watered heaven with their tears,
> Did He smile his work to see?
> Did He who made the Lamb make thee?

I had little notion of what those words meant; but the sound of them, the amazing ideas they represented, rushed through me like water in a parched desert; it was as if these were my own verses rediscovered, the very poetry of my soul. I read the whole book through— not a very great undertaking— sitting there: drinking it in, alternately delighted and saddened, as the author of *Songs of Innocence and Experience* revealed in such holy naive language the wonder of God's world, and the depths and poignancy of man's distress amid it.

Excited by the effect of these verses, I got up and wandered down to the Gorge, leaving Lucretia busily adding colour washes to her land and seascape. Standing on the brink of the sheer rock face, looking up the narrow channel between the three islands rising abruptly from the sea (pacific enough today, ruffled by the soft steady northerly wind but without a swell), I could see the gantry on the apex of the cliff at Gunver Head, and the whim which was bringing up the iron buckets full of ore mined from the rock face. Here were men risking their lives for a pittance, to bring copper up 'to grass' and supply the insatiable demands of industry and commerce. Warships, I knew, were now copper-bottomed to guard them against borers. Every steam engine, working across the country, whether pumping or milling or pulling goods wagons, needed brass boilers and pipes. Bed-warmers, jugs, kettles, saucepans, lanterns, rods and levers of all kinds - all were being made of copper or brass. Cornwall, indeed, was known as the Copper Kingdom. And here, amid the glorification of industry, the making of wealth, was a voice crying, crying to God and man to see the awful slavery which came with the worship of commerce and riches.

And was Jerusalem builded here
Among these dark Satanic mills?

We had our own Satanic Mills— I had seen them in West Cornwall, where men were old at thirty, and women and children worked long hours at the spalling sheds breaking up the ore the miners brought to the surface. I saw now what the poets of Nature meant: that man was born to liberty, with the right to appreciate and enjoy the open air and the bounty of natural things which the Creator had given us; that we must refuse the blandishments of industry and so avoid the drudgery and death-inviting toil it so surely would bring with it. I felt a call to be part of the fight against such slavery. I did not doubt that it was God himself telling me to take up arms against Mammon.

'James!'

I turned. Lucretia had left her books and drawing, and come some way limping and stumbling over the rocky outcrops on the steep valley side. Her face betrayed alarm. I hastened back to her, and took her weight to prevent her falling.

'What is it, my dear?'

'I was so afraid— you looked lost, I was so fearful you would fall into the Gorge.'

True, I had been standing on the very edge, wrapped in my vision, utterly unconscious of the eighty feet drop below me which could have meant death or mortal injury. I said, 'You are my guardian angel, Lucretia. If you could only always be near, to counsel and warn and save me.'

'My dear love, I could not bear... to lose you so soon...'

'Ah, Lucretia... do you really feel so much for me?'

We lay together in the soft grass of a hollow, dug out many years before by other miners seeking to win their riches from the ground, and I held her in my arms, soothing her and whispering that I would always be careful of my personal safety for her sake.

'Have you finished your picture?' I asked after a while, when she had got over her fright and was nestling contentedly against me.

'Not quite. It won't matter, though...1 can take it home and put the finishing touches to it.'

A pair of skylarks rose above us into the clear cold air, giving out their jubilant songs, weaving tapestries of pure joyous sound above us. We listened together, then she said, 'I must read to you Shelley's Ode to a Skylark:

'Hail to Thee, blithe Spirit!—
   Bird thou never wert—
That from Heaven, or near it
   Pourest thy full heart
In profuse strains of unpremeditated art.'

She went on to quote three or four more stanzas from memory, then recited the last:

'Teach me half the gladness
   That thy brain must know:
Such harmonious madness
   From my lips would flow,
The world should listen then,
   As I am listening now.'

'I don't believe I could ever write like that,' I said. 'I suppose Shelley went to Oxford.'

'No doubt. But I'm sure Oxford could not teach him to write like that. Mr Shelley is an original genius.'

'I think my verses will always be quite simple,

and direct.'

'I hope so,' she said. 'Do you know why I brought along that little book by Blake?'

'No. Well, I suppose, you thought I ought to read it, and 'tis certainly quite wonderful.'

She leaned up on an elbow and looked down earnestly into my eyes. 'Not just that. I think the poem you wrote and gave to me is very like some that William Blake wrote. You have the same kind of visions. The same philosophy, or attitude to life and the world. You both instinctively know what is really valuable, as distinct from the things that only seem to be valuable.'

I smiled. 'Do you really think that? You're not saying it just to encourage me?'

'Of course I say it to encourage you. But it's also true, James. You will write more like it, won't you?'

'I will try. For you. No: not only for you. Just now, on the cliff edge, I was watching the miners at work on the rock face, and I could see thousands, hundreds and thousands, of men and women and children in dangerous and cramped conditions, labouring and mining, striving to serve the great machines in factories and workshops all over the country. If anything can make me write more poems, it will be those kind of thoughts.'

She sighed and drew me to her, laying my head on her breast as a mother might clasp and comfort her favourite child. The larks stopped singing and dropped to earth again: I had observed, for many times watching and listening to them on the cliff top, that they never stayed up singing for more than ten minutes at a time, before descending, as if exhausted for the time being by such an intricate ejaculation of song. I heard now the rattle and whine of the gantry and chains coming down to us, drawing me back to thoughts of material things and how to make money.

'Lucretia,' I said, 'I have been thinking hard about how to raise enough money to go to College. Mr Nanskivell estimates that I shall need something over three hundred pounds, unless I can win an Exhibition, which might bring me in some seventy pounds or so a year. As a Master Mariner I think I can only save, at the most, thirty pounds a year; so I must find a way to raise more.'

'I think I could help you' She was now sitting up, clasping her long tweed skirt about her knees, watching a dark furry caterpillar, one of the last of that year, working its way across the grass through clumps of dry dead thrift. 'I have nearly two hundred pounds a year, an annuity left to me by a maiden aunt whose favourite I was; she and I both had literary tastes, you see. I could easily spare you the hundred, or whatever you should need if you gain an Exhibition.'

That was not at all what I had been leading up to. 'Lucretia, my dear,' I said, sitting up also. 'My dearest love, thank you, but I could not accept it. Never. Don't be offended, but I would rather— work in the mines, or on a dreadnought, anything rather than owe you a penny. No, I must do it myself.'

'Are you really so proud?'

'I call it self-respect. Anyway, there is another distinct possibility, but I feel I must have your approval, or I shan't entertain it. My employer, Mr Thomas Rowlands, thinks well of me. I believe he regrets having to stop his free-trading activities, but he might, I think, allow me to continue them, by chartering me one of his ships. I know the trade, I am as good an agent as any, and I'm sure that within a year or so, perhaps sooner, I can make enough profit on four or five runs to Brittany and back, to raise what I need.'

She looked round at me with dark troubled eyes. 'It will be dangerous,' she said. 'I don't need to tell you, of course; but I should fear every day and night for you.'

'I doubt if there's much risk of my being killed. The ship might be wrecked, but that is always possible. It wouldn't be for long; I should give up smuggling as soon as I achieved what I need. You wouldn't object, though, to it, as a matter of principle?'

'Principle? No, James, how could I? My father himself finances free-trading syndicates. He might well back you, as you have such a rising reputation. Useless for me to object, even if I had strong views against the trade.'

'It does help the poor greatly,' I pointed out. 'Our people round the quayside live on salted pilchards or herrings for most of the winter; they can't afford meat. Salting down a barrel of fish costs a pound and three shillings if the duty is paid on it; but only eight shillings if they can get salt from us runners. And the pigs they keep; it would cost nearly ten pounds to salt down a pig when 'tis killed, duty paid. How many do you think could afford that? That's nearly a years earnings for most of them. They would starve if they couldn't get their free-trade salt, and sugar, and tea. Not to speak of spirits and tobacco, to give them a little ease and cheer.'

She nodded. 'I do not blame them, or you. No doubt in their place I would do the same, and flout the law without thinking twice about it. No, it is the danger to you, now that the Revenue men are stronger, and there are battles. One thing I must implore you: please try to avoid fighting and violence.'

'It may not always be possible. If they fire on us first...'

'Promise you will do all you can to avoid it.'

I sighed, took her hands and kissed them. 'I'll do all I can. It will be a matter of luck, or God's favour I believe. Through good judgement I haven't caused anyone's death yet.'

I could only hope that those words would assuage her fears. We gathered her things together, as the sun was now lowering in the west and shadows were lengthening down into the valley. I helped her mount her pony and walked back with her as before. We did not talk much, both being sobered by the matters we had discussed, but as we neared the last bend in the lane before Devereaux Place she said, 'When will you go to see Mr Rowlands?'

'Tomorrow. Before we sail, on the forenoon tide.'

'You will let me know what you arrange with him?'

'I shall get a note to Susan for you. Daniel or one of my sisters will deliver it.'

'Tell them to take it to the kitchen and give it personally to Mary Cribbens, the cook. No one else. Now, my dear independent, proud young buccaneer, kiss me. Take these books to sea and read them when you can, but put your Latin studies first. When shall I see you again?'

'We'll be back inside a week.'

'*Au'voir*, my dearest. I shall think of you

constantly.'

We kissed, rather chastely, she leaning down from the saddle. I noticed that the leaves on the elms and sycamore trees, which surrounded the great house and rose above the hedge behind her, were already showing spots of yellow and rust at the approach of autumn.

CHAPTER 19

THE PROPOSITION

That evening at half-past seven, I went along to Mr Nanskivell for my first Latin lesson. I was greeted on arrival by Mrs Nanskivell, as pale and 'wisht' as we would say, as any woman not long for this world. Later I heard her at the back of the cottage, admonishing a servant girl, and scolding one of her children who had arrived home late for the evening meal; between these activities she coughed loudly and violently. For an hour then I was instructed in the indicative present conjugation of the verb *Amare*, to love, and the declensions of the noun *Mensa*, a table. Leaving me poring over *Regare*, to rule, and *Ode*, a song, Mr Nanskivell went upstairs with his candle to see to his wife, and settle her down for the night; though from his lined and grey face I could well guess that he would get but broken sleep from the spasms of her congested lungs.

After pouring us both a glass of raspberry cordial, Mr Nanskivell set me some exercises to do, as best I could during my forthcoming voyage, and told me to order from a good bookseller a copy of the Reverend John Wesley's 'A Short Latin Grammar'; Bristol, he said, was a thriving city, where I might find it stocked as well as anywhere; and bade me goodnight and safe voyage.

I was about early the next day, stowing my clothes and books in my tin box (the same I possessed since I was ten years old, though now I had a leather portmanteau and canvas kit-bag as well); and breakfasted on fried whiting and 'bubble and squeak'— fried mashed potato, mixed with cabbage stalks and turnip — prepared by Susanna, aged fifteen. I kissed my mother and sisters goodbye, and stepped out onto the quayside, carrying my box and portmanteau, while Daniel shouldered the kit-bag to put aboard the Sprite. It was a fair day, and at eight in the morning the tide was creeping in around the old stone jetty at the entrance to the harbour. From quay wall to quay wall one could almost walk across the decks of smacks, barques, cutters, sloops and schooners, all either awaiting cargoes, discharging goods, or awaiting repairs. The noise of caulkers' mallets tapping oakum into their timbers, of carpenters' hammers and chisels, the cries of the auctioneer taking bids for catches of fish brought in during the night, with the clatter of horses' hoofs and the screech of iron-rimmed wheels as carriers' drays turned out from the narrow streets onto the quaysides, the steady groaning and tearing of timber as a huge baulk was cut lengthwise at the sawpits: these and a score of other familiar sounds met the ear and fused into a great concatenation of industry, as the port of Lodenek began once more to earn its daily bread.

After finding all in order on the Sprite, I bade Daniel take good care of the family in my own and my father's absence; and sent him whistling off to school, to learn the lesson of the day from Mr Nanskivell, to hand on to thirty others.

At ten minutes to ten I was waiting at the shipyard office when Mr Rowlands arrived there. The great baulks of timber on the other side of the harbour, seasoning in the water, were now moving on the rising tide. The Sprite was almost afloat; soon we would be sailing up-river before the still prevalent north wind, now backing to the west, to load with slates. The old seadogs on the public quayside seat known as the Long Lugger were saying there would be rain before nightfall.

Mr Rowlands, I perceived, was not in the best of moods; a concentrated frown creased his forehead and he walked slowly at a deliberating pace. However, he seemed to brighten on seeing me standing there by the clerk's desk.

'Ah, James. Ready for another voyage?'

'All ready, sir. May I have a few words with you before we sail?'

He took out his watch, a huge silver piece and examined it. 'I can give you ten minutes,' he said, and, opening the door of his office, beckoned me in. Seating himself at a small desk he said, 'Now then. Anything troubling you?'

'No trouble, sir. But I have an idea— a proposition, perhaps. I want to earn some money. I need about three hundred pounds. I like my work, I like the Sprite, but I can't help thinking that the coastal trade will never bring me in much.'

'And how do you propose to earn more?'

'I'm sure there is still a great deal of profit to be made from free-trading. I know you've set your face against it, but I wonder if you would help me to organize my own runs, and to distribute the goods at no risk to yourself.'

He frowned at me for a few seconds, then, picking up a pencil which lay beside the pad of writing paper on the desk, began to tap it rhythmically on the soft surface. 'How?' he said.

'If you would charter me one of your vessels, preferably the Sprite,' I said, 'I could show you what trade can be done.'

'No doubt,' he said. 'And what if before you had brought in much, the vessel was captured by the Revenue, or sunk by them, how would things stand? I should lose a good ship with nothing to show for it.'

I had not anticipated that; though, mentally kicking myself, I knew I should have.

'I should guarantee you would be repaid,' I said.

'A ship like the Sprite is worth over two hundred pounds,' he said. 'How can you guarantee that, young man? What property, or valuables do you have, that you can pledge me as security?

'None, sir. But I can give you my word of honour that I would make good any loss. By hard work over the years.'

'James, James,' he said, 'I thought you had a better grasp of business. However, I must admit that the coastal trade has not been so profitable recently. And like you I yearn for the grand old days of free-trade. But the coast is closely watched, and the game isn't worth the candle now.'

'I shouldn't land here, in this district, Mr Rowlands.'

'Where then?'

'Further up the coast, between Port Isaac and Boscastle; or further north. There are plenty of handy coves and beaches, with good valleys running up to farms; we could pretty soon get the goods out across the Moor to Launceston, Plymouth, even Exeter. There are far fewer Preventive men and coastguards up there.'

He sat, tapping his pencil quietly on the pad, and looking at me, then staring out of the little office window at the forest of masts and spars that occupied the inner harbour, then staring at me again.

'I will think about this,' he said, standing up. He laid a hand on my shoulder. 'I have great confidence in you, my boy. You are right, there are still great profits to be made, by an enterprising and cunning trader. Mind you, if I agree, I shall want my share of the venture. And if you get caught my name must never be mentioned, except as the ship owner. You understand that?'

'Of course, sir.'

'Come and see me - not here - up at the House, when you get back from this trip. Now— *bon voyage*, as the French say— I wish you fair wind and weather.'

I left the office believing that we understood each other, confident that together we should work out a satisfactory arrangement. On board the Sprite, I wrote a short and hasty note to Lucretia, unable to say anything definite, but glad of the excuse to communicate with her. I sealed it and addressed it to Susan Roberts, Devereaux Place; and before we cast off to sail up to the quarries, I went ashore to find a likely messenger. Luckily my sister Emma came out onto the quayside at that moment, bound on a shopping errand for my mother; and I prevailed upon her to take the note as soon as she was free to do so, enjoining her to go to the kitchen at Place and give it to Mrs Cribbins the cook.

That evening about six, having loaded the helling slates, we got out of the estuary under our own sail, the wind having gone back to the west, though fitful and blustery. After passing under the rock face of Stepper Point, surmounted by golden flecks of autumnal gorse flowers, and out into the Atlantic, I handed over to Enoch and went aft to my cabin, there to begin to study my Latin exercises; but the ship began to plunge and sway in a rising gale, and I had to give it up. I went on deck and was met by a harsh stinging squall; Enoch had given orders to reef the jib and mizzen sails, and we were driving forward under our mainsail alone, well ballasted by the cargo. Not until we were off Lundy did the wind slacken, and knowing I would get little rest, I stayed on the bridge with Enoch, who chewed tobacco phlegmatically; he accepted a nip or two of brandy, gazing from the binnacle to the dark sea ahead, and the intermittent light of constellations glimpsed between the clouds, and back to the binnacle again. Set Enoch a course, and it would be followed with undeviating accuracy

'No chance to get to my books tonight,' I said. 'I need a steady light for that.' Enoch chewed solemnly and nodded. 'Tis hard work, I don't doubt, consecrating on they pages,' he said. 'I wadn't struck on that when I was schooled, and never managed to read much.' After a while he said, as if brooding on great themes, 'Do 'ee reckon this booklearning do mean much, when all's said and done? Why should a clever young chap like yerseif, master of a good craft like this, want to do such a thing?'

'Only to better myself,' I said. 'To broaden my horizons.'

'Mine are broad enough, I b'lieve. Went to 'Mericky twice, Newfoundland too; soon be time for me to sit out on the Long Lugger with th' old men, but like all they, I've bin here and there, and can tell a few good yarns.'

'I mean, there are things you can't get to know by seafaring, and travelling,' I said. 'History, for instance. What went on in the past. And classical languages, so that you can study the great writers.' Enoch shook his head. 'Tis all beyond me. But I dearsay you've got some great scheme in that head of yours, Mr James, and whatever 'tis I'm sure you'll bring it to pass. Your father always said you was a determined devil, and that you wouldn't rest 'til you got whatever 'twas you wanted. I only hope 'twill all be worth it for 'ee when that do happen.'

We made Bristol the following day about noon and discharged our cargo; the next day we shipped several crates of china ware and various articles of ironmongery, along with Nottingham lace and Leicester hosiery, and embarked on the return voyage to Lodenek. I had the evening and most of the night to study, and made some progress; the weather being calm, in between my watches I continued my Latin exercises, and also read *Tom Jones* and William Blake. Later on the voyage I began to compose another poem for my dear Lucretia.

We berthed again alongside the quay at Lodenek that Saturday evening, and on the Monday morning I went to see Mr Rowlands at Sandry's Hill. As I walked up to the house and entered the drive I wondered if Emily would be there; and sure enough, I saw her in the shrubbery, snipping off little pieces of laurel and euonymus to add to a flower arrangement.

'Hullo,' she said, 'Father is expecting you, James.' She came out of the bushes, holding a pair of secateurs in her gloved hand, and the snippets of stems and leaves in the other, and walked up to the house with me.

'Did you have a good voyage?'

'Fair,' I said. 'Not exactly exciting. Only to Bristol and back.' I wondered what effect the news of my studies would have on her, and said, 'But I have plenty to occupy me. I am studying Latin, and reading some of the great English authors.'

'Indeed.' She looked at me with some surprise, but quickly said, 'What will you do with Latin, when you learn it?'

I hesitated. 'Tis the gateway to a full education. I want to improve my prospects. Perhaps I shall go up to Oxford or Cambridge to study.'

Emily thought for a moment, then said, 'If you do that, there will be great prospects for you indeed. I doubt, though, if you would settle down in Lodenek then. Who knows what you might do?'

She seemed to envisage that I would go off across the world, in Government service perhaps, or find some lucrative post in London or another great city. The thought of leaving my home town and taking up a career elsewhere now struck me forcibly.

'I hope I shall return to Lodenek, at least every now and then,' I said.

'Yes. You would miss the old town, I daresay. I'm sure I would too, if I had to leave it.'

She meant, if she were married and had to go away. I was still pondering on this when we reached the portico, and Mr Rowlands himself appeared in the open doorway.

'Ah, James. Come in, my dear fellow.' This mode of address appeared promising. 'Emily, ask Simmonds to bring us some Madeira, will you?' He led me into the same small parlour, as before, as Emily left us with a lingering wistful glance.

'My daughter is restless,' he said, indicating a chair for me to sit on. 'It will be time for her to marry soon. I shall be giving a party for her twenty-first birthday. Next month. She would like you to attend, James, and has promised me that she won't play any silly tricks on you this time.'

'I will come, sir, if I can.' I looked at him expectantly.

'You mean if you are in port at the time. Well, you will no doubt be your own master, and will be able to arrange things how you will.'

I took this to imply that he was amenable to my ideas. The footman appeared with a decanter and glasses on a silver tray, and put them down on the small Queen Anne table. Mr Rowlands poured out the wine, lifted his glass, and said, 'To a new partnership, Captain Spargo. One that will materially benefit us both, I sincerely hope.'

'To our partnership.' I drank mine, sipping it warily, remembering the sherry I had so rashly drunk down on the occasion he had appointed me as Master. But the Madeira was blander and altogether less potent, it seemed to me; a pleasant glow, no more, in my throat and stomach as it went down.

. 'Now to details. I have given this considerable

thought, James. Firstly, the Sprite is rather too small for our purposes, but I have no other craft as speedy. So I am buying a new ship, a barquentine of about a hundred and fifty tons, which will give us a decent profit on each run. The results must be worth the risk. She is called the St Malo and is at present lying at Plymouth. I shall want you to go up and sail her home. I think you will like her; she'll draw less water than the Galatea, but has a good hold and fair deck space.

'Secondly, I shall draw up a legal agreement, whereby you will charter her, and as you suggest, at a nominal figure of twenty pounds the year. But between you and me, James, the arrangement will be that twenty-five per cent of all profits you make will come to me. You will bank with my Lodenek Bank, and I shall arrange for the account to be adjusted accordingly. So it will be entirely up to you to make the whole venture pay. Agreed?'

I had no choice, I saw, but it seemed a reasonable arrangement.

'Thirdly. You will need some funds to begin trading with, to pay your crew, for the goods and the landing. I shall make a hundred pounds available — by opening an account in your name and crediting you with that amount. If you fail, then I lose that advance. If you prosper, I shall expect it to be repaid in three years time. Agreed?'

'Agreed.' Again, a fair proposal, and no option.

'Fourthly. You may trade wherever you will, and how you will. I don't wish to know of any of your arrangements. As far as the outside world and especially the Revenue are concerned, I am simply your banker, and the provider of the ship. Agreed?

'Agreed.' I saw good sense in that: the arrangement protected his position in case of my arrest.

'Fifth. If the St Malo is captured or sunk, during the time our agreement runs, you will pay me back the value of her to me: which is three hundred and twenty pounds, the price I am paying for her. That will be written into the charter agreement.'

I stared at him. He had said that he would drive a hard but fair bargain; but three hundred and twenty pounds represented the total sum I hoped to raise for myself. 'What if,' I said, 'she should be lost or taken before I have been able to put that sum into the bank?'

'That is something that must be faced if and when it happens. I risk losing the greater part of it, of course, but all business is a risk, and I have sufficient faith in your abilities, your experience and daring, to make the venture pay.' I supposed that three hundred or so pounds would be no terrible loss to him, great as it seemed to me; and if I earned the sum I aimed at, which at least must be four hundred pounds, he would profit by one hundred pounds, and still at the end of the venture have a good ship to trade with.

'So it is a gentleman's agreement that you shall deal only with the Bank,' he said. ' Let us shake hands on that.' We stood up and grasped each other firmly by the hand. Then he refilled our glasses and said, 'Let us drink again to your success.'

We drank, sat down, and he smiled, relaxing now that the main business was over.

'When should I go to Plymouth, sir?'

'As soon as you please. She lies at Millbay Dock, having new sails fitted; by the time the coach gets you there she will be ready. You will need to engage some hands to sail her; I shall write a letter to introduce you to the present owner.'

'How old a craft is she, and where was she built?'

'She's no more than ten years old, built by Came's at Saltash. I'm sure she'll do, but if you find anything much against her, then come home again. As yet I've only paid a deposit.

'I'll go tomorrow.' I was in business in a prosperous way at last, and was impatient to begin. I sipped the Madeira, feeling now quite euphoric. Catching sight of Emily out on the lawn now playing croquet with a younger sister and a brother, I smiled, remembering our antics on that sports day five or six years ago. So she was soon to be twenty-one. My own twentieth birthday was imminent, and would be marked by this great new venture.

'You remember, no doubt, James,' Mr Rowlands said musingly, following my gaze, 'what I said to you about girls, and not becoming too fond of them. Is that still the case with you? No one you're getting fond of?'

I did not feel I could lie to him; I felt myself colouring, but said, 'There is a certain young woman I am much taken with, but I shall still put my business first.'

He grunted, and was silent, drumming his fingers upon his knees whilst his children banged the croquet ball with their mallets outside, giggling and laughing. I could not help comparing Emily, so charming, active and vivacious, still full of youth and impetuosity, darting here and there after the ball and admonishing her siblings, with Lucretia: who was plain, so serious and sage, handicapped but uncomplaining, so full of deep thoughts and mature philosophy. Much as I had hitherto been impressed and intrigued by the one, the other now eclipsed her in my mind, as the earth might eclipse the moon.

'I wish I were twenty-one again,' Mr Rowlands said. 'There are a few things I would do differently. But you, James have great prospects, and all your adult life before you. Keep your head and you will succeed.'

A soft step was heard outside. 'Is that you, my dear?' He got up and went to the door.

Mrs Rowlands entered the room. She was tall, buxom and stately, with eyes of the same green and violet hues as Emily, I now noticed. 'This is the young man I spoke of,' her husband said. 'James Spargo, master of the Sprite— but now he's to have a new ship.'

'I am pleased,' the lady said, as I stood respectfully. 'I hope she will be a great success and will answer your purposes.' I wondered if she knew what sort of arrangement we had made.

'I shall find out tomorrow, ma'am; I'm off to Plymouth to see her, and sail her back to Lodenek.'

'How is your father, dear Captain Spargo?' Mrs Rowlands enquired.

'He's pretty well, thank you. At present on the high seas, bound for the Baltic, I believe.'

Mr Rowlands nodded. 'If James proves as capable a sailor and manager as his father, my dear, I shall be more than satisfied. We're going through some difficult times, with trade falling off, at present; but we shall weather it and see better, I have little doubt.'

Mrs Rowlands smiled. 'Have you seen Emily to speak to, James?'

'I did see her as I came in.'

'And you will be coming to her twenty-first?'

'I shall certainly hope to come, ma'am.'

She nodded graciously, as if much pleased. 'I do trust you will. I should like all Emily's Lodenek friends to be there. She has many acquaintances outside, you know, among the gentry and farmers and the officers; but her real friends are here in this town, as I believe her heart is.'

I remembered Emily's strange plea to be taken away to sea, on my last visit to the House; and wondered whether the parents really did know their own daughter. But her remarks to me as I arrived at the House did seem to indicate a great attachment to Lodenek; no doubt she was now confronted by the prospect of being married and moving away, and was perhaps apprehensive. I wondered whether Mrs Rowlands' remarks contained some hint that I might be welcome as a suitor for Emily.

I said, 'She was always keen to help at the School, I know.' At this point the outer door was flung open and Emily herself, with Ralph and Maria, came rushing in, laughing and joking among themselves over the croquet. On seeing me, Emily immediately composed herself and walked demurely enough across the hail towards us, whilst the other two ran off up the stairs.

'Captain Spargo is to have a new ship, and go into business on his own account, Emily,' Mr Rowlands said.

'Really?' she turned upon me her emerald and purple gaze, solemn enough now, as if realizing I had grown up ahead of her. 'I am so glad, James, and wish you great success. I am sure you will do well. I should like ...' I had an idea she wanted to say, to sail with you; but after a slight hesitation she said, 'to see your new ship.'

'I shall be glad to show you over her, when we bring her home,' I said; it would have been churlish not to have offered as much. 'Well, I must make preparations for the journey. Thank you all for your encouragements. I hope and intend to be worthy of your confidence.'

As I walked away down the drive, ruminating on Emily and her parents, I became conscious, or so I believed, of their combined gazes, and the weight of their various expectations, bearing down upon me.

CHAPTER 20

THE St. MALO

It was fortunate that Reuben's ship docked that afternoon at Lodenek, and, as he had three or four days before she sailed again, he was pleased to accompany me to Plymouth. Daniel, hearing of my news, which mightily intrigued the whole family (except my father, who would not hear of it until the Galatea returned from Scandinavia) immediately wanted to accompany us to see the St Malo. 'I could be galley monkey for you, and foretopman, 'he said, his eagerness making us all smile.

Remembering how dearly I had wished to go to sea at his age, I said, 'Well now, I should think a trip round land back to Lodenek would be a useful start to learning seamanship, wouldn't you, Reub?'

Reuben considered, his face puckering up with some mischievous thought, while Daniel waited, agog; then he said slowly, 'I dunno whether he's ready for it. Can 'ee make tea, and a good obbin, Dan?'

'Reckon he can,' said Emma. 'Though he burnt the last one on our griddle iron.'

'Weather seems settled, eh, Reub?' I said.

'Ess— shouldn't like the poor shammick to get blawed out o'the craw's nest,' said Reuben.

'No fear of that— I shall hold on like a leech!' Daniel said stoutly. 'What do ee think mother?' I said; for whatever my views, she would decide.

Mother put down her sewing and said, 'Well, I daresay you'll be off to sea like the others soon enough, whether I like it or no, Daniel. I doubt if you'll be in better hands than James' or Reuben's. But who else will you have, James? Surely you won't be sailing a big ship like that with only the three of you?'

'We'll hire three or four hands in Devonport, Mother, don't fear. They can work their passage back from here, or sign on for Cardiff or Christiana, if they'd rather.'

Daniel pleaded, 'I can go, then, Mother, can't I? Don't say no now.'

She smiled, a shade wanly. 'If only you knew how I worry and pray for you all when you are away on the ocean. Sometimes I wish my family was all girls, like Mrs William Henry Thomas up to Punnion.'

'Get out, Mother, you know you'm prouder of we than any other mother of sons in Lodenek.' Reuben kissed her on the forehead. 'You needn't fear for us— we all got salt water in our veins, Father always do say.'

'Yes. And Daniel's the same. Well, what can't be cured must be endured, I suppose. I'll look out a few things for you, Dan. But mind, James, I won't have him going up the rigging. Put him in the galley and make him useful on the deck— I rely on you, now.'

Reuben went out to meet his sweetheart, indeed his betrothed: for he had overcome his shyness and succumbed to the charms of Mildred Morcom, who, having apparently decided that I was not to be anybody's intended except perhaps Emily Rowlands', had turned her winsome attentions upon him. My father and mother approved of this, though they warned Reuben he was not in any position to support her yet.

I went up to our bedroom and composed a short

letter to Lucretia, which I was going to send up to Place by Emma the next day:

My Dearest L,

I am leaving for Plymouth tomorrow to bring home a new ship, called the St Malo, which I am to captain and, by arrangement with Mr. R., to trade with on my own account. I promise you I shall make enough on this to pay my way to Oxford. I think of you every hour, and read your books. When I get back we must meet as before, if the weather allows. My eternally devoted love to you,

Your slave and buccaneer,

J

and I copied out, in my best copper plate, the verses I had composed on the voyage home from Bristol.

OCEAN THOUGHTS: FOR LUCRETIA

When thro' the squalling storms we fly
Or ride beneath the moon
By quiet tides or mists enfurled,
Past headland or by dune,
Of thee I dream, my dear.

From Ushant's shore to Scilly's rocks,
And on the Northern seas,
Where'er we sail, in Winter's blasts
Or through the Summer's breeze
Your voice alone I hear.

Borne on the Atlantic's rolling crests
Or Channel's deepest surge,
Along the coast of Brittany,
I nurse this lonely urge:
Such love for you I bear, my dear,
Such love for you I bear.

We set out the next day by ferry to Wadebridge on the morning tide, arriving there about eleven in the forenoon, and secured places on the mail coach calling at the Molesworth Arms. We rode outside, and enjoyed the sharp October air rushing through our hair and around our ears, as the coach and six horses bowled along the new macadamed turnpike road up the valley towards Bodmin. At Dunmere Bridge all able-bodied passengers, the coachman and postillion, had to alight and walk up the hill, whilst the horses slowly drew the almost empty vehicle up to the town. Bodmin was very important, in Cornish eyes, because it housed the Summer Assizes and boasted the grim fortress of its Gaol, where criminals were incarcerated and hanged publicly on the tall cliff-like walls; as well as the County Asylum, where dangerous lunatics were locked up for their own and other's good.

The mail coach went on up to Launceston across the moors. We alighted in the long crowded street inside the town wall, and after asking, found a carrier going on to Liskeard; so for a small fee we rode uncomfortably on the backboard of the dray, drawn by four slow cart horses, through the Fowey valley to that sleepy market town. There we took lodgings for the night at an inn. As I was careful with my cash, not wishing to spend yet any of the hundred pounds capital Mr Rowlands had allotted to me, the three of us shared one bed with a pedlar, a travelling horse dealer, and numerous fleas and bedbugs. It was noon the next day, having ridden with another carrier to Saltash, and taken the ferry across the River Tamar, that we actually arrived in Devonport and made our way down to Millbay Docks, and found the St Malo.

Surely she was a sight to gladden the heart of any prospective Master. Broader in the beam and drawing more water than the Sprite, she was nearly twice as long. With a foremast carrying a stout square sail and a gallant, a jib boom, and main and mizzen masts with good long booms and gaffs, I could see she could put on a broad canvas and run well before the wind, or sail close to it, still bearing well. As Mr Rowlands had said, her cargo capacity was considerable: more than twice that of the Sprite, and almost equal to the Galatea's.

I spent some time going over her with the agent for the company who was offering her for sale. Abaft there were some half-rotten futtocks, and it looked as if her keel and bottom had not been properly cleaned and tarred over the last several years. But such matters could be righted easily enough in our own shipyard. There was little leakage below the waterline, at least. She would sail back to Lodenek well enough, Reuben and I agreed.

That evening after walking along the Hoe and admiring the Sound, I went so far as to stand my brothers a decent dinner at the best inn on the Barbican; after which we went back to sleep aboard the St Malo in hammocks, fully clothed, having nothing else to cover us. Fortunately it was a mild night for the time of year. The next morning I stepped ashore to seek a couple of deck hands for our voyage back, and was confronted by a strange but familiar figure: Job Peters, rolling barrels of salt herrings out of a warehouse and down the gang-plank of a loading schooner. He was now even wider across the shoulders than he had been as a lad of fifteen, though he was then easily the biggest boy in Lodenek; I could make use of those strong arms and legs, I thought. 'Job,' I said, 'Job Peters,' wondering whether he would turn his surly glance upon me as always, remembering our past rivalry.

Instead his eyes lit up to see someone from Lodenek, and he was most respectful. 'James Spargo,' he said. 'What are you doing here in Plymouth?'

'I've come to sail the St Malo back home,' I said pointing to the ship. 'She's my command now.'

He looked at me, then at the vessel, with some longings. 'I wouldn't mind taking a trip home to Lodenek,' he said. 'Haven't seen my poor old mother for near on a year now.'

'Then ship with us before the mast, eh? You've done some seafaring , I know.'

He had to think for a moment. 'How much?'

'What are you being paid here?'

'A shilling a day.'

'I'll pay you one-and-six, and pay your passage back here if you want.'

'Right, Cap'n. Done. When do we sail?'

'As soon as I've found another hand.'

Within half-an-hour I had engaged an older, experienced seaman from several I found loafing around the docks, and sent him off to get his bundle for the voyage. I sent Reuben and Daniel off to buy provisions, and went over the St Malo again with Job, raising each sail and inspecting every gasket, halyard, shroud and cleat, finding most to be satisfactory and seaworthy. An hour later we cast off and were towed by a gig out into the Sound, where we tacked and veered most of the afternoon against a steady sou'wester until off Looe. As night fell the wind increased, going round to north-west, and we dropped all sail, Reuben and I taking the watch together, to ride the wind out in the lee of the Dodman: to proceed any further in the darkness with our makeshift crew would have been foolhardy. Daniel, helped by Job, proudly produced a piping hot mutton stew and a great thick hobbin, only slightly burned on one side. He and the great lousterer got on well together, Job instructing and helping the boy to handle and secure the stays, and reef the sails on the main and mizzen booms.

By early morning, before dawn, the wind was nor' east and we got under way again, putting on full sail, passing Falmouth and Carrick Roads about noon and rounding Land's End at mid-afternoon. By tacking and sailing close to the wind, our square foresail reefed, we arrived off Stepper Point about midnight and hove-to in the still prevailing nor'easter; and finally made Lodenek harbour at ten next morning on a falling tide.

CHAPTER 21

A FAMILY ALTERCATION

Mr Rowlands was waiting to greet us as we moored in the Pool off the harbour walls, and were rowed ashore in the gig sent out for us. I reported that all was well with the St Malo, except for the stern timbers which needed replacing, and that she ought to be scraped and cleaned in the repair yard; he agreed to make arrangements for these things to be done without delay. Job Peters went home to see his mother who lived in one of the tiny cottages in a court at the back of the market place, and Reuben, Daniel and I went home to tackle three of my mother's largest pasties, baked just in time for our arrival, full of good potato, onion and turnip, and tasty lumps of mutton. Mother and the girls made a fuss of Daniel, who boasted he knew all the sails on the St Malo and how to handle them, and how to make an Irish stew.

A letter awaited me, inscribed with a flowing neat hand which, although I had never seen it before, I knew immediately to be Lucretia's.

'Delivered here by Susan Roberts, Miss Lucretia's maid,' said Susannah, with knowing glance at Emma.

'And what can they want with you, up to Place?' demanded my mother.

I opened it and ran my eyes over its contents. 'Tis an invitation to a Literary Circle Miss Lucretia wants to start,' I said. 'Meeting on Tuesday evenings at Devereaux Place.'

'Well I never,' mother said. 'Literary Circle, is it. And you learning Latin and Greek. Sure I don't know where 'twill all end, James.'

'Nor do I, Mother. But getting educated is difficult enough, and I must take what opportunities I can.'

The fact that I was invited up to Place impressed the family more than anything else I had done so far. Who had ever heard of any of our people from the quayside being invited up there, except to sing carols at Christmas?

'He'll be writing books next, I dearsay,' said Emma, proudly.

Daniel's eyes widened. 'What sort of books, James? Will they be sea stories?'

'Maybe, Dan, in time. All in good time.'

As it would take several days to put the St Malo in order, I had time to study, and visited Mr Nanskivell for more lessons. He was pleased with my progress, and said that if I continued at the same rate I should be able to sit the Matriculation examination within a year, and begin studying Greek. He talked to me about his antiquarian researches, and told me that he too had been invited to attend Miss Devereaux's Literary Circle.

'We are very fortunate that Miss Lucretia has such an interest in literature,' he said. 'I am sure it was she who persuaded her father to subscribe to my book.'

'Are the subscriptions coming in still?' I asked.

'Yes, but slowly. I still need twenty more.'

'I should like to subscribe for a copy myself.'

'Would you, James? I should be most pleased to inscribe it for you when the time comes.'

Daily I went to the shipyard, inspecting the repairs to the St Malo; then I would go home and read or study, or go for a walk if the weather was fair, or row downriver fishing with Daniel, the tide being full in the afternoon. I could hardly wait until the next Tuesday when I should go up to Place for the meeting. Meanwhile, on the Saturday, the Galatea put into port and my father came home.

I was very glad to see him; our paths had not crossed for almost six months; we were seldom home together these days. But when he had had a hot bath in the tin tub before the kitchen stove, my mother scrubbing his back, and had changed into clean clothes, and had eaten a good hot meal, there took place the usual exchange of news around the family hearthside, he sitting in his favourite semi-circular backed armchair; and it was Susannah who said, 'Our James had got a new ship, Father. He's to go trading on his own account now.'

'What's this, James?' Father turned his dark serious eyes upon me. I noticed that his face was more heavily lined now, his dark beard flecked with grey and even white; the hair on his temples was also thinning and greying. He was in his mid-forties, I suppose; still a lean, strong figure of a man, hut somehow slower in his movements, not as agile as I had known him to be hitherto.

'Tis true,' I said. 'Mr Rowlands is chartering me a new vessel he's bought. The St Malo. She's a harquentine, nearly the size of the Galatea, and they're doing her up in the yard now. We sailed her home from Plymouth this week.'

'And I helped, too,' said Daniel. 'Didn't I? I was

galley-monkey. Reuben came as well.'

Father continued to look at me searchingly, as if thinking, 'There's more here than meets the eye.' Finally he said, 'Trading on your own account, eh? What will you use to pay for goods?'

'That's all arranged. Mr Rowlands is lending me... some money.'

'How old are you, James?'

'Nearly twenty,' I said. 'As you know, surely.'

'Surely I do. Now look, my son, you seem to have forgotten one thing. Until you're twenty-one, and while you live in this house, I have a right to know whatever you're doing, planning, scheming, arranging, with your life. You're my responsibility. I've always seen you were clothed and fed properly haven't I?'

'Yes,' I said. 'Certainly you have.'

'And we've always been good friends. Eh?'

'Yes, Father.'

'And now I come home and find you making these great plans and arrangements without waiting to consult me.'

I sat there, perplexed. It had not occurred to me that he would question what I was doing; he had always been so proud of my career as a seaman and agent, but in his absence I had assumed he would approve of my attempt to advance myself.

'But he's not after doing anything wrong, is he, Edward?' my mother said anxiously.

'Wrong?' said my father, his eyes afire. 'Wrong? Is it wrong for him to get himself involved with risks like chartering a ship— and not even twenty yet— without consulting me, his father and guardian? In law 'tis wrong,

I'll tell you that. All of you!' He stared around us, his face flushed and angry in the flaring light of two candles and the sea-coal fire; and we stared hack, struck dumb.

'I didn't realise... Mr Rowlands and I discussed it all, every detail, and agreed...' I said, fumbling for words.

'Mr Rowlands be damned! He may he my employer, and yours, but I should have been brought into these arrangements. God only knows what you've let yourself in for, my boy; this could be the ruin of you, and of me too.'

'I'm sure we can trust Mr Rowlands,' I said, 'to look after our interests as well as his.'

'Little you know! Mr Rowlands is a business man, a clever merchant venturer, but I wouldn't trust him more than another in these affairs. There are plenty of things being said about him to make me doubt if you've done the right thing. Now listen. I shall want to know everything about this agreement, and your intentions, or by Heaven I shall go up to Mr Rowlands and tell him what I think of him!'

'Now, please, Edward, don't be spoiling your first night home after so long away,' pleaded mother. 'You two must talk about this tomorrow; go out somewhere alone, and have it all out between you. I won't have my peace and quiet disturbed any more tonight.'

My father sighed, shook his head, and said more calmly, 'I'm sorry, Harriet, but this riled me. I'll say no more at present. Now then, young Dan, come and tell me what else you've been up to all this time. I've got a little present for you here...' and he drew from his pocket an intricately carved wooden Swedish whistle, on which he proceeded to play various sweet and sad folk-tunes and sea-shanties. Reuben soon excused himself, and went out to keep a tryst with Mildred. I went up to our bedroom and tried to concentrate on another chapter of Ivanhoe, but found my attention wandering, thinking worriedly of what Father would say when he finally heard all my plans; for it did not occur to me to be devious and withhold anything from him. In our house, his word had always been law, and had never before been questioned by any of us children; I realised that if there were to be any deep disagreement I should have to forsake our home and find somewhere else to stay when ashore.

On the morrow, which was Sunday, we all went as a family to church; a rare occurrence for us Spargos, in that time, as at least one of us was usually away at sea. I took my place in the choir stall, from which I could have, if I but turned my head slightly, a good view of the Squire, his wife and family, including Lucretia, all sitting in their high box pew; and also of Mr Thomas Rowlands, with wife and family including Emily. I chose not to look at either, afraid of drawing undue attention to myself, and of giving any hint of my feelings, which might be wrongly construed.

After the service my father proposed that he and I should take a walk along the lanes above the town, whilst mother and the girls went home to cook the Sunday dinner: the one certain meat meal of the week, apart from offal of various kinds: tripe, giblets, chitterlings, and so on. Today we were having a loin of pork, from neighbours who had just killed a pig. Most householders in Lodenek kept a pig in their outhouses or 'crows', feeding it scraps and skimmed milk, and sharing the meat with one another when killing time arrived. We did not keep a pig ourselves, but paid for our portions in household goods and provisions brought home by Father, Reuben or me from our trading.

My father and I ascended the hill past the battlemented walls and grand iron gates of Devereaux Place, and trod the stony lane up towards Trethillick hamlet, the same way on which I had escorted Lucretia several times previously.

'Now then, James,' Father said to me in a kindly yet determined manner, 'I want to hear all about these plans of yours. It seems I've got a good deal to catch up on in my absence.'

I had thought about this moment, on and off, for most of the preceding night; and began as I had decided to do, at the beginning. I told him how I had met Lucretia on the cliff top, how our friendship had grown, and how she had encouraged me to learn Latin and Greek and aim to get myself a proper education. Father listened in silence, walking slowly along between the hedges, through the autumn leaves falling from the Cornish elms and hawthorns, among withered stalks of cow parsley and alexanders, avoiding the barbed and clutching tendrils of brambles nodding in a moderate west wind. From time to time he stopped, eyed me attentively, and said, 'Go on,' or 'Then what?' I told him how I had prevailed on Mr Nanskivell to teach me, and of my discussions with Mr Rowlands and of our agreement, keeping nothing back. By the time I had finished we were a good mile or so from Lodenek, walking west, and could hear the steady roar of surf on the rocks at Porthmissen and Trevone bays. I finished by saying, 'I'm truly sorry you haven't been told of all this before. But you have been away at sea for the last several months, and so have I. If you'd been at home, I would have consulted you first. But I thought the advice given to me was good, and came from people who are concerned to help me.'

'Yes, I can see that,' he said. 'I'm not angry with you, not now. I realise you have the aptitude and ability to go on learning, something I never had. I don't blame you; though hoping to go to University is something I never even considered; but then, we had so little to help us in the way of schooling. In my day, it was a wonder we managed to read and write and count. But this does worry me, James; I have a feeling you're aiming too high for a lad from Lodenek quayside. Now, I want a straight and true answer to this; what are your feelings for Miss Lucretia?'

'We are very fond of each other.'

'You're not thinking of marriage, by any chance?'

I said, very slowly, sensing some opposition in his tone of voice, 'We have considered it. Of course 'tis very difficult. One way to it would be for me to get a degree and enter a profession. Her family would certainly object otherwise.'

'Would they, indeed. Has it occurred to you that your own family— your mother and me— might also object?'

I stopped, staring at him in consternation and amazement.

'No, I see you've never considered that. Well, I tell you now, before this goes any further, I do object. And so, I'm sure, will your mother.'

'But why, Father? Surely...'

'You should have learned by now, my son, that each one of us on earth has our own appointed station in life. What have all the lessons from the Bible, and all the vicar's sermons, taught you, if not that?'

'I can't recall anything forbidding someone like me to love and marry someone like Lucretia.'

'We may be allowed to look a little higher than our present stations,' he said. 'I haven't objected to your friendship with Miss Emily Rowlands, for instance. Indeed, your mother and I have thought that, as you were getting on well, and making a successful career, and you are certainly favoured by Mr Rowlands himself, you might well be able in time to make a good match there. But to dream of marrying a Devereaux! — My dear boy, you must put that right out of your head. Even if she loves you, which I doubt— these young women with fancy educations and ideas do sometimes raise a bright young man's hopes, only to scorn or ignore him in the end— even if she should genuinely love you, I assure you the thing won't work. It will lead to bad feelings. Can you see Squire Devereaux agreeing to meet me and your mother on equal terms? He'd throw Miss Lucretia out and disown her, rather than that.'

'If he does such a thing, I shall support her. Anyway, she has some money of her own.'

We walked on in silence for a while. Above us a pair of buzzards circled, planing effortlessly on the wind currents in a clear sky, their sharp high-pitched cries reaching down to us a hundred feet or more down below.

'I shall say no more about that,' Father said, 'for the time being. I believe that in time you will find this notion of yours to be a false hope and dream. At present I'm more concerned for your safety, and that of anyone else who sails with you, in your free-trading ventures.'

We had reached the field, cottages and farmhouse at Trethillick, and could glimpse, a mile or so away, the humped headland of Trevose and the sparkling sheen of water before it, broken by restless surges of white water. At the crossroads we turned down another narrow lane that would bring us, by a circuitous route, back to Lodenek; hens scratching in the dust moved out of our way, and a large sow and six piglets thrusting at her teats lay in the sun inside the farmyard gate.

'Do you think I can't organize a run for goods, as you used to. Father? I thought you considered me a capable skipper, and agent. After all, you trained me.'

He sighed, and put a hand on my shoulder. 'My dear James, you know as well as I do things are not at all the same now. The Channel and Western Approaches are full of naval sloops and Revenue cutters watching and searching everything. What do you intend to do? Arm the St Malo and fight your way through?

'No. We shall carry guns, but for self-defence only.'

'What do you mean by that?'

'I mean that if we are so closely pursued that we can't get away, we should have to fire at the other boats' rigging, that's all. I have promised... Lucretia, not to get involved in battles if I can possibly help it.'

'Hmm. She's got some sense then, it seems.'

'Much more sense than any woman I've yet met. She's genuinely concerned for my advancement and welfare, Father. You must believe that. Anyway, I've worked out that four good runs, five at most, will bring in the profit I need. Then I'll stop, for I hope to matriculate and go up to Oxford, in a year or so.'

'If you don't get captured or sunk in the meantime.'

'Yes. But, by working from different ports across the water— St Peter Port, Cherbourg, Roscoff, Brest, Concarneau, St Nazaire, I reckon I can keep the Navy and the Revenue guessing; and by sailing well west of the Scillies, then north and east, we should get clear of all trouble. And I plan to land farther north from here, between Port Isaac and Bude. The main thing I need now, and I was hoping you would find me the right people— is a good experienced Lander, and two or three reliable clerks. You must know some people along Boscastle or Trebarwith or Crackington Haven, surely?'

My father walked on, frowning; then, with a hint of a smile, he said, 'By George, if you aren't a cool customer, James Spargo. Well, I suppose it might well work. Though I tell you I don't like it, I don't like it at all. So far as I'm concerned, the University can be damned; I'd far rather see you go on as a lawful merchant captain. But I see you are aiming high, and I doubt if anything I say will stop you from trying. Have you signed the agreement with Thomas?'

'Not yet. He's having it drawn up.'

'So there's still time for you to change your mind, and withdraw.'

'How could I do that? He's bought the St Malo especially for me. He believes in me, Father. He's backing me.'

'At very little risk to himself. You carry all the

dangers. And all because you met a young woman you've no business to be consorting with.'

I was silent, flushing angrily, at a loss as how to answer him. Hot tears sprang to my eyes; he must have seen them. He sighed, perplexed, and stopped in the narrow rutted lane, with muddy pools lying between its cart tracks.

'I shall have to think this out, and discuss it all with your mother. All this education makes little sense to me— I don't trust it. We Spargos don't rise to it; we've always trusted to our native wits. Well, I do know of one or two people up along that coast. But this is something not to be rushed into, James. 'Twill weigh heavily on my conscience if I give you the wrong advice, or encourage you against my better judgement.'

We turned out along the main coastal road that leads from St.Merryn into Lodenek, and passed the new Vicarage, an imposing Georgian-style edifice, with its stables and a lawn; the Church Commissioners had built it at the request of the Reverend William Rowlands. He had found the previous Vicarage next to the church too small for his large family, and also wished to avoid the contagion of typhus and cholera with which our insanitary town was only too often visited.

In silence we walked back, downhill past Place gates, both thinking our own thoughts. But I had a growing feeling that, after deep cogitation, and discussion with my mother, Father would finally consent to help me in my plans.

CHAPTER 22

A LITERARY CIRCLE

And so it proved; it was my mother who turned the scales of my father's mind in my favour. When my plans and hopes were all explained to her, she said, 'Well, Edward, you must realise that James has done specially well. It doesn't amaze me one bit he wants to go on to something better than captaining a merchantman. If you ask me, he takes after my Uncle Michael. Look what he did for himself.'

'Your Uncle Michael had help and patronage, so you've told me enough times,' Father retorted.

'Ah, but without the brain to study he could never have gone to Cambridge, and ended up the Rector of Smallheath in Birmingham. I'm sure James will do as well, or better.'

My mother's paternal uncle, it now transpired, had been born in a village just outside Cork, and showing himself an exceptional scholar at the little Church of Ireland School there, had been taken up by the vicar of that place and had been coached by him to take Matriculation; he had indeed gone to St John's College, Cambridge, partly supported by a scholarship and partly by a grant from a Church Educational Fund. I had heard of Great Uncle Michael, of course, hut he was a remote figure I had never met, and had died ten years before; so he had not previously assumed much significance in my mind. Now, however, it seemed to me vastly encouraging that someone related to me (and from humble origins) had done something similar to what I intended.

'Tis my side of the family has the real brains,' I heard mother say in a voice that brooked no argument, 'and don't be making any mistake on that score.'

The outcome was that father agreed, but still with considerable misgivings, to help me find the best people to run the landing and distribution of free-trade goods in the areas I intended to work. He proposed that he and I should travel up to Trebarwith and St Gennys to talk to various trustworthy persons who could, as he said, 'arrange things.' I was now well content, seeing the fruition of my hopes in sight. But first, there was the meeting of the Literary Circle at Devereaux Place.

On the Tuesday evening I went up the hill past the church, and walked in through the tall iron gates under the square battlemented towers, up the drive between shadowy laurel bushes and a privet hedge, to the Elizabethan mansion. Lights were lit in the library at the west end, and I could see a fire blazing on the hearth; and Lucretia was at the door leading into the hall, welcoming Mr Nanskivell and Matthew Pook, who had arrived just before me. Matthew was now a clerk in the Lodenek Bank, and I was pleasantly surprised to realise that he too took an interest in literature.

'James, I'm so glad you could come.' Lucretia greeted me as a friend, without fuss, but held out her hand and pressed mine lightly but meaningfully as the others entered the hall before me. There, under the family portraits staring lugubriously from the wall, we paused. Lucretia's maid, Susan Roberts, came forward to take our coats. 'Please go into the library, Dr Harley is in there,' Lucretia bade us.

We went up a flight of several steps, led by Mr Nanskivell, who had evidently been to Devereaux Place before, and along a narrow passage and into the library. I was amazed to find the whole room book-lined, shelf upon shelf, up to the very ceiling, filled with leather-bound volumes— most of which appeared never to have been opened. Dr Harley, a middle-aged physician, one of the two medical practitioners in Lodenek, was a hearty balding man of about fifty, with a considerable paunch covered with a white snuff-stained waistcoat, and pince-nez on his nose. He looked up from a volume of poetry he had been perusing.

'Ah, Nanskivell! Good to see you. And two likely lads, eh?'

'James Spargo, and Matthew Pook ,' said Mr Nanskivell.

'How de do,' the Doctor nodded to us. 'You're a sea-captain now, I hear, Mr Spargo.'

I nodded, 'Yes, sir. I shan't be able to join you on many Tuesdays, but I'll come whenever I'm home in Lodenek.'

'Matthew and James were both monitors at the School,' Mr Nanskivell said. 'And both good readers of poetry, as I recall.'

'Splendid, splendid. Just been re-reading the Ancient Mariner,' Dr Harley said. 'What a tale, eh? Quite amazes me every time I look at it.'

'Ah, yes, the Mariner,' said Lucretia, entering with a younger woman. 'We must read and discuss the Mariner.' She glanced momentarily at me. 'This is my sister Sarah,' she said, introducing Matthew and myself to her. Sarah was not unlike Lucretia, rather taller, with a less pronounced nose, and a pale plaintive sort of face; her eyes, like Lucretia's, were dark, liquid and responsive. She smiled at us and sat down near the fire. We all took our seats on the leather-padded chairs with ornate walnut backs.

'Now!' said Lucretia. 'I have long had this idea in my mind, that we should have a Literary Circle in Lodenek. I don't wish it to be a close little coterie, so if any of you know anyone else who is fond of reading, or of writing of any sort, do please tell me. If necessary we can meet elsewhere in the town, if numbers should require it. If we can interest enough people we might raise funds to equip our own Literary Institute, in time.'

I glanced at Matthew. 'I propose Matthew Pook as treasurer. He's got the Bank behind him.'

There was general laughter at this sally, which put us all at our ease. Soon we were animatedly discussing what books we had read, were reading, or hoped to read. After several minutes of this Lucretia, who seemed to have appointed herself Director or Chairman of the meeting (by common consent, I must add, for she assumed this role quite naturally and vivaciously, and we were only too pleased to be directed by her) called on Mr Nanskivell to read something from his *Antiquities*. Which he did, a little diffidently at first, but gathering confidence and strength as he went on, describing the stone circles and henge monuments of Bodmin Moor, and speculating, like Dr Borlase, that the Druids of old had used them for their rites; though he himself doubted if they had actually erected such features, believing them to be considerably older than the ancient Celtic people themselves.

We were each asked to read something; Matthew read a passage from Cowper's *The Task*, Sarah a chapter from *Persuasion*, and then it was my turn.

'Would you read something of your own?' I heard Lucretia say. 'Captain Spargo, you know, is something of a poet.'

I was struck numb with fright. To compose verse was one thing, and to read in private to Lucretia herself another; but to be called upon without any warning to read one's own fledgling work before company was quite something else, utterly beyond my expectations or imagining. ' I haven't brought anything with me,' I said; but there, I saw, put before me on a small table, copied out in Lucretia's own handwriting, was the first poem I had presented to her.

'Why not read this?' she said, smiling at the rest of the Circle. 'James lent me some of his verse to read, earlier this year. I liked this one so much I copied it out—I do hope that was all right?'

'Oh... yes. Of course.' I looked through the poem, frowning slightly, wondering what they would all think of it.

'I'm sure it must be worth hearing, James,' said Mr Nanskivel, 'if Miss Lucretia thinks well of it.'

So I read it, not very well, for the thing was so sprung upon me, and also I could not avoid speculating on what the company must have thought about my having shown any work to Lucretia previously. It seemed to me she was deliberately using this occasion to make an announcement of our particular friendship. They were all very kind, and commented favourably on it, except Sarah, who sat watching both me and Lucretia with a secretive little smile; I was sure she was in her sister's confidence, and knew something of her feelings for me.

I was relieved when tea and coffee were served for the ladies, and glasses of port for the gentlemen. Matthew and I partook of the latter. More conversation flowed, not entirely about literature. Mr Nanskivell complimented me on my poem and said, 'You must go on and write more, James. I declare you have a regular penchant for it; don't you agree, Doctor?'

'Eh? Oh yes, to be sure. What a thing for us, here in Lodenek, to have a budding poet indeed, a Romantic, as well.' I saw that Dr Harley was evidently following the latest developments on the poetic scene; and indeed, to finish the evening, after Lucretia had read us some Shelley and Byron, he read us the whole of the Ancient Mariner. He read in a quiet undemonstrative manner, his voice rising slowly and falling like the tide; quite unlike Mr Nanskivell's dramatic fashion, which I well remembered, thinking back to our enraptured class listening to the poem as he had read it in School. Something about Dr Harley's smooth inflexible tones, precisely emphasizing certain phrases, intensified the terror of the story; and I found myself deeply disturbed by the predicament of the Mariner, who had, with one thoughtless action, condemned his crewmates and himself to a living hell. The idea of his penance struck home to me; forever he would wander, seeking to relieve himself of his guilt by telling his story to whomsoever he could prevail upon to listen. I saw there was a great need in us all to confess our misdeeds, to be shriven, as the Mariner sought to be by the Hermit; yet the guilt remained, and would remain as long as he lived.

'Is it he?' quoth one, 'Is this the man?
By him who died on cross,
With his cruel bow he laid full low
The harmless Albatross.

The spirit who bideth by himself
In the land of mist and snow,
He loved the bird that loved the man
Who shot him with his bow.'

The other was a softer voice,
As soft as honey-dew:
Quoth he: 'The man hath penance done,
And penance more will do.'

And I had a sudden brief vision of myself, as the Mariner, who had made some terrible mistake of judgement, and bringing destruction and sorrow upon those I loved. As the Doctor read the end of the story I felt as if a knife were being driven into my heart and very soul. I saw Lucretia looking at me; I suppose I went pale and looked distraught; she was evidently much concerned for me. But once the reading finished and the others murmured their comments— they were all deeply impressed by the Doctor's performance— my clouds vanished and I managed a smile to show my hostess I was well enough. And as we bid her, individually, good night, she pressed my hand again in hers, then saw us all to the door.

On reaching home I found that in the inner pocket of my coat was a letter.

My Dearest James,

I have been reading and re-reading your latest poem, each time weeping for joy to realise how much I mean to you. Such beautiful verses and sentiments surely must be true— how can I doubt that? — and I return your love a hundredfold, my dearest.

I am glad you have made your arrangements, and hope the St Malo is all you can wish a ship to be.

Now— I fear it is going to be difficult for us to meet during the autumn and winter months, which is one reason why I am starting the Literary Circle. At least we can, on occasions (when you are home in Lodenek), be together and can converse, albeit in the company of others. I have chosen the first members very carefully, for they are all intelligent but discreet. They will surely be able to conclude from little things they witness— gestures, glances, perhaps implied meanings— that we have a deep regard for each other. But I think we can rely on them not to gossip, indeed they will protect our relation with each other. With time, and as you study, there will be opportunities to meet my father and other members of the family, so that gradually I hope, they will come to accept you as a deserving and valuable friend. I only beg you to be patient, my dearest, until next spring, when I shall be able to visit our beloved cliffs and shores again, and meet you there.

You will always be closer to my heart than anyone else, and I shall rely on your devotion to keep you true to me, until the day, in two or three years time, when we can contemplate marrying. (Can you imagine what a wonderful thrill of emotion it brings me, even to write such a word in a letter? Yes, I want to be your wife, your helpmeet, your eternal companion and closest friend. Write to me soon, dearest, and continue writing at every opportunity, telling me of your adventures and hopes and dreams— indeed everything.

I remain, as I must henceforth ever be,

Your loving

L.

CHAPTER 23

MAKING ARRANGEMENTS.

The Galatea was due to sail again within a week; my father, quietly enjoying his respite from the seafaring, spent two or three days seeing old friends, yarning with the old men on the Long Lugger, and sitting at home by the fire in the evening, reading a three weeks-old copy of the Sherborne Mercury I had brought home from Mr Nanskivell's. On the evening after I had been up to Place— and having told the family, all eager to know what went on at such grand doings, how I had fared there— Father said, 'Well, James, if we're to make these certain arrangements for you, we'd better set about it. Tom Jonas is going fishing up off St Gennys tomorrow, and we can ship there with him. Be up by five, he's leaving on the flood before six.'

Daniel wanted to know where we were going and why, but mother hushed him, saying it was important business he would only understand later.

So taking a couple of mutton pasties, some cheese and cold potatoes in their jackets, the next morning, as dawn flushed the sky over St Breoke downs, we were on quayside in a sharp east wind, watching Tom Jonas and his crew of four making ready aboard their smack with its dark red sails and black-tarred hull. They were going after mackerel, coley and whiting; their nets were rolled in readiness, with cork floats fastened across the top edge and lead sinkers along the bottom.

It took us until mid-afternoon, tacking and box-hauling against that wind, to arrive off St Gennys High Cliff, its seven hundred-odd feet high apex towering above the bushy undercliff which ran below it. The smack towed a skiff, used to pay out the net and bring it around in a full circle; so we were rowed ashore in it, landing at Crackington Haven. Here a coasting schooner was discharging iron-ware and coals in the narrow inlet, between the jagged reefs of rock formed by upended stratas of slate: as dangerous a place to berth in as ever I saw, but, in that east wind, a calm and sheltered cove.

We made our way up to a weathered slate farmhouse by the church, which was built below the inland slope of the headland known as Pencannow Point. Here we made the acquaintance of Mr Samuel Pearn, the farmer, who did not seem surprised at our arrival. Rubicund, with pale blue bulging eyes, comfortable in corduroy breeches with leather leggings and an ancient heavy broadcloth coat, which in some lights looked green and in others a rusty black, he bade us into the spacious slate-flagged kitchen, and to sit by a small log fire in the immense grate, upon three-legged stools; and proceeded to offer us rum, brandy or gin in pewter mugs. He then lit a long clay pipe from a number laid out on the hearth; and offered us one each, filling them with reeking strong dark tobacco. I have never been a great smoker, but sitting there by the fire as the afternoon faded out across the valley below and the moors to the west, sipping brandy and water and puffing that powerful weed, I felt content and dreamy, and began to wonder what I was striving for so desperately; and whether a quiet life on the land, with a buxom comfortable farmer's daughter for wife, had not a great deal of attraction for a man. But the vision of Lucretia, pressing me to her bosom, writing me that letter of sincerest avowal, put such thoughts out of my mind.

Farmer Pearn was telling tales of smuggling, recounting how the Revenue men had been outwitted along these shores, how landings had been made at places believed by the Excise men to be impossible. ‘’Tis a fearsome coast, as you must know, Captain Spargo; it do take a very cute man to bring a cargo in along of here. The Revenue cutters give it a pretty wide berth as a rule. And as for hiding places, I could take you to a dozen barns with trap doors under bales of hay, and cellars underneath; and here in this very farmhouse— well... just you listen.’ He kicked aside an old hessian mat in the centre of the floor and stamped the slate flag with his boot; a dull echo sounded from below. I noticed a series of deep nicks along the edge of the stone, no doubt made by crow bars when lifting it. ‘Many a keg of rum and brandy have been stowed down there, to be distributed when the time was right.’

‘Do you see much of the Revenue along here?’ asked Father.

‘They Riding Officers come round now and then— not a great deal. There’s two of ’em stationed at Boscastle, four miles the other side of High Cliff, and another four up to Bude; that’s about eight miles from here. A difficult beat for ‘em, I’d say. Though once, two or three year ago, I remember we was surprised late one evening when us had a landing just about to begin; the ship was lying off the Haven down below and everything was ready to bring her in when we got a signal from Pencannow that the Revenue was making this way. We just had time to send four or five good men up along here, and they met a couple of Searchers just by the kissing-gate that do lead into my field from Dizzard Cliff beyond; in no time they was trussed up together, one each side of the gate, and left there till four in the morning after we had the goods landed and stowed. Then we sent a boy up through the furze bushes with a knife to cut 'em free. 'Twas a good dark night and they never knowed who did it.'

After several such yarns we got down to business. Until recently Mr Pearn, it seemed, had been the Lander for a group calling themselves 'The Choughs'; there were half a dozen groups then operating in the district, all taking their names from local birds. The Choughs had been successful for about fifteen years, but their Venturers, the Squire of Trencreek and the Vicar of St Gennys, had both died, and there was now no-one to finance the operation.

'And if you found another Venturer, Mr Pearn,' said Father, 'would the Choughs be interested in handling a few more runs?'

Farmer Pearn tapped out his pipe gently against the hearth. 'Well, now,' he eyed us both quizzically, 'it have often seemed to me a great shame that we've got all this here wonderful ghastly coast, which the good Lord seem to have made specially for free-trading, and nobody much taking advantage of it. I'm getting on, you know— seventy-two this year— and I aren't sure that I personally want such excitement at my time of life; but I've got a son, struggling along to make ends meet, and bringing up a largish family. This farm don't feed more than a few mouths, d'you see. I should certainly consider any offer very carefully.'

Father explained that I was to be the Venturer, having the backing of a well-known business man in our own district; that both he and I were well-experienced in free-trading, and skilled in sailing into inshore waters. He could offer the Lander, whoever he was, the sum of fifty pounds to organize a team and the disposal of the goods, that sum to include paying twenty men ten shillings each to bring the goods ashore. After a few more questions from Mr Pearn, and a dish of tea and a hot squab pie—pigeons spiced with apples, currants and onions—brought in by Mrs Pearn, the farmer said he would make arrangements to employ a team of men, and a Writer. He believed old Josiah Jelbert, the retired Parish Clerk who had done the latter job for him previously, would welcome a little money to keep him out of the Poor House. We agreed on a date the week after, by which orders from various landowners, farmers, clergy and merchants in that and neighbouring parishes would be taken, and sent to Lodenek. We would then send them back word as to the date and time we should expect the St Malo to arrive off Crackington Haven, where the landing team and their horses, donkeys and mules would be assembled.

'Well, gentleman,' Mr Pearn said, 'we must drink one more glass, to the success of The Chough's revival.' And he poured out more liquor for us all, with which we toasted the new venture. 'There's one small detail, however,' he said then. 'In this part of the country the custom is for the Lander to be paid his fee in advance.'

I had not expected this, but father had; he said cheerfully, 'Naturally. It shows good faith. Well, James, I suggest you write out a Note of Hand, to be drawn on the Lodenek Bank; will that satisfy you, Mr Pearn?'

'I think it might, sir, thank you. That Lodenek Bank has got as good a reputation as any.' So I obliged him by writing my Note, on paper which he provided.

The outer door of the farmhouse was now heard to open, and voices could be discerned in the dairy, that of Mrs Pearn and a newcomer. 'That'll be my son, George,' the farmer said. 'Getting dark now, he've finished his work. Ah, George'— as the kitchen door opened and a curly-haired sullen-faced man of about forty came in. 'Two gentlemen from Lodenek here with a very interesting business proposition. Captain Edward Spargo; Captain James Spargo.'

George nodded, eyed us both warily, and sat down on the stool; he warmed his hands, as large as dinner plates, at the fire, which he livened by kicking the smouldering logs with his miry boots, sending sparks flying. He listened dourly and without comment, while his father went over the scheme and then took out my Note, which he waved before his eyes.

'What d'you say to that?' he finished.

'I say,' said George slowly, 'I should say— 'tis a fair offer. We han't had a good run here for several years. The Revenue reckon we'm all gone to sleep.' He thought for a little, then picked up one of the several clay pipes in the hearth, gesturing to his father for tobacco. Filling the pipe, he lit it and drew on it strongly for several seconds; and then said, 'Things getting a bit hot, like, down your way?'

'They certainly are,' I said. 'Which is why I've chosen to come up here to see if you're interested.'

He nodded, closed his eyes for a minute or two, and then, opened them wide and said, 'How many runs and how often?'

'Well,' I said, 'that will depend on the success of the first run. If all goes well I should hope to make one a month, perhaps one every six weeks. Success will also depend on what orders you can get, of course.'

'I can get orders, all right. We'm a bit scattered up yure, 'twill take a few days to get about. Yes; one a month or every six weeks— 'twould be about what we could handle.'

The brandy and rum was offered again, and George became rather more affable, though he never actually smiled. But we covered all the necessary details, and agreed well on all matters. And as it was far into the evening when we concluded the business, Mr Pearn would not hear of us leaving the farm then, but called his good lady and commanded her to make up a bed for us; we could go on to Trebarwith the following morning.

After a sound night's sleep in a deep feather bed, we were aroused at six by the farmyard rooster; and by seven, as light strengthened above the uplands behind the valley, we were breakfasting on fried eggs and bacon cut from one of the great flitches that hung from the kitchen beams. Farmer Pearn saw us off, directing us up the muddy lane to the highway; of George there was no sign. As we plodded along, avoiding the runnels and pools between high slate hedges, I said to Father, 'What did you make of the Pearns?'

Slowly weighing his words he said, 'The old man talks a lot. Rather too much, I thought. But George is a deep one. He's all there, though you might not think so on first acquaintance.'

'Well, so long as they can organise the landings,' I said, 'all should be well,'

Father merely grunted and increased his pace. The lane became drier as we mounted the valley side, and after a couple of miles we came in sight of the inn at Wainhouse Corner. At the smithy beside the public house was a carrier's dray, with four horses, one being shod. We paid sixpence to be taken on down the highway to Delabole, from where we walked down another thorny tortuous lane to the tiny village of Trebarwith, overlooking another splendid valley running down to the sea between two immense humped clifftops.

Here we made the acquaintance of one Ezra Johns, auctioneer and valuer; who, after we had explained our business, invited us to share a cold rook pie, bread and cheese and ale, declaring himself to be delighted to be able to organise a series of landings on that stretch of the coast. Trebarwith Cove and Port William (where there was a rudimentary quay), Backways and Tregardock and Trerubies, he said, had a long history of running free-trade goods, which still went on in a quiet way; he opined that the Revenue services, being much stretched along this coast, paid relatively little attention to the area. He could obtain plenty of orders through his contacts with farmers and gentry far inland— indeed, he said, as far east as Launceston and south to Bodmin. He was sure that the only reason that there were not more landings thereabouts was that ship's captains were too much afraid of the coast, with its narrow inlets and huge towering cliffs. It was true, he said, that few boats could be mustered to take goods off the merchant men, but it was generally practicable to run a ship ashore on an incoming tide, given favourable wind and weather, and to unload her before the ebb. It had been some ten years since a ship was seized here, though there had been a couple of wrecks due to unexpected squalls coming up from the west.

I could see that father did not like the idea of beach unloading, but I recalled that the St Malo was broader in the beam and drew less water than the Galatea; she would sit easier on the sands. So with Mr Johns we walked down the valley to Backways Cove, then climbed up Start Point and walked the cliff top to Tregardock beach; which, Mr Johns averred, was the perfect landing place, safe for the ship, far enough from any centre of population to be overlooked, yet with good lanes and tracks along which goods could be carried briskly. Several farm houses in the vicinity offered cover and storage, as well as mine adits and deep caves above the tide lines. I felt that here was an opportunity I could not refuse. So we struck the same kind of bargain, and made the same type of arrangements with Mr Johns, an affable and direct man, as we had with the Pearns.

On returning to his house, a choice villa in its own grounds at the east end of the hamlet, we sealed the matter by drinking together a bottle of excellent claret; after which he drove us in his own gig down to Port Isaac, where we arrived at late afternoon and found another Lodenek fishing smack about to cast off to drive the first shoals of herring then arriving off our shores. We spent most of the night sailing back and forth across the mouth of our estuary, while the fisherman cast out their nets and brought in a fair catch; we lent a hand to bring the fish aboard and to sort them into baskets for the morning market. Among the hundreds of silvery herring were small numbers of scad, wrasse, and eels.

And so we got home at dawn, to retire and sleep in our own beds; and, for my part, to dream of new adventures and successes.

CHAPTER 24

EMILY - AND ISEUT.

A week later, at the end of September, having received the orders I required from George Pearn at St Gennys; having checked and double-checked everything on the St Malo (now repaired, scraped and thoroughly caulked, and her stays and halyards renewed and overhauled); and having engaged as good a crew as I could find in Lodenek— including Enoch Penberthy as mate, my old friend and mentor Tom Permewan as cook, Job Peters and Davy Bligh as deck hands— I was stowing my gear aboard on a fine mid-morning as the tide rose, and a brisk south westerly ruffling the waters of the Pool as they lapped the Town Bar, when a shout from the boatswain brought me on deck.

'Captain— lady asking for you.'

The lady proved to be Emily, accompanied by her younger brother Ralph, the one I had seen playing croquet on the lawn at Sandry's Hill House. I came to the bulwark and looked up at them as they stood above me on the quayside.

'Good morning, Captain,' Emily called; 'may we come aboard? You said you would show me over your new ship, you know.'

On the half tide the St Malo was some ten or twelve feet below the quayside; the crew used the iron-runged ladders fixed to the wall, and we had no gangplanks.

'Of course you may,' I shouted up. 'But there's only the ladder, it may be slippery.' Grease and slime from the fish scales were the two main hazards, as I had known from early childhood.

'I shan't mind. If I fall you must catch me,' Emily said, with a humorous lilt to her voice; and bending down, gripping the heavy iron mooring ring beside the ladder top, she turned herself around and got her feet to the first rung. I saw several petticoats and underskirts, slim calves and ankles and fine white lisle stockings, descending upon me; and felt my colour rising, recalling again the scene at the Whitsun sports wheelbarrow race. I noticed some of the men on the deck gaping and grinning, and snapped at them, 'Belay there— bosun, get these men to work.'

'Aye, aye, sir.' Martin Crews, the boatswain, was soon sending them scurrying to their duties, coiling ropes, shaking out sails, shining brasses and swabbing down the quarter-deck.

As Emily neared the decks one of her dainty little shoes came off and bounced down beside me; I was about to pick it up when she gave a little gasp and, missing her footing, hung there with two hands on a rung and one foot on the gunwhale. 'James!' she cried with a frightened little laugh. I leapt up on the gunwhale and took her by the armpits, saying, 'Let go, I've got you,'— and lowered her gently to the deck, where she retrieved her shoe, much amused by the incident and not at all embarrassed. I helped Ralph down beside her, jumped down, and said, 'I hope nothing is spoiled?'

'I don't think so. What a business it is getting on board. Quite an adventure.' She glanced up at the quayside. 'As long as father isn't here to see it. Now— show me all around. I want to see everything.'

'Jolly nice little craft, ain't she?' Ralph said. 'I'll wager she can sail pretty smartly.'

'She'll do well, I think,' I said. 'We haven't much time, we're casting off in half-an-hour for Guernsey.'

'Ah yes.' Emily nodded. 'But are you sure that's wise?'

'I think so, why not?'

'I have heard there has been some trouble there. The Government has sent Revenue Officers to the island, and the Guernsey men don't like it.'

It was true, I recalled: Guernsey, technically a British possession, but self-governing with its own constitution, acknowledged no right of any London Government to interfere in its own affairs. The Revenue men were there to suppress free-trading, of course; St Peter Port would indeed be a poor choice for a first trip. I whispered to Emily, with a nod to young Ralph, 'Not my actual destination— which I cannot tell you— you understand.'

They nodded, exchanged meaningful glances, and began to talk about the ship. 'I'll show you my cabin,' I said, leading the way across the deck to the poop.

Emily was deeply interested in my quarters, cramped though they were: the narrow bunk, the swivel chair bolted to the floor, and the little folding desk screwed to the bulkhead, at which I would write when studying. 'I shall be able to think of you, whenever you are away, sleeping here in this dear little place,' she told me. 'Now may I see over the crew's quarters?' I did not think that advisable, neither did Ralph; because we believed some of the men would not be presentable, might well be partly or wholly unclothed and at their ablutions; Ralph because he thought he and Emily were taking up too much of my time. 'Just a *peep*, James dear, *please*,' she said, turning her wide winsome eyes on me and fluttering her eyelids once or twice. 'I do so want to see how other people live. I feel I live such a sheltered life, you know.'

'Oh, come along, Em,' Ralph urged. 'Captain Spargo has a great deal to attend to, I'm sure.'

'It is almost time to put out,' I said. 'Besides, the companion ways are steep and narrow, and you'd probably lose your footing.' A problem suddenly presented itself to me. 'How are we to get you up the quay ladder?' I said. 'You'll need one hand to lift your skirts, surely.'

She considered this and gave a little laugh. 'Dear, dear. Now James, you really must think of something.'

I had visions of getting one of the men, perhaps Job Peters, to climb up with her on his back; clearly those layers of skirts down to her ankles would prevent her mounting by her own efforts. 'Well,' I said, 'if you can climb down, as you did, do you think you could manage a rope ladder, over the side into a dinghy?'

'I might,' she said, with her merry roguish smile. 'But I should have to do it barefoot. These shoes are quite useless on rungs, it seems.'

I called Enoch, who went shinning up the ladder and got a skiff, his own, anchored some way along the quay; and he was soon alongside the St Malo. We let down the rope ladder; Ralph went first, ready to catch his sister if she fell. Then, throwing down her little kid shoes into the boat, she began to descend, helped over the side by me. She paused, looking over the gunwhale, her eyes dwelling on me. 'I shall be thinking of you, James, every day. *Bon voyage*, my dear.' She climbed down slowly, feeling for each rung of the ladder, and made the descent without mishap; then sat on the stern thwart of the skiff, her reddish gold hair flaming against the grey-green water and the old slate harbour walls, like a princess in a royal barge, graciously waving goodbye to me as Enoch rowed her and Ralph to the nearest slipway.

On the afternoon of the next day, after a change of wind to nor' nor' east, and a fast uneventful trick, we ran into Brest and proceeded to load with orders for St Gennys: brandy, port, rum, spices, salt, sugar, tea, silks and lace. We embarked from Brest the following night about eleven, and set a course west-nor-west, which would bring us west of the Scillies; but the wind backed to due west and we made slow progress, heavy rain clouds sweeping in over us as we laboured through the deep troughs. Enoch had given orders to strike the main and mizzen top sails and the gaffs, our square foresails having been taken in since we left port. I left my studies in the cabin and came up on deck to see how we fared.

'Don't think much of this, Cap'n,' Enoch said, peering into the thick gloom. 'Might as well ride it out as try to tack to and fro against this.'

I agreed with him. 'Set the trysail and strike the rest,' I said. 'Keep her dead into the wind. If it eases or goes round then we'll make for'ard.'

There were still two hours left until my watch on the bridge; I saw the larboard watch working in the driving rain, in their oilskins, to secure the sails to the booms. I went down to learn more Latin verbs and translate out of English some sentences Mr Nanskivell had set me. After half an hour, the ship's motion being too great to continue, I lay on my bunk, holding onto the rail, and tried to doze.

The storm blew half the night, all through my watch; and then, about six as I was being relieved by the second mate, it began to subside; as dawn appeared the clouds were parting, and we looked out across a grey expanse of wintry, clashing waters. And bearing down on us from the north was a Revenue cutter, carrying ten guns.

'All hands on deck,' I shouted. 'Set full sail! Put about— course due east!'

During the time in which it took our half sodden sleepy crew to hoist sails and turn the St Malo before the wind, the cutter came within range and spoke us through a loud hailer. 'Ahoy there! His Majesty's Revenue cutter Nomad. Your name and destination if you please!'

They had the wind with them; no doubt their guns were primed, and we might well get a broadside if they could bring their craft around in time. 'Run out and prime the chasers!' I ordered.

Our two stern carronades were soon in place, just as, the St Malo turning to catch the now fitful wind, and our sails billowing out as we got under way, the cutter fired four of her forward guns. One shot buzzed overhead harmlessly; one landed on our quarter-deck, scoring a yard-long scorch mark and smashing into the starboard gunwhale; a third carried away one of our halyards— no great matter, as we were able to run up another fast enough to replace it— and the fourth tore a hole in our mizzen sail just above the boom, necessitating a running repair executed by the bosun and a seaman skilled with a sail-maker's bodkin. Setting her jibsail, the cutter looked now like overhauling us; I waited until she was well within range, then, ordering the stern carronades to aim for her rigging, gave the order to fire. They were two excellently effective balls, one carrying away a main backstay, and the other crippling her gaff, so that the sail flapped and yawed. She was obliged to reef sails so that the backstay could be repaired, otherwise her main mast might have snapped in a sudden gust; so we got out of range, and with all possible sail now on, held to our lead, though she seemed from time to time to gain slightly on us.

The chase went on for most of the morning, as we passed Ushant and ran with the Breton coast in sight; about eleven in the forenoon the cutter gained on us sufficiently to get us within range again, and I was obliged to order another four rounds of shot from our stern chasers. This time we splintered her bowsprit, sending her jibsail flying free. But it was evident that, well-loaded as we were, she now had a significant advantage; so, the wind now veering to nor' east by north, I decided to run for Roscoff, where she would not dare challenge us. Thus at mid-afternoon we entered that now familiar port, the cutter firing several shots at us in desperation, the balls falling short by ten or twenty yards.

We moored up and I sent the larboard watch, with Enoch, ashore; they had earned a respite from such excitement. They were warned to be back to ship by eight that evening so that the starboard watch, the bosun and second mate could be relieved. I remained in my cabin, thinking. We must stay in Roscoff for a day or two, out of harm's way; it would allow us to make good the damage done to us, at least. But we should lose nearly three days in my calculation, so that the landers at St Gennys would be kept chafing against our return; the only way to make up some of the time would be to sail between Land's End and the Scillies on the return voyage. I was loath to do that, but supposed that we might manage it safely enough at night. I wondered how I might get word to them of the delay; but short of sailing to Falmouth, in the teeth of coastguards, Riding officers and cutters, to get a man on a mail coach as far as Jamaica Inn— an unthinkable proposition with no guarantee of his arriving before our planned time— I could see no way to warn them. I remembered then how my father had put a man ashore at Mullion, to ride up to Porthcothan with news of our delay. But St Gennys was another thirty miles on; that would mean finding a change of horse somewhere en route, and we should lose more time getting our man ashore.

I changed my jacket and trousers, and went ashore, leaving the St Malo in good hands, and went along the quays still thinking of how I might best warn the landers; and, walking through the streets of the town, found myself outside the house of Monsieur Renan in the quiet square I remembered. I decided I ought to pay my respects to the good merchant, since I had fetched up here; so finding a bell with a chain attached to its clapper, on the outer wall beside the door, I gave it three good clangs. As I did the Eglise clock nearby struck six.

The door opened and Iseut stood there in a white apron covering her from her neck to her ankles. She drew a sharp breath. '*Jammes! mon cher Jammes!*' And in a second she was in my arms and kissing me. I was overcome with surprise, amusement, and embarrassment;

she showed no such niceties, calling out, '*Papa! Viens ici, je vous en prie*,' between her embraces.

Monsieur Renan appeared, in his long waistcoat and shirtsleeves, a pipe in his hand. '*Ah, Monsieur Jammes!* Capitain Spargo! Please to enter.'

And then I was in their long dining room where a meal was about to be served, and had to tell them of my adventures and why I was there, and what I intended to do next. Iseut, her eyes shining, listening intently to my every word; her father nodded sagely, pointed his pipe at me and said, 'You do not like to live, it seems, *sans le danger*.' He poured wine for me and insisted I should dine with them; not only that, but there was no need to go back to my cramped quarters on the St Malo that night, for there were good beds unoccupied in the house.

It was indeed refreshing to behold Iseut so happy and pleased to see me. She had certainly grown and matured since I had last visited there; the memory of the passionate kisses she had given me in the walled garden at the back of the house returned to me as I saw her presiding over the various dishes which she took from the elderly maid and served herself, every so often allowing her glance to dwell on me just a second longer than was necessary. Her every action seemed to say to me, '*Je t'aime.*'

After the meal I sat by the stove with Monsieur Renan, more out of politeness than pleasure, for I was now very drowsy, having lost most of my previous night's sleep. He plied me with good cognac and a dark liqueur I have never met before; it tasted of oranges and came, I believe, from the West Indies. He offered me a pipe to join him in smoking, but I declined. Iseut was in the kitchen, attending to various duties; or perhaps she was seeing to my bed. When he had enquired after my father we talked, in our halting way, partly in English, partly in French, of the difficulties facing the Trade these days. He was still prospering, he said, though not as much as hitherto. The British Navy and Revenue Service were everywhere; one had to be very careful. I told him something of my plans, and explained that I could not sail to Roscoff as often as I would wish. 'Iseut,' he said, 'has often wish to see you. We think you sail across the world to America or Africa. Cornwall is not far away, one day sailing from Brittany; *peut-être* you will return here *encore plus souvent*.'

'*Peut-être*,' I said, my eyes half closing and the fumes of the liqueur hazing my senses. '*J'éspere pour cela...*'

Iseut now came in, without her apron. She knelt beside me and smiled gently, her great black eyes appearing to swim with compassion and amusement. '*Pauvre Jammes, il est fatigué, n'est-ce pas? Il faut que tu dorme, mon cher.*'

'*Excusez-moi, si'l vous plait,...*' I mumbled. 'I think I really must...go to bed.'

I believe that Iseut, who led me upstairs with a candle which she set down on a chest beside a bed with a plain white coverlet, actually did more to undress me than I did myself— I have a faint recollection of trying to get my shirt off and finding her tugging it over my head, and of her kneeling on the floor pulling my boots off. She drew two scalding stoneware hot water bottles out of the bed, pulled the blanket and feather quilt back, and got me, mother naked, in between the sheets; and as I drifted away to slumber I felt her lips fasten on to mine and heard her whisper, '*Noz da, Jammes ker. Cusk ynta.*' (Sleep well.)

I must have slept, deeply and dreamlessly, for at least four hours. Then I heard the church clock striking twelve as I became half awake, conscious of moonlight entering the room through the horizontal slats of the shutters. I turned over and was beginning to sink Into sleep again when I felt the bedclothes being drawn back, and a warm female form slip silently in beside me. I turned back into the arms of Iseut, who whispered, '*Sssh. Dorme, dorme, mon amour. Pas de bruit, if faut que mon père n'entend pas...*'

It would not be seemly for me to describe here the delights and sweet sensations I experienced then for the first time. Even now I can hardly regard them as sinful, although no doubt they were in the sight of heaven; for it seems to me now that we were simply two children huddling together for comfort in a world of loneliness and danger. Whether Iseut had the conscious design of entrapping me into marriage with her, or whether, innocently overcome by my presence in the house she instinctively wanted to caress and comfort me, I have not to this day been able to decide. Who can divine with any certainty what causes a woman to act, especially when she loves a man? So we loved and caressed through the remainder of the night, until the church clock gave out four weary notes; and though afterwards I knew years of such fleshly union with my dear wife, nothing has ever erased or eclipsed the memory of that night with Iseut. But I was sufficiently aware of what I was doing to withhold that which would have inevitably brought shame and opprobrium to the dear girl, and a lasting remorse to myself. Perhaps, in that, I baulked her intent for her own good.

Towards morning when the moon went down and the first cocks crowed on a farm half a mile away, she told me she had two suitors in Roscoff, neither of which were to her taste.

'*Tu es mon vrai amour, Jammes, seulement tu.*' I thought of Lucretia reading my poem on the cliffs, watching the skylarks with me, kissing me in the cleft of rock where we sheltered, the rain glistening on her shoulders and breast.

'*Je t'aime aussi, Iseut,*' I said. '*Oui, je t'aime beaucoup; mais...*' I paused; she was silent, suddenly withdrawn in my arms.

'*Tu aimes un autre.*' She turned on her back, staring up at the ceiling. Then, sobs shaking her form, she turned over facing away from me. '*Je le connais, je le... connais... mais j'ésperais...*'

I kissed the nape of her neck. 'I'm sorry, my dear *Iseut... Pardon-moi, si tu peux.*'

She ceased to cry and sat up in the bed. '*Et vous serrez marriés*?'

'Oui.'

'Quand?'

'Peut-être— après deux, trois années.'

She flung herself down upon me, not crying now, clinging to me like a lost child. '*Ni a veiz warbarth whez* (we shall be together still)!' she breathed, almost stifling me in her tight embrace. '*Viens ici souvent, pour mon plaisir, Jammes ker.*' We said no more. I lay there kissing her and fondling her, wondering if I had broken her heart, until, as the clock struck six she got up, put on her nightdress and stole quietly back to her own room to dress and begin the day.

*

An hour later, after a breakfast of crêpes, honey and coffee, brought by the maid servant, I took my leave of the Renans. Monsieur saw me to the door *en deshabillé*, a dressing gown over his shirt, his kneebreeches minus stockings. Iseut was quiet, perfectly composed, wishing me '*Bon voyage*' and '*Au revoir*— till the next time.' There was a mere hint of disappointed yearning in her eyes, but after saying farewell, she turned and marched firmly down the passage into the interior of the house.

I went back to the St Malo, sought out Enoch, and discussed with him the question of sending word to St Gennys about our delayed arrival. Enoch, chewing his quid tobacco in my cabin, scratched his head and frowned, and took his time about replying.

'I don't see any good way of getting a message up to they parts,' he said finally. 'Mullion's no good— too far, by horse or by mail coach. We sh'd be there as soon as the messenger. There's a ketch in here from Plymouth, but even if we could get somebody to take word back that way, 'tis a good day's journey from there to Lanson and Crackington— maybe more. No; I don't see how.'

'We've got Davy Bligh on board,' I said. 'He comes from Boscastle.'

'Ah, that's more like it. Can he ride a nag?'

'I don't know. We'll ask him.'

Enoch went on deck and bawled to the bosun. After a minute or so he came back with Davy, who had been glad to sail with me after his voyaging far and wide during the previous several years.

'Now, Davy,' I said. 'You may be able to help. Can you ride a horse?'

'Tolerable well,' he said. 'My uncle've got ponies and nags on his farm, back o' Boscastle; I've jaunted out on them now and then.'

'Could you ride one, the best, from Boscastle to St Gennys Churchtown?'

'Could do, s'pose, if I had to.'

'How long would it take to do that?'

'Dunno. 'Tis 'bout six, maybe eight miles. Hour, hour an' half, say.'

Enoch and I looked at each other, and both nodded.

'The only problem is the moon,' 'I said. 'Sets around four in the morning. So we'll want him ashore at Boscastle by about ten the evening before, to ride to St Gennys and get George Pearn alerting his landers. They'll have given us up, three or four days after the time we arranged.' I explained the plan to Davy, first swearing him to secrecy; he fell in with it eagerly, especially as there was an extra thirty shillings for him if he successfully discharged his task.

'Your uncle won't object? He shall have ten shillings for the horse.'

'He'll be delighted, even if I do get'n out of bed. Uncle Albert was a great free-trader hisself back along.'

We got under way from Roscoff as night fell and beat back to a position two or three miles south of Tol-Pedn-Penwith by two the next morning, the moon gleamed fitfully between banks of high slow-moving cloud; and though we passed several other craft, I took none of them for Revenue Cutters or naval sloops. So far so good. Handing over the watch to Enoch I went below and got three hours sleep, during which, with the aid of a brisk south-westerly, we ran smartly up between the Longships and Land's End, and altered course for North Cornwall, keeping well out.

By midday we were off Lodenek, and soon would overshoot our mark; so I gave orders for the drogue to be dropped, and we took in all sails. Our position was ten miles due north of Pentire Point and some twenty miles south-west of Bude. I had the starboard watch in readiness all afternoon in case an inquisitive Searchers' craft should bear down on us; but though sail after sail appeared and went by, going east or west, and one or two south from Ireland into Lodenek, we had no trouble that day. Several craft spoke us, enquiring if we were in distress; but we were able to assure them that we were merely waiting for the tide to flow in order to enter my home port. As darkness fell we set the mizzen sail and winched up the drogue, and made our way to Boscastle, the wind having now veered to a light nor-west by north.

We lay off Boscastle, surrounded by a number of fishing boats; the half-moon was full overhead, but there was plenty of cloud cover. Conscious that we were within range of a good telescope from the coastguard station on Forraburry Head, as soon as the ship's boat was lowered, with Davy and two strong oarsmen in it, I gave orders to set the main sail, mizzen and gaff, and we went about close to the wind, clear out of range as soon as possible and to get into Crackington Haven by four as the moon set, for the unloading. On arrival, the night had become so dense and black that we were momentarily at a loss to know how to get into the beach between the massive rocks; but, after we had exchanged signals with the shore and made our way slowly in, the nor'wester propelling us gently forward with mainsail and mizzen struck and foresail half reefed, we became aware of three or four pinpoints of light on our larboard bow, and a similar number on the starboard. They turned out to be candles inside hollowed out mangle-wurzles, of the sort children make for hallowe'en: the small apertures gave sufficient light to guide us but could not be seen out to sea, nor of course from the land. Thus we made safe landfall by drifting in between them, and the discharging began.

Our changed plan worked well; indeed I was later assured by George Pearn that the Choughs team was very much impressed by the way in which a venture they had begun to believe had been abandoned, perhaps through shipwreck, storm or arrest, had been revived and successfully concluded. Certainly it boded well for me; landers must have every confidence in their Venturer and Captain, and they were all paid promptly. Despite our delays and damage, that first run in the St Malo brought me a welcome profit of fifty-five pounds, after Mr Rowland's share and all expenses had been deducted.

CHAPTER 25

EMILY'S GRAND BALL

Shortly after this run my twentieth birthday arrived. I was actually away from Lodenek on the day, engaged in my first run to Trebarwith, bringing goods from Concarneau to Tregardock. All went well; the landing was effected on a moonless night, the St Malo beaching gently at two in the morning, being unloaded by half-past three and floated off on the high tide with a west nor' west breeze. We then sailed on to Cardiff and brought back a cargo of steam coal, to be distributed by Thomas Rowlands to various pumping stations at mines and quarries in north Cornwall. Thus we allayed any possible suspicions of the Lodenek Customs Officers.

On berthing and arriving home I was presented by Reuben, in the absence of my father who was at sea, with a magnificent new mariner's chronometer inscribed 'James Spargo, from his Father, Mother, brothers and sisters. 7th October, 1820.' I was greatly touched, knowing how much such an instrument must have cost; only father and Reuben could have contributed much towards it, although Emma, who was apprenticed now to Miss Sloggett, the milliner, might have spared a shilling or two. Daniel insisted he had saved up his pennies earned by running errands and making deliveries for Mr Chellew, the grocer and chandler, to add to the funds. He was fascinated by the time piece, and wanted to know how to wind and set it, and what part it played in the art of navigation: one day, he said, he too would own one when he was a ship master like me.

Perhaps, I reflected, the present was actually a hint to me to stick to sea-faring. I knew that whatever might happen to me in the course of following a career, I should never be parted from this chronometer; and I have it still here on my desk as I write.

Among the gentry and rising merchant classes, it was of course *de rigeur* that an eldest son or daughter should have a ball to mark the occasion of his or her twenty-first birthday. So, a few days afterwards, I looked out my best jacket and white duck trousers, bought myself a new tailored shirt from Mr Oatey and a pair of high-heeled calf-hide shoes from Mr Curgenven, dressed and went up the hill at six o'clock to Sandry's Hill House for Emily's grand ball: the high point of her life and, as it turned out, the last large event to be held in that mansion.

I was greeted, as before on the occasion of her sixteenth birthday, by Emily herself and her mother. Now as tall as Mrs Rowlands herself, Emily was quite resplendent: in her dress of shimmering emerald Shantung silk which matched her eyes and flamed with light from the chandeliers, her hair now lifted above her head and coiled into auburn plaits, she seemed confident, regal and grown up. From a girl who had seemed afraid of the world, yet eager to find adventure in it, she appeared with one stride to have conquered it, being intent on dominating this occasion, as was her right. There was no mistaking the intense pleasure she took in greeting me.

'My dear James— how good of you to come. I trust your voyage was successful?'

'Indeed yes, despite contrary winds and slight damage to the St Malo. But soon repaired.'

Mrs Rowlands nodded, smiling at me also. I bowed to her; she said, 'Welcome Captain Spargo. You will know some of our guests, I hope. Do make yourself at home and enjoy yourself.'

The orchestra was playing light airs and marches, and there were some thirty or more guests sipping wine and making an animated buzz of conversation. I nodded to Matthew Pook, who was engaged in talking to Jane Pellow; he actually proposed to her that evening, I later learned. I found Mildred Morcom, Reuben's fiancée, who was as glad to see me as Emily had been. Reuben himself had been invited to come, but had had to go to sea again. Now that she was spoken for, Mildred treated me with far less awe than hitherto; indeed, by the end of the evening we were on quite familiar terms as prospective brother-and-sister-in-law. And I danced with her three times, as she did not appear to mind my clumsy gyrations on the floor.

Professor Boldini's orchestra had been expanded by the addition of four violins, a mandolin and another cello: the sound of the twelve instruments swung us all immediately into the festive mood expected of us. Emily was marking her card with the names of various young beaux, in uniform and out; I went over to her and said, 'I can't pretend to have improved myself at dancing, but if you'll suffer me for a waltz or the Valeta, I shall be glad to do my best.'

She gave me her most brilliant smile, and that sparkling emerald and violet gaze, and showed me her card: against a waltz, the Valeta and the Three Handed Reel, my name had already been pencilled in. 'You see, James, I was certainly not going to let you off; but try not to tread on my toes, will you?'

'I shall do my utmost to avoid it,' I said, smiling.

And watching Emily, as she went through dance after dance with such gay abandon, the veritable queen of the evening, I could not but feel a pang of regret that she would not, could not now, be my betrothed. For so long she had been my unattainable ideal, the near-goddess I had dared to make my friend; whose confidences I had received and of whose high and impish humour I had been the willing butt; and now, when at last she was attainable, I must, I saw, make her understand that I was not for her; that I was committed to another. I thought also of Iseut: dear, passionate, yearning little Iseut, to whose growing up I had recently and painfully contributed. Yes, I loved her also; I loved Emily; but above all I loved Lucretia. I was reminded of the song out of *The Beggar's Opera*, sung by a visiting tenor at a concert in Lodenek a year or so before, in which occurred the unforgettable lines:

'How happy could I be with either,
Were t'other dear charmer away!'

How I wished I were a Sultan or a Bedouin sheik, who was allowed three or four wives, and could embrace them all without impropriety, finding approval under the law of Allah!

'Well, James, I trust you are pleased with the St Malo?' Mr Rowlands was at my elbow a glass of madeira in his hand.

'Very much so,' I said. 'She handles well in most conditions. Though we had a narrow escape a couple of weeks ago off Brittany...'

He put his free hand on my arm, silencing me with a

warning look. 'Remember,' he said, 'no details. I don't want to know anything of your voyages or trading.'

'Of course.' I stared at him. He was thinner of face than he was wont to be, his eyeballs more prominent and of a yellowish hue; yet the pupils had a kind of unnatural brilliance. Altogether he seemed to have shrunk, as if he had lost weight due to not eating well. I knew little enough about doctoring, but I thought immediately of yellow fever, the jaundice, or worse, the plague.

'Are you enjoying yourself?' he enquired, releasing my arm.

'Indeed yes, sir. A wonderful occasion. And Emily looks quite magnificent tonight.'

'Ah yes. Does she not? I have done all I could for my daughter. Perhaps we have spoiled her, but I doubt it; some innocence is still there, I am glad to say. At heart she is a simple girl. She knows what she wants, James. Whether she can have it— that's another matter.'

I thought he was talking feverishly; perhaps he had had rather too much wine. Was he alluding to Emily's feelings for me? I was at a loss as to how to reply.

'She will likely get a proposal of marriage tonight, I understand,' he went on. 'Perhaps two, or even three. She will make a handsome wife for some dashing lieutenant or squire's son.'

'I certainly hope she will find happiness,' I murmured.

'You say that as if you don't think she is happy,' he said sharply, fixing me again with that strange glitter in his eyes.

'We all have to find our own happiness— indeed to earn it,' I said.

'Ah, you are wise beyond your years. You will go far, I know it. I understand you have designs to go to a university, is that so? Though why, I cannot conceive, when here in Lodenek, if you continue, you will rise to some power and wealth in commerce. My own firm will need a fresh hand soon, a new broom, perhaps, when I retire.'

'But surely, your sons...won't Ralph take over the business?'

'Ralph? Pshah! At present all Ralph wants is to go into the army and cut a dash as a subaltern in the Dragoons. No business interest or sense there, I think. One of the younger boys, Richard, may have possibilities. Well, we must wait and see. You have other ideas; it is no business of mine, and I have no right to interfere or try to advise. But I am your friend— your teacher in a sense, James, isn't that so?'

I could not deny that I owed him a great deal. 'Of course it is, and I shall always be grateful to you, Mr Rowlands.'

'Never mind gratitude, make your way...you'll get what you want, I can see it, though whether it will make you content is altogether another matter. Now drink up... but you have no glass, James!'

'I shall take something directly. I don't indulge much, even aboard ship; besides, you remember the last time I came to Emily's ball?'

'Aha!' he clapped me on the shoulders. 'I do. You were down in the dumps that night. You've learned a great deal since though. Well... good luck, James. *Bon voyage*— and many of 'em.' And he was gone in among the spectators, who were standing about laughing and watching the dancers. At that moment the Three- Handed Reel was announced, and I sought Emily out.

So the evening went on among the glitter of epaulettes on dress uniforms and the bright silky colours of girl's dresses, the flickering incandescence of the chandeliers and the brilliant sounds of the orchestra. Professor Boldini, quite bald now on his pate but with a shock of white hair standing up around it, worked himself up into a frenzy conducting the faster waltzes and the Lancers. Then the interval was announced.

I took a glass of brandy-fizz and a cream cake, and found a corner of the stairs, where Matthew and Jane had ensconced themselves. We passed some quiet remarks about the occasion, and I sat there thinking about Lucretia, who would never participate in such events— I reflected it was as well I did not much care for dancing, on that very account— when Emily herself approached.

'James: I wonder if I could have a few words with you in private?' She was still regal and outwardly composed, but I detected some suppressed agitation in her face and in the look she gave me.

'Certainly, Emily. Is there something wrong?'

She led me into the small parlour of the hall and closed the door. She sat down with her hands tightly locked together, on the little sofa, indicating that I should sit beside her.

'James,' she said, twisting her hands together, and looking at me with a tremulous gaze— excited but, I swear, frightened also— 'I have just had a proposal of marriage.' Then I saw there was actually tears beginning to start in her eyes.

'My dear Emily,' I said, 'I am so glad for you. That

is, if it is someone you like and can love.'

She shook her head. 'I don't know... perhaps... but it is so sudden... I thought I must tell you.'

'Me?'

'Oh James. Surely you know why.'

My feelings were in turmoil. I wanted to take her and crush her to my breast, to soothe her, kiss her, yes, love her; and knew that whatever happened I must not. 'Dear Emily, dear friend,' I said. 'I did promise to be your friend, always, and I hope there will never be any reason to break that promise.' Her hand crept into mine; I held it, caressing it, making it a substitute for my natural feelings to comfort her more thoroughly. 'Who is the young man?' I asked.

'Philip Rashleigh.'

'Ah.'

Young Rashleigh, a handsome if, in my opinion somewhat effete young lieutenant in the Dragoons, was the eldest son and heir of Charles Rashleigh of Menabilly, at that time High Sheriff of Cornwall, and owner of extensive estates between Fowey and St Austell. 'Well,' I said, 'he will no doubt be a very desirable match for you. I daresay your father and mother will be delighted.'

She looked miserably up at me, her lightly rouged cheeks splattered now with weeping, and said, 'Say the word, James, only say the word, and I will refuse him.'

'My dear, dear Emily...' I felt the situation slipping well beyond my grasp. The wrong words now could end our friendship and make us mutual enemies. 'I respect you, honour you, yes, I love you, as a friend loves another. But I cannot marry you, even if your parents would have me. I have... committed myself to a career; and to someone else... who is to be my wife.'

'Who? who?' she blazed at me, anger and jealousy flaming in her face. Then she quickly controlled herself. 'I am sorry: I have no right to insist you tell me.'

'I would certainly tell you, but I'm sworn to secrecy for several years... until I can earn enough money to go to university and find a profession.'

'I see. People have been saying that you're in love with Susan Roberts, a lady's maid at Devereaux Place.'

I began to laugh at the very idea, but checked myself. Of course the letters passing between myself and Lucretia via Susan had inevitably sparked off such a rumour. 'I assure you it isn't Susan I love. In time you and everyone will know. When I have proved I am worthy of her.'

She sat thinking, sobbing a little from time to time, then bravely attempted to smile at me. 'I hope you will prove it soon. Of course you are worthy of her, whoever she may be. I only hope she will prove worthy of you.' She stood up. 'We must return to the ball. I must accept my destiny, somehow, I suppose. No doubt in time I will come to like and perhaps love him.'

The door opened; Mrs Rowlands stood there. 'Are you quite well, Emily?'

'Yes, mama. James and I...' she paused, not knowing how to explain our being closeted together.

'I was only giving Emily some private advice, Mrs Rowlands, at her request. Will you excuse me now?' I bowed to them both, and left them to discuss the proposal behind closed doors.

In the hall I stood watching as the dancing got under

way again; I saw Matthew and Jane whirl past in another waltz, and Mr Rowlands himself partnering a squire's lady from near Bodmin. But the music washed over me like waves over a rock; there was a hidden ground bass in it, which I alone there could hear. I felt a great sadness, a nostalgia for our youth together, and reflected that Emily, so long my ideal of femininity, was about to depart from my world. I had my Lucretia (who had written to me again, another warm loving letter, received on my return from the voyage), and wanted no other; yet Emily had somehow gained a deep fond hold on my heart, and she would always be the lover, the sweetheart, I almost but never had. Despite her impetuosity and wilfulness, her naivety and unpredictability, she would always be with me, at the back of my mind, whispering into my ear, entrancing me with those brilliant ill-matched eyes: the belle of my life's ball, who perhaps after all, despite her brave coming of age, would never quite grow up.

Half an hour later, as the great twenty-first birthday cake with blazing candles was brought in, I saw Emily with the tall, thin Philip Rashleigh, who was bending over her in slightly awkward and inane manner; she was smiling bravely up at him, evidently quite resigned to having the betrothal announced. And after the candles were blown out and we had all toasted her in wine, Mr Rowlands did indeed inform us all that he had the happy duty to announce the engagement of Emily Lavinia to Philip Charles Rashleigh, lieutenant of His Majesty's Cornish Light Dragoons, of Menabilly and Prideaux House, Luxulyan. And we toasted the couple and gave them three hearty cheers.

But Emily, when saying farewell to her guests an

hour later, seemed on the brink of tears again as she took my hand in hers, limply letting it drop, and failing to meet my eyes for more than a brief half-second.

CHAPTER 26

GOOD RUNS AND NARROW ESCAPES

During that autumn and winter I made four more highly successful runs— two to Crackington and two to coves near Trebarwith— which brought my total profit up to over three hundred pounds. But these were not uneventful ventures; looking back now I truly believe that Providence smiled on us, so narrowly did we, on three of those occasions, escape being caught.

In November we ventured as far as Douarnenez, on the southern coast of Brittany where, armed with a list of goods required at Trebarwith, Delabole, Camelford, Bodmin and Launceston, and a bag of golden sovereigns from the Lodenek Bank (for we had had no previous contact with merchants in that port, and could not expect credit), we loaded the St Malo with rum, brandy, geneva, playing cards, tea and tobacco. We found a fair wind on our return journey, and westered round the Scillies and then up the north coast of Cornwall, taking three days and two nights. We lay off Tregardock, well out to sea, and sent a boat ashore under Martin Crews, the boatswain, to alert the landers; who were all in position that evening, with no interference from the Revenue, at that stage. The unloading took place quietly, goods being run up to various farm houses and an inn at Delabole, where they were stowed in deep cellars. But some hint must have reached the Searchers, for a Riding Officer from Boscastle and six Dragoons were seen approaching early the following day. By that time the St Malo was well out to sea and heading for Bideford, where we expected to sell artichokes, onions and swede turnips which we had also bought from Brittany. What took place at the Quarryman at Delabole was related to me afterwards by Ezra Johns.

The Excise, it transpired, had had suspicions about the inn for some time. The landlady, Mrs Eliza Carkeek, had been selling liquor at remarkably low prices, it was reported; so the Searchers required her to account for every cask and anker she had on the premises, and to show evidence in the form of receipts as to whom she had bought it from. They found her sitting in the taproom, peaceably smoking the briar pipe she favoured; she was told, in no courteous manner, to stay exactly where she was while her premises were searched. This order she obeyed without arguing, even though she had to sit there for the best part of an hour. After examining everything, including the blackboard on which she chalked her prices, they could find nothing to charge her with. Her ledger, made up to the previous day, revealed only legitimate purchases, namely of beer; there was indeed only one container of spirits, a cask of rum, clearly marked with a customs clearance, and only a quarter full. The Riding Officer ordered the men to search the bedrooms, the outhouses and stables, with no better results. They left, quite frustrated in their endeavour; upon which the landlady arose, having concealed under her skirts an anker of good cognac, and beneath it the flagstone which covered the entry to the cellars containing our previous night's delivery.

Our next run, in December, was made to Roscoff; I debated with myself for some while before deciding on that port. I now had sentimental reasons for wishing to avoid it, fearing that M.Renan, if not Iseut herself, would not welcome me there now. I overcame that objection by remembering that there were a number of other merchants well established there who could supply me with goods — some of them of Scottish and English origin who had been there generations, and were now regarded by the French authorities and Breton natives as subjects of France itself.

In the event M. Renan was pleased to see me arrive, as a customer, and even insisted that I come back to the house to dine with him and Iseut; which I did, finding that no embarrassment was my lot, since we merely talked as old friends; and, later that evening, took leave of each other in a quiet atmosphere of good will. I reflected, as we sailed on the midnight for Cornwall, that Iseut had seemed resigned and a little regretful, but was certainly putting a calm brave face on the affair. She even allowed me to kiss her forehead lightly on parting.

The choice of Roscoff had been forced on me because, during the brief dark days of December when weather was more changeable than at other times of the year, it was as well to have as short a voyage as possible; easterly or north-easterly winds could add several days to our calculations, and to go to other Breton or French ports would add to any delay. Not only that, but the orders for the December run were unusually heavy, with Christmas and New Year festivities in mind. It was essential to arrive back off Crackington Haven, our destination for that run, no later than a week before Christmas itself, In order to get the cargo distributed in time for the festive season.

One of George Pearn's landers was a mason and

stone carver named Cantrell, who also did undertaking as a side line. Cantrell's hearse was a new-fangled object in the parish; a closed conveyance for a coffin was not something the people of St. Gennys had previously thought necessary. However, it not only did away with the need for bearers to trudge for miles along miry lanes carrying corpses to their burial, but provided a most useful way of transporting contraband goods, which for some months deceived the Searchers. At last, after the Riding Officer from Bude had noticed the hearse at a certain farm for the second time in six weeks, and on making enquiries of the Vicar, could not trace anyone who had died there, the game was up. The hearse was searched— fortunately before being loaded with free-trade goods stored at the farm; and thenceforth was carefully watched. The next time it was used it was stopped and searched, and the coffin it carried actually opened in order to ascertain that it carried a real body.

The incident of the farmer's wife in labour is still talked about today, and will very likely go down in history as one of our most famous smuggling incidents. We had arrived off Backways Cove, at the head of the valley immediately below Trebarwith village, from Douarnenez, in mid-February; the weather was stormy, and we had difficulty landing our cargo since the strong north-west wind bore us in on a huge surf. I could see that we should be dashed to pieces on the rocks of that narrow cove, attempting to beach the St Malo. Accordingly we took several reefs in our mizzen and main sails, having furled the square foresail, turned close to the wind, and made for Tregardock, where a wider beach gave us a better chance. We were being watched, of course, from the shore, by a lookout up on the cliffs; I could only trust that the landers would realise our intentions and would follow us along the coast. Which they did; and we came hurtling in on a tremendous roller that lifted us high onto the sands, so that I feared we should never get her off again. The unloading was achieved with remarkable efficiency, men appearing in the surf up to their waists to take off the ankers and bales; because of the change of plan they took most of it to the nearest farm, a quarter of a mile up the lane, where concealment was limited. Some of the spirits were hidden among bales of hay and in furze ricks; but most of the cargo were simply taken into the kitchen, dairy and living room of the small building, hardly bigger than a cottage. The farmer, Henry Carslake, one of the stalwarts of these operations, realised the danger he was in, and sent word to Ezra Johns to organise the distribution of contraband as soon as possible.

Meanwhile, after unloading, the sea rose with the tide round the St Malo's stern, but she did not float; her bows were still partly buried in the sand and shingle. I set the crew to work, in the darkness of the moonless night, flayed by spray and rain, to dig her out; but the tide was already receding, and we had lost our chance. We were stranded there until the next tide, at three in the afternoon.

It was fortunate that we had loaded potatoes and mangolds at Douarnenez, and thus could show the Revenue we had a legitimate cargo when they arrived in the forenoon to inspect the ship. A stranded vessel can never escape attention, however remote her landfall; but after looking her over, and questioning me about our destination— which I told them (quite truthfully, as far as the vegetables were concerned) was Barnstaple— they left, apparently satisfied that we had been blown off course by the gale and had been lucky to escape being wrecked. What led them to Tregardock farm, whether it was need for refreshment or actual suspicion that free-trading was being conducted there, I never knew; but when I saw them marching up the lane and in through the farm gate, I truly believed that all would be discovered, and my enterprises doomed then and there.

What I did not know was that Henry Carslake's wife was at that moment in labour, her sixth child being imminent; and that the local doctor, a friend of Henry's and an enthusiastic customer for free-trade goods, was in attendance upon her.

The three Revenue men— the Landing Waiter and two Searchers from Boscastle— happened first to enter one of the barns at the entrance to the farm, and found a cow munching hay from one of several bales there; she had dislodged the bale, revealing three or four ankers of rum behind it. On moving the other bales they found then more ankers, and seized them, and, entering the farmhouse, demanded to search the entire place. Henry Carslake complied, professing ignorance of what they had discovered; how it came to be there he couldn't guess, unless of course a team of smugglers had decided, without his permission, to hide it there. Such things had happened before.

The Searchers went through the house, finding nothing else, but were halted at the head of the stairs by the doctor, who told them that the wife was in labour in the bedroom. They were welcome to search anywhere else, but he would not have his patient distressed by strange men entering her room. And indeed, anguished cries were heard from behind the door, piercing enough to cause the men to turn pale. They made a quick examination of the other rooms and left, announcing their intention of returning later that day to complete the search and confiscate the ankers in the barn; they left one of their number on guard there.

The wife bore her child in a room stacked with kegs of brandy and rum, sacks of sugar, packets of tea and bales of silk and tobacco. When the Searchers returned, however, there was not one item of contraband to be seen; the woman lay there sleeping, her new-born son in a cot beside her. And in the barn, dead drunk beside a broached anker of rum, was the Searcher who had been left on guard. The rest of the goods had been moved to safer hiding places up the valleys at other farms, and some were now on their way along the lanes and moorland tracks to Bodmin, Wadebridge, Launceston and further afield.

The Searcher's story was that he had been seized by three men whom he could not describe, since they wore scarves round their faces and, a cask being staved in, was forced to drink several cupfuls of over-proof spirit, effectively rendering him unconscious. However, the version told to me afterwards by Mr Ezra Johns, was that Jack Rouncevall, one of Carslake's farmhands, had engaged the Searcher in conversation, remarking how cold it was in the barn, and inviting him inside to warm himself at the fire; upon the Revenue man's refusing to budge from his duty, Jack got a mallet and chisel and offered to knock out the bung of one of the casks, saying that a pint or two would not be missed, and a few drams would warm the Searcher's veins against the bitter wind blowing through the barn. The man succumbed to this temptation, with the desired result.

Meanwhile, down on the beach, we had dug a good trench round the stranded St Malo, so that the afternoon tide, aided by our two ship's boats, each pulled by six oars, lifted her off the sands; so we were well out to sea by the time the Riding Officer and reinforcements arrived. There was no evidence, of course, that we had conveyed the missing casks. We sailed on to Barnstaple, and from thence to Cardiff and Liverpool, to bring back to Lodenek a considerable cargo of sheet iron, kettles and boilers, Manchester velvet, long cloth and cotton yarn.

CHAPTER 27

MRS DEVEREAUX - AND THE SQUIRE

During that March and April I made no runs across to France; my idea being to allay suspicions on the part of the Revenue Services by making a series of fairly short voyages to bring in legitimate goods: coal from South Wales, ironware from the Severn ports, cotton goods from Lancashire, and linen from Belfast. This also gave me more time at home to study; moreover, on three or four occasions I managed to meet Lucretia on the cliffs near Tregudda or Butterhole.

Our feelings for each other had increased in intensity until, on the last of these rendezvous; I was moved to tell her that I could hardly bear to part from her. She evidently felt the same towards me; and said, ‘But it cannot be long now, surely, before you will have earned the money to go to College.’

‘Two or three more free trading runs will do it,’ I said. ‘I'm to sit the Matriculation examination in June. Mr Nanskivell has talked to the Reverend Rowlands, who has written to his old College— Exeter, I believe— at Oxford. And if I pass I shall be able to go up to study in the Michaelmas term.’

‘And if you pass,’ Lucretia said boldly, her brown eyes dilating to a golden amber as the sunshine searched into them, ‘we ought to be married immediately, so that I can go up with you and live in your chambers as your wife.’

I stared at her, having envisaged a further three years of study before our marriage. ‘That would be truly wonderful, my darling. But how... are you sure?'

'Quite sure. I've been giving it a great deal of thought, James. It is time I entered some wider and more intelligent Society than Lodenek and Cornwall can offer. I believe Oxford will suit me very well.'

'No doubt it will. You'll soon make friends there. But what will your family say?'

'My family will accept it. So much the worse for them if they don't. I can live without my family. I couldn't live without you, James. Not now, my dearest. Not now.'

We embraced, tears freely running down both our faces at the tremendous joy this brought, to be able to declare our commitment to each other in such terms. Yet I had an overriding sense of disbelief that this could actually happen: the proposition seemed too simple, too miraculously easy an arrangement, bringing me my heart's desire so much more quickly than I had counted on, that I could only pray silently to God that this amazing scheme could be practicable.

And afterwards, reflecting upon it, I could not see why it should not be so. Lucretia had her own small fortune; I would have my trading profits. The Matriculation should not be too difficult, nor (in those days) were the Tripos studies themselves too onerous for those with a modicum of intelligence and application. Yet I could not still that nagging, insistent doubt. Could Squire Devereaux stop the marriage? Lucretia was of age and independent; how could he? Perhaps some illness or accident— perhaps shipwreck— perhaps...?

I put all this from me, and trusted to Providence and my own native wits to see us both through to the great day of our bliss.

Devereaux Place
10. v. 1821

Dearest,

Make sure you come on Tuesday. I have several things arranged, very important for us both. And I have written a poem I intend to read! (You see you are not the only one in Lodenek who can put verses together, though I make no pretence that mine are better, or as good as yours.) Do not fail me, my darling. I can hardly wait to see you again, to be in your presence, if not your arms.

Ever yours,

L

So I ascended the hill past the church and entered the great iron gates beneath the mouldering slate archway, on that quiet May evening, cogitating as to what Lucretia had arranged. Blackbirds, robins and thrushes fluted and shrilled through the trees about the churchyard, through that clear luminous peace which rain-washed air brings when the wind drops; it had blown and rained hard nearly all afternoon. I had been at home with my books, having delayed (at Lucretia's behest) the St. Malo's departure for Cork, and thence to Brittany; for it was time for another run, this time back to Crackington Haven. Bright tremulous beads of water stood on the laurel and box leaves, scattering profusely as I brushed against them. The church clock struck eight as I arrived at the main entrance.

Inside, already assembled in the library, were

Lucretia, her sister Sarah, Matthew Pook, Dr. Harley; and Mrs Devereaux. I felt some awe at the Squire's wife, who was an imposing lady, regal in her attitudes and gestures. Observing her in church from the choir stalls, I had formed the private opinion that she ruled her family and household with an iron will. She was tall and handsome (without that aquiline nose, which was a Devereaux feature, repeated in generations of paintings up and down the stairs and in the hall), and had always seemed to me to be larger than life. Some of her magnificent certainties and gestures being repeated in Lucretia herself, it was little wonder that I had taken some while to overcome my diffidence and veneration to claim the daughter: now I had to face a magnification of those doubts and apprehensions before the mother. Though I confidently believed in myself and my plans for the future, to be unexpectedly confronted by a person so evidently superior in every way as Mrs Devereaux threw me off balance, and some of my confusion must have shown.

'Ah, James, so good to see you,' Lucretia was saying, as much the chairman of the proceedings as ever. 'This is my mother, who is joining us tonight.'

I bowed and took Mrs Devereaux' outstretched hand.

'I am indeed glad to meet you,' the lady said, comfortably ensconced in one of the leather padded chairs. 'Lucretia has told me all about you.'

All? I wondered. I hope not, yet at least. She was smiling at me in such a regal yet sympathetic fashion that I was immediately put at my ease.

'How are your studies progressing?' she continued. 'I wonder how you can find time, being away at sea so much.'

'I do find— that is, I make time, to study at least two hours every day, wherever I happen to be,' I said. 'Whether at home or abroad, or on the high seas. Only the worse storms prevent me, ma'am, now and then.'

'I do admire dedication,' she said. 'Surely you deserve to succeed.' And gave me again that warm welcoming smile, almost as if I were already one of her family.

'I am sure he will,' Lucretia said. 'Now, if we may begin... I fear poor Mrs Nanskivell is much worse, so her husband will not be here tonight.' I knew that to be true: my mother and sisters had been going up to help the dying woman, taking broth and egg custard and other light delicacies; but she was sinking fast, and was not expected to last more than a few days. Dr. Harley's grave look, as he nodded, merely confirmed this.

'Who shall start, then?' Lucretia said. 'Matthew?'

'If you wish,' Matthew said. 'I've been reading Fielding's *Joseph Andrews*. It's the tale of an upright and virtuous young man servant, very handsome and admired by all the ladies and servant girls, and the temptations he's exposed to in Society.'

I noticed Sarah and Lucretia exchanging amused glances, with a flutter of eyelids, and then hastily composing themselves to listen. Having read *Tom Jones*, I had some idea of what to expect. Matthew was evidently much taken with this story, and put a great deal of enthusiasm and liveliness into his rendering of a couple of racy chapters. I could see, however, that Mrs Devereaux was not nearly so amused as her daughters; she sat through the reading with a cool smile of reserve.

'Damme, rollicking good stuff,' said the doctor,

heartily, when Matthew had finished. 'Beg your pardon Mrs Devereaux— but Fielding always cheers me up, y' know.'

I sensed that Mrs Devereaux did not consider *Joseph Andrews* as the best choice of the evening. 'May we not have some poetry?' she asked.

'Of course, Mother.' Lucretia looked at Sarah, who said, 'I am quite struck by John Keats, who has really been writing some very beautiful odes— so well constructed too.' And she read the *Nightingale*, which was a revelation to me, as much as Shelley's *Skylark* had been when Lucretia had quoted it from memory on the cliffs at Guddra. The rich languorous words, the tone of poignant melancholy, the visions of the past it opened up— and the sense that death was near the poet (who indeed, at that very time was, though unknown to us, dying of consumption in Italy) — brought to me the realisation of how personal poetry could now be, portraying one's own griefs and tragedies, yet at the same time identifying them with those of all men, and women, everywhere. We are all human, the poem seemed to be saying; we all feel pain, and know sorrow, which is heightened by the sense of passing beauty; yet, as in the nightingale's song, beauty and grief are eternal, and eternally entwined.

I thought then, and still think now, that it is a great poem, perfectly conceived and sustained; some of Keats' Cornish and Celtic ancestry, it seems to me, must have been responsible for its noble melancholy and extreme sensitivity.

'My heart aches, and a drowsy numbness pains

My sense, as though of hemlock I had drunk..'

Sara read it quietly, phrasing it well— she had evidently rehearsed it aloud— and when she ended there was a profound silence in which we all sat unmoving, none of us daring to break it. The clock on the mantelpiece ticked sonorously; the trees outside the library window dropped pearls of moisture onto the lawn; there were tears about to brim in several eyes, including mine.

Lucretia spoke at last. 'I am sure that was extremely moving,' she said. 'We shall hear much more of Mr Keats in the future— I believe he will soon be accepted as one of the truly great poets, despite the views of some unkind critics.'

'But what poet has been without criticism of the most destructive kind, however great he was?' the Doctor said. 'Especially if he breaks new ground. Wordsworth and Coleridge have had their fair share, for sure.'

'It must be so hard to bear,' said Sarah. 'Especially if one can write such sad heartfelt verse as Mr Keats.'

'Shall you read your own poem now, Lucretia?' enquired Mrs Devereaux.

'I think not now, Mother. Not immediately after the Nightingale. My poor attempt would seem quite pathetic. James, what have you brought?'

I had been thinking still about the Ode, wondering also how I should find the audacity to attempt to write more verse of my own after beholding that peak of poetic achievement. But then, I supposed, great poets lead on lesser ones, who lead on mere amateurs like us— but show us all the way, at least, to sincerity. At Lucretia's request I put John Keats from me, and opened the book I had brought.

'Lord Byron,' I announced. 'A favourite passage of mine, from *Childe Harold's Pilgrimage.*' I stood up and read out boldly, intent on achieving a dramatic effect, sounding out the grand organ effect of that dissolute peer's feeling for the sea.

Roll on, thou deep and dark blue Ocean— roll!
  Ten thousand fleets sweep over thee in vain;
Man marks the earth with ruin— his control
  Stops with the shore; — upon the watery plain
The wrecks are all thy deed, nor doth remain
  A shadow of man's ravage, save his own,
When, for a moment, like a drop of rain,
  He sinks into thy depths with bubbling groan—
Without a grave— unknelled, uncoffined, and unknown.

They all saw immediately, of course, why I favoured those lines; I read the following five stanzas, trying to portray in my voice the ocean's moods, from playful and serene to tempestuous. When I finished, on the quiet note of a boy sporting in the waves and trusting the sea as a friend, they actually applauded me.

So the evening passed pleasantly, with Mrs Devereaux reading Collin's *Ode to Evening*, and the Doctor an Essay of Addison's from the Spectator; until, at last, Lucretia sat there, all eyes expectantly upon her, about to read her own poem. I must confess I was quite curious about this; I expected something clever or deep, and finely wrought, for she was a voracious reader, and had she not the benefit of all those calf-bound volumes about us, the collected works of every poet of note from Homer and Virgil to Chaucer, Shakespeare, Pope and Gray? And I was sure she had studied them all.

What we heard astounded me, and I think also the others, by its grave simplicity. As she read I remembered her comparing my own first naive verses to the poems of William Blake.

COMMUNION

I walked the wondrous ways of earth,
  The mountains bleak and seashore strand;
I saw the sky's vast pageants spread
  Before me like a mythic land,
        But worshipped them alone.

In deep communion with the cliffs
  The whispering heather bells and thrift,
I wandered like a spirit pure
  With avid wings of lark or swift;
        Yet always was alone.

Bright sheen of lakes, the chattering streams,
  The hedgerows and the rolling moors:
With every breath of zestful air
  My soul aloft transported soars
        In ecstasy— alone.

But now, oh love, I see you come ,
  A soft light in your dreaming eyes,
Surveying what I hold most dear;
  Two solitudes in mute surmise
        Meet here: no more alone.

'Tis God himself, his face unmasked,
We love in all these gorgeous scenes;
'Tis God who once, each thousand lives,
Allows two souls such plenteous means,
And binds them into one.

I am sure that of all we said, or read, that memorable evening, we all felt that this was the most remarkable offering. Not that as poetry it could rival Keats, or Byron, or even William Collins; but that one of our circle, known yet unknown, had dared to express in such words the innermost yearnings of her soul, and to read it to us in such a modest yet determined manner, made us pause and wonder. It was, as I realised almost from the first lines Lucretia spoke, a declaration that quite evidently involved me. It seemed to be a direct response to my poem about my feelings for her when away at sea: in fact, the very rhyming scheme, if not exactly the rhythm, was the same. And all there knew who the poet's love was, with whom at the end she was united; though no one so much as looked at me in any direct way as if to say so.

'Ah, Lucretia, the Muse's true voice has spoken in you,' pronounced the avuncular Doctor. 'Which makes a marriage of true minds, if your words are to be taken literally.'

Lucretia smiled and said nothing. Mrs Devereaux, I saw, was now watching me, and so was Sarah. It seemed I was expected to comment. 'She has out-done me, I think,' I said after a pause. 'Perhaps the poem is prophetic. I hope so.'

'Amen to that,' Mrs Devereaux said. 'We always knew that Crish was talented. She reveals more gifts as time goes on.'

'Have you written anything else, Miss Devereaux?' asked Matthew.

'Nothing I would show anyone. I hope I have high standards,' Lucretia said, this time glancing at me.

The Doctor rose. 'I must be away now, I fear,' he said. 'I must look in on Mrs Nanskivell on my way home.'

'Will you not take a glass or two before you go?' Mrs Devereaux offered.

'Not tonight, if you will excuse me. It has been a delightful evening. A refreshment to the mind and soul. Dear ladies, I bid you goodnight. And James, you have a rival in verse— I expect you to respond next time we meet.'

Matthew stood up and also took his leave; I suspected he wanted to call in on Jane on his way home. I wondered if I should go also. But something in Lucretia's gaze held me there; and I remembered her note— something of importance, beyond her poem itself, it was plain.

Mrs Devereaux rang the bell and a manservant appeared bringing the port, followed by a maid with coffee in a silver pot on a tray with delicate Staffordshire cups and saucers.

That I should find myself sitting there in the library of Devereaux Place, comfortably partaking of refreshments with Lucretia, her mother and sister, was something I should have entirely disbelieved had it been forecast a few months previously. What did we talk about? I hardly remember. Mrs Devereaux was still trying to put me at my ease, as if, it seemed to me, I were about to be subjected to some great test; and the way in which Lucretia looked at me seemed to support this. At first I answered all questions warily, committing myself to no forthright views; then, I recall, the lady asked me if I believed that education ought to be extended to everyone, as far as possible, even to the poorest and lowest in the land, and that I said that I hoped I lived to see the day when that actually happened. I suspected that, as a member of the gentry, she might not be pleased with that; but she nodded sagely, and said, 'We must all do our part in overcoming ignorance, which I believe is the chief cause of all unhappiness and misery in the country.' And then, to my utter surprise, Lucretia and Sarah rose and each made some excuse to leave us— though Lucretia made it clear she would return— and left me alone there with Mrs Devereaux.

She came straight to the matter in hand. 'My dear James, I am so glad to have this opportunity to speak to you alone. My husband will be home shortly; I hope you will have some words with him in private. Now you and I, James, must be friends— or all will be lost. You realise it is of Lucretia I am thinking. Sarah and she have been secretive, but I have realised for some time that there has been a strong feeling between you and dear Crish. She means a great deal to us all, you know. Despite her disability, she is a wonderful girl— I needn't, of course tell you that; but we all think so much of her, and if she is to marry and settle down as a wife we must all feel quite certain that she has found the right man. Of course we have looked at all the possibilities, but none of the young men we are acquainted with in our somewhat limited circle are acceptable to her. You see, James, Cornwall is small enough, and not even Devon and Somerset seem to provide anyone intelligent or sympathetic enough for Lucretia to consider. Of course she is extremely sensitive. I know she had more or less resigned herself to a single life, with her books and painting. And if such were to be her fate she would have accepted it, and risen above it to do some worthy work in life. She is a very determined young woman, and knows her own mind.'

'I am fully aware of it, ma'am,' I said.

'And she certainly knows what she wants now. I personally would not object— I shall, in fact, do all I can to further her happiness and yours. I believe you will succeed in life; surely you have given sufficient proof already of your enterprise and will to rise in the world. But some of us'— she hesitated, as if considering what term to use, not wishing to offend me— 'us so-called people of *society*— are not ready to accept persons, however worthy, from outside their ranks. I warn you my husband has some difficulty in so doing. I myself am aware that, in the past, the nobility and even our Royal family have been strengthened and renewed by marriages to men of the rising merchant class.'

She was right; I was aware, from my discussions of local history with Mr Nanskivell, that several of our County families had risen or been revivified in such a way: the Robartes of Lanhydrock, and the Treffrys of Fowey, to name but two instances. 'My own family, the Elsworthy's, made their fortune through lead mining in the Mendips, a century ago,' she went on. 'So I have some sympathy with those who better themselves. It is rather different with my husband, though; you see, the Devereauxs came over with the Conqueror, and have been here at Lodenek since the fifteenth century.'

I was considerably heartened to find such an ally in the great lady of the house, and said, 'Perhaps he will make an exception in Lucretia's case. I intend to be a husband worthy of her, and if he will accept a professional man...'

'He might, in time. We must give him time, James. And as to that, what profession do you contemplate joining?'

'I have been thinking about the law, ma'am.'

She was silent a moment or two, gazing out of the window. Hoof beats were heard in the drive; and turning I saw an open landau with a fairly bedraggled Squire and his son Robert in it, with several fishing rods projecting behind them, driven by a groom in a shining wet cape. 'Here he is,' Mrs Devereaux said. 'I'm not sure about the law, James. Not such a respectable profession, though in time you might become a Judge. My husband doesn't trust lawyers. Why not the Church? I understand you're a good Anglican, like the rest of your family, and you sing in the choir.'

I smiled to myself, never having thought that such qualifications fitted me for entry into Holy Orders. Privately I was still quite sure that I could never become a parson without receiving a genuine call. Aloud, I said, 'I have considered it, ma'am.'

'Then perhaps that would be the best thing; tell him you're ...considering it.'

Conversation languished then in expectation of the Squire's appearance. Mrs. Devereaux seemed to go into a reverie, her eyes still gazing out of the window, but not at the scene beyond it. Then I heard Lucretia's voice outside, entreating the Major.

'But Father, you did promise me you would talk to him.'

'Did I? Did I?' the Squire's voice was petulant. 'That was before I set out on this damn fool angling expedition. All Robert's idea— hardly a trout rising, no flies out— now I'm wet, confoundedly miserable, and hungry into the bargain...'

Please God, I thought, let it be some other time, if I must meet him. The Squire had a reputation for a hasty temper and for ill-judged decisions.

'I'll go to him. Please— wait here,' Mrs Devereaux said.

'Don't you think, ma'am, that another time might be best?'

'Perhaps. But if you could just wait ten minutes or so...' She indicated the bookshelves. 'Do look at anything that interests you, and help yourself to the port.'

There was a modest fire burning in the grate. As I was not going to be dismissed, and must obviously face the Squire if he could be prevailed upon to see me, I might as well make the most of the situation. Seated there before the flickering logs, a glass of rich port at my side and a volume of Marlowe's plays in my hand, I began to see myself as a country vicar in his study, writing my sermons, and composing poetry, which I would later read to Lucretia for approval and criticism. Those ten minutes stretched to twenty; I had read several scenes from *Tamburlaine the Great*, and begun to wonder if I had been forgotten by everyone, when the doors opened and Lucretia came in. She moved with her hobbling gait quickly to my side as I rose. 'James, he says he'll see you... he's changing into dry clothes... My darling, you will see this through, won't you, for my sake... He's all bark and very little bite, he usually gives into anything I want... Oh James!' And she was in my arms, kissing me, breathing in an agitation I had never seen upon her before.

I had not time to remark on this, however. Outside I heard, 'All right, Cissy, very well, let's get it over with. You know I can't stand these upstarts. People who don't seem to know their station in life.'

'Cissy' was Cecilia, Mrs Devereaux. I started at the word 'upstart', but the port glowed benignly in my chest and stomach, and I felt a confident amusement at the Major's pejorative tone. A humorous tolerance, I saw, was the best, indeed the only effective answer, to such insults from one's so-called superiors.

Dressed now in his dark green evening coat and fortified by a large glass of brandy, he entered the room staring at me critically, even offensively: a stout sandy haired red-faced man wearing a small peruke, his Devereaux nose scored with purple veins and a small wart on the left nostril, his jaws working as though he were biting on something very unpleasant indeed; and stood there a full ten seconds. 'H'rrmph,' he said and nodded to himself. 'Ahaw.' This sound, resembling a clearing of the throat, was an habitual one with him, by which he could express approval, disapproval, or criticism of whomsoever he was talking to.

'Father, this is James Spargo. Captain James Spargo,' said Lucretia.

'How de do,' Major Devereaux muttered, still glaring at me. His eye fell on the half-full decanter of port. I thought he might disapprove of my taking wine under his roof; but he said, 'Sit down, young man. Glass of port?'

'Thank you, sir, but I've already had some.'

'Got to learn to drink, y'know. And how to hold your drink, too,' he said, refilling the glass I set down. 'Better join you, I dessay. Beastly business, drinking alone. Haw.' *Blurt.* He broke wind quite loudly, as he bent over the decanter, but without blinking, handed me my glass. This, I was aware, was a habit which was apt to punctuate his conversation and activities, even sometimes in church.

'Father...' began Lucretia anxiously.

'Shush now, Crish. Don't want you interruptin'. Man's business, this. Better leave us, there's a good girl. Haw.'

Lucretia, for once, appeared helpless and perplexed. She looked from me to her father, then back again. 'Oh... very well,' she said, and limped out of the room.

'Your health,' muttered Major Devereaux holding up his glass and sipping deeply.

'And yours, sir,' I replied. We drank in silence for a space, then he said, sitting down opposite me with the smouldering fire between us, 'Fish at all, do you?'

'I've done a fair amount,' I admitted.

'What kind of fishin'?' *Blurt.*

'Bass from the rocks. Cod and hake from fishing smacks...mullet, round the Doom Bar; mackerel, of course... and salmon, once or twice.'

'Rod and line?'

'Net, sir.'

'H'rrmph!' Not, this implied, a gentleman's way of catching the most valuable fish in our river. 'Ought to know better... just as bad as all Lodenek men...not a sportsman among 'em. Haw.'

I hesitated to reply; he was, I saw, deliberately trying to provoke me. Yet something told me that if I did not defend my fellow townsmen he would despise me; so, quite deliberately, I rose to his bait.

'We can't actually be concerned with sport or fair play, Major Devereaux. Rather with helping to feed families with hungry mouths.'

He paused, finished his glass of port, eyed me narrowly; and then re-filled his glass. He held out the decanter to me, but I refused by shaking my head. 'Good point,' he said then, as if such a thought had never occurred to him in his life. 'Damn good point. Haw. Well now, my lad, if you come up river with Robert and me, up beyond Grogley Woods— y'know, it's no good this side of Grogley, water's ruined with mining waste— we'll show you how to catch trout with flies. Now there's an art and science for you. Whole books been written about that. I've even read one or two.' He paused, thinking. 'They tell me you want to go up to Oxford. Why?'

'To better myself. To enter a profession, sir, if I can.'

'What profession?' *Blurt.*

I spoke slowly and carefully, remembering what Mrs Devereaux had said. 'I haven't yet properly decided... I shall have a year or so in which to make up my mind. I might well read Divinity, to become a parson. Or perhaps read the Classical Tripos, to become a Fellow. I want to write books of some sort. To be an author.'

He stared at the fire, shaking his head. 'Haw. Never had authors in the family. Not unless you count old Dean

Henry...' He looked up at the darkened varnished portrait of one of his ancestors over the chimney breasts portrayed in a long eighteenth century wig and clerical bands. 'We've got his books of sermons and commentaries on the Old Testament here somewhere,'— he indicated the shelves of books behind him— 'though must say I've never read any of 'em. Quite famous in his day, they tell me.'

Silence. We sipped the port; I still had a few drops left in my glass. The evening closed in and the light faded out between the oaks and beeches beyond the library wall.

'Never saw much point in education, myself,' he said. 'Went to Eton, y'know; only thing I was good at was the Wall Game. Had couple of terms up at Balliol — learned to drink four bottles o' claret in an evening— Haw— did a bit of rowin'— bit o' wenchin'— then came home to the estate. Father ill. Well...'

I could see no comment I could, or should, make to this. He lapsed into silence again. The fire rustled and a half-charred log slipped, sending up ash and sparks in a little cloud.

'Trust our Crish to want to marry an author,' he said then. 'Tell you what, though, you're a plucky one to take her on. She's a stiff proposition. Haw. Shouldn't want to try it m'self.'

'Lucretia and I are very close. We know each other's minds.'

'I hope you do, young sir. She's too clever for me. I could never have married such a gel. Haw.'

'Strange.' I was emboldened by the port, no doubt, or I never should have said then, 'I was thinking how much like her mother she is. Fine, noble, full of consideration— with a wide grasp of sympathies. You married such a girl, sir.'

He put his glass down and stared at me, a small vein pulsing on that inflamed curving nose. 'I did, you say? Did I now! Haw. Well, damme, I suppose I did. Wonderful woman, my wife. Knows how to get her way, too, I must say. Well... women, you know... necessary evils, eh? Life can't go on without 'em; more's the pity.' *Blurt*— loud and prolonged.

I again decided that no reply at all would be suitable here. He took the decanter and poured for himself the last glass. Then jerking his head at me, as if suddenly having remembered the most important thing of all, he almost barked, 'Understand you work for Rowlands, eh?'

But I had anticipated this. 'Mr Rowlands, sir, is not my employer any more. I trade on my own account now, and merely charter my ship, the St. Malo, from him.'

He stared at me, the vein on his nose pulsing alarmingly as if it might at any moment burst; then he seemed to relax. 'Haw. That so, eh? Well... glad to hear it. What're you tradin' in?'

'Whatever needs to be brought into Lodenek.'

'Doin' much free-trade now?'

I wondered how much he knew, though I thought it likely that Lucretia had told him something of my activities.

'A little, here and there. Rather more difficult these days, you know. It needs very careful planning and arrangements.'

'Haw. Good old days gone now, eh? Well, wish you luck, m'lad. You're a cool one.' There was a certain gleam of approval in his eyes now, mellowed by the wine.

We talked on for another five minutes, until a gong sounded somewhere in the depths of the house, and the door opened: an aged butler with a reedy voice said, 'Supper is served, sir.'

'Haw. Capital. I'm starvin'. Gives you a damn keen appetite, fishin' y'know, whether you catch anythin' or not.' We both rose. 'Well, James Spargo, been most interestin' chattin' with you. I must say I respect your views. Come back and see me in a few days time, eh? Need a little while to think this over.' *Blurt.* 'Ferris, show Captain Spargo out, will you.'

'Thank you, sir. I'll call on you after my next voyage, beginning tomorrow.' As I was conducted along the corridor and into the hall an urgent voice whispered, 'James!' Lucretia was at my side. 'What did he say?' She put her hand on my arm, searching my eyes for the answer she wanted.

'He's considering it. I'm to see him again when I return from this next trip.'

'Good! If he hasn't refused, I think we'll be all right. Mother and I will persuade him. How long will you be away?'

'Four or five days, I should say.'

'My dear love.' The butler, waiting now across the hall, inhibited her from embracing me. 'For you,' she said, holding out a paper. 'A copy of my poem. Take it with you. Read it every day.'

CHAPTER 28

THE FINAL RUN

On May 20, having received orders worth some six hundred pounds from George Pearn at Crackington, we sailed in the St Malo on a fair north-easterly, ostensibly for Wexford but in reality for Brest; where, arriving two days later, we took on a cargo of two hundred ankers of rum, three hundred and fifty of brandy, ten bales of tobacco in the leaf, thirty sacks of brown sugar, twenty of salt, twenty pieces of fine calico and twelve of silk taffeta, a quantity of fine Breton lace, and twenty-four boxes of East India spices. The duty on salt at fifteen shillings per bushel was still grievously high, despite the efforts of Cornish Members of Parliament led by Sir William Lemon to get it reduced; although within two years it was to be lowered, and four years afterwards abolished altogether.

There were no thoughts in my mind, as we set sail for the return voyage, that this would actually be my last free-trading run. True, according to my calculations and the latest report I had had of my savings mounting up in the Lodenek Bank (Mr Rowlands having deducted his share of the proceeds of my trading), I now had sufficient funds to pursue my aim of going to Oxford: something very near four hundred pounds would stand to my credit if this particular voyage paid off as others had done during the preceding autumn and winter. However, I saw no reason to call a halt yet; the schemes I had devised were working on the whole very well; and another run was being arranged to supply our Trebarwith and Bodmin district customers in three weeks' time. But, as events proved, that venture was never to be undertaken.

My youngest brother Daniel, now aged thirteen, had persuaded me to take him on board as a foretopman. Like Reuben and myself before him, he was now chief Monitor at the National School, and Mr Nanskivell's right-hand man; especially latterly, when the poor distracted Master, worried about his desperately ill wife, could hardly concentrate on what lessons he was giving. So much in fact devolved upon Daniel, that he, rather than Nanskivell himself, had been the teacher for the previous two months. Quiet and assured, he oversaw all preparations, instructed the younger Monitors in their lessons early in the morning, and, during the afternoons when the Master himself was frequently absent, read poetry and history to the class, and organized drawing lessons and nature studies. My father afterwards always said that Daniel had the best brain in our family, and should have gone far. He was tall for his age, with more than a touch of my mother's red hair; he was certainly more handsome than I myself had been at thirteen, a veritable young Apollo much admired by the girls and young women of Lodenek; though he had not reached the point at which their attentions drew from him any great response. Seafaring was his whole ambition and desire; again I saw myself in him, as he pleaded to be taken along for the run. My mother resolutely opposed his going. Always conscious of the dreaded possibility of losing her sons at sea— she was unhappy at having us all away on voyages at the same time: and, my father and Reuben both being on the high seas, having shipped away the previous week, she got herself into a state of wretched anxiety as soon as she heard me tell Daniel he could come.

'I'll only be away a few days, Mother,' Daniel said, putting his arm around her as she stared miserably from him to me and back again.

'I'll see he comes to no harm,' I said. 'He's very handy about the ship and knows the rigging. And if he's going to sea for his livelihood, now is the time to learn all he can.'

Her chief terror, it appeared, was his falling from the crow's nest or a stay: which seems strange to me now, since she had never evinced any such fear on behalf of Reuben or myself.

'Well, I can't tie him to my apron strings, I suppose,' she said at last, wiping her tears away, but clinging to Daniel the more; he thought it amusing, and tried to joke with her.

'I'll be back soon enough, like the bad penny turning up, Mother.'

'Oh Daniel— you simply don't know how I feel... 'tis God's will, I suppose, whatever happens,' she said finally releasing him. 'We're all in His hands, to save or take as he wills.' She had never been overtly religious, and this utterance struck home to me, for a second or two stirring my own anxieties. All I could say was, 'There are people dying around us from disease and accidents all the time. There's no more danger on the sea, if you are a good mariner.' I thought of poor Mrs Nanskivell, now dead— she had passed away that night on which our Literary Circle had met, a merciful release, but still a great sorrow to us all. I thought of little children being buried every week, dying of cholera, typhus, or consumption. I thought of various cruel accidents that happened from time to time: people being thrown out of shays or gigs and killed or maimed, being trampled by runaway horses; falling from the cliffs gathering eggs or samphire; falling into the holds of ships, like poor Sammy Littlejohn who a month previously had broken his neck whilst loading a barque at Lodenek quayside. And the continual accidents in the mines, with men buried under falls of rock, or being drowned by flooding, losing their holds on ladders at the ends of weary cores, or failing from cliff-faces in our own district.

So Daniel came, and I was pleased by his sober and grown-up demeanour, his keen application to his duties; though he was always a cheerful and merry lad, ready for a laugh and full of odd quips and sayings. He was tremendously popular with the crew; Enoch Penberthy had a particularly soft spot for him, and was sure he would in time become Mate and Master, like his father and brothers.

I recall in vivid detail the conversation I had with Daniel as we sped back towards the Scillies on our return, a spanking north-east gale driving us hard towards the Isles; I was relying on the wind changing as we neared them, for I could see a difficult haul northward to come around west of the Bishop Rock to begin our course up the North Cornish coast to Crackington. It was about ten in the evening; Daniel was off duty, but instead of going below he came to the bridge, as he loved to, watching everything I did with acute interest, asking questions whenever he thought I would not be distracted from my watch. We were proceeding by dead reckoning, but the clouds would now and then part briefly and I gave him his first lesson in reading the sextant.

'Tis plain to see you'll want your own command one day like the rest of us, Dan,' I said. 'But 'twould please our mother far better, you know, if you'd study for another and safer career.'

'All very fine for you to say that, Jim. You always wanted to go to sea as much as I did, and you've done it all right.'

'Yes, but I can see the dangers of it now— one doesn't at your age, you see. Anyway I'm thinking of giving it up soon, if my plans work out.'

'Can't really see you as some lawyer or government secretary,' he said, as the clouds flew past us and the St Malo dipped into troughs between heavy waves, sending showers of foam over our bows. 'You'd be always itching to get back to this sort of life, wouldn't you?'

'Maybe. But something drives me on to other things.'

'You mean you're in love.'

I glanced at him, a youngster new to the great conceptions of life and its deeper purposes, seeing only the immediate attractions and goals of youth, and passionately wanting those alone.

'You'll be in love yourself before long. But that's not all— there's much more to a man's life than seafaring and making love, if he has a mind of his own and some ambition.'

He studied the compass on the binnacle, checking our course, which I had set at north-west by north. 'I suppose I shall find a nice girl and marry her,' he said, 'all in good time. But I can't see much wrong with a home and children in Lodenek, like Father has, and a good command and interesting ports to sail to. I don't think I shall ever look to become a gentleman like you, Jim.' This greatly impressed me; it was as if in his innocent way he was criticising me for trying to rise above my appointed station in life. His words brought back to me what Father had said on our long talk that day regarding my hopes and marriage to Lucretia. It was difficult, I saw, for them to realise what opportunities there were to grasp, if one went about things the right way.

'A gentleman? I wonder if I shall ever be accounted that,' I said. 'The gentry would say one has to be born a gentleman. Though I see it quite differently, Dan: you or I or any other with some intelligence and application to study, or enough money, could turn ourselves into one. Under their veneer and manners and high living they all have the same desires and appetites and feelings as we have. Mrs Devereaux was only saying to me the other day that her family were merely successful merchants a few generations back. Now they're accepted as gentry. The Rowlands family are doing the same thing in Lodenek, though rising rather faster than the old county families approve of.'

Daniel thought about this for a moment or two; I could see new and revolutionary ideas invading his mind. Then he said, 'You mean that all these grand people aren't really our betters at all?'

'Not quite, Dan. I mean that we can be as good as them— in God's eyes at least— if we work to improve ourselves and live a good moral life. They are born to great advantages, which they don't always use for the best. In my view they could do much more to help those less fortunate than themselves. If I achieve a place in their society I hope I shall, by example and precept, be a good influence on them.'

I thought of Squire Devereaux, living it seemed only for his hunting and fishing, disapproving of Lodenek men for netting salmon; and of his father, old Sir Robert, who had had the blackberry bushes in his fields tarred so that our poor people should not pick the fruit there and disturb his pheasants. I thought of the vicious man-traps which so many landowners set in their woods to maim poachers, and of the laws which could hang or transport to the colonies those starving persons who stole sheep or loaves of bread; of the infamous Corn Law which kept the price of bread artificially high even in times of recession. I thought of the interminable burden of Excise duties imposed upon the poor. It seemed to me there was a great deal to do to convince the gentry that their immense privileges should he used to help the lower classes on whom they depended for their wealth and well-being. I was sure that Lucretia, with her acute perceptions and sympathies, would agree with me in this.

From that conversation with my young brother, who was seeing, as I was, these weighty questions and problems for the first time, began my quest for moral and political improvements, fuelled by a rising wave of moral indignation, which was later to change my life entirely. But first there occurred a catastrophe which cast unforeseen doubts over my career and dearest hopes, causing me to re-examine in the greatest depth and detail my intentions and ambitions.

Twenty-six hours later, just before midnight, after beating up the Atlantic between Cornwall and Ireland, we arrived off Crackington. In the weak light of a waning quarter-moon, through my telescope I could just distinguish the humped shape and sharp nose of Cambeak, the headland bounding the western side of the Haven. The tide was on the flow, and our arrangement was to land the cargo about two hours after midnight. There was a moderate and growing swell which faintly worried me, though I said nothing to Enoch, whose watch it was. We hauled in sail and rode there quietly for an hour or more; I knew the landers would be there watching us, and hoped that no Revenue men also had us in view. Light clouds drifted across the moon, which set just after one a.m; when I gave orders for the mizzen and gaff sails to be set, and we moved silently nearer the coast on a light due north breeze. Somewhere near Bray Rocks I whistled to Daniel, who was up in the crow's-nest, to give the signal. His three flashes were immediately answered by a spotsman upon Cambeak, which was now on our starboard, indicating all was well. Striking the gaff and loosening the mizzen we moved across to the eastern side of the Haven, under Pencannow Point which towered above us, a sheer black mass delineated only occasionally by starlight along its apex. Lines of small flickering lights appeared as we expected, along the frozen violence of the broken rocks, guiding us in along the deep-water channel towards the cliff-face where great iron rings, driven into the rock, would secure us. A few minutes later a voice hissed, 'Throw out your painter,' and our bowsman, standing ready, hurled the mooring rope in the direction of the voice. Gang planks were put out, and the landing began, relays of men appearing out of the dense gloom and forming a human chain; soon they were passing keg after keg, anker after anker, down the line to a clear space on the sand where the goods were loaded on to trains of waiting mules and donkeys.

This, however, had not been proceeding for more than fifteen minutes, when a beacon suddenly blazed forth on the cliff-top at Pencannow, immediately above us. At the same time two Riding Officers on horses and a party of Revenue men appeared at the end of the lane where it met the beach, with flintlocks primed. The landers ceased their activities, surprised by the glare of the beacon: they themselves always maintained a small amount of kindling and gorse branches on Pencannow to warn any ship in danger of going on the rocks, and also as a signal to any free-trader such as myself that it was unsafe to land The coastguards, knowing this, had cleverly utilised the store of brushwood and, dousing it with train oil, had produced a mighty though short-lived conflagration illuminating the whole of the beach and Haven below.

Shots now rang out, the balls flying over our heads, and a voice bellowed, 'In the name of the King, I confiscate those goods: stand where you are and be recognised!' This challenge had the opposite effect upon the landers, who were some forty strong. Those on the beach disappeared behind the mules and donkeys, and took cover behind the rocks; those by the ship scrambled off across the sharp rocks and deep gulleys with whatever contraband they were handling, intent on concealing the kegs and bales in any cave or pool or fissure they could find; and knowing every inch of the shore, they were not long about this. Meanwhile several of them, after muttering among themselves, produced pistols and a musket or two and sent shots back at the Revenue party. Firing now came from the Coastguards on the cliff, their missiles splashing in the water beside the St Malo, and a couple striking the deck where I stood supervising the discharge of cargo. I heard one of the landers say, 'George Pearn— where's George?'— as if he expected Pearn to take charge in this emergency. But George Pearn was nowhere to be seen.

'Run the guns out to starboard,' I called, not too loudly; 'Enoch, put out the larboard longboat. Somebody fetch me an axe.' There was a bare possibility, I thought, that if we cut the St Malo's moorings and towed her out into the bay amid the fracas, we might escape, despite the strengthening wind and the swell.

The Revenue party were now advancing across the beach; the pack animals, disturbed by the firing, were now braying and running amok, which deterred the officers for some while. Two of our carriage guns were now ready; I had no intention of firing on the Excisemen themselves, and gave instructions to aim high above them. 'Fire! Fire!' I yelled, and attacked the hawser where it stretched over the gunwhale; with three axe strokes it parted. Our two balls boomed across the beach, causing more confusion and uproar among the thirty or forty animals, which were now bolting across the sand and rocks to escape up the lane. I heard a loud splash behind me; the longboat was in the water. Enoch Penberthy, his eyes dancing and a grin of pleasure at the excitement on this face, threw out a rope ladder and was the first down it himself, the wind and swell driving the small craft up under the stern of the St Malo. Others followed him down into the boat. The landing party were now scattering across the rocks towards Cambeak, firing indiscriminate shots at the Revenue men as they went; in the waning light of the beacon I saw a Searcher fall, and others kneel to tend him. Our guns spoke again: I saw the Revenue party split into three groups, one working around under Pencannow to come at us from the north, our portside; one creeping forward to the west, along towards Bray Rocks, and the other cautiously advancing in the centre. I went aft to see how the longboat was faring, and witnessed in the fitful light of the dying beacon a sight that remains engraved on my memory today, and which haunts and disturbs my dreams even now.

The longboat was almost full with nine men, including Daniel; the tenth, my old friend and mentor Tom Permewan, was descending the rope ladder. At sixty-four, Tom had failed somewhat, but was determined to take part in whatever action and excitement offered itself as a relief to his cook's duties; and he prided himself on being a good oarsman. Now he lost his footing on the last rung of the ladder, but being near enough as he supposed to the gunwhale of the longboat, let go the rope; he got one foot onto the gunwhale, but the swell suddenly buoying up the boat, knocked him back against the hull of the St Malo, and with a brief cry he disappeared into the water between the two vessels. 'Push her clear!' I heard Enoch shout from the stern sheets; the longboat was pushed off by several oars. Tom's head appeared, several yards away from the boat; he threw up a hand as if seeking help gave a choking gasp and disappeared again. I saw Daniel poised on the bow of the longboat, stripping off his seaman's jacket; and saw him dive into the depths of the black water.

For his age he was a strong swimmer, and liked nothing better than to breast the waves. After what seemed an interminable age, though it could have lasted only ten or fifteen seconds, we saw him come up with Tom in his arms. The longboat was a mere ten yards away; but ten yards might have been a mile in that icy water (as cold in May as it ever is), and Enoch's commands to row two strokes got them to that spot only to see them both disappear. 'Daniel!' I heard myself shout, my voice tearing the air with its frenzy; I was divesting myself of boots and jacket, and, with hardly a thought for what I was actually doing, was climbing down the rope ladder; then I was in the water myself, swimming hard for the longboat and the place I had seen my brother and Tom surface.

Before I got there Davy Bligh had also dived in, and had come up with Tom, more dead than alive; the longboat crew were hauling them on hoard. I was no great swimmer myself, and by the time I reached the longboat needed to rest and recoup my strength; two crewmen and Davy and myself then went down into the pitch dark waters about twelve feet deep, encountering the broken jagged edges of the rock formations running out along the shore. On my third dive, well-nigh exhausted myself, I touched a soft inert form, and groped a pair of legs and tugged, but the body would not move, apparently being caught and trapped by something. I let go, rose to the surface, and shouted, 'I've found him: can't move him!' Davy came over and dived with me; the two of us found Daniel again, more by touch than by sight, for in that deep gloom, among a forest of waving bladderwrack, one could distinguish almost nothing: the only dim light was reflected from the grey shelves of rock and their patina of pinkish corallina below low water mark. Standing on the rock we groped round that silent lifeless form, and found his head jammed into a deep fissure. My worst nightmares, across all these years, have been of trying to prise him free; dreams which seem to go on and on with my tortured desperation increasing, until I wake up sweating and screaming.

But get him free we did, doing some inevitable damage to his face and skull; and broke the surface with him in my arms, my lungs almost bursting, in time to see a Revenue cutter appear off the Haven, rounding Cambeak and heaving to some way off.

All thoughts of escape, however, were now submerged in my grief for Daniel. 1 knew he was dead, that there could be no hope that any spark of life still lingered in him; yet in such circumstances hope struggles with reason, and I could not be utterly convinced until we had got him on board the longboat and examined him properly. No pulse, no suspicion of a heartbeat: even then I persisted in trying to pump the water out of his lungs in a forlorn attempt. Tom Permewan, it transpired had been saved, but only after a fashion; they had done what they could, laying him across the thwart on his belly and pressing his back, so that the water he had breathed in was expelled, and he recovered consciousness; yet, having been minutes under water and in effect drowned, he was never the same again. His brain had been turned, as we used to say, by that awful experience; for the rest of his life he was to sit at home in his chair by the fire, a vacant look on his face, uttering only incomprehensible monosyllables, having to be fed and washed and attended to by his wife and daughters.

But Daniel— how those terrible moments of vain hope and gibbering fear return to me, in my waking and sleeping moments, whenever I am reminded of him!— Daniel was dead. Never should I take him fishing again, or instruct him in navigation and seamanship. Never would he come smiling and joking, delighting us all with his youthful love of life. Truly the best are taken early— they are too good, some say, for this evil world— and our only consolation is to submit to God's will. But always, lurking like a serpent at the back of my mind is the guilty sense that I was at least partly responsible for his death. If I had only listened to Mother's impassioned plea not to take him along— if I had but recognised that her intuitions were right, that danger and doom lay in wait for him! From that very moment we laid him down in the longboat, a dead form with battered head and face, and his young godlike looks torn and destroyed, I began to question and repent of my involvement with free-trading. Not only Daniel and Tom, but at least one Excise man was affected (later we learned he died, of a ball received in the chest, leaving a widow and six children). And now coming home to me with a fresh horror, was the sorrow and grief that was to be visited upon my mother and father, my sisters and Reuben also. The price I was to pay for my enterprises was, all too suddenly, it was revealed, far too high.

And as the Revenue men took the St Malo, and shouted to us to come ashore and give ourselves up, I could see staring at me the ruin of all I had worked for, all my schemes and desires.

CHAPTER 29

THE RECKONING

As Venturer and Captain of the vessel apprehended in the act of bringing undutied goods ashore, I stood accused as the main offender. I made no attempt to escape; there was little point in doing so, for they would have traced me easily enough, and short of fleeing to Brittany or America and so abandoning all my plans and ambitions, there was no prospect of evading prosecution. My runs were over; prison no doubt awaited me, and I could only hope that something could be salvaged from the wreck of my fortunes in order to start again.

But I own I had no heart for the struggle. The death of my brother now seemed to me a divine retribution for my illegal enterprises. How could I have hoped to avoid dire danger to myself and others in such circumstances? I cursed my aspirations, all my attempts to improve myself, even the luck I had until now, which had lulled me into a sense that I bore a charmed life. I stopped short of cursing dear Lucretia, though I could not help but recognize that if I had not met her and come to love her so deeply, I should not be in this trapped and tragic situation.

I was taken, in handcuffs, on horseback to Bude, where I was lodged in a tiny cell for the night next to the Custom House. The Revenue party were cock-a-hoop at their capture, for despite the secrecy of our operations my notoriety had grown and I had become a sort of folk-hero, a Robin Hood, among the people of North

Cornwall. So much so that a reward of five hundred pounds had been offered by the Revenue for information leading to my arrest or the apprehension of my vessel. Most of the cargo had been seized, though the landing party had managed to conceal some ten ankers of rum and perhaps fifteen of brandy, plus some packages of the silk, in caches along the seashore; and about a dozen of the mules and donkeys had run back to the farms, carrying kegs which had been rapidly concealed. The crew of the St Malo dispersed, taking the body of Daniel home to Lodenek by carrier. The ship herself was towed by the Revenue cutter to Bude, where she lay, an object of great curiosity and a warning to all, until my trial was held.

The absence of George Pearn at the scene of the landing was explained when it was known that the reward for laying information had been claimed. Naturally, the Customs authorities would not divulge who had claimed it; but as Pearn disappeared from the district, going, it was said, to Canada, the conclusion was obvious to all. He was in fact away for seven years; only when his father lay dying he returned, a man without friends and associates. A year or so afterwards he built a row of four cottages in the parish, which he let out to men working the nearby slate quarries; but the memories of Cornish folk are long, and he was never again accepted as one of the local community. His treachery became immortalized in the nickname which locals gave his cottages— 'St Malo Row.'

After a brief examination by the local magistrates the next day, I was sent for trial at the Assizes. From Bude I was taken in a coach and four, guarded by two

Revenue men, to Bodmin Gaol. The Customs Collector would have a month or so to prepare his case, and would need that time, because this was no petty lawsuit; and well-knowing the propensity of local juries to give those accused of smuggling the benefit of the doubt, he was determined to present as much damning evidence as possible. So I lodged in the new prison, which had been built some thirty years before. Until then the infamous gaol at Launceston had housed most of Cornwall's important miscreants, but its terrible conditions becoming too much for even the heartless administrators of the time, and its remoteness from West Cornwall being inconvenient, the more central Bodmin gaol had been built to supplement it. Yet, such were the difficulties and deprivations of the age, forcing poor persons to resort to petty crimes and worse, that it was already overcrowded: built to house a hundred prisoners, male, female and debtors, it now contained scores in excess of that number.

I was housed in a cell with four others: a fourteen year old lad from Illogan, who had broken into his employer's house and stolen some silk handkerchiefs; a farm hand from St.Mabyn, caught poaching rabbits on the local squire's estate; a cooper from Mevagissey, who had wounded his wife and her lover, attacking them with a knife; and a seventy year old vagabond, who had begged from parish to parish for many years, who had succumbed to extreme hunger one night and stolen some turnips from a farmer's field. They would all, like myself, be tried at the Summer Assizes in Bodmin, due in five weeks time.

I had enquired of the Bude magistrates of the possibility of obtaining bail; but that was, as I had feared, a forlorn hope; it was granted in the sum of one thousand pounds, an impossibility apart from the remote chance that Mr Rowlands, or perhaps Squire Devereaux could be persuaded to deposit such a sum. And I was in no mood even to ask for their help; my increasing guilt over Daniel's demise and that of the Revenue man now drove me to accept it as natural or divine justice that I should suffer those weeks of imprisonment upon remand as part of my well-earned punishment. What else would follow I could only speculate; I fell into a dull and depressed condition of mind, utterly desponding of myself and what seemed the futility of my endeavours over the past two or three years, so that I was prepared to accept whatever sentence was to be meted out to me, whether it meant long imprisonment, transportation to Botany Bay, or even hanging; though as far as I was aware no one yet had been hanged for the act of smuggling. I thought in my despair, however, that the death of the Searcher on the rocks at Crackington might be construed as murder, and that I could be held responsible for that crime as well.

I was to some extent distracted from these fears by a visit from my father, who arrived two days later. I was taken out of that crowded malodorous cell and taken to a yard on the western side of the Gaol, beneath the thirty feet high cliff-like walls built of solid rock, where we were able to talk alone. My father had paid for this privacy, which under the emotional circumstances was most welcome. On seeing me he clasped me to him, a thing he had hardly done since I was a very small child, for he was not normally demonstrative. 'Ah, James, James, my son— what a pass things have come to!'

I all but burst into tears at this. We clung together

for a long minute, mutely comforting each other, as though we were striving desperately to salvage somehow the wherewithal for a new life from the wreck of my old one. Then, releasing me, he regained his customary self-control.

'And how are you, my boy? How are they treating you?'

'As well as I deserve, I think, Father.'

'Deserve? Who is to say what you deserve? Only the Lord himself, I say. But you are fed well enough?'

'I can eat most of what is brought to me.' The food we received was adequate, plain though unappetising.

'I've brought some things for you— two of your mother's big mutton pasties— she insisted on making them for you— and a saffron cake of Emma's. You hear such terrible reports of prison food.' He had with him a basket covered with a cloth, which he had placed on the ground. 'They all send their love; you must keep in good heart— your family won't desert you, whatever happens.'

'I know. Thank them all for me, won't you... How is Mother?'

'Grieving badly, but I think she'll mend. At first of course she was utterly distraught, but after a day or so she calmed down and now says it was God's will, and that she knew all along it would happen to one of us one day. She is a brave woman, James; you must know what fears and anxieties she has undergone on all our behalves over these years. But she loved Daniel, he being the youngest, somehow more than all.'

'Yes. So did I. He had such a way with him— such innocent love of life...'

'Don't dwell on it, my son. And you mustn't blame yourself. How could you foresee such a thing? D'you know what I think? If it was to happen, it would have come about whatever we could do to prevent it. If he'd stayed at home he'd have met with some accident or fatal illness.'

In such circumstances, I saw, a deep fatalism is one of the best consolations. 'Perhaps you're right, Father. As they say, the Lord giveth, the Lord taketh away. I hope Daniel is rewarded with eternal bliss— he brought happiness into our lives.'

Father was silent a moment, gazing at the great walls about us and the rows of barred cell windows ranged along the inner side of the yard. We took a turn up and down, and he said, 'I have news which may add to you troubles, I fear. Mr Thomas Rowlands has been laid low with a stroke, and has been lying very ill at Sandry's Hill House these three days past. It seems doubtful whether he'll mend. Meanwhile there has been a run on Lodenek Bank, everyone wanting their money out; the Bank is now closed, and we're all waiting to see what will happen.'

'What does that mean, then— that he's in financial trouble?'

'It may be so, as too many fear. But panic, of course, due to ill founded rumours, can cause a crash. It happened to Vercoe's Bank at Truro twenty-odd years ago, when the Wheal Eliza mines failed. The trouble with Thomas's business empire is that it all depends on Thomas himself— no natural heir or successor, it seems to me. Young Ralph is now in London trying to raise a loan to see them through.'

I remembered what Mr Rowlands had said to me, implying that he would happily take me on as his protegé and successor. This challenge would give Ralph a chance to prove himself, perhaps. Then I remembered the agreement I had made with Thomas, and a cold fear descended on me for the credit I had accumulated at the Bank. I told my father of the arrangement, concluding, 'The St.Malo has been impounded— she'll surely suffer the same fate as other smuggling vessels. They'll take her apart and sell her off. And I shall owe Mr Rowlands over three hundred pounds, most of what I've earned— even supposing I can get the money.'

Father shook his head. 'Perhaps. We're all in the same boat. There's several hundred pounds of my own, and all Reuben has earned, in the bank. Well, it's in the lap of providence now, James. As for you, we must all pray for a sympathetic jury and a merciful Judge.'

'Does Mr Rowlands know of our capture? Or is he too ill to be told?'

'I'm not sure of that. When I get back I shall go to enquire. If he recovers perhaps he'll see me. No doubt you're thinking of asking some help from him.'

'He knows many persons in high places— remember he's been High Sheriff and deputy Lord Lieutenant.'

'Yes— and he always made a favourite of you. I'm sure he will do what he can, if he lives to do it.'

There was one thing on my mind of which we had not yet spoken. 'I haven't had any word from Devereaux Place. Is all well there? Do they know what has happened? I thought that Lucretia would have written to me, at least.'

Father looked solemn, and frowned a little. 'I'm sure they have heard— all Lodenek surely knows, and is talking of little else. I've heard that Miss Lucretia has not been well, but I don't know what ails her.'

'Perhaps you could find out? If you send a note to her for me; Susan Roberts will take it.'

'I'll do more than that, James. I will go to see her, or Squire Devereaux, myself, on your behalf. Goodness knows what garbled version of events they may have received.'

We parted soberly and full of dark thoughts for the future. 'Give them all my love at home,' I said. 'Especially Mother— tell her I'm well, and hope to escape the worst penalty. I don't know how I could face her now, though.'

'Your mother loves you, James. She will never hold this against you. For her, it is God's will, and she accepts it.'

Those words quietened my agonized self-accusations, and I too underwent the following weeks with something of that resigned acceptance of what must be. The other inmates of my cell viewed me with some suspicion at first, but I shared with them equally my pasties and the cake, and when they heard what I was accused of they regarded me as if I were royalty: they wanted to hear all my adventures and exploits, the St.Mabyn man especially, for he had heard of the now legendary young captain who had been supplying rich and poor along the north coast with contraband goods. I was in no mood, however, to act the hero, nor to recount my history; so I begged them to leave me alone for a few days to adjust to prison life. When, despite this, they would still comment and enquire, I told them of my bereavement, for which I blamed myself to a great extent, and they had the Christian grace to desist for a while.

Twice a week we had to scrub out our cell with soap and hot water, which kept the nauseating smell left by our slops to a more or less tolerable level. As remand prisoners there was no compulsion upon us to work, but we were invited to join in the activities of the prison, whereby we could earn a few pence a day. The prison Governor, who acted here as a Venturer, provided employment for the men: sawing up timber into planks and joists for the building trade, cutting and polishing gravestones from slate and granite slabs, weaving at the looms in a large workshop, and picking oakum for the Navy. The women prisoners in another part of the Gaol spun and carded wool, and made and repaired and laundered the clothes and bedding for the whole prison. The Governor bought in all materials, and profited from the sale of the finished articles. I decided that I must relieve my brooding and despondency by some activity, and tried my hand at picking oakum— of which I had already some experience, as a boy on the quayside at Lodenek. It is a matter of teasing out into long thin strands the ends and pieces of old rope which would be of no use for any other purpose, being half rotten: such strands would be tarred by seamen and rammed into crevices and joins when caulking their vessels. But picking oakum is tedious work, and each four-hour stint was enough for me, having filled a couple of sacks with the frayed out strands. This would be followed by exercise in one of the yards beneath those high forbidding walls; we could walk, run, indulge in our own exercises, or join in those organized by one of the turnkeys for the prisoners in the Bridewell, or house of correction for local persons committing small misdemeanours. The able-bodied were kept running up and down the yard for five minutes or so, then ordered to bend and stretch and swing their arms for another five minutes. This sort of thing was most beneficial after the oakum picking; but when I chose to saw up timber for four hours, a quiet walk was all the exercise I wanted afterwards.

Prisoners sentenced to hard labour were forced to work half-hourly shifts on the treadmill, followed by an hour of sawing. The treadmill, a newly installed device, was feared and hated, the talk of the prison, town and surrounding district. Holding a fixed bar above his head, the prisoner had to tread each step of the great revolving mill-wheel as it descended against him, at a rate of fifty steps to the minute. If he flagged, the next wooden step coming down struck him on the shins. After his spell even the strongest convict was well-nigh exhausted; often the weaker ones, having suffered injuries, had to be taken off it. Some men deliberately inflicted wounds on their legs in order to avoid the dreaded device. When I was in the Gaol a riot took place one day when a certain Luke Tregenza, a Truro man convicted of affray and assault on a constable, refused to work the treadmill; he and several other hard labourers broke up the wooden rail surrounding the mill and, arming themselves with pieces of it, kept the gaolers at bay for two hours or more. The Governor called in dragoons from Bodmin barracks, and, using the butts of their firearms, the soldiers forced the men to submit. The others were sent back to their cells;

Tregenza, ordered to ascend the mill again, refused; he was held down and flogged until he agreed to go on it again.

Occasionally, despite the high walls surrounding the Gaol, there were breakouts. One agile prisoner, a small man from Portloe used to climbing cliffs, actually scaled the wall at the back of the prison, where it was less high due to the hillside behind it, spent an evening at the Barley Sheaf inn enjoying the hospitality of those who were intrigued by his daring, then returned after midnight to his cell by the same route. So as not to be noticed he had gone without his prison coat of brown serge uniform with red stripes on it, wearing a sack round his shoulders as it threatened rain.

The prison chapel provided an experience I shall remember always with affection and wonder. Sunday was a day of rest for hard labourers and Bridewell alike, the only exercises taken being quiet perambulations in the yard. We attended morning and evening service in the chapel. The hymn singing, the intensely felt praying and emotional exhortations of the prison chaplain, an evangelical cleric who had been greatly influenced by Messrs Wesley and Whitfield, gave us all an immense relief of pent-up feeling, an escape of fervour which at first surprised and shocked me. Used as I was to the well-ordered services in the church at Lodenek, with our restrained choir directed by Mr Tremayne and the hour-long closely-reasoned High Church sermons of the Reverend William Rowlands, I could not at first enter into the abandoned spirit of this worship. I soon began to see, however, what the appeal of Methodism and Bible Christianity really was: an opportunity for the poor to obtain release from the squalours and drudgery of their lives, into a world of spiritual hope and promise of celestial joy. Although looked upon with suspicion by the repressive government and squirearchy of the day, who still feared a Revolution as had happened in France, and thought of themselves as sitting on a boiling cauldron of rebellion, it did in fact give the lower classes a huge compensation for their lot; if only the Church and aristocracy could have seen it, this was a safeguard against chaos and turmoil. I think it is not too much to say that John Wesley and the preachers who followed him saved Great Britain from the terrors of revolution, though in so doing they prolonged the misery and deprivations of working men and their families for several decades.

But in the prison chapel I was caught up in a tremendous surge of uninhibited song glorifying Jesus, fervent prayers that we should endure our punishments as our Saviour had borne his Cross and died on it, that in another world soon we should be united in His love for ever. I was able to pour out all my guilt and sorrow, and make promise of atonement. I would live a pure new life from henceforth, accepting gladly whatever sentence was to be given to me, and would work for His Kingdom on earth, spreading the love and forgiveness he taught us.

'Rock of ages, cleft for me,
Let me hide myself in Thee:
Let the Water and the Blood
From thy riven side which flowed,
Be of sin the double cure,
Cleanse me from its guilt and power.'

Each time I hear that hymn of Isaac Watts' I see before me the prisoners in the chapel at Bodmin Gaol singing it with such passion, hearing the high excited voices of the women in their screened-off section, the bass moans of the men in theirs, and tears come to my eyes.

Looking back now I see that experience as a great turning point in my life. The chaplain, Reverend Leonard Jarvis Boon, was an earnest young man who lived as fully a Christian life as ever I saw a man do, applying every principle gleaned from the New Testament to his daily life. He saw to it that the poorest inmates were fed properly, and, if they were ill, received medical attention. He visited our cells and prayed with us, forwarding any complaints we had about our treatment if it were too severe. In him a light shone, the joy of knowing he was doing his Saviour's work, and I saw that he wanted every man and woman there to be brought into a state of Grace.

Leonard and I had several serious and intense discussions, during which I posed him the question of whether what I had done, in my free-trading career, was truly wrong in God's eyes— especially as in conducting such a career I had surely helped to relieve the lot of my poorer customers by avoiding onerous and, in my opinion, immoral duties on some of the necessary goods of life. He thought long and hard at this, and said that he was sure I was at heart a good and conscientious young man, but had been led astray by circumstances. He would think the matter over and come to me. Which he did two or three days later.

'There are undoubtedly unjust laws,' he said, 'which in time we must hope and pray will be repealed.

Indeed there are many humane and mercifully minded men in Parliament who have been trying for years to change them. I trust that they will soon prevail. Meanwhile I am sure that God himself is merciful to the poor miscreants forced to steal in order to feed themselves and their starving families. Of course there is always Parish Relief, but I know how ashamed they often are to accept such degradation. As to your own case, the duties on many goods may be unjust, but your great offence is not in evading them, but in the manifold deceptions you have engaged in order to do so. Once you embrace the trade of bringing in uncustomed goods you must, perforce, lie and deceive when questioned. And, as you have seen, the situation leads to worse— to violence, at first in self-defence, but then to dangerous events — of which of course you are fully aware. So I can only counsel you to renounce such a life, and use your intelligence and undoubted gifts to improve your lot, and that of your fellow men, in other, legitimate ways.'

And we prayed together that I should find a new career untainted with such deceits and dangers. I believe it was mainly to the Reverend Boon that I owed my decision to study divinity and to become a parson— provided that, despite the reversal of my fortunes, I could still go to Oxford; or, if that were not possible, to join the Methodists and become a preacher, and like Mr Boon himself, find a vocation in succouring the outcast and despised. Whether Lucretia would approve of the latter was a question to which I did not then address myself; but I verily believe now that if it had come to that she would not have forsaken me.

My mother, at least, would support me in such an

endeavour, I felt sure; and indeed, when my father brought her to visit me a week or so later, and I told her of my inclinations (after an emotional reunion during which we both wept in joy and sorrow intermingled), she confirmed these thoughts. 'Ah, James, my own dear boy, 'twould give me the greatest pride and pleasure to see you take up such a career. Never mind about Oxford, if it isn't to be, the other course will be just as good and rewarding— though not in terms of stipend. I know you have the ability to help others and advise them. Isn't that so, Edward?'

I could see that my father was not so keen on such a course; he nodded but kept silent. 'I feel sure that all this is part of God's plan for me,' I said. 'Out of this time of trial will come my reward and penance; whatever it is.' George Uren, from St.Mabyn, was likely to be transported, unless the judge was merciful— an unlikely prospect in those repressive years. The Mevagissey man, John Holland, might have been accused of murder if his knife had found a vital artery. I felt we were all living under a black cloud through which the angel of death might soon descend.

So I was moved to hold prayers in our cell at evening, before we went to sleep on our hard wooden bunks with their straw mattresses; and the others, at first out of sheer respect for me, but increasingly because they saw that I was devout, joined in, and shut their eyes, and occasionally murmured 'Amen' or 'So be it Lord.' I would speak somewhat along these lines: 'O Lord (who knoweth the heart and soul of every poor sinner, and loveth him, despite all his dire deeds), mercifully hear our prayer tonight; for we know we have done wrong, though often because of desperate circumstances. We pray to Thee to give us strength to bear our sentences with fortitude and, if we be allowed to continue our lives here on earth, to live henceforth in diligence and honesty and love for our fellows. We ask this in the name of thy beloved Son, our Lord Jesus Christ, who came to save us from our sins for ever.'

These evening prayers grew into an informal service, for they were eager to talk about their situations and how they had been misled, or driven to perpetrate their crimes. And, since they asked me questions, which I answered as best I could, I became their counsellor and comforter. With Mr Boon's help (for I could not satisfy all their queries and perplexities from my own store of education and experience) I prepared them, I hope, to accept whatever would be their penance, and to turn to religion as their guide and touchstone thereafter.

And so we passed those weeks until the judges arrived at the end of June for the Summer Assize, the only one then conducted at Bodmin; and we were brought to trial.

CHAPTER 30

A LETTER

Devereaux Place,
30 V 1821

My Own Dearest Love,

Following the news of your being apprehended I wanted so desperately to see you at once, and would have ridden all the way myself to Bodmin; but I had succumbed to a heavy cold which then settled on my chest and produced a fever which raged for over a week. Dr Harley said it is severe bronchitis, and I am forbidden to go out although I am much better now, thank heaven; so you may imagine my delirium, in which I raved— so Sarah and Mother tell me— all day and night, believing myself to be on my mare Joanna, riding up and down endless gullies and over moors and cliff-tops, trying in my deranged mind to reach you at Bodmin, and never getting there. Oh my darling, I can't tell you how much I feel for you immured in that place, even though they say it is a good modern prison and quite unlike the dreadful hell Launceston Gaol has become. I know you will bear all with fortitude, and I am sure you will emerge from this ordeal with renewed determination to make a career for yourself despite all.

It is my fervent hope, and I think the saving grace of this situation, that though you may be convicted of illegal trading, no great stigma will attach itself to you hereafter, affecting your career. Dr Harley sees no obstacles to your continuing your studies at some future date, even if you should have to serve several years of imprisonment. And I shall be able to visit you, as will your family— so bear up, my dearest James, and when life in Gaol becomes too much for you, think of your loving Lucretia who in every single one of her waking hours thinks of you tenderly, and prays for a merciful outcome.

My father is very concerned and even distressed at what has happened. It surprises me to see how he takes it. I think you have impressed him far more than we thought. He promises me that as soon as I am well enough I may go up to Bodmin to see you. Indeed I am told that all the people of Lodenek, your friends and your family, even the Vicar, Mr Rowlands, are all anxious for your welfare.

If there is anything you need that we can provide you have only to ask. I am sending with this letter a little gift which will sustain you, when you have opportunity to read it. It is one of my most prized books, but you have need of it more than I just now. So treasure it, along with my love, my own dearest, and bring it back safely to me in time. Your Father has been here to see me and my parents, to tell us how things are with you behind those walls. So you see I can picture you there, doing your daily work, and trying to cheer up the other inmates of your cell.

I am sure you will be a help and consolation to those other unfortunate souls caught in the grip of our harsh laws.

I can write no more now, not being strong enough to address myself to putting words on paper, though my heart is full of emotions and reflections I should dearly wish to set down - they would make several whole books, I daresay, if I could do it. It is evening now, the sun is shining through the high trees beyond my window. I must sleep. Goodnight, and God bless you, my dear, my only love, the light of my life.

Your ever loving wife to be,

Lucretia.

The gift Lucretia sent me was a small leather bound volume of Robert Burns' poems. I have it here on my desk as I write; inside is inscribed 'To Lucretia, with much love on her birthday from her Mother. 6. VIII 1817'. I read it whenever I think of my dear wife; and there has never been another poet, save only Shakespeare, who in such pithy words and sentences put so many human situations before us, so that we recognise our own hopes, yearnings, failures and loves. Truly Burns speaks to all mankind everywhere. And I often read again those verses which sustained me so well when in Bodmin Gaol:

Till a' the seas gang dry, my Dear
  And the rocks melt wi' the sun;
And I will luve thee still, my Dear,
  While the sands o' Life shall run.

And fare thee weel, my only luve!
  And fare thee weel, awhile!
And I will come again, my luve,
  Tho 'twere ten thousand mile!

CHAPTER 31

TRIAL AND JUDGEMENT

The date of my trial was fixed for June 10th. A week before that I was visited in gaol by Mr Nathaniel Venning, a lawyer from Launceston, who had been commissioned by my father to defend me. We were conducted to a private room in the Governor's wing and allowed an hour for me to brief him. I had not anticipated having an attorney to defend me, being intent on acknowledging my guilt and accepting whatever judgement would be delivered upon me; and I wondered how on earth this gentleman's services would be paid for, in the light of what my father had told me about Mr Rowlands and the Lodenek Bank. I found out afterwards that Father had raised a fund for my defence, travelling with Reuben around the countryside, obtaining contributions from the wealthier gentry, parsons and farmers who had been my important clients and who had much benefited from my free-trading runs. Even Lucretia and Squire Devereaux had promised twenty pounds each towards the account. Mr Rowlands, who I am sure would gladly have donated towards it, had not been asked, since he still lay so ill.

Mr Venning was a heavy florid man of sixty, much addicted to taking snuff at every opportunity— as was witnessed by deep golden-brown stains down his long waistcoat, of the antiquated silk embroidered kind worn by gentry and professional men in the later eighteenth century. He wore a small grey peruke, which was powdered only now and then, and presented a shabby appearance; he evidently liked his port and brandy, for on each of the occasions he visited me, and when in Court also, he fairly reeked of those liquors.

'Now then, my dear zur,' he began, in a rich Westcountry brogue, with the kind of accent one finds in north-east Cornwall and west Devon, 'we must establish the facts as yew knaw them. Now Ah take it yew will be pleading not guilty?'

'No. I shall plead guilty.'

Mr Venning stared at me for what seemed minutes altogether. He then carefully removed the small round spectacles he had perched on the end of his nose, rubbed his pale blue eyes, blinked at me, and said, 'Do Ah yure yew rightly, Mr Spargo? Did Ah trewly yure yew say Guilty?'

'You heard me correctly. I intend to plead Guilty. In any case, how could I plead otherwise? I am the captain of the St Malo, which was taken with a cargo of contraband on board. Everyone knows it. I was arrested with the ship. That is the plain truth, Mr Venning, and I don't see how it can be avoided.'

Mr Venning sniffed, took out his snuffbox, opened it with great deliberation, and offered it to me. I declined. He took a couple of pinches and sniffed them up his wide, inflamed and hairy nostrils. Staring at me solemnly with those pale watery eyes he said, 'Trewth, yew say. Now Ah tell yew this, young zur, and tez somethin' we must get right in tew that there haid of yours yure and now. Ah'm a lawyer, and Ah'm not concerned with trewth, or findin' out the trewth, but awnly the justice. That's what Ah'm yure for, to git justice for yew, Mr

Spargo. Now ask yerself what's just— for yew to plead Guilty and go to gaol for three, mebbe five or six years; or even git yerself transported to Botany Bay, like Sam Ellison up to Brixham? He wus caught smugglin' awnly last year, and now he's on his way to New South Wales— or for yew to protest yer innocence and let me defend you as best we can. Ah knaw a few tricks, yew may depend; Ah bin practisin' in Lanson and Bodmin for upward o' forty year, and there's witnesses to yer good character, I can tell yew, waitin' to come and testify. And yew must realize, zur, that the jury will be on yer side tew a man— they dawn't like the Excise and the terrible evil duties they dew put on us people. I dearsay even the Judge'll be sympathetic in his awn heart, though he's bound tew be hard on yew, if yew are convicted; for the Government is doing everything it can tew stamp out free-trading, and Judges are being directed to give out harsher sentences these days. So in my honest opinion, which is what yew want, and what yer father came to me to git, yer best chance is tew plead Not Guilty, and let me and the Jury dew the rest.'

I stared back at him, amazed at this, my first encounter with the sophistries and machinations of lawyers. Of course I was well aware, in the matter of smuggling, of the outrageous verdicts of Not Guilty brought in by juries all over Cornwall and the West Country, despite often damning evidence to the contrary. But my whole objection to pleading as Mr Venning advised was decidedly moral. Not for the life of me— literally for my life, that is, my moral and spiritual well-being thereafter— could I see how I could honourably marry Lucretia and become either parson or minister, preaching moral edicts and Christian conduct, if it were all founded on a blatant lie, which not only myself but everyone else would recognize. No, I thought, this is not my course; I should regard myself as a hypocrite for the rest of my days, as bad as any trickster or fraudster.

'Mr Venning,' I said quietly, 'I am sure you are a very experienced and clever lawyer. If any man could win my case for me it is you. But my conscience will not allow me to perjure myself— isn't that what they call it? — by lying in Court before all. I simply would not have the audacity to do it. If my lips spoke the words, my face and demeanour would shout otherwise. I can't help it, Mr Venning. I shall have to plead Guilty; you must call your witnesses to say whatever they can on my behalf, and we must leave the rest to God and the Judge.'

And there the matter stayed. Twice afterwards he came and tried to persuade me, the second time with my father, who, upright and honest man that he was, was certainly uncomfortable, I could see, about the whole thing; but I held steadfastly to my conviction, which with thought and prayer increased a hundredfold over that week. And after the trial, Father admitted to me that it had troubled him deeply to attempt to persuade me otherwise, and he greatly admired me— more, he was proud of me— for holding to what I knew was right.

*

The trial, when it came, was short. I was led into the dock and sworn in, made my plea, and Mr Venning was invited to speak on my behalf. The Judge, Sir Montagu Summerson-Devine, lifted a world-weary face under his massive wig, and ran his eyes over me with a flicker of interest; no doubt mine was for him an unusual case, far removed from the theft, murders and woundings, forgeries and bigamy he was used to hearing.

The Court was overbrimming with the public, for my apprehending had caught the general imagination and attracted widespread attention: on a bench to one side were correspondents from the West Briton, The Royal Cornwall Gazette, The Western Luminary and the Sherborne Mercury. Not only that— which amazed me, for I was ill-prepared to face such fame, or infamy, after being shut away in the Gaol for a month— but I perceived, on looking among the spectators, my mother and father, sitting with Reuben alongside, near the front; and further back, on the other side, my dear Lucretia, with her brother Robert. To see them all there, especially Lucretia (who looked pale and hollow-eyed, evidently just recovered from her illness) produced in me a strange mixture of emotions: delight and gratitude that they should be there to support me by their presence, mingled with shame and distress that I had to stand there before them, and be the object of such public interest and wonder. I also sensed that there was a definite undercurrent of sympathy for me from everyone there, even the officers of the Court: the general view was that I was a hero who had been treacherously delivered into the arms of the law.

Mr Venning was not ill-pleased to give the Court the benefit of his impassioned oratory. In London, I reflected, he would have caused immense amusement, with his broad accent and country ways of speech; as he spoke I noticed some satirical looks and ostentatious yawning on the part of the prosecuting counsel and the Clerk of the Court. But he knew how to sway the spectators, if not His Lordship himself.

'Me Lord, this young man, I dew submit to yew, have found hisself tew be a victim of circumstance. Now what dew Ah mean by that? Ah mean, zur, that he've bin brought up by honest parents— his father bein' a well-knawn an' respected ship's captain in the port of Lodenek. He've bin brought up to be a Christian worshipper at church, a choirboy and a Monitor in the National School at Lodenek; an' be all accounts Ah've yurd, a clever and 'ard workin' pupil, and now a brilliant seaman commandin', at the age of twenty-one, his awn ship. Mebbe, yer Lordship, 'twas lack of experience an' Judgement in wan so young that have led'n into misguided ways: but Ah put it to yew that the people of this bare and rocky land of Cornwall do not live in any luxury. No, zur, far from it. Yer Lordship 'ave travelled awver our barren moors. Perhaps yer Lordship 'ave seen our terrible cliffs and coast, where ships be wrecked in dozens, — nay, scores— every year. Ah, 'tis a hard life for honest poor people yure, the kind of stock that Captain James Spargo dew come of. An' when yew take into dew account the imposition of onnerous duties on nearly everythin' the people dew eat an' drink an' wear on their backs, why, zur, can it be any cause for wonder that they turn tew free-tradin'— the deliberate evasion o' they duties— I will not mince my words fine, zur— tew *smugglin'*? Why, free-tradin' is held down along o' we, me Lord, to be an 'onest and respected profession. An' why not? The Cornish would far rather risk bein' caught an' put in gaol, or even transported, than tew starve or go on tew Parish Relief. No, zur, we be a proud race, an' us dawn't submit to poverty and shame without a mighty gude struggle. An' life, as Ah say, is one long struggle for most o' we.

'So Captain James, yure, have seen it as a kind action, — a dewty yew could call it— to supply the wants of the poor an' destitute, along with others better blessed, by bringin' in from France an' Brittany the salt an' sugar an' tea an' calico they needed, along with a few little extras such as brandy and tobacco tew maake life a mite easier for 'em all. Misguided, zur, yes, 'e wus. An' if you question 'im, 'e'll admit it. Repentant 'e is, Ah can assure your Lordship. An' wishin' to turn to a better life, to use the gifts God 'ave given 'im to Christian ends. He 'ave bin studyin', me Lord, an' 'e dew tell me 'e 'opes, still, to take the Matriculation examination at Oxford to go up to University, so that he can pursue some 'onourable profession. If yur Lordship will take into account his background and all the circumstances, and 'is future haspirations, and can find it in yur 'eart tew be merciful in sentencin' 'im, then Ah believe 'e will go on to fulfil those 'opes. And in so doin' 'e will, Ah dare prophesy, prove that out of crime can come public gude.

'Now, yer Lordship, Ah've said enough, Ah trust an pray, to cause yer gude self to think that mercy rather than a harsh sentence will be the just outcome of this yur sad case. If Ah may, with yer permission, Ah should like now to call two witnesses to testify to the otherwise gude character of the accused, who is, as Ah said, truly repentant of his misdeeds.'

The Judge gave me a searching steely look. I tried to appear as humble and contrite as I could, but returned his gaze, hoping he would not reject Mr Venning's request. 'Very well, Mr Venning. I hope this will not take too long. We have a long list of other cases to hear today.'

'Ah will be as brief as Ah can, yer Lordship. Call Mr Henry Nanskivell.'

I was surprised and pleased to see my old mentor and friend ascend to the witness box. Despite, or perhaps because of, his recent bereavement, he looked younger and less bowed down with trouble. Having been sworn in, he was asked to outline my educational attainments and plans for the future, which he did fairly and succinctly, including my studies of Latin and Greek.

'And in yer experience, Mr Nanskivell, 'ave yew ever knawn a young person in Captain Spargo's position, sailin' a ship on the 'igh seas, comin' and goin' as 'e dew, who could find the time an' determination an' persistence to study in this way?'

'I certainly have not. I consider Captain Spargo's application to his studies to be wholly admirable and quite astonishing, under the circumstances.'

'An' Ah believe yew 'ave been advising 'im on 'ow to obtain entry to one of the Colleges at Oxford?'

'I have done my poor best to assist him in that regard.'

'Would yew say, Mr Nanskivell, that a young man in 'is station of life could earn the money to support hisself at college be the normal means he had at his disposal?'

Mr Nanskivell said, 'He could not. I did advise Captain Spargo on how much a year he would need to go up to Oxford.'

'And 'ow much extra finance in yer estimation would 'e need to help 'im through College?'

'He would need to earn at least three hundred pounds to support himself at Oxford, in order to obtain a degree.'

'And dew yew consider that the reason he tuke up free-tradin' was as his best means of gittin' that extra sum?'

'I do. He had, I am sure, no other means, save begging the assistance of some rich patron, of achieving that aim.'

'Ah see. Thank yew, Mr Nanskivell.'

The prosecution saw no point in questioning Mr Nanskivell, and he was told to step down. Next called, to my greater surprise, nay amazement, was the Reverend William Rowlands. To see this venerable patriarch ascend to the witness box, his whitening hair haloing his face, his clerical bands well in evidence, was like beholding a visitation of Elijah or another of the Old Testament prophets. Having taken the oath he turned to the Judge, meeting his gaze on calm and equal terms, and composed himself to answer Mr Venning's interrogations.

'Yew are the Reverend William Rowlands, Master of Arts, and Vicar of Lodenek?'

'I am.'

'Would yew kindly tell us how long yew 'ave bin vicar there?'

'Twenty-six years.'

'Reverend Rowlands, Ah believe yew knaw the accused, Captain James Spargo?'

'Quite well. I have known his family since I first

came to Lodenek.'

'How would yew describe the accused's character, zur?'

'I should say, without doubt, he is an intelligent and industrious young man, and until now at least, a credit to his family and the town.'

'Ah b'lieve, zur, yew have had somethin' to dew with advisin' Mr Spargo on his intended future career?'

'I was pleased to know of his studies under Mr Nanskivell, and I encouraged them. I have indeed made arrangements for him to go up to my old college at Oxford to sit the Matriculation, which will take place in a month's time— if he should be at liberty—' here the Vicar paused briefly and looked directly at the Judge— 'to do so.'

'And how dew yew personally, zur, assess the future prospects of the accused, providing o' course, he will be able to follow such a Hacademic career?'

'I have great hopes that he will make his mark in one of the professions. I understand that he has shown considerable aptitude in poetry and verse; I shall give him every encouragement in that direction. He has, undoubtedly, a strong moral sense, otherwise I believe he would have not pleaded guilty here today.'

'Thank yew, Reverend Rowlands.'

No questions from the prosecution. Mr Venning summed up, in very few words, his case for clemency, and the Judge asked me if I had anything to say. I considered that all had been said, by Mr Venning and my witnesses, as well as it could have been. So in a sentence or two I told his Lordship that I was heartily sorry for the crimes I had perpetrated, the trouble and grief I had brought on others, then announced my intention of pursuing my studies and devoting myself to a law-abiding life and career thereafter.

The Judge now rose; it was half-past one in the afternoon and a recess was needed.

So I was kept in some suspense for another hour, until Sir Montagu returned, fortified by a good lunch and several glasses of claret, as I guessed from his somewhat more lively and benevolent expression. As he took his seat and nodded to the Clerk of the Court a complete hush fell on the assembly.

'Accused, be upstanding.'

I stood and faced His Lordship. He regarded me in silence for several seconds, quite impassively. Someone coughed nervously. I had visions of a prison sentence: of picking oakum and sawing wood for two or three years at least. I wondered what Lucretia, my father and mother, could be thinking.

The scene is fixed on my memory like a daguerrotype. It is as if I am outside and above the Court, seeing all, the Judge about to impose the sentence, the people gripped and in that silent expectation, myself standing rigidly there, returning his Lordship's penetrating scrutiny as manfully as I can manage.

Sir Montagu spoke, in a quiet slightly reedy monotone that bored into my ears and brain like a fine drill. 'James Spargo, I have heard of your career and misdemeanours with great concern. It is clear that you are a young man of some ability, who has been, understandably perhaps, led into illegal trading in order to provide yourself the funds which, I fully accept, you intend to devote to furthering your education and improving yourself. But, however laudable your desires in that direction, you have wilfully chosen to flout the laws of this kingdom, defrauding His Majesty's Treasury of many hundreds, perhaps thousands of pounds in duties. This is a grave offence which carries severe penalties, and it is the duty of justices such as myself to apply the law with utmost rigour; for if Customs and Excise duties are to be ignored and evaded by everyone up and down the land the Government would become bankrupt and anarchy would prevail. I take your Counsel's point that many of the duties are heavy, and cause some distress and hardship, especially in poorer districts such as these; but these duties are *law*, and until Parliament should see fit to lower or abolish them, there is no choice for me but to impose upon you the penalties of the law. I therefore direct that the ship you command, now impounded, shall be destroyed by being sawn into three equal parts and her timbers and fittings to be sold at public auction; and that you shall serve a term of imprisonment of six weeks, and pay a fine of one hundred pounds to the Clerk of this Court, in default of which you shall serve a further six months in prison. Call the next case.'

There was an immediate hubbub as the spectators stood up; some cheered, others waved at me; I could see my mother sobbing for relief into my father's arms, and tears on Lucretia's face also. The Sergeant.-at-Arms bawled, 'Silence in Court— silence I say!' but it was fully two minutes before order was restored. Meanwhile I was marched out of the dock by two constables and taken to the Clerk's office at the front of the Court building. My mind was in a confusion of doubts, hopes, relief and fears for my future. The six weeks imprisonment had already been served on remand; but the hundred pounds— how was I to pay it? and the St Malo was to he destroyed, as I had foreseen; which meant that I owed Thomas Rowlands three hundred and twenty pounds, with my profits still tied up in the closed bank at Lodenek. I presumed that I should have to go back to prison unless somehow the money for the fine could he found.

'A hundred pounds is the amount, Captain Spargo,' said the clerk at the desk. 'Can you pay?'

'Not for a day or two, at least,' I said. 'Perhaps, in a week or so.'

My father arrived with Mother and Reuben close hehind him. 'Excuse me, officer,' he said. 'I'm not sure if I can help... Isn't there a means of giving you a bond?'

'I can't take personal bonds or promissory notes, sir,' the clerk said. He sounded sympathetic; the constables took their hands off my shoulder and stood back while the matter was discussed. 'My instructions are, strictly cash or bank notes; I can take notes of hand only if the signatory is personally known to the Clerk of the Court or the Sergeant-at-Arms.'

'And what if,' said a woman's voice at the office door, 'the signatory is known to the Judge?'

We all turned. Lucretia stood there, with Robert behind her. She smiled at us all, acknowledging us as a family, and included in her smile the clerk and the constables. 'I am sure,' she said, coming forward to speak directly to the man at the desk, 'we can resolve this by speaking to Sir Montagu. He is a family friend, indeed my sister is his god-child. I am willing to write you a note of hand myself. I am the daughter of Major Devereaux, of Devereaux Place, Lodenek.'

The middle-aged clerk had never been faced with such a proposition. Evidently it appeared to him to be quite irregular, hut the great Sir Montagu's name having been invoked, he felt obliged to pursue the matter; Lucretia's presence and bearing appeared to overawe him. 'I'm not sure, Miss Devereaux... we can't interrupt the hearing...'

'We must, of course, wait for the next recess. Sir Montagu will want some refreshment, I imagine, at about four o'clock. I will write him a letter to explain. May I have pen and ink and paper?'

The clerk stood up and offered her his chair; when he had placed the materials before her she wrote, vigorously and clearly, a request to Sir Montagu to vouch for her note of hand. When this was done, sanded and folded, the clerk gave it to one of the constables to deliver as soon as the Judge ordered a recess, or the jury retired to consider a verdict. 'Would you very much mind,' Lucretia said, smiling sweetly, 'if we stayed in your office while we wait? It is very draughty in the corridors, and I have not been well, of late.'

The clerk acquiesced to this most willingly, sending the other constable out for more chairs; Mr Robert Devereaux was introduced to us all, but then excused himself, saying he wanted to smoke a cigar and see to his horses. We then passed an emotional hour there, discussing the case and comforting each others. Lucretia was kind and affectionate to my mother and father, who soon warmed to her and chatted without embarrassment; we were all united in our relief and joy at my avoidance of further imprisonment, as we hoped and now expected, and looked forward to a return to Lodenek to take up our lives again as we wished.

Only Reuben sat there, hardly speaking, gazing in wonder as Lucretia and I held hands in the intervals of the conversation, gazing mutely into each other's eyes. 'You know, Captain and Mrs Spargo,' Lucretia said eventually, 'that James and I are very close and mean a great deal to each other. In fact, I dare claim we are practically engaged to he married; there is only the business of obtaining my father's approval— I don't need his *consent*, you understand— which I am quite sure will soon be given. Especially now, after this outcome.' I wondered whether Father's own reservations about out marriage still held; but if so he showed no sign of it, reacting amicably, even cordially, to her remarks and comments.

This reunion went on until the clerk came back and said that, the jury having retired in the case following mine, Lucretia's letter had been delivered to Sir Montagu; who had informed the Clerk of the Court that he recommended him to accept Miss Devereaux's note of hand.

So Lucretia wrote out her note, and I tried to thank her; I declared that she should he repaid in full, whatever happened, but she silenced me, her eyes dancing with love, and said that we would come to some arrangement later. She told me that she might be away from Lodenek visiting a relative for a week or so, and that I must be patient a little longer, until we could meet again. Robert then appearing at the door, impatient to get home again, she kissed me delicately on the cheek, smiled at my family and took her leave.

Before we left the court buildings to take the coach back to Wadebridge, and then the ferry down to Lodenek, Mr Venning came out of court, the Judge having risen for a short recess; and my father was able to pay him there and then for his advocacy, with a leather bag containing a hundred sovereigns. He thanked the attorney for his efforts on my behalf.

'Oh, yew must think nothing of it, dear zur,' Mr Venning said, taking the money with one hand and administering to himself a good pinch of snuff with the other. 'Tis all in a day's work, as yew might say. A very interestin' case; Ah awnly wish, yew knaw, that this yure young man 'ad pleaded Not Guilty. *Then* we should ha' had some real fun wi' the prosecution. Never mind, Ah only 'ope 'e dawn't live tew regret 'is decision.'

'No,' said my mother, 'I can assure you that he will stick to what is right, and do his Christian duty; or he's no son of mine, Mr Venning.'

The lawyer bowed, somewhat ironically I thought; and we left, a sober chastened family, free except for our debts and concern over lack of money.

When I heard afterwards of the fate of my cell mates I was amazed at the lightness of my sentence. John Holland had been given ten years hard labour for wounding and affray; George Uren, three years of the same for poaching; the old vagabond, Peter Dymond, was sent to the Bridewell for eighteen months for his turnip stealing; and poor Jimmy Martin, aged fourteen, was to be transported to the colonies for ten years as a result of his theft of the silk handkerchiefs. Clearly Sir Montagu had been swayed by no pity for them, nor of course had they had the benefit of any lawyer to defend them or plead mitigating circumstances.

Many years afterwards I learned from Lucretia that Squire Devereaux, hearing that Sir Montagu had been appointed judge of those Assizes, had written to him privately asking for clemency on my behalf; for the Major and he had been at Eton and Oxford together. When I heard that, I was ashamed and saddened that I had been so favourably treated, and swore to myself that I would devote my efforts, such as they might be, to alleviating and changing the system which administered one law for the rich and another for the poor.

CHAPTER 32

A HOMECOMING

My sisters and brother Reuben, when I arrived home, all held me in awe. Not only had I been in prison, but was now declared a suitor for the hand of Miss Lucretia Devereaux; to them it was as if I were proposing to marry into Royalty. My father and mother seemed hardly less stupefied by the events of my trial and Lucretia's gesture of paying my fine, though they had known, of course, of our close friendship. 'I can't believe, though, that Squire Devereaux will allow James and Lucretia to marry,' Father said. 'Something tells me his position simply won't allow it.'

'Not if James goes to Oxford? And maybe becomes a parson?' Mother said. 'Surely then he wouldn't object.'

'Perhaps not,' said Father. 'But 'tis a feeling I have— to me this is just a castle in the air, for a Spargo to think of marrying a Devereaux.'

'And who, after all,' replied Mother tartly, 'are these Devereauxs? Are they any better than us, just because they have a big house and so many acres, which they filched from somebody else, because they supported William the Bastard of Normandy? Our James can hold his own with any of 'em, I'll be bound, Edward Spargo.'

My father knew better than to argue any further when she was in her revolutionary mood, as he called it. He took his cap and went out, muttering that he had to see to the rigging of new sails on the Galatea, which was due to sail the following day for Kingstown and

Liverpool.

The first thing I did the day after arriving was to go to the churchyard and put flowers on Daniel's grave. There was no headstone— that had been ordered from the slate carver, Mr Trescowthick at Crugmeer; only a small wooden cross with 'D.S. in rough tarred letters marked the mound. I went alone, and spent a full half-hour there on my knees praying and remembering my brother, recalling the happy times we spent together, with many a sigh and tear that his great promise and hopes would never be fulfilled. I prayed desperately, with tears running down my cheeks, to be forgiven for the part I had played in his death. And I vowed to my Maker that I would do all I could to help deserving youngsters such as he in their struggle to find a good and honourable place in life. Finally, I thanked God for granting Daniel, in his short span, such enjoyment of childhood and youth as he had experienced— thinking of the hungry and deprived lot of so many children I saw around me.

There in the corner of the churchyard, under the cliff of beeches and sycamores that surrounded it, by the old slate wall covered with ivy and toadflax, I felt I wanted to remain: out of the strivings of the world and its calamities, at peace there in the sunshine and rain, hearing only the slight sway and creak of the yews when the small breeze reached their top branches, and the flitting of chaffinches and wrens about me. 'Peace, Daniel,' I whispered. 'May you be blessed in your peace, in heaven and in the earth.'

But other considerations pressed; I got up from my knees and left the graveside, knowing however I should have to return to it at least once a year during the rest of my life. A few days later I wrote this Lament for Daniel:

And art thou gone, our dearest and our best?
  And hath the Lord conveyed thee to thy rest?
O brother, son, companion, who didst give
  Thy life to save another, mayst thou ever live
The life eternal now beyond our strife.

Was ever such a glorious youth to see,
  So comely in thy strength and verity?
With quick enquiring mind and happy mien
  Thou pleasedst all; loved in return hast been
By all who shared thy eager, zealous life.

Short thy days, but wreathed in love were they;
  Laughter and kindness broughtst thou every day,
As if thou cam'st from Heaven's climes to bring
  A glimpse of joyous plenitude, to sing
A jubilant cantata, all too brief.

Now art thou laid deep in our Cornish earth,
  United with the land that gave thee birth;
Thy promise unfulfilled; yet He above
  Shall more than compensate thee with His love,
And thus assuage our ever-present grief.

My family were much moved by these verses; my sister Emma, who had the best hand of any of us, was commissioned to inscribe them on a piece of vellum, which Father framed and hung in our best room, reserved for important visitors and our own Christmas gathering.

After leaving Daniel's grave I next sought to enquire after Mr Thomas Rowlands. Seeing Nan Thomas in the town I accosted her on the subject.

'Aw, he's awful bad, poor gen'leman,' she said. 'Doctor do come every day, but he d'just lie there. Hardly speak now, they say. Jus' fadin' away.'

'Does he see any visitors?'

'Only the family to my knowledge.'

'Would you... mention to Miss Emily that I would like to see him, if 'tis allowed?'

She pressed her lips together dubiously. 'I'll ask her, Mr James. They can't but say no.'

'Tell her I shall fully understand if they do.'

I wandered about the quayside, talking to this one and that, for I was an object of wonder and, I found, some veneration (at least among the young and the poor, who regarded me as a hero); several made a point of shaking me by the hand and complimenting me on my light sentence. Enoch Penberthy, Davey Bligh and others of my crew, who had not yet found another ship to join, told me how they had worried for me in gaol, and feared that I would be given a long term in prison. They all mourned the destruction of the St Malo.

'She was a good-tempered craft, and sailed like a mermaid in a fresh wind,' Enoch said. 'You did a good job choosing she, you and Mr Thomas between 'ee.'

'Yes,' I said, 'she served her purpose well. Perhaps too well.' I brooded a little on Daniel's and Tom Permewan's fates; I had just been to see the old sea-cook, sitting in the doorway of his tiny cottage in Jacob's Court, catching the morning sun, his mouth dribbling as he stared vacantly at the hens scratching and pigs rooting about him.

'You mustn't be too upset 'bout it all,' Enoch said. 'You got the rest o' your life before you to recover and make amends. Eh, Cap'n?'

I smiled wanly and put my hand on his broad shoulder. 'Reckon you're right, Enoch. No sense in mourning forever.'

In a fortnight I was to go up to Oxford to matriculate, and I should have to make arrangements to get there. I had no money; I owed Lucretia a hundred pounds, and most of my credit at the Lodenek Bank was forfeit to Mr Rowlands for the St Malo. The bank was still closed, for Ralph had apparently not been able to satisfy Messrs Coutts and Company, and no new loan had been forthcoming. Coutts, it seemed, would not move in the matter until they knew the outcome of Thomas' illness.

I went to see Mr Nanskivell and the Reverend Rowlands to thank them both for their testimonies on my behalf at the trial. I found the former at the National School, supervising a young assistant master who was taking the combined classes in drawing. Leaving the new teacher in charge, Mr Nanskivell took his hat; we went out into the narrow street and walked some way along the field path above the estuary, planning what I should do to get to Oxford for the examination.

'The best way is to ship to Bristol and take a coach through Gloucester to Oxford. You may be lucky enough to find a vessel going to Gloucester itself,' my old mentor said. 'I have a relative in Bristol who would give you a night's lodging; I'll write you a letter of introduction. In Oxford the College will offer accommodation for examinees. You will come to me for final revisions, I hope, James? You have a week or more, so use it well.'

'I will come each evening, if it is convenient.'

'Not Tuesday; it is our Literary Circle. Had you forgot?'

I admitted I had indeed forgotten, among all my anxieties.

'And here,' said Mr Nanskivell, a strangely eager light springing in his eyes, 'comes another of our Circle.'

It was Miss Sarah Devereaux, with a small pug-dog on a lead. She had just appeared through a wicket gate leading from Place, for the path we walked on ran beside the high stone wall of the deer park fronting the house itself. She seemed to affect not to see us, being concerned to pull the little animal along, for it was interested in sniffing various plants and tufts of grass where other dogs had passed.

'A very good afternoon to you, Miss Sarah,' Mr Nanskivell said, raising his hat with something of a flourish, whilst I respectfully touched my cap.

She looked up, colouring slightly. 'Oh— Mr Nanskivell! How do you do... And Captain James... I am so glad to see you home at last. I've heard all about your affairs from my sister, of course... How wonderful to think that they released you. Surely you must be glad to be home.'

'I am indeed, thank you, Miss Devereaux.' There was a pause, a slight awkwardness; I sensed there was something unspoken between her and Mr Nanskivell, to which I was not yet party.

'We were discussing James's journey to Oxford,' the schoolmaster said then. 'He goes up to Matriculate the week after next.' We all moved slowly along the path as he explained to Sarah how I was to get to the College. Below us the wide waters of the river mouth spread, the incoming tide all but covering the Town Bar, and a couple of gigs were towing in a schooner from Points against a light south-west breeze. The ferry to Black Rock on the opposite side to Lodenek was plying its way slowly under two pairs of oars manned by the ferryman and his son. My two companions made light remarks on the splendour of the day, for the sun now shone in glory on the lakelike river, bringing out delicate and brilliant tones of green and blue in the water, turquoise where it covered the sand and deep violet and ultramarine in the channels. I felt they wished to talk more intimately between themselves than they could in my presence, so I sought the first excuse I could to depart from them. On reaching St Saviour's Point, where a pile of hewn rocks, the ruins of a medieval hermit's abode, stood grey-green and bright gold with lichen, a branch of the path doubled back towards the town, lower down the slope above the river; so I bade them *au revoir*, saying I had some business to attend to, and that I would see them both on Tuesday evening. On looking back I saw them dallying there, on that promontory above the waters, much more interested in examining each other's faces as they talked than in the scenery about them; while the pug-dog, now unleashed, nosed happily among the ruins and the surrounding blackthorn bushes.

I wondered whether their friendship was serious enough to lead to a proposal of marriage, since Mr Nanskivell seemed infatuated with Sarah; there was a difference of some fifteen years in their ages, she being a year younger than Lucretia, but he was still relatively a young man and in his prime. What on earth the Squire would say, faced with another daughter wishing to marry beneath herself, I could only speculate— with some amusement, thinking of his choleric face and that purple-veined aquiline nose. I reflected that Mr Nanskivell's book on Antiquities would be published soon, and would bring him enhanced status, if not riches. But probably this was all mere dalliance, an association which if nothing else would compensate the schoolmaster for the trials he had just undergone in nursing his departed wife. I had more important matters to concern me.

It was all very well to plan how to reach Oxford, I brooded as I reached the quayside among the manifold noises of sawing, caulking, and loading ships; but without any certain income how could I accept a place at the College if it were awarded me? How safe, I wondered, was the money I had put by in the bank, and how much would be left after the St Malo was paid for? Perhaps I should give up all idea of going to Oxford, and return to seafaring; by honest and legal trading I might save some three hundred pounds or so in six to eight years, and then go up to the University. It seemed a daunting prospect indeed. Would Lucretia wait for me so long? I should be twenty-seven or more before we could marry. In this anxious and despondent frame of mind I went through the town, up the streets past the church, and out along the high road to the Vicarage, barely acknowledging or speaking to those I met and who greeted me.

Vicar was at home, said the elderly maid who answered the door; she would see if he would receive me. I was left waiting in the hall of the large Georgian house, watching the vicar's gardener tending some rosebushes on the lawn. I stood there for some minutes. wondering whether I had called at an inconvenient time; then the maid returned and said, 'His Reverence will be with you in a minute' and vanished. The minute went on, and I began to think I would simply have to go away again; then the door at the far end of the passageway opened and the Vicar's white hair and eyebrows could be discerned in the half-gloom. 'James Spargo,' he said in his ministerial boom. 'This way, if you please,' and led me into his study.

It was as if I had come to he admonished and lectured by an Augustan headmaster. No doubt I deserved it; no doubt the Vicar had my best ends in view; but I found this harder to stomach than the Judge's remarks before passing sentence.

'I came to thank you, sir, for speaking on my behalf at the trial,' I said.

The Vicar stood, his back to the window, framed against the afternoon sunshine, his face in shadow and all detail lost to me. The strong light caused me to blink and squint. His voice came out of the blaze surrounding him, yet he himself was dark and indistinct, as if he were God speaking to Moses on Sinai 'Why,' he said with stern and righteous accusation, 'do you think I did it? Why should I inconvenience myself with a journey to Bodmin and back— a journey which took me away from my parish duties for a whole day— an *uncomfortable* journey at that?'

I mumbled that I did not really know.

'I will tell you. Your father came to me, explaining the case and your position. Your father is a good man, an *upright* man; your mother is a good respectable woman; they have brought you up as a member of the Church and a Christian. You, sir, have heard me preach often enough against smuggling, and disobeying the law. By any standards of justice you should now be serving a term of several year's imprisonment. Do you not agree?'

I agreed, humbly and wholeheartedly.

'Yet the Lord is merciful. I believe He has work for you to do; I was gratified, in talking to Mr Nanskivell, to find that you had applied yourself so well to your studies, even on board ship. It is my view that such enterprise and intelligent activity as you are capable of should be channelled in the right direction. I have prayed long and hard over your case, James Spargo. I have earnestly sought God's guidance; and I have been encouraged to be merciful. So I spoke for you, and my prayers were answered. The verdict is a sign from heaven that you should now devote yourself to improving your lot, to be worthy of whatever career you will be called upon to follow. I am confident that you will go to Oxford; that the Way will be made plain to you there. But, James Spargo, there are great temptations and snares for students in that city. In my own day I witnessed them, and by report they have not diminished. You will meet those who are rich, and will want to lead you into gambling on horses, and cockfighting and dogfighting; there will be loose women beckoning to you on every corner; there will be those who will invite you to drink yourself into stupor and bestiality with wine and spirits. I cannot allow you to go up to university without being warned of all this.'

'Sir,' I said, now recovering my confidence somewhat, 'I thank you sincerely, for your warnings. But I shall have little money to spend on such things, if indeed I am able to keep myself; for my situation is difficult, my savings being closed to me with the Lodenek Bank. But I give you my word as a Christian that if I do find the means to study there, my whole endeavour shall be directed to gaining my degree— in Divinity.'

He was silent for a moment, and then gave a gruff 'Ahem,' moved to his desk, and sat down behind it on the leather-covered armchair. He indicated a smaller chair for me to sit. His whole manner softened and he became fatherly and considerate. 'Divinity, you say?'

'Yes. I have decided that I definitely want to become a parson, sir; and if I can't get to Oxford, I intend to join the Methodists and be a preacher.' I went on to outline to him my experiences in prison and the effect they had wrought upon my religious convictions. He listened intently, nodding to himself now and then, staring at me with his pale blue intense gaze. When I had finished he grunted with some satisfaction and said. 'Did I not say that the Way would be made clear? Yes, James, I see there is indeed work for you to do— you are called to do it. I fervently hope, however, that you will perform it in the bosom of Mother Church, and not under the regime of the Wesleyans; and God forbid that you should join the Bryanites, for they hold to the idea of Free Grace: they believe that a man can sin as much as he pleases, provide he repents once a week. That creed will lead you into damnation.' He thought for a moment or two, and then said, 'As you seem to be in financial straits, despite making great profits from your ventures, I advise you to apply for an Exhibition. I will give you a letter for the Bursar of the College, who will tell you how you may sit for one; I believe there are several available, but there is bound to be competition for them. It will mean writing an extra paper or two, and you will have to stay on at Oxford for perhaps a week. My letter will also recommend you to be given a room in College at special rates for indigent students. When do you leave?'

'In ten day's time, sir.'

'Come and see me again in a week. Continue your studies; pray night and morning; take Communion on Sunday; and, my son, take this with you, and whenever you put it on or take it off remember my words.' From a drawer he took out a small wrought-silver Celtic cross, on a fine chain, and pressed it into my hands. 'A talisman,' he said. 'It will remind you of your home and Cornwall, and may it bring you back among us in God's good time.'

I was amazed and gratified at his giving me this token, and muttered my thanks. The patriarch had suddenly become a friend and counseller. He told me afterwards that he had had the cross made for one of his sons, who had been intended for the ministry, having shown great earnestness and promise in his youth; but the lad had died at the age of seventeen from fever contracted through visiting sick and destitute parishioners, and it had lain in the drawer of his desk ever since. It seemed to me a confirmation, setting the seal of others' hopes upon me. Surely, I thought on leaving the Vicarage, there can be no turning back now, or I shall disappoint not only my own hopes, but those of my mother, Mr Nanskivell, Lucretia, and the Reverend Rowlands himself.

I still wear that precious little cross, with its

interlacing knotwork, and have it on me now as I write; and each evening I take it off and lay it beside my bed as I sleep, and still think of that august and unapproachable, yet essentially kind pastor of ours.

On reaching home I found a letter awaiting me, with Emily's handwriting on the envelope. It was not the careful conscious copperplate of our young days; the hand was agitated, jerky and spiky, though I recognised her ornate J and the extra curl she put on the S of Spargo.

My dear James,

It was kind of you to enquire after dear Papa. He is indeed very ill, and has slowly sunk over the last several weeks as to be almost unrecognizable as the man we all knew. I cannot find it in me to expect anything but the worst. He does not receive visitors now, but when I told him you were home again, and what had befallen you, he asked especially to see you. I am sure you will come, and soon. The sooner the better, dear friend; to humour a dying man.

Yours ever truly,

Emily.

It was about five o'clock; my mother was directing my sister Susannah in the kitchen, and the evening meal would not be ready for some while; it would be mackerel and potatoes, I knew, the staple diet of those on short commons. I put the letter inside my jacket pocket and went out, climbing the road to Sandry's Hill House, where I entered the gates and went up to the great pillared portico, with grand scrolls on its capitals, and a bas-relief of sheaves of corn and fruits on the facade. No kitchen entrance for me now, I thought. As I neared the steps I saw Emily watching from the window of the small parlour; she waved and as I reached the doors she opened them herself.

'Ah, James. Do come in. So good of you to come. You had my letter?'

'Yes.'

She seemed well enough herself, but had evidently been weeping. 'He has been muttering all kinds of nonsense this afternoon since I told him about you. I can't make head or tail of it, but your name comes out among it all. It's the doctors, I'm sure they're killing him with their blood-letting, but what can I do? My mother won't listen to me, nor my brothers. He needs building up, not bleeding; don't you agree?'

'I'm not a doctor, Emily, but I think I do agree. Shall I see him now?'

'This way.' She led me up the great circular stairs to a large bedroom overlooking the harbour. There lay her father in the depths of a massive four-poster bed, its curtains half-drawn against the evening glow of the sky; a nurse sat with him, nodding sleepily. As we entered the sick man turned his head and recognition sprang in his eyes. I heard him breathe a long quavering sigh of relief. He was almost a skeleton, it seemed, a travesty of himself. His face gaunt, grey and wasted, the cheek bones and jaw all but showing through the ivory coloured skin; he looked as if he had already been embalmed. Yet his eyes stared up at me as if they might leave his head.

'Only a minute or two, Miss Emily.' The nurse was fully awake now, warning us both.

'Very well, Tonkyn. Captain Spargo won't stay

long.'

Mr Rowlands feebly stretched out a shrunken arm, and I took his hand and pressed it firmly. He whispered something, which I failed to catch; I knelt down by the bed and turned my ear to him, listening closely.

'James... wanted to see you, before... always a good servant... should go far... must tell you... the St Malo...'

The shadow of a voice faded; he lay exhausted for a moment or two. I studied his face as he closed his eyes; the slight wrinklings of a frown indented his brow. I was about to get up and leave him, thinking he ought perhaps to sleep, when he opened his eyes, gripping my hand with sudden urgency. 'St Malo...' he repeated. 'Don't worry... made provision... be all right. I've seen to it...'

His voice trailed away, and a stertorous breathing took over. The nurse came forward, waving me away, and lifting him up, doll-like, with one strong arm, she administered a sip of brandy-and-water with the other from a cup; he spluttered a little and finally relapsed on the pillow, sleeping. Emily and I crept out of the room.

As we went down the stairs we met Mrs Rowlands ascending. 'Captain Spargo... Thank you for coming,' she said. Her face was lined and concerned, as if she had lost much sleep. 'My husband always thought a great deal of you. I fear there is little hope. How is he?' — this last to Emily.

'The same, but he was glad to see James,' Emily said. 'He's sleeping peacefully now.'

Mrs Rowlands swept on up the stairs past us.

Emily took me into the small parlour and carefully closed the door. She regarded me solemnly for a few moments, then burst into tears and flung herself into my arms. I soothed and caressed her gently, kissing her forehead as she wept against my breast.

'Oh James, James,' she mourned, 'What's to become of us? If he dies, we shall be ruined, I know it.'

'Surely not, Emily. Your father is too good a business man to fail to provide for you. He has a great deal of property in the district, you know.'

'Ruined,' she repeated. 'I can feel it, I know that something terrible is going to happen. You will help me, won't you? You always said you'll be my friend.'

'I'll do whatever I can. But surely you'll be married soon.'

She stopped crying, looking at me piteously, and dabbed her eyes with a small handkerchief produced from her sleeve, an article quite inadequate for the purpose, so that I had to lend her my kerchief— which reminded me of the previous occasion, that of her twenty-first birthday ball, when I had lent it to her. 'I hope so,' she said in a strangely hollow tone. 'I hope so. Though I don't want to marry at all, really.'

'Tis a good match, everyone thinks.'

She twisted her mouth in an expression of disgust at the notion of a good match. 'You know what I feel,' she said, 'if anyone does. I have no faith in marriage. No faith in Philip Rashleigh, nor in myself. We've been engaged now for more than six months, and we can't agree on a date for the wedding. When I think back only a year ago... everything seemed wonderful then, it was all mine for the asking, except that you...' She did not pursue that thought. 'I'm sorry, James, to burden you with my worries. You have had enough trouble and tragedies of your own to hear. But... sometimes I really do believe I'm going mad. Mad!' Her eyes stared at me, the whites showing starkly as the lids opened wide, and I was shocked to see the wild ungovernable fear in them. It was only a moment, however; she quickly regained control of herself, and impulsively took my hand, stroking it between both hers, looking at me humbly and suppliantly. 'Don't desert me, dear friend,' she breathed. 'You will not desert me when I need you, will you?'

The scene rises before me again like a *table d'étude*, with those two figures staring at each other, she distraught— he, myself, startled and puzzled; and I still hear her quick apprehensive breaths as she stared imploringly into my eyes. 'Of course I shan't desert you, if you need my help and sympathy,' I assured her.

I left the house, my mind confused by many doubts, trying to recall and assess what Mr Rowlands had tried to tell me, disturbed by Emily's behaviour and her prophecies of disaster. I went home to join my family around the table, but could eat little of the food put before me; and stayed silent all evening, withdrawn and anxious, turning these things over and over in my mind until I began to feel obsessed and haunted by them. I went to bed early and slept poorly.

The next day the news spread that after receiving a last Communion from his brother the Vicar, Thomas Rowlands had died peacefully in the night.

CHAPTER 33

THE FUNERAL — AND AFTER

It was, without doubt, the largest and most impressive funeral held in Lodenek for a decade—certainly the greatest of its kind since the death of the Squire's father, old Sir Robert Devereaux. On that occasion the Colonel of the regiment of the King's Cornish Light Dragoons with fifty men on horseback had come down from Bodmin, for in his time Sir Robert himself had been their Colonel.

Now we witnessed, as well as the family mourners (which included the large family of the Reverend William Rowlands) both the Lord Lieutenant and the High Sheriff of Cornwall, several magistrates and dozens of business and social acquaintances of the deceased. Mr Mackenzie, our former Collector of Customs, was there to give the funeral oration from the pulpit, since the Vicar himself had decided it was not his place to render it for his brother.

We Spargos, Father and Reuben and myself, attended, sitting at the back of St Petroc's church with the servants of the Rowlands, the tenants of Thomas' farms and inns, and his employees, sailors, shipwrights, agents, managers and clerks. Sitting behind us I found Enoch Penberthy and Captain Dick Stribley, himself very frail, who had insisted on coming although Dr Harley had forbidden it.

This was a men-only funeral, which was becoming frequent in those days; even so, the church was full, with some standing in the choir vestry and the south porch. The atmosphere was heavily charged with the sense of the end of an era: Thomas had personified a new age of enterprise and competition, born and intensified against the background of the French Wars. Now that he was dead we all expected great changes; few of us dared hope they would be for the better.

He had left Lodenek a greater and more significant commercial port than he found it, so declared Mr Mackenzie, in his soft undemonstrative Scottish tones. Sixty ships now traded out of the harbour, and more were being built each year; when Thomas had arrived there had been but twenty; he had been the first to send his vessels to the Baltic and Russia. He had brought the town immense increase in employment, and had encouraged better farming through the rotation of crops. He had been a generous contributor to local charities and foundations, the church and the National School in particular having benefited. He had served conscientiously as Justice of the Peace, Deputy Lord Lieutenant and High Sheriff, and, as President of the Lodenek Harbour Association, had instigated improvements to the channels, the erection of capstans to haul in ships against the wind, and the acquisition of Lodenek's first lifeboat, the Mariners' Hope. He had been a kind employer, a considerate landlord, an upright Christian gentleman, a worthy example of the best type of British businessman. He was also a most devoted husband and generous loving father of his children. So it went on: as impressive a list of achievements and endeavours as ever a man might hope to hear of himself.

Yet somehow, I could not but think, the real man

had been rather different from this catalogue of admirable qualities, this dead and historical account of his life and works. In actuality Thomas had been vulnerable, regretful, sometimes frustrated, often angry, worldly-wise, yet somehow innocent in all his strivings. I remembered his attitude to me and my ambitions: his fatherly counsel, his criticisms of Emily, his encouragement and warnings. I recalled his advice to me to return to the Ball, on the occasion of my debâcle at Sandry's Hill House, aged fifteen; and his insistence that I should not get married too early in life. I saw again his waxen pallid face and urgent gaze, trying to tell me something about the St Malo. Tears came into my eyes; I was not the only one to be so moved, for Mr Mackenzie's quiet dispassionate speech was having an increasing effect on dozens of men there. I verily believe that if there had been women present the whole churchful of us would have broken out in sobs and lamentations.

A light rain was falling as the bearers shouldered the coffin out into the churchyard to the newly dug grave among the yew trees. An unaccustomed silence was upon the whole town. Not a caulker's mallet, neither saw nor hoist nor winch was heard; there was no loading or unloading: the port had, since mid-day, ceased its customary operations, as a mark of respect to Thomas Rowlands. Ships rode inside the Points, on a calm tide, waiting for gigs. As the Vicar read the burial service the yews dripped steadily and the earth was turned to clammy clay as the mourners filed past the grave, a long slow procession lasting nearly half-an-hour, dropping clods of it on to the oak box with its name-plate engraved with scrolls and copper-plate. Raindrops glistened upon unhatted hair and beards. I wondered what the Reverend Rowlands thought of his brother, remembering his consistent condemnation of smuggling, his denunciations of private greed and warnings of the immorality and dangers of amassing riches. Yet the old patriarch seemed moved, his voice trembling and hoarse at times, his white beard and moustache shining in the rain as he drew upon himself tears from the heavens.

'Almighty God, we give thee hearty thanks, for that it hath pleased thee to deliver this our brother out of the miseries of this sinful world; beseeching thee that thou mayst of thy gracious goodness, shortly to accomplish the number of thine elect, and to hasten thy Kingdom; that we, with all those that are departed in the true faith of thy holy Name, may have our perfect consummation and bliss, both in body and soul, in thy eternal and everlasting glory...'

Afterwards, walking away from the churchyard into the town, talk among the men was muted. They spoke only respectful commonplaces. 'Shan't see the like of he again.' 'He was always good to us servants. Always interested in what you was doin'. 'Never passed you by without a nod or how d'ye do.' I sensed behind all this a yawning void: the void of apprehension as to what was to happen to them all, to their town, now that Thomas was gone.

We knew soon enough. Following the funeral there was a family gathering at Sandry's Hill House at which the lawyers read Thomas' will. I cannot recall what bequests he made, nor do they matter here, save one. The next morning another letter for me arrived, from Emily, in writing more agitated than before.

Sandry's Hill House,
16th June 1822.

My Dear James,

I write this in haste so that you shall know as soon as possible. My Father in his Will has left the St Malo to you. I think you will have been worried that you would have to stand surety for her— if so, this will greatly relieve you. He has left great debts, and we have been warned not to expect to he able to live as we did. I don't know what is to become of us.

Ever your friend

Emily.

I understood now what Thomas had been trying to tell me on his death-bed. At one stroke a huge yoke was lifted off my shoulders, to think that I should not have to reimburse the family or the estate for the ship I had commanded. Now I would he able to use what money I had, assuming I could get it out of the bank, for my own purposes. I was surprised that Emily understood my situation so well; perhaps Thomas had confided in her at some point. I reflected that she must have been distraught to have written to me so— she was evidently unable to control her need to pour out her anxieties to me, so fearful was she of what was to come upon her and her family. I would gladly have gone to her then to offer what comfort I could; but I could not intrude upon a family so grief-stricken, and my intentions might have been misunderstood had I dared to do so. After some thought I wrote a note of thanks, telling her how much I owed to her father, and that I would never forget his encouragement of me; and that if I could help her or her family in any way, my services were at their call.

*

Two days later an Assessor from Messrs Coutts and Company arrived from London, and went into the Lodenek Bank with Ralph Rowlands and the family's lawyers, where they were closeted for the best part of the day; a lunch of cold ham and fowl was sent into them, with wine and ale. When they emerged at late afternoon Ralph, in particular, looked very downcast.

For two weeks afterwards their clerks and agents went around the various inns, shops, cottages and farms, and the shipyard owned by Thomas Rowlands, cataloguing every item of furniture, livestock, implements, and goods for resale or for shipbuilding. By the time they had finished I was on the way to Oxford in a ketch bound for Gloucester, having borrowed from the Vicar twenty pounds to cover my expenses. His offer of a loan came unexpectedly and just in time; for I had almost been at my wits' end to know what to do, having refused to borrow from Lucretia.

I arrived in Oxford, found Exeter College, and sat the Matriculation: a paper in Latin, one in Greek, and the next day a general paper in English. I did not find them difficult, and was sure I had done well. Accommodation in a student's rooms (the undergraduate being on vacation) was offered me at two shillings per night, and tolerable meals could be had at various inns for modest prices. The Bursar of the College informed me that he had received the Reverend Rowlands' letter, and had enrolled me for an Exhibition examination, to take place three days later. I spent those three days studying my Latin and Greek books, and learning a long passage from the *Aeneid* and another from the *Iliad*; both of which stood me in good stead, when I took the paper along with four other poor students. I then revisited the Bursar, found I had matriculated with Credit, and took the next mail coach back to Bristol, where I stayed the night with Mr Nanskivell's cousin and his wife; and next day found a lugger sailing with china and ironware to Barnstaple. I joined her as a deckhand, for by now I had but seven shillings or so left of my loan; slept the next night uncomfortably on Barnstaple docks upon a heap of old rope awaiting the oakum pickers, and thence was able to work my way on a barge bound for Lodenek to load slates for Barry. Thus I arrived home, to find the town seething with rumour, contra-rumour and sensation. On the doors of the Bank, and also at various prominent places in the streets, were affixed notices announcing:

AN AUCTION SALE
will be held at the Britannia Inn, Lodenek
on Wednesday July 10th 1822
at 10 o'clock in the forenoon
offering the following excellent vessels:

Brigantine	*Galatea*	*250*	*tons*	*burthen*
Lugger	*Sprite*	*90*	*tons*	*ditto*
Sloop	*Fair Maid*	*110*	*tons*	*ditto*
Ketch	*Dawn*	*70*	*tons*	*ditto*
Schooner	*Emily*	*200*	*tons*	*ditto*

Also baulk and other timber, deal, spars,
iron, marine stores, and many other articles
of merchandise, all being the property of the late

THOMAS ROWLANDS, ESQ., OF LODENEK.

Catalogues of all on offer are now available at
the counting house of Thomas Rowlands and Son
South Quay, Lodenek.
ALSO
FOR SALE BY PRIVATE CONTRACT

A large stock of wines, brandy and rum
in cask and bottles lying in the
cellars of the above firm.

In payment for any of the above articles, notes of the firm of Thomas Rowlands and Son, payable to the bearer on demand, will be accepted.

It was the beginning of the end of the business empire which Thomas had created. In the Truro newspaper the West Briton, which was published two days later, an advertisement appeared:

CREDITORS OF THE LATE THOMAS
ROWLANDS, Esq.
of Sandry's Hill House, Lodenek are desired to send to Messrs Cantrell & Co., Solicitors, of St Austell, accounts of the nature and amount of their respective demands, calculating interest of such debts as carried interest.

Not only that: the Lodenek Bank was now open, for six days only, to pay in full all who held credit there, and to take in exchange for cash all bank notes issued by Thomas Rowlands and underwritten by Coutts and Company. People were coming in from the countryside about, from farms and villages, to join Lodenek residents themselves and retrieve their savings. Father and Reuben had been among the first to apply, waiting among a crowd of creditors buzzing with speculation and ill-founded comments. I went in immediately, having got my account book out of my tin box in my bedroom, and was paid bank notes drawn on Coutts and Company, Chancery Lane, London.

Having honoured all claims upon it, the bank was closed, its clerks and accountants discharged, and the company liquidated. Meanwhile I had written a joyous note to Lucretia to say I would call on her with some excellent news.

CHAPTER 34

A REUNION

Since arriving home from Bodmin I had seen Lucretia only once, at our Literary Circle, where we had no opportunity to discuss my affairs. The day after the Circle she and her mother had departed for a short visit to her maternal great-aunt in Gloucestershire: a tiresome duty forced on her, she said, because all the able-bodied members of the Devereaux family at that time of year had various other summer activities which they insisted in pursuing. Her aunt, a lonely and wealthy widow, demanded that some members of the family visit her, and she had to be placated; and Mrs Devereaux was convinced that a change of scenery would do her daughter good after her illness. Lucretia's only consolation whilst at Amberley lay in painting water-colours of the Cotswold Hills, when the weather permitted. But now she and her mother were back; and I was impatient to see my fiancée and dearest friend again.

I walked up the drive of Devereaux House to find her sitting on the lawn by the library window, with Sarah and Mrs Devereaux. Sarah's pug dog was wandering about the flower beds, nosing among lilies, pelargoniums and forget-me-nots, occasionally lifting its leg over the plinths of two marble statues— a Mercury and an Aphrodite— which stood among the plants. Lucretia, I noted as I approached, was still paler and thinner of face than usual. The three women made a charming scene in their hooped bonnets and light-coloured summer dresses, and behind them the little Greek-style temple, designed by Lucretia's grandfather, a classical devotee who had brought home the statues from Italy. Mrs Devereaux was sewing a sampler and Lucretia was reading to them when I arrived; but she broke off and stretched out both arms, crying 'James! My dear! Tell us all about it, how did you fare at Oxford?'

So I was made to sit down on the lawn, and take tea, which was brought out by a footman and two maid-servants, and had to tell them of my experiences in that city of colleges and chapels. 'So I've matriculated, well enough,' I finished, my mouth half-full of cherry cake, 'but I shan't know about the Exhibition for a week or two.'

'How much is it worth?' asked Sarah.

'Ninety pounds a year. It's the same one that Reverend Rowlands himself won to go up to Exeter College nearly forty years ago.'

'Then it's going to be all right,' said Lucretia, 'whether you're awarded the Exhibition or not?'

'Yes, I think so— I've got my savings out of the Bank; not only that, but Mr Thomas Rowlands has left me the St Malo in his will, which means I'm absolved from repaying him or his estate. The only thing is... I won't be able to repay you, Lucretia, for the fine, not for several years, you realise.'

'I doubt if I'll starve,' she said lightly, 'for want of that. In time you will repay me handsomely, I've no doubt, perhaps in other ways.'

It was understood, of course, that what was hers would soon he mine; so it was really neither loan nor gift, but rather a payment on account. Mrs Devereaux was probably reflecting as much. She said, 'And when shall we hear of the wedding plans? Presumably you intend to get your degree first, James?'

I looked at Lucretia. Certainly there appeared to be no hindrance now to our marrying immediately, as she had declared she wished to. But Lucretia merely smiled, and raised her eyebrows, throwing back on to me the onus to answer her mother.

'I have been thinking,' I said, 'how marvellous it would be if Lucretia came to Oxford with me; to live there as my wife. Mature students do take their wives to live with them in chambers. What do you think of the idea, Mrs Devereaux?'

The lady appeared quite startled by this, and dropped her sampler; retrieving it from the grass she said. 'Really now, James, that is a notion I had not considered. I hardly know what to say...'

'It would he great fun, Mother,' Lucretia said, with a mischievous glance at me.

'I think it's a capital idea,' commentated Sarah, grabbing the pug, which wandered up to her now, and feeding it with crumbs off her palm. 'You'd love it up there, Crish, I'm sure. So much to do. Boating on the river, and excursions into the country. They say the Cumnor hills are lovely. Why *not*, Mother?'

'Well, we must consider. I see no dreadful objection to it. Though perhaps your father will think it all too rushed.'

'I think he'll agree,' Lucretia said. 'He's quite taken to James, I believe. Now, my dear Exhibitioner, let's drive out to our favourite cliffs. I haven't been out to Butterhole since I was so ill.' She beckoned to the footman, who stood at a respectful distance near the library window, and gave him orders for the head ostler to harness a pony and trap.

'*Au revoir, chére Maman*,' she said, '*et toi*, Sarah.'

'*À bientôt*,' Sarah said, smiling. I could see that she was greatly enjoying the contemplation of our romance, and wished it to prosper as she would wish her own with Mr Nanskivell to do.

'Dinner at seven, Lucretia,' Mrs Devereaux said, commandingly. Lucretia nodded, took my arm, and we made our way round to the stables; and were soon bowling along the lanes out towards Trethillick and Crugmeer, with Lucretia handling the reins. The children of those hamlets stopped their playing to see us speed through, and farmers' wives and dairymaids smiled and pointed us out to each other. Surely, it seemed to me, the whole world must know and approve of our intentions; how could the Squire possibly stand between us now?

We took the rough track out on to the cliffs, I jumping down to open gates as we passed through; and before long stood at the very spot where I had first talked to Lucretia and found her reading Wordsworth. As then, the full panoply of summer spread above and about us; a score of larks were in full song, rising above us to pour out their encouragement and celebration; the ocean lay benign and sparkling about the offshore islands and beyond Trevose Head, with the full sails of traders moving slowly in a soft south-westerly breeze across the horizon.

'How long is it,' asked Lucretia, 'since we first met here?'

'Three years and four months, I believe.'

She looked at me with such intense joy and happiness that I could not forebear taking her into my arms and kissing her. 'Oh James... to think of our plans... our dreams... that they should he coming true in this way!'

'I couldn't believe they would... I can still hardly believe it, after what I've been through... I'm so amazed at it all, I'm sure 'tis all meant... part of a Divine Plan. Do you feel that?'

'Yes,' she whispered, as I held her close against me. 'I do feel that it is Destiny, Providence... or God's will.'

I was glad she could attribute our mutual desires to the Creator. I wanted to tell her of my new-found calling, to relate in detail my prison experiences, of my firm decision now to pursue a life of ministry. But other feelings and urges were rising to cloud that need. 'I've so much to say to you my dearest,' I said. 'I will tell you it all, very soon; but we must celebrate this day, mustn't we, as another of God's great gifts; a signal to us that our life together shall be as calm and good as the creation we see about us.'

'My darling,' said Lucretia, 'you do sound like a preacher.'

'I may become one,' I told her, 'if I can't get a degree in Divinity at College. For that's what I've decided I want to do. Can you see yourself as a vicar's wife?'

She burst out laughing, sat down on the turf and, taking my hand, pulled me down beside her. Now she verily assaulted me with embraces, kissing me on every part of my face and neck she could reach, bubbling with little spurts of laughter as she did so. I succumbed in amusement, protesting a little at first, then joining in the frolic and reacting to her movements so that, after some minutes we sat up, both breathless, regarding each other solemnly; then burst out with gusts of merriment again. She had become dishevelled, her hair, partly released from its carefully trained mode, hanging down over her shoulder on one side, the tiny pearl buttons of her dress undone upon the nape of her neck; her breast heaved intriguingly under the flower-embroidered cambric. She moved nearer to me, her mouth open, inviting more kisses; and for the life of me I could not have resisted the longing and hunger I saw on her face and in her eyes. Forgetting then the gorgeous scenes, the trilling pealing larks, the entire possibility that some farmer or fisherman might come by, we mounted such a wave of passion and desire, commingling spiritual and bodily love with natural and righteous emotions, that to hold back, not to give ourselves utterly to each other, seemed to us both then a crime. So our first consummation took place in that spot, which has since become hallowed in our minds, and which we revisited again and again later, whenever we returned to Lodenek to see our families.

After this tremendous event, our final committal to each other, we sat soberly, hand in hand with my arm around her shoulder, looking down on the soft surges over the rocks below, watching the tendrils of oar-weed swirling as the small waves moved in and out. Shags and oyster-catchers sped over the waters and disappeared. A couple of Lodenek fishing smacks sailed past, trailing lines for mackerel. For a very long space we said nothing at all, being absolutely content to be there so close together; I remember a deep sensation of communion with sea, sky and cliffs, of drinking in the sunshine through all my exposed pores (for I had taken off my shirt and rolled up the bottoms of my trousers to the knees) and exuding intense goodwill to all the world in return; I am sure Lucretia felt much the same, her stillness and content having such a real and tangible presence beside me there.

How long we stayed there thus I cannot be sure; it might have been an hour, perhaps less. The sun was lowering behind a thin gauze of cloud when we stirred, and Lucretia said, 'We had better go back. Something may be said if I am too late for dinner. But I don't care really, my love— this is worth more than any family considerations.' She began to put her hair into place.

I said, a darker thought crossing my mind, 'I suppose what we have just done is a sin, in the eyes of God.'

'I can hardly believe it,' she said, her eyes glowing at me as she took my arm to get up. She adjusted her dress and, with my assistance, closed up the neck at the nape. 'Will I do? At least to get back to the House and my room?'

'I think so.' She looked more beautiful than ever to me, though wisps of hair were still wandering about her ear; her large brown and agate eyes, dwelling on me with such love and satisfaction, blotted out all other physical considerations.

'We're not the first, you know, nor certainly the last, to make love before marriage,' she said as we went haltingly, indeed regretfully, back to the pony, which cropped near the gate leading from the field. 'Love is all that really matters— true and sincere love; for love is the great driving force of the Christian religion, is it not? Perhaps in God's eyes we're already married. Haven't we solemnly vowed each to the other often enough?'

I could find no answer to such an argument. And even now, almost forty years afterwards, having devoted myself to the ministry, I cannot believe there was any sin in our union on that most memorable day.

'You didn't answer my question,' I said as I helped her up into the trap, and untethered the pony, 'about becoming a vicar's wife.'

'My dear,' said Lucretia, 'if that is what you want; if you really have decided— then of course I will do all I can to support you. Though I may not be as well fitted to the duties as an able-bodied woman, you know.'

I got up beside her and kissed her lightly on the ear. 'I knew you'd say that, my darling.'

We drove smartly back to Devereaux Place, delivering the trap at the front door to the footman. Lucretia kissed me, lingeringly and longingly, as the conveyance and pony were taken away; then fled indoors. Dinner itself was half over when she came down, she told me later. Sarah smiled secretively to herself, the Major raised his eyebrows above his glass of claret, said 'Haw...,' and nothing else. Mrs Devereaux eyed her elder daughter speculatively, noting the extraordinary glow which she possessed after her excursion, but said little except, 'I see you have benefited from the sea air, Lucretia.'

CHAPTER 35

A BROKEN TROTH, AND A SETTLEMENT

Fair Haven,
Harbour Row,
Lodenek,
15th July 1822

My Dearest,

More good news— I have been awarded the Exhibition! The letter came today, and it means that my tutorial fees, books and so on, will be paid for. I have written to confirm my rooms at the College, hut of course I don't know whether there will be sufficient accommodation for us both in them, or whether indeed you will be coming with me as my wife. Has your Mother talked to your Father yet about this? I hope and pray that it can be amicably agreed, as it would be a poor and inauspicious beginning to our marriage if we were to incur your parents' displeasure. Also, my darling, please consider that if it should become known that we eloped in order to marry, it would not stand me in any good stead at the start of my career as a minister; indeed, I doubt if I should ever be offered a curacy. So we must trust in God and your Father for the present. When shall we be able to meet next?

Your parsonified lover and eager friend

J.

This letter I sent up to Devereaux Place, and awaited a reply with growing anxiety. I was beginning to feel that Lucretia, rather than myself, was the impetuous partner in our engagement. I also considered that, tempting though it might be, and a great source of joy, to have my love there at Oxford with me, as my wife, would distract me from my studies. Without her I could surely apply myself so much more effectively. So I was torn between disappointing her for my own (though ultimately also her) advantage, and pleasing her at my certain cost.

A letter in reply came the next day:

Devereaux Place
16.VII. 22

My Only Love,

Such wonderful tidings about the Exhibition! My sincere and admiring congratulations! Surely you will do well when you go up.

Whether our deepest desire to marry will have my Father's consent I am beginning to doubt. Mother has put the case to him, but so far he appears quite adamant that we shall not have his approval. I heard them arguing loudly yesterday; all is quiet today, but an ominous silence prevails. Whatever his decision, I think it high time you came to visit us as my prospective suitor, and that you should be treated honourably as such. The least he can do is to hear you put your case. I hope to have an interview arranged soon.

Courage, mon brave— we shall be together sooner or later: eventually, no one can prevent it. I hope that the mere suggestion of an elopement will bring mon père around. Yours in ever-growing affection and love,

L.

I waited a week for that summons, or invitation, to go up to Place and discuss our affairs with the Squire. Meanwhile events in the town increased the passionate interest all Lodenek people took in the affairs of the Rowlands estate. More notices appeared:

All or any part of the

FREEHOLD ESTATES

of the late Thomas Rowlands, Esq.,

are now for SALE BY PRIVATE CONTRACT

on very reasonable terms.

Persons interested in the above are

invited to apply to

Cantrell and Co., Attorneys

at South Street, St.Austell.

Allowance will he made to Creditors of the

aforesaid Thomas Rowlands

against the purchase monies, towards the

liquidation of their claims.

And this:

FOR SALE BY AUCTION

at the Golden Lion Inn, Lodenek

at 11 in the forenoon

on Thursday 27th July 1822

All lease-hold dwelling houses, gardens

and fields of the late Thomas Rowlands, Esq.,

in or near Lodenek, held by him for the remainder

of several terms of years on the lives of persons now living.

Promissory notes and dishonoured drafts of the

late firm of Thomas Rowlands and Son will be taken

in payment of the purchase money.

These offers attracted purchasers, and the free-hold and lease-hold estates were thus sold off, to pay the very considerable debts incurred by Thomas' high living. It was rumoured (and later confirmed) that Squire Devereaux had bought Sandry's Hill House, its grounds and plantation. The Rowlands family had already moved out, the women, including Emily and Mrs Rowlands, and the two youngest boys, taking up residence once more at

St Petroc's House, half-way down the hill towards the harbour: the only good property the family now retained. The older sons went to seek their fortunes elsewhere; one lodged at the Vicarage with the Reverend Rowlands, and later, like myself, took Holy Orders. Ralph was given a fairly lucrative position in the Counting House of Messrs Coutts and Company in London, where he did well for himself; he later became a partner in his own commercial bank, and married a lady of considerable substance.

But it was Emily who suffered most from this upheaval. Even before the death of Thomas, reports had come to her that Philip Rashleigh, her fiancée, had been seen consorting with the younger daughter of Colonel Paynter of Carnanton, in St Mawgan-in-Pydar. Perhaps it was an innocent action on young Rashleigh's part to accept an invitation to a house-party there; the Paynters were old friends of his family. The report, not malicious in substance, but repeated maliciously, suggested that Philip had paid too much attention to young Caroline Paynter, and was even seen walking unchaperoned with her in Carnanton woods. Much disturbed when this got back to her, Emily awaited Philip's next visit in order to confront him and demand an explanation. The visit was never made. Instead, a further report from well-meaning friends came, indicating that Caroline was a guest at the Rashleigh residence, Prideaux House near Luxulyan, at a birthday ball given for Philip's sister. Philip was seen to dance with Caroline far more than with any other young lady there.

Emily wrote him a letter, demanding to know his intentions; by this time her father was extremely ill. No reply had been vouchsafed her when I visited Sandry's

Hill House; which explained her anxiety and confusion when I mentioned her forthcoming marriage. When Thomas died no member of the Rashleigh family attended his funeral nor did Philip write to Emily consoling her; nor did his father or mother write to Mrs Rowlands. After a space of three days, during which Emily underwent tortures of indecision, on the advice of her mother she sent back to her fiancé his engagement ring. It was not acknowledged. Six months later, just before Christmas of that year, the engagement was announced of Caroline Paynter to Philip Rashleigh.

*

My interview with Squire Devereaux took the form of a formal invitation to dine with him and his family; which caused another sensation among the Spargos, and raised my hopes that the Major was about to give his consent to my marrying Lucretia, perhaps even giving his blessing on our living together in Oxford.

I had already been to Mr Oatey to be measured for a new cut-away coat in royal blue serge with brass buttons, and a pair of dove-grey trousers, slightly flared as became my nautical background. I had also ordered a new pair of chrome-hide shoes with square toes and brass buckles from Mr Curgenven; I considered I had better spend some of my savings on a decent outfit, so as not to appear too indigent when I went up to Oxford. Now, having three or four days in hand before going up to Place, I called on those worthy tradesmen and hurried the work on, having fittings that very same day.

Dinner with the Devereaux family was, I supposed, to be my final test. If I could not conduct myself in an acceptable manner, I felt, I should never gain the Squire's approval. However, on arrival I was welcomed warmly enough by them all; as Lucretia had divined, the Major had a certain admiration of my past exploits which, I hoped, would cause him to excuse any gaffes or social solecisms I might unwittingly perpetrate. We all laughed and chattered over a bowl of cold punch in the sitting room overlooking the statues and the drive, before the butler summoned us into dinner. The long table with its array of silver and pewter ware, the many different knives, forks and spoons, the footmen awaiting us, the lugubrious portraits around the walls, relieved only by a large coloured engraving of Lodenek harbour done by Polwhele at the turn of the century and dedicated to old Sir Robert Devereaux (who had subscribed, and partly financed, his *History of Cornwall*): all this naturally overawed me. But Lucretia squeezed my hand and told me to sit opposite herself, and to watch what she did so as to get the mechanics of the cutlery correct. And we began a very large meal, with a variety of wines, such as I had never before contemplated.

Afterwards Lucretia admitted that the dinner had been a much more thorough affair than the family would normally have had on their own at that time of year; one wine only, usually claret, was sufficient for the Squire, provided of course he could have his port after the meal.. Lucretia herself was intrigued to see how I would comport myself through the repast; but though I was continually surprised and impressed by the various dishes and wines, I managed to betray little of what I felt. I watched Lucretia narrowly as each course came, and used the same implements as she did. I was careful not to volunteer any remarks, and to confine myself in conversation to answering questions directed to me, which came mainly from Mrs Devereaux and Sarah, and young George Arthur, home from Eton for the vacation: who was desperate to know of my experiences of smuggling and prison, and disappointed that I had not witnessed an execution whilst I was in Bodmin Gaol. His mother soon forbade him to pursue this, saying it was not good dinner talk. 'I expect James will he pleased to tell you all about it on another occasion,' she said. 'I am sure there will be other opportunities.' She looked at her husband, at the other end of the table; he twitched his eyebrows and nose, grunted a 'H'rrmph!' and gave the briefest of nods.

The weather being very hot, there was no soup (for which I was heartily glad): we began with a *compôte* of fresh garden cherries and pineapple, laced with lemon juice, sugar and rum, served in crystal. glasses on a tray packed with ice. (Like all landowning families, the Devereaux had an ice-house, theirs being a tunnel in the woods behind the mansion, where ice made in winter was stored in boxes packed with straw.) The *compôte* was deliciously cold and sharply refreshing. It was followed by several trout, which the Squire claimed he and George had caught in the Petherick River a mile or two above Lodenek the same day. They were served with asparagus and a bread-and-fennel sauce, being brought in on silver salvers and accompanied by bottles of Barsac, a wine which until then I had not tasted. Sarah watched me with some amusement as I handled uncertainly the fish knife and fork, also new to me. That course being removed by the flunkeys, it was succeeded by quails in aspic, a dish I had heard about but never actually seen; though I had eaten quails' eggs, having as a boy stolen some from the Squire's own preserves. In those days one could often hear the strange cry of that secretive bird from hedges and low bushes, and occasionally see bevies of eight or ten of them feeding in fields or on open heaths. I dismembered mine delicately, successfully imitating Lucretia's actions, feeling that I might after all hold my own in society at Oxford. The quails were served on beautifully decorated Spode plates, and a light dryish hock was poured to complement them.

By now I was feeling fairly replete, and wondered if we might now have a sweet course. But no; there appeared, on a vast pewter charger, a great roast sirloin of beef, done to a turn, still sizzling in its gravy. It was a meal in itself; Squire Devereaux carved me a generous portion, to which was added both boiled and roast potatoes, broad beans and cabbage, and horse radish sauce. I wondered what the wine would be; it came, a dark rich red burgundy, full-bodied and slightly sharp to the palate, but a delightful draught with this titanic traditional dish. By the time I was halfway through I was wishing my trousers were a size larger; but I battled manfully on to do it justice, and left only a small heap of cabbage and half a potato.

Until now the conversation had been spasmodic, of which I was glad, for I did not believe I could eat properly and use the correct cutlery whilst trying to talk as well. Now there was a pause before the arrival of the sweet; Mrs Devereaux asked me, 'And have you decided definitely, James, what you will be reading at Oxford?'

'Yes, ma'am,' I replied. 'I intend to read Divinity.'

She regarded me with an intent gaze before saying,

'So you mean to enter the Church?'

'If I gain a good degree.'

'I rather thought you would want to study literature, take Greats, perhaps.'

'I have decided I must do some good work somewhere. I suppose you could call it my conscience working, after all the unlawful, perhaps sinful, deeds I have done; I really don't think I could justify my going up to Oxford or marrying Lucretia, unless I could make up for my past in such a way.' I hoped that did not sound priggish and self-righteous, but I said it humbly and sincerely, feeling that it was only right that they should know why I was contemplating such a course. I saw Lucretia's eyes smiling at me with encouragement and compassion. The Squire said, 'H'rrrmph... Goin' to be a parson, eh?'

'Yes, sir.'

'Well, y' could do worse. I know one or two good ones. Tolerable fellows on a horse, decent shots, too. Not that our fellow, Rowlands here, takes part. Too evangelical— not one of the old school.'

I had to admit to myself that the idea of Reverend William Rowlands riding to hounds, and bagging braces of partridges and pheasants, was unthinkable. I could see that I should be expected to join in such activities, and though as a boy I had enjoyed birds' nesting and shooting pigeons and rooks (using catapults and home-made bows and arrows) I could not fancy killing any wild animals or birds now. I might, however, go fishing with the Major and his sons, which would gain me some sort of approval in their eyes, especially if I proved expert enough at their kind of angling.

The sweet arrived: a huge summer pudding made with plums, pears and raspberries, topped with chopped almonds and walnuts, and flavoured with just a hint of sherry: not sufficient to destroy the luscious and tart flavours of the fruit. An ornate silver dish full of crusty clotted cream was passed around; we ate out of blue Wedgwood bowls decorated with white Greek designs. It was the perfect conclusion to an excellent meal, and I enjoyed every mouthful of it. Cheese was offered after it, hut I had to decline, feeling that my trousers would give way if I took another bite. At this stage the ladies rose and returned to the drawing room; whence George Arthur, after being allowed to stay for a few minutes to sip a glass of port, was bidden to join them.

So I was left alone at the table with the Squire, who offered me a cigar and passed me the decanter. Soon I was relaxing, sipping the wine and puffing a strong Havana, feeling every inch a lord.

'Glad none of the others are here, actually,' the Major said, lighting his own cigar. 'Robert's off to Italy and Charles is gone fishin' in Scotland with some College friends. Our eldest son Edward is out in India with his regiment, y'know. Haw. Now we must talk seriously, you and I, James.' *Blurt*. I felt full of flatulence myself, but despite his freedom I could not bring myself to pass wind so openly in his house. But he saw my discomfort, and said, 'Warm still, ain't it— take your coat off. Loosen your belt, my boy don't suppose you eat like that every day.' So I took off my jacket, for I was beginning to sweat like a navvy, and loosened my waistband, and was then able to converse in comparative comfort.

'Right. I have decided, after consultin' with m'wife,' he said, the vein in his nose pulsing gently, 'that you and our dear Crish may marry.' He sipped his port and fixed his amicable but still somehow critical blue stare on me. 'But there's one condition. You must go to Oxford and get your degree— and not only a degree, but a place as a curate, at least, before the marriage. If you'll agree to that I propose to settle five hundred pounds a year on her, with more to come in my will when I die.' He drew deeply on his cigar, still, examining me with that pale blue gaze, trying to gauge my reactions.

I was not at all put out by this. My first reflection was that he might well be right: that whatever Lucretia might desire, we could not have everything just yet; the main thing was his approval. 'Thank you, sir. I shall do everything I can to be worthy of her. You know how I regard her.'

'Yes, yes. But look here, James, there must be no nonsense. There's some idea—some feelin'— that she might talk you into an elopement. Well, now, understand me on this: I won't have it, d'you hear? Could never face the County after that sort of scandal. If you and she go off and get married before you're established as a parson—curate, whatever it is— you may change your mind and go for medicine or somethin' else— *before*, d'you hear— before you're established in whatever it's to be— then I shall cut her out of my will, and neither of you will be welcome here or on my estates.' *Blurt*: an unquestionable full stop.

'Very well, sir, I accept that.'

'You won't let her talk you out of it?'

'I will not, sir. I have been thinking that it

wouldn't help me, indeed it would be a bad beginning as a clergyman to have any sort of scandal attached to me. Much as I would desire to marry her tomorrow, and have her love and company at Oxford.'

'Ah. Good man. Knew you'd see sense. You can think ahead—good sign. Wish my own boys had that sort of attitude to life. Beggars seem to live for the day, and never mind tomorrow. Mind you, must admit I was like that when I was young. Sowing wild oats, gambling, that kind of thing. Haw. Now there's Sarah, she's stuck on the schoolmaster, whatsisname, Nancarrow?'

'Nanskivell.'

'Haw. Well, damned if I know what to do about her. She's young and silly enough to run away with him, though he hasn't a penny to his name and couldn't keep her in any style.'

'I'm sure Mr Nanskivell has too much sense to propose or agree to any such thing, sir.'

'Think so? Haw. Hope you're right. Got this book coming out soon, thought it might turn his head. Might decide to go up to Town and try his luck. Sarah'd be off too, I shouldn't wonder.' He poured more port, and passed me the decanter.

'I hope the book will succeed,' I said. 'He is a very worthy scholar and a good sound man; I used to be Monitor under him. He has tutored me well in Latin and Greek. I think he's wasted here in Lodenek.'

'Hr'mmph.' The Major did not sound impressed.

'One thing that might keep him here, however,' I went on, exploring an idea that only now occurred to me, 'would be for him to have his own school, with fee-paying pupils. There's only a very poor salary in being a

National school teacher, as you realise.'

He sniffed, drained his glass, poured more port, and lit another cigar. 'Have his own school, eh? How could he do that?'

'Perhaps, if his book brought him some money—or if he had a backer. A venturer, in a manner of speaking.'

'Is there money to be made runnin' a school?'

'There are no decent establishments in this part of Cornwall that I know of. Nothing like Blundell's or Marlborough College. A proper boarding school, if he employed several good teachers and a decent matron, and so on... 'tis an idea, I suppose. There must be businessmen, farmers, merchants, and so on, who would he glad to send their sons to a good school fairly near at hand.'

He thought about this, the vein on his now glowing nose beginning to twitch faster. 'If Sarah is so keen on him, might be a way of keeping her in Cornwall,' he said. 'Suppose I could put up a few hundred; there might be others to do the same, hey?'

'*Pro bono publico*?' I said, sipping the heavy strong wine, and feeling my head beginning to swell drowsily.

'Eh? Oh yes. Quite.' *Blurt*. 'Well, dammit, you're full of ideas, my boy. Something else to think about, hey? Must say you're a deep one, like Crish. You're a good match for each other. Another cigar?'

This I declined, finding the one he had given me rather too powerful for my taste. Gratified by his comments, I broached something else which had occurred to me. I felt somewhat reckless now; could I do wrong that night? Nothing ventured, nothing gained. 'I have also been thinking, sir, about Lucretia's great-aunt, in Gloucestershire; the one she and Mrs Devereaux have just been visiting.'

'Aunt Martha? Bit of a termagent. A real old battleaxe, between you and me. Haw. What of her?'

'I believe she likes to be visited.'

'Well?'

'Is she lonely? Does she have a companion?'

'Now and then. Gets these genteel widows, and so on to stay. They don't last. Nobody can stand her for more than a week or so.'

'Ah.' I reflected that perhaps the idea was not a good one, after all.

'What's on your mind, young man?'

'I was only thinking... that if Lucretia could go up to stay at Amberley for a while during term time, I could travel over to see her at weekends.'

'By George... see what you're drivin' at. H'rmmph. But y'don't know what you'd be subjecting Chrish to. Still, the old dragon would love it. And if Chrish could only stick it for a while, she'd leave her a nice little packet. Haw. But it would be hell for the dear gal; she probably wouldn't even consider it.'

There we had to leave the conversation; the combination of rich food and various wines was suddenly having its effect on me, and I had to ask the way to the closet to relieve myself. When I came back the Major was stubbing out his fourth cigar. 'Better now, my lad? Have a brandy?'

'No thank you sir.' I could take no more liquor of any sort.

'Haw. Well, we must join the women, I suppose, for chit-chat and coffee.'

I own I was apprehensive of the way Lucretia might take her father's decision. When he announced it, before the family, and said that I had accepted the conditions he requested, there was a profound silence, and all eyes were turned upon my love; who sat in the armchair by the window, an empty coffee-cup beside her, as the twilight gathered outside on the crenellated stone walls and the deer park beyond. For seconds she seemed frozen; then, getting up in her awkward way, she held out her hands to me; I crossed the room and took them in mine; and she said quietly, 'Thank you, Father. If James accepts, then I accept. I can wait two or three years, no doubt, while he reads for his degree.'

'Haw. Capital, capital,' snorted the Squire, and, sitting down, beckoned to Sarah to pour out coffee for him; there were no servants present.

'Oh my dears,' said Mrs Devereaux, getting up and holding out her arms; she embraced us both simultaneously, with a warmth I have seldom experienced among the gentry or aristocracy. 'I am sure you will both be supremely happy, and that it will be all worth waiting for. Now James,'— releasing us both— 'you will study hard and be an excellent husband, won't you? I rely on you to look after our darling Crish for the rest of her life.'

'I shall be only too happy to devote myself to that, Mrs Devereaux,' I assured her.

'Oh, Mother— of course he will,' said Lucretia, half-laughing. 'Though I'm not an invalid, and I intend to help him in every way I can when he enters the Church.'

I was certainly relieved that she had taken this so well. Perhaps, I reflected, my letter had made her see that her idea of marrying me now was impetuous and ill-considered. After more congratulations, from the Squire himself, Sarah and George Arthur, and the drinking of a toast— a bottle of champagne being called for— Sarah said, 'and will you announce your engagement now?'

'No,' said Lucretia firmly. 'I should prefer this to be a well-kept family secret for as long as possible. And I will not have James spending the money he needs for Oxford on a ring for me. Our love is the only proof I need for our future together. Don't you agree, James?'

I was pleased enough to keep our plans on an informal footing, foreseeing various invitations and functions ahead for us if we made any announcement— events for which I did not feel well-prepared. Better, surely, to let Oxford teach me what it would before facing more society. So I agreed readily. After taking leave of the family, I walked with Lucretia down the drive, watching a half-moon rising between the tall beeches and the elms over the churchyard below, and I told her of my idea that she should stay at least some of the time in Gloucestershire with her aunt. She stopped and looked hard at me, then began to laugh in her frank and ready way. 'James, James, it is sweet of you to think of that— but I wonder what you'll say when you meet our Aunt Martha. I really don't think I can commit myself to more than a week or two. But we'll try it and see. Perhaps we can both travel up to Amberley and stay a few days with her before you go to College.' She laughed again, her voice echoing in the gloom of the trees and down to the great archway over the entrance;

and there in the drive among the laurel bushes, in full sight of the house, she embraced me so warmly, with such deep and loving affection, that I felt, as I held her in my arms so close to me, hearing her every breath pulsing through me as if it were my own, that Providence was indeed working out its Plan for both us both.

CHAPTER 36

THE DEMISE OF SANDRY'S HILL HOUSE

I spent the rest of July and August in a strange limbo, an indefinable life between that of a working sea-captain and a gentleman student. It was an unaccustomed lull in all my activities, which might have been called a holiday; except that I was at home, and restless, and felt that I did not now properly belong anywhere. I began to suspect that my father had been right when he had talked of our being appointed each to our own station in life, and that we tried to change it at our peril.

Yet looking back now I suppose it was for me a necessary time of lying fallow, of slow desultory preparation for what was to come. Some days I went off fishing from the rocks at Stepper Point, glad to be alone, communing with the crashing waves and the spume blowing about me, having only sea-birds and seals and the shipping entering and leaving the Harbour to distract me from examining and re-examining my great purpose in life. And was it not after all an inspiring cause, to preach the Gospel and try to teach, by example and precept, the truly Christian life— to alleviate the lot of the poor and sick and imprisoned, to bring peace to those in dispute with each other, to comfort the bereaved, and bring children into grace at the baptismal font? I felt more than ever that I owed it to all who had helped me, and especially to the memories of Thomas Rowlands and my dear brother, Daniel, to go forward now the way was made clear. I was eager to be off to Oxford to begin my studies; but the Michaelmas term would not begin for another eight weeks yet.

When the weather held fine I could expect to meet Lucretia, to accompany her to our favourite places on the cliffs. The mine at Guddra Head had 'gone scat'— bankrupt— after producing about four hundred tons of copper; Squire Devereaux had been paid some royalties, and the local men employed there had had three or four months' pay; but the adventurers had lost most of their money. We could now wander through the remains of the gantry and the whim, look down iron ladders fixed to the cliffs and see empty adits and levels below us, where gulls and shags would now nest. We read the poems of Scott, Blake, Cowper and Byron; we discussed novels and essays; we lay in the sun, teasing and whispering loving nonsense to each other, and kissed with devoted passion. I was more in love with Lucretia than ever, yet beyond and above our love-making I admired her, was continually amazed by her maturity, good sense and judgement, leavened by her sharp sense of humour. So great was the gift being offered to me that I was still incredulous that it could come my way, and I needed all her reassurance to believe that I was worthy of it.

At home at night, and alone on my walks, or even out in the boat when I would row gently on the incoming tide to a pacific tree-lined inlet up river, I would read whatever I could get my hands on; books lent by Lucretia and her mother, by Mr Nanskivell and the Vicar. I devoured everything hungrily, as if making up for the time I had lost over the previous ten years or more whilst I was at sea. I read Thompson's *The Seasons, The Rape of the Lock, several of Shakespeare's plays, Roderick*

Random, *Humphrey Clinker*, the amazing *Tristram Shandy, Evelina* by Fanny Burney, and *Heart of Midlothian*. The squire gave me permission to use the library at Place, and I would spend hours there on a dull or rainy day poring over the massive tomes which he and his forebears had collected and subscribed to, though seldom actually read. Huge seventeenth century botanical works illustrated with folio-sized woodcuts; medieval herbals, bestiaries portraying magnificent incredible monsters, ancient atlases with strangely shaped continents; the complete works of Homer, Herodotus, Plato, Virgil, Ovid, Martial, and Caesar, in Greek or Latin; Dr Johnson's Dictionary, Pryce's *Lexicon Cornubiensis, Lhuyd's Archaeologica Brittanica*, volume upon volume of sermons with uncut pages, and the works of Dean Humphrey Devereaux including his life of Mahomet (very disparaging to Allah and his Prophet) and his esoteric commentaries on the Old Testament. At random, unadvised and at my own whim, among those shelves of majestic calf-bound works I sampled and dipped and browsed, enjoying myself immensely and wondering at the vast amplitude of the world of knowledge I was about to explore.

In September, however, I was directed to some extent by the Reverend William Rowlands, who, thinking it his duty to prepare me in some way, promoted me in church to the capacity of unofficial lay-reader. I used my fairly capable tenor voice to intone the versicles; I read the lessons, and served at Holy Communion. He invited me to come and study with him at the Vicarage on Friday afternoons, when he spent two or three hours preparing his sermon for Sunday. I found the various theological and doctrinal points he expounded to be, on the whole, interesting; though I was much more interested in *applying* the principles of the Christian religion than I was in examining them, and said so. But he replied, 'You cannot expect to practise what our Lord and St. Paul and the Fathers of the Church have laid down, unless you thoroughly understand it. That is why you must go to College, my boy: otherwise you will be no better than the hedge-preachers and the Bryanites; may God have mercy on them.'

I visited poor Tom Permewan several times a week, bringing him various small titbits; a mutton pasty, a figgy hobbin, or a mackerel or bass if I had caught something; and would take him, clutching my arm, supporting his other side with a stick, out of that especially malodorous little court, reeking of pigs and human refuse, along the quayside. He would smile vacantly and nod to people who spoke to him, but hardly an intelligible word came from him. Yet I felt it was doing him some good, whether or not he could tell us so; I was thankful I could do this small thing for him, and privately vowed to myself that I would continue to do as much for him whenever I was at home in Lodenek.

I also saw Captain Dick on several occasions. Although frail and also unable to stand unassisted, the old man was still spritely in his mind, eager to reminisce about his past seafaring, and how we outwitted the Revenue; and to discuss the latest news, being an avid reader of the *Western Luminary,* which he perused minutely, missing nothing. 'Damme, James,' he would say, 'pour us out a finger o' rum each and sit down on that there stool. What have 'ee got to tell me now? Have

’ee heard about the Foreign Secretary shooting hisself?’ (This was Lord Castlereagh, who had just committed suicide.) ‘Not ’zactly popular, eh? Coffin hooted on the way to Westminster Abbey— what d’ye reckon to that? What do ’ee think to this ’ere man who’s going to be hanged up to Bodmin for killing his father? And what d’ye think will happen to Sandry’s Hill House now the Devereauxs have bought it?’ And he would go on, telling me of the world’s sensations and its ills, asking my opinion, but hardly listening to any replies I could squeeze in between his words. He was delighted to have an audience, for his wife would never stay to hear all this among her household duties, preferring to gossip with her neighbours when she had some time to herself.

Except for being with Lucretia, I enjoyed myself best at this period in the company of Mr Nanskivell. I helped again at the school, teaching the older boys literature and history, until August when the holidays came. Often in the evenings I would visit my old mentor and we would talk, over a glass of cordial, of books we had read, of travel and art. He would read me verses he had composed, some of them being love poems obviously written with Sarah in mind, though he would not actually admit that she was the subject. I hoped that Sarah would receive them with the understanding and sympathy with which Lucretia had received my own efforts at love poetry, but had some doubts on that subject.

Two or three times I accompanied him to the printers in Truro, travelling down on the morning coach and staying overnight at the Red Lion Hotel in Boscawen Street; we spent the afternoons poring over and correcting the proof sheets of his book, which was now about half printed. It was a new experience for me, to see the type being set up, to smell the warm ink, to examine the copper engravings of Mr Nanskivell's drawings, and to watch the apprentices gathering and folding the sheets ready for stitching and binding. (It whetted my appetite to produce a real book of my own one day; something which in later life has come to pass, indeed several times over.) We had a printer in Lodenek, of course, but posters, pamphlets and broadsheets, wedding invitations and funeral cards were the mainstay of his business. The next day we returned home, rolling through Tresillian and Ladock leaving clouds of dust behind us, to refresh ourselves with ale at the Blue Anchor inn, standing alone on the gorse and bracken-clad heath; thence to St Columb Major and via the tortuous by-lanes to St Eval Five-Turnings, Rumford and Lodenek itself, in time for the evening meal prepared by my mother and admiring sisters.

During this time I became a regular guest at Devereaux Place, dining there about once or twice a week, and lunching there, mainly before driving out with Lucretia, on other occasions. Lodenek, I am sure, knew what was in the offing, or thought it did; my own family said little, and never had any expectations that we should marry until I had completed my studies at Oxford. But I felt people's eyes upon me, and was an object of wonder and curiosity whenever I walked through the town; it was not a comfortable feeling, to be so marked out from one's fellows and erstwhile friends. Some of them, Matthew Pook for instance, seemed to be almost embarrassed now to talk to me. But my great happiness and joyful anticipation bore me through all this, and I tried to chat unaffectedly with them all as if nothing extraordinary was occurring.

It was at one of the dinners at Place— or rather, after it, when the Squire, Robert and Charles (the latter both now home for the game season which began on September 1st) and myself were sipping port, smoking and talking, that I heard what was to happen to Sandry's Hill House.

'Saw Stonehouse today,' the Major said to Robert. Stonehouse was the Estate Steward. 'Fixed up the sale. Best thing, actually; don't want anybody else comin' in and buyin' the House and playin' Squire here again.'

'So that'll be the end of the Rowlands empire, eh?' said Charles. 'Not surprised, Pa; they were obviously living well beyond their means.'

'Clever business man, though,' Robert said. 'If he'd lived on, he'd have pulled it all together, I'd wager. If the Bank in London had gone on backing him they'd still be there.'

'Here's the man who knew him as well as anybody,' the Major said, indicating me. 'You got on well with Thomas, eh, James?' *Blurt*.

'He was certainly very good to me, and gave me my opportunity,' I said. I owed it to Thomas not to disparage his memory in this company. 'He seemed to see me as his young self, all over again— perhaps the kind of son he wished he'd had.'

'Haw. These entrepreneurs all have their day, then it's over.' The Squire drank down his port and refilled his glass.' 'We've seen 'em come and we've seen 'em go. Still, must say he put Lodenek on the map...'

'What actually is to happen to Sandry's Hill, sir?' I made bold to ask.

He eyed me steadily, his aquiline nose pulsing gently. 'Goin' to be sold off— lock, stock and barrel, every brick and plank. Nice lot of Portland Stone there— should get some decent offers for it.'

'Must say,' said Robert, 'It'll be something to look out of our windows without having to see it stuck there across the valley.' He indicated, with a languid wave of his hand, the prospect across the town where Sandry's Hill House rose, solid and formidable in its apparent Georgian permanence beyond the church tower and the treetops about it.

A week or so later the following advertisement was placed in the West Briton newspaper, and posted about the town and countryside, and far across mid-Cornwall:

TO BE AUCTIONED ON SEPTEMBER 18TH 1822
AT 10 IN THE FORENOON
AT THE LATE NEWLY-BUILT MANSION HOUSE
OF THOMAS ROWLANDS ESQUIRE,
SANDRY'S HILL HOUSE IN LODENEK:-

all remaining furniture and furnishings, beds,
kitchen utensils and equipment,
crockery and china, and many other items.
Inspection of lots may be made on the previous day
from two in the afternoon until five.

AND ON SEPTEMBER 20th AND 21st
AT THE AFORESAID MANSION:-
In small lots for the convenience of purchasers,

the floorings of the chambers, stairs, balustrades, mouldings,
skirtings, doors, door cases, window shutters,
handsome marble and other chimney pieces,
hearth, stove and other grates, locks, bolts, etc,
of the said house; all of which are nearly new,
of the best quality, and within a very short distance of water carriage.

The 18th, a Tuesday, dawned fair and mild. I had at first decided I could not possibly attend the sale, since it would bring back too many memories, and the thought of seeing the Rowlands' family possessions dispersed— although I was sure that their dearest and intimate possessions must have gone with them to St. Petroc's house and elsewhere— would sadden me too much. But then the idea that I might bid for and gain some small item to retain for myself, a talisman or love-object to remind me of those happy aspirations of my youth and the encouragement given to me by Emily and her father, overcame my diffidence; and I dressed soberly, putting on my best new coat and a dark cravat (the cravat was just then coming into vogue, in place of the stock wound round the throat) as a private expression of my mourning for the great days of Thomas' sway. I breakfasted in almost total silence, hardly answering my mother's and my sister Susannah's chatter as to what was being offered for sale (for they had been up to the House to view on the previous afternoon), and the speculations as to who would buy what. I knew Mother would go up early to try to secure a particularly fine copper tureen and kettle she desired, if she found she could afford them; my father had given her two pounds to spend on any necessary household items she could buy.

When we arrived it seemed that most of Lodenek were there— that is, the women, most of the children, and the more respectable persons not engaged in trade or in the port. I saw Dr Harley, Mr Nanskivell (his deputy was evidently running the school), Nan Thomas, Mr Pawley the ex-butler, Simmonds the former footman, many of our neighbours, and even Captain Dick Stribley, who had been brought up the hill in a dog-cart hired especially for the event. There were no members of the Rowlands family there, nor any of the Devereauxs; though I saw Susan Roberts, Lucretia's personal maid, and several others from the kitchen at Place.

It is, I suppose, a natural human trait to wish to be in at the death, as huntsmen would put it, to see the last of something that has loomed large in one's life and home town; and though Sandry's Hill House had not been there long— a mere seven years, in fact— or perhaps because its term was so short for a grand mansion— the wonder and drama of its demise was greatly heightened. And to secure, for a reasonable or a knock-down price, something from the great house, of which one could say to future generations, 'Look— that came from Sandry's Hill House; your grandmother paid five shillings for it,' or whatever price had been agreed, was a temptation few could resist, if they could find the wherewithal to bid. Who does not like auctions? They are the best of plays, a combination of instant wagering and venturing; and even if one is beaten by a more persistent bidder, one has lost nothing, and gained the thrill of it all.

Thus I reflected, seeing beds, chairs, settees, settles,

stools, tables, curtains, pictures, sheets, blankets, pillows, cushions, feather ties, china and brass ornaments, desks, escritoires, bed pans, pictures, table cloths, doileys, runners, cups, saucers, plates, dishes, bowls, knives, forks, spoons, condiment dispensers, sugar casters, saucepans, griddle irons, brandises, baths, tubs, scrubbing boards, a great mangle with wooden rollers, kettles, tureens, pots, spades, shovels, brooms, rugs, brushes, mats, carpets, fire irons, fire dogs, and so many other possessions put up, described, bid for, and knocked down, to this or that highly delighted person. My mother got her tureen and kettle for fifteen shillings, and for half a crown a brandis (an iron ring with three legs that would sit in our living room fire and boil many a kettle and pot in future years); and she and Susannah went off home well satisfied.

Dr Harley bought a crimson and purple Turkey carpet for five pounds, and a mahogany long case clock (Joseph Mayell, Lostwithiel, 1764) for three pounds ten shillings. Nan Thomas bid fiercely for a feather tie, and got it for four and threepence. Mrs Curgenven, the bootmaker's wife, had the huge mangle for thirteen shillings. Captain Stribley fancied a teak barometer, but fell out of the bidding at six shillings; then successfully bid for a writing case and holder with pen and inkwell attached, for four and eight pence. Mr Nanskivell had two polished oak bookcases for a pound, and then for two shillings the engraving of Paris and the three Goddesses. I almost entered the bidding for that picture myself, for it would have been a powerful memento; but I am glad now that I did not. I have since reflected that I could see myself as Paris holding the apple; that those Goddesses might have been the three women that I have loved, each in a different way: the fair-haired beauty on the left being Emily, the small dark charmer on the right, Iseut; and the statuesque lady in the centre with the long Grecian nose, Lucretia. But I could not have lived long with the picture, knowing later what became of Emily, and realising my unwitting part in her fate.

As the auction went on people became more and more excited, laughing and joking amongst themselves, so that their first attitudes, of awe and wonder that they could be involved with such an event, were utterly forgotten; and the auctioneer, having disposed of most of the impressive items, began to add sly comments on the lesser ones now offered. Sickened by all this and near to tears that they should now all be so disrespectful, I was about to leave the House— we were all in the great circular hall, with the auctioneer conducting the proceedings from the stairs— when he held up an object and said, 'Now here's pretty thing— a lovely thing— a silken bell rope.' He held it up, pulling it gently through his fingers; the rose-red hue of the strands and the tasselled ball at the end glistened. A slight hush fell. 'Now surely there's somebody here who could find a good use for this? Dr Harley, will you bid a shilling? No? Mrs Curgenven— keep your servants hopping with it?' Mrs Curgenven, who kept only one little maid, shook her head, smiling, half-embarrassed, 'What am I bid? Come now, ladies and gentlemen all, it will come in handy to impress the neighbours, even if you haven't got a bell.' They were laughing now; for most of us there a bell-pull would have been the least useful object in the whole house.

'I'll give a shilling,' I heard myself say.

'A shilling— from the young man there. Captain Spargo, isn't it? Am I bid more? One and sixpence, anybody? No? Very well, a shilling to Captain Spargo.' He hammered the little table set up precariously on the stairs. A murmur went round as I went up to take possession of the rope. I knew what they were saying— 'What on earth do James Spargo want with that? S'pose he think he'll have it in some big house one day, as he's courting the Squire's daughter. Getting ideas above his station, if you ask me.' But that day I merely wanted the bell-pull as a keepsake; it was the one Emily had used to summon Nan Thomas on that first occasion we met in the little sitting room, when she had offered me lemonade so winsomely and hesitatingly. And I have kept it ever since; Lucretia never objected to it, realising what it means to me. It hangs now in my study, having found at last a good use again, to summon my housekeeper when I need her. But I often handle its glossy texture with regretful admiration, remembering Sandry's Hill House, and the Rowlands family in Lodenek.

The next day, the day of the builders, the tradesmen, land stewards and other business people intent upon realising what they could for their own advantages from the wreck of Rowland's fortunes, was a very different affair. The furniture and furnishings auctioned to the public had all been removed, the smaller articles having been taken away by their new owners, the larger ones being stored in the stables at the rear of the house to be collected later. Now an utterly serious, indeed grim auction began; at which the auctioneer suggested a starting price, and taking a briefly upraised finger, a wink or twitch of an eyebrow or a scratching of an ear, as a sign of increase, brought the price up steadily to where it stuck: not a word exchanged, not a smile, a joke or facetious comment. Lodenek merchants were competing with those from St Columb, Bodmin, St Teath, St Breoke, Egloshayle, and even Truro. Farmers from a radius of twenty miles were there, as well as landowners, agents, church representatives and others.

By noon most of the small lots had been disposed of, being marked with the buyers' names in red chalk, and listed by the auctioneer's assistants: each one was given a number also, which represented its place in the order in which it was to be dismantled. The fireplaces, chandeliers and chimneys were numbered first; followed by the helling (roofing) slates, ridge tiles, rafters, roof beams and bearers. Graduating down, the upper floor, doors, windows and frames, cupboards, floorings and joists came next. Then the staircase; and so on down to the ground floor, including picture rails, skirting boards, kitchen sinks and slate flags. All were sold off, including the stout new walls of Portland stone, the window glass, and the great south-facing Ionic portico with its scrolled bas-relief depicting a cornucopia of wheat and fruits. This latter was bought by an elder of the Wesleyan Church at St Austell, where it now graces that otherwise austere building; having been carefully dismantled, the sculptured sections loaded onto drays, taken down to the harbour, carefully packed in hay and shipped around Land's End by my father in the Galatea (now owned by Mr Tredwen who had the Higher Shipyard) to Pentewan; from whence it was carted up to its new home. The rest of the mansion was scattered about mid and north

Cornwall: granite coigns and lintels went as gateposts to various farms, the slates graced the houses of gentry and farmers; whole roofs and interiors were rebuilt with the pitch-pine Thomas Rowlands had imported from the Baltic for his own use. The staircase was removed in eight pieces and later incorporated into a grand new house being built in North Devon.

All this took some months to accomplish, by which time I had gone up to Gloucestershire with Lucretia, to stay nearly a week with her Aunt Martha before going on to Exeter College and immersing myself in my studies. Gradually as I moved further away from Lodenek my confused feelings about the great collapse resolved themselves into a sense of being confronted by some implacable fate, against which neither protest or sorrow would avail. To the young, pity and compassion come, perhaps, too easily. The town would soon enough get over these great and tragic events, though they would be talked of for generations; whereas I, affected closely by them as few others were, knew I would never be able to forget, and believed I would go to my grave wondering why it had all happened, and whether it could have been averted. And amid all these speculations the pale sleepless face of Emily rises, ever questioning and accusing me. For I know that had I married her instead of Lucretia, she might well have been alive and well even now, and sitting beside me here as I write.

Chapter 37

AFTERMATHS AND CONCLUSIONS

The charming William and Mary facade of St. Petroc's House, at the bottom of the hill just above Lodenek's Inner Harbour, has always been counted one of the best features of the town. It has five bays, a small pillared portico, and is hung with local slate over which at one side a clematis climbs; there is a long wing at the rear, and kitchen gardens and terraced lawns rise to a coach house and stables above it. Until the erection of Sandry's Hill House this was the largest residence in the town apart from Devereaux Place.

So, although in reduced circumstances, the Rowlands had come back to their first house, which they still owned; and so could hardly be said to be indigent. Enough had been saved from the sale of the estate and business after paying off creditors to allow them a reasonable style and comfort, though they had now only one footman, a cook, two maids and a coachman to serve them. I was pleased to hear it reported that the family had fitted in well to the old house, in which they seemed now somehow much more at home than in their grand Mansion. Mrs Rowlands, it was said, was conducting herself with great fortitude and dignity; she was level-headed, was well advised in her affairs by her brother-in-law, a large farmer at St Wenn; and in this situation exuded an air of complete acceptance, tinged perhaps with relief that she no longer had to play the part of a gentleman's wife and hostess: for they could entertain very little now. The younger sons and daughters appeared to take their fate well enough. Only Emily still failed to come to terms with her lot.

Three days before Lucretia and I were due to go up to Amberley I received a letter from Mrs Rowlands.

St Petroc's House
20. 1X. 21.

Dear Captain Spargo,

I believe you are to leave for Oxford in a few days. Knowing of your past friendship with Emily, I would esteem it a great favour if you would call on us, preferably in the afternoon, before you leave. My daughter is much changed, I fear, and you may be able to help. She often speaks of you.

Sincerely,
Maria Rowlands.

It had been in my mind to enquire after Emily, had I met any of the servants or younger members of the family; but the occasion had not presented itself before now. I showed the letter to Lucretia, explaining my past acquaintance with Emily; generous and sympathetic as ever, she said, 'Of course you must visit them, my dear James. The poor girl must be distracted or distraught by what has happened to her, through no fault whatever of her own.'

I went to see Emily the day afterwards, and I can

never forget the experience of that hour's visit. I own it marred my happiness for months afterwards, despite Lucretia's love and the best application I could make to my studies. When we are young and have found our happiness, our life's joy, we are blind and deaf to the likelihood of another's pain and misery: until we are actually confronted with it, when it confounds us and causes us to question the vagaries of life, and wonder whether it may not be our turn to suffer next.

Mrs Rowlands was awaiting me, it seemed. No sooner had the footman answered the door than she was there in the small vestibule at the foot of the stairs, greeting me. Her eyes seemed sad and weary to me: those green and violet eyes she had given to Emily. She took me into the sitting-room and said, without asking me to take a seat, 'Thank you for coming, James. I may call you James, may I not? I feel you are Emily's only friend outside the family.'

'Of course, Mrs Rowlands,'

'We will go up to Emily's room. She refuses to leave it most days. But I must warn you, all this may be quite useless— it is possible she may refuse to see you at all. I am at my wit's end as to know how to deal with her. Dr. Harley has been and says she must be got away from Lodenek— from Cornwall, in fact. But she absolutely refuses to leave this house. Oh, James, it is almost too much to bear, to have this after what we have been through.'

I never thought to see the lady betray such emotion, such vexation; for I felt it was not so much pity and concern for Emily as inconvenience to herself that was uppermost in her thoughts. I murmured my sympathy, however.

'Whatever help I am able to give is yours, Mrs Rowlands.'

'We can only try to prevail upon her to see the sensible course. Will you come this way?'

We went up the stairs to the upper floor, along the landing to a room at the end, where she knocked. There was no answer. She knocked again. 'Emily? Here is a friend to see you. May we come in?'

There was silence for a moment or two, then a shuffling or rustle was heard from within. 'Emily, do you hear me?' Her mother asked, in a rather more exasperated tone.

The door was tentatively opened to the extent of an inch only. 'Who is it?' Emily's voice whispered.

'It's me, James Spargo— your friend, Emily,' I said.

The door was shut very promptly. 'I have no friends,' Emily's voice muttered from within.

'Please, Emily— James is going away in a few days. He only wishes to say farewell,' her mother implored.

'No need, no need. Dead, dead. All dead,' I heard her say, as if to herself.

'Emily, may I say goodbye to you? I don't wish to leave home without seeing you, just for a few moments,' I urged.

Silence, followed by an irresolute rustle and pacing within.

'You have always been so good to me, Emily— always interested in my career, and so encouraging. As your dear father was. He would want you to continue so,

I am sure.'

A step or two on the other side of the door which opened and Emily said in a low voice. 'Just a few moments, then.'

She retired into the boudoir. It was a small room done in rose and mauve furnishings, on the corner of the house overlooking the hill outside, down which people, horses, drays and chaises moved; opposite was the stable yard of the White Hart Inn, the oldest hostelry in Lodenek. Without leaving this refuge Emily could watch many of the goings on of the town; and from it she had a view out over the river to the uplands of St Minver opposite, to where the ferry plied under its sail and oars. She had the sunrise to watch and the panoplies of clouds to entertain her. But now she stood with her back to it all as if it meant nothing to her; the curtains were more than half-drawn, allowing little enough afternoon light in which to move about. A book lay on the ottoman by the window, with a leather mark in it, which I thought was a good sign, and a piece of embroidery lay half-complete on a little satin-upholstered chair near the other window.

She was very simply dressed, and her hair now hung down straightly about her neck with not even a ribbon to adorn it. Her face was deadly white, as if she had powdered it with chalk; her lips were pale pink, tinged with mauve, her eyes large and lustreless. I could see she had lost considerable weight. She stood there saying nothing. The atmosphere in the room was close, even stifling, for the weather was still warm.

'My dear Emily, you should open a window or two,' her mother remonstrated. 'It's surely unhealthy in this weather to be so closed up.'

‘I get cold if there’s a draught,’ Emily said.

‘Well, you hardly eat enough to keep yourself warm,’ Mrs Rowlands said, revealing again the underlying frustration she felt.

‘Wouldn’t you like to go out, perhaps into the garden?’ I asked. ‘We could talk there.’

‘No, thank you.’

‘I am leaving to go up to Oxford on Monday,’ I said. ‘I suppose I shall come home for Christmas, but I wanted to see how you are before I went.’

‘I cannot say I am well. You know what has happened, I suppose.’

‘Yes. I am so sorry about your engagement. But you mustn’t take it too hard— he couldn’t have been worth your love, could he?’

‘Love? What had that to do with it? I was expected to marry, that’s all. A mere duty. Girls must marry and raise families. Sometimes I think perhaps I’m lucky, I can escape all that. But what else is there? I shall end up a half-crazy maiden aunt. Everything used to be mine— now I have nothing. What have I done to deserve this? You, James Spargo, you know what I desired— needed— the only thing that could make me happy in this world...’

‘Emily, please— don’t speak in that way,’ Mrs Rowlands said. She looked at me apologetically.

‘He knows! He knows! Now he’s going to marry the crippled Devereaux girl. God help me, I can think of little else— what has she to offer— money? position? Are you so ambitious, James? I never thought that of you, but now what other explanation can there be?’

‘Please, Emily, don’t distress yourself. Perhaps I

shouldn't have come... I have only the kindest of feelings for you: but these things happen to a design, a plan we cannot foresee. I love Lucretia; she and I share a life of the Spirit, a love of nature and a love of literature.' I was now almost overcome with remorse and compassion for the poor girl, and had great difficulty in not succumbing to the guilt she obviously wanted me to feel. 'I was so happy to think you were to be married,' I stumbled on. 'But if you can only face the world bravely and hold your head high, I am sure you will meet another, a better man; better than me, someone who will truly love and respect you.'

She was silent, turned half away from us, staring now out of the window. I turned to Mrs Rowlands. 'I had better go. I don't think I'm doing her any good.'

'I am sorry I spoke like that,' Emily said then. 'You have a wonderful life before you, and I hope you will be happy in your love. No doubt you are right; it is fate, and I must accept it somehow.'

'Shall I write to you perhaps, and call to see you when I come home again?'

'No...I think not... it upsets me too much. Please let me be. I don't know what's to become of me.'

'You must go away from here. Your mother wants it, and the Doctor says...'

'I will not go. I *don't...want to live.*' It was said with a low frightening intensity, and Mrs Rowlands and I could only stare at her, in silent perplexity.

'Come away then, James,' the mother whispered at last. Emily gave one huge sob, still standing by the window, twisting her hands together. I wanted to rush over to her, to take her in my arms and kiss and comfort her; but how could I? I see her now, as I see her every so often in my dreams, that pale wraith-like figure in a loose white muslin dress, her auburn hair hanging loose about her, tortured and silently grieving, before I had to leave.

At the bottom of the stairs I turned to Mrs Rowlands. 'I'm so sorry, Ma'am... I haven't been of any help, have I?'

'Who can tell? Sometimes to confront one's troubles like this clears the way for the real solution. I felt we ought to try it. I'm sorry, it must have been very upsetting for you.' Mrs Rowlands had recovered her equanimity; she had done what she felt she ought to have done, and now, it appeared, had washed her hands of the whole strange affair.

'I am her friend. I love her as a friend, Mrs Rowlands, and always shall. If ever I can help... in any way... you have only to call on me.'

'Thank you, James. I wish you all success at College, and happiness in your marriage.'

I felt as I left the house, that if only the mother and daughter were closer, if they could but love and understand each other, all would yet be well. But Mrs Rowlands' lack of warmth towards Emily, the impression she gave of intending to do her duty but not a jot more, left me fearing for Emily's health and sanity.

*

I went with Lucretia to her Aunt Martha at Amberley Court, a solid limestone mansion in the Cotswolds, providing as great a change of scenery and architecture as I could imagine; we seemed to step into another world of settled and unchangeable ways, far from the bustle of our sea-port and the manifold doings of its inhabitants, used to seeing sailors and cargoes from across Europe and from Canada and America. Here were close-clipped box hedges sculptured into elegant forms, pear shapes, cones, bowls and arch-ways; a formal rose garden; an intricately designed knot garden, and shaven lawns. It was all a little too elegant and civilised for me, and I confided to Lucretia (who agreed with me) that the not quite tamed gardens and shrubberies of Devereaux Place were to be preferred

Aunt Martha was indeed, I found, a sharp and crotchety old lady, yet she took to me from the first; I was respectful but firm in my views when asked for them, which seemed to please her. In the evenings I would read to her some of her favourite works— mainly the novels of Scott and Fielding; she had a taste for romance, and for both high and low life in town and country. When I entered Exeter College, Lucretia stayed on for several weeks to amuse her in my stead.

The close friendship (and secret engagement, as it turned out) of Sarah Devereaux and Henry Nanskivell came to a head the following Christmas when Major Devereaux announced to the family, myself now included, that they would be married the following summer. He also told us that he and several other gentlemen and businessmen were to set up a boarding school which Mr Nanskivell would head. It would open in the refurbished stables of Sandry's Hill House, the only building left intact on the site, for much of the mansion itself had already been demolished. (Work in dismantling the rest would actually continue for another two years.) Henry's book, A *Survey of the Antiquities of Northern Cornwall*, was to appear at Easter: two hundred copies bound in calf leather at five pounds each and two hundred and fifty in buckram at three pounds, had been subscribed for: this, I estimated, would give the new headmaster a profit of some twelve hundred pounds.

In June 1822, after completing my first year of studies, I was present with Lucretia at the wedding; the couple went to live in Henry's house which had been decorated and refurnished for them by Mrs Devereaux as a wedding gift. So Sarah started married life as the step-mother of three children, the eldest of which, a boy of twelve, attended his father's new school. The second child, a girl of ten, was a pupil of the National School under a new master, and remained there; the third, a boy of six, stayed at home and was taught his letters by Sarah herself. The couple seemed rapturously happy; they have since had two children themselves (now grown up and married), and have remained devoted to each other over the years, though Henry, now seventy-four, is in failing health. His school—Devereaux College, as it is called—flourished, and within three years was removed to more commodious premises in Bodmin. He himself retired as headmaster, aged sixty-three, in 1849. His book was a considerable success, and brought him invitations to lecture at the newly formed Royal Institution of Cornwall, and later to the Royal Cornwall Polytechnic Society at Falmouth. He projected a second volume, on the *Antiquities and Medieval Works of Fowey Moor*, but has not completed the drawings; and now, not being able to travel to make sketches at the places he has described in great detail, will almost certainly not be able to finish the work himself.

I duly entered Exeter College and was able, by

diligent application to my studies, eschewing most of the distractions of university life, to complete the Divinity course in two years, and took a First. My only sport was rowing, mainly for exercise— but then, I had always enjoyed it, even as a small boy, on our own Lodenek river. I rowed for the College, and during my second year was a member of the university team rowing against Cambridge, though we lost by less than half a length. Lucretia stayed at Amberley for increasingly long periods, and I would take the mail coach over at weekends, arriving on Friday evening and leaving again on Monday morning. Aunt Martha came to life at those weekends, demanding that we played whist and picquet during the winter evenings or when the weather was poor, between hearing spells of an hour's reading, usually undertaken by Lucretia and myself alternatively. In spring and summer weather, she would sit outside on the terrace and watch us play croquet or indulge in archery, taking a certain malicious pleasure in ordering her gardeners about, and interfering in their plans for the well-ordered beds and shrubberies.

But she was evidently gratified at seeing us enjoying ourselves, and, I think, was especially delighted to witness how Lucretia blossomed in my company under the tender consideration I could not but show my dear love. Now and then she would say, 'I want to go inside now and rest a little— you two go for a walk in the grounds, or take the chaise and drive out somewhere,'— thus providing us with the opportunity, at some point during the weekend, to be absolutely alone for an hour or two, and enjoy the soft delights of nature in that gentle rolling country, to visit those villages of mullioned limestone cottages and gracious villas; and, in some sheltered nook of trees or on the hills overlooking the Gloucester vales, caress and kiss and commune together in passionate contentment.

When I came down from Oxford with Bachelor of Arts after my name, Lucretia and I were married at our church of St Petroc in Lodenek by the Reverend Rowlands. My father, mother, Reuben and sisters all attended, Reuben being my best man, and I had the great satisfaction of seeing them dine at Devereaux Place afterwards as the bridegroom's family. I told them all beforehand to watch me closely and use whatever cutlery I employed for each dish; and so they acquitted themselves pretty well. The wedding over, Lucretia and I drove to Falmouth, where we stayed our first night together as man and wife at the Killigrew Arms, and next day boarded a packet which took us to Lisbon. Aunt Martha's wedding gift was a Tour of the Continent—which at that time usually meant Paris, Nice, Pisa, Florence, Rome and Vienna; but, neither of us enjoying extended coach travel on unpredictable roads, we elected to get to Italy by ship, which we did, being blessed by fine weather and a calm Mediterranean sea. Landing at Naples we then reversed the usual order of things, travelling to Rome, then Venice and back to Florence, and thence by coach to Paris and London. And in the Piazza San Marco at Venice, one afternoon when Lucretia was taking a siesta, I met, walking with her newly wedded husband, Iseut Renan.

She looked radiantly happy, though she coloured shyly and seemed confused on first seeing me; but then recovering herself, she introduced her husband, the son of a well-to-do farmer near Roscoff. He was decently educated, and had a certain determined look about him, that to mind augured well for them both. How Iseut would take to a large farm or landed estate I could only guess; but her skill at managing her home and at accounting would no doubt prove most useful.

'*Et ton père, comment va-t-il?*' I enquired.

'*Ah, mon père est très content— il est marrié encore maintenant*!' Her chosen lot, her dream of marriage and a family of her own, was about to be realised.

I said, '*Je suis très heureux pour toi, chère Iseut.*' And on parting, kissed her lightly on the cheek.

*

Soon after returning to Great Britain I was appointed curate to the vicar of Longsworth in Hampshire, where I served two years, and where our first child was born— a son we named Edward Charles, after my father and Lucretia's father. Longsworth is but three or four miles from Portsmouth and Spithead, which I visited from time to time; and when a vacancy occurred among the Chaplains to the Fleet, it seemed natural to apply to fill it, which I did for the next three years, enjoying my experiences on board the great men o' war that lay in dock there. Many a time I yearned to go to sea with them on long voyages, but my chaplaincy was shore based, and the most I ever did there was to go to Gibraltar and back on the battle cruiser Dauntless, in place of her own appointed Chaplain who was ill at the time.

I was then collated to my first parish, Redhill in Bristol, where I served ten years, and where Lucretia brought three more children into the world: two daughters and another son, though one of the girls died of cholera, then endemic in the city, before she was six months old. Lucretia and I worked among the poor in Bristol, nursing them in their own cottages and hovels when sick, feeding the hungry when trade fell off and bad times came; and together we ran a school on the monitorial system in our own Church Hall.

Finally, at the age of thirty nine, I applied for the rectorship of this parish of Forrabury-with-Minster, where I now reside, a widower; for my dearest wife died after a fall on the cliffside while walking one wild winter day, breaking her arm and two ribs and contracting pneumonia as a result. My children are now grown up, have married and found homes for themselves elsewhere; and my daughter Jane comes over to see me most weeks from Delabole, where her husband has a farm, and I visit them in return.

Here as I write, in my study which looks out west to the sea in one direction, and south to the rising moors in another, I set down in solemn truth the various events in Lodenek which followed the death of Thomas Rowlands. My father died twelve years ago, but my mother is still alive, at eighty-four, though becoming frail; she now lives here with me at the Rectory, and keeps house, as she calls it, ordering my housekeeper, cook and two housemaids about as she pleases; and because they have grown fond of her they humour her by appearing, at least, to do her bidding. Reuben, a Master Mariner, is still at sea, though he intends to settle down any year now, he says. He has been married to Mildred for nearly forty years. My sisters are all married with families of their own. I return to Lodenek twice a year to visit them all, enquire after their health and their doings; I visit Daniel's grave, and my father's near it; then go back into the town to pass, as if drawn by a magnetic force, St Petroc's House wherein I last saw Emily, before going off to Oxford.

For two years after that last meeting, each time I was home in Lodenek I went there to enquire after her. Each time I was met at the door and told she was indisposed, but that she would be told I had asked. The first time Mrs Rowlands saw me; thereafter, only servants. I accepted the situation, and decided to go there to enquire no more; though once, on passing the house, I saw a curtain move at that window on the corner and detected a shadowy feminine form behind it watching me. Five years later the news came that Emily, after increasingly becoming a recluse, only going out of her room at night and wandering the house when everyone was asleep, had died of her own devising; she had thrown herself out of the window and broken her neck. Today there is a marble tablet in Lodenek Parish Church commemorating Thomas Rowlands and his wife, with spaces for the names of their children, two others of whom have already gone to their maker. But Emily's name is not on it, nor ever will be; she is buried outside the church yard wall in unconsecrated ground. It is said, by those who swear they have seen it, that her ghost walks the corridors and kitchens of St Petroc's House on certain nights; and I cannot doubt what they say.

Each time I pull my bell-rope I remember her, but it is mainly as a vivacious domineering girl with all the world to chose from and win. I see those gorgeous ill-matched green and violet eyes smiling at me, and feel myself trying to dance with her. Then I think of my dear Lucretia, of her wise counsels, our poetry readings on the cliffs, our manifold joys and cares of our family life together; and ask God why Emily was denied such things, for which she yearned, and which should have been hers.

*

Major Charles Devereaux was killed by a fall from his hunter some eight years after Lucretia and I married; Mrs Devereaux died only last year, aged eighty-eight. Their eldest son and heir, Captain Edward D'Arcy Devereaux having previously died of typhus at Rawalpindi, Robert succeeded to the House and estate. Lucretia and I used to stay there for a week or so, several times a year. I enjoyed my visits, but never felt at home in that great Elizabethan house.

I often went fishing for trout and salmon with Robert, and we came to understand and respect each other tolerably well. Over the years he has become almost a model Lord of the Manor, building good cottages for his farm workers, and paying decent wages to his servants, so that to work 'up to Place' is an occupation much sought after in Lodenek; he has recently made a handsome contribution to the provision of new closed brickwork sewers in the town, as recommended by the Board of Health, which we all hope will extinguish the horrors of cholera and typhoid fever so rampant at times in the past.

The great days of Lodenek's ship-building and trading are now over; four of its shipyards have closed and the coastal and import trade is falling off, as huge new steam vessels bring goods into the larger ports for the railway system (at present spreading its tentacles all over the country, and now into Cornwall) to distribute. Lodenek men, and sometimes whole families, are now migrating elsewhere to look for work and better wages; they leave by emigrant ships, which sail from the port almost weekly now, taking unemployed Cornish miners and agricultural workers to Canada, the United States, and Australia. Jane and Matthew Pook's eldest son having gone to Cardiff and successfully established himself there in business, the whole family, parents and seven children, have now gone up by the weekly steam packet to join him; for South Wales, with its steam coal, iron and tinworks, is booming.

There is very little smuggling in Cornwall now, the duties on all goods except spirits having been lowered or abolished altogether; though occasionally a run is made, usually from the south coast or the Scillies, when gigs row or sail over to Roscoff and back under cover of moonless nights. Last year a lugger was apprehended at Falmouth, the Captain being fined five hundred pounds and sent to prison for six months. The Coastguard and Revenue Services have stations all around our coast. The golden age of free-trading will, I dare prophesy, never now return.

The Reverend William Rowlands has departed to his glorious rest after fifty-one years as Vicar of Lodenek; much mourned, a legendary patriarch, he too now has his great tablet in the church on which, one by one, the names of his wife and children are being inscribed as they also pass away. I travel once a month to Bodmin Gaol, to assist the Chaplain there, to talk to the inmates and counsel them as best I can. It impresses them when they hear of my past misdemeanours and, I hope, inspires them to reform their lives when they realise what I, with the help of God and my Lucretia, have been able to make of my life. Like the Reverend Leonard Boon, I conduct a hearty evangelistic service there, with plenty of good rousing hymns for the prisoners to sing their Creator's praise, and I lead them in devout and often emotional prayers. Hangings are not public now, though they still take place at the Gaol, and such doom-ladened events cast a pall of tragic gloom over the town when they occur. Life is always deemed precious, however wretched and deprived it may actually be; most of us cling on to it desperately until, due to failing health, we lose the will to go on, and succumb to our approaching end. Each time I drive into Bodmin and view that great arched portal of the Gaol I remind myself that within it, but for the mercy of the Almighty, I should myself have been immured for several years; and can only thank Him that it has been otherwise with me.

Now I write my sermons and poems— I have had several books of verse published, and two novels, moral tales which have found some favour with the public. I take my daily walk along these beloved Cornish cliffs, which I used to enjoy with Lucretia; and never fail to give thanks from a full heart for the years in which she and I shared such wonders of Creation, and for our twenty years of marriage during which she continued to encourage and inspire me in my work. And so I visit my parishioners, comfort and succour them, exhort them and give them Holy Communion, content to go on fulfilling my vocation during what time may still be allotted me here on earth.

I look back on my youthful and somewhat nefarious activities with a mingling of remorse and nostalgia for the adventure of it all. I hope and believe, however, that I may be absolved by all-merciful Providence for my past activities in avoiding that heartless regime of extortionately high taxes. I can only pray so, every day, amid my ministrations to my parishioners.

-FINIS-